"Seth Rudetsky belts a high comedic note in this HILAR-IOUSLY reflective, mile-a-minute insight about the real people who travel the Great White Way."

—**Ana Gasteyer,** Actress/Singer, *Saturday Night Live, Wicked*

"No one out there KNOWS BROADWAY or can tell a story like the *a-mahzing* Seth Rudetsky."

—**Jonathan Groff,** Tony-nominated actor/singer, *Spring Awakening*

MR. CONDUCTOR, IF YOU PLEASE . . .

It's been said (actually, it's been sung) that when a Broadway baby says goodnight, it's early in the morning. But what about those nights? The thrill of being on stage, the adulation, the applause, the stage door fanatics...

Stephen Sheerin has no such life. Sure, he dallies on the Great White Way, but when he does have a job it's beneath the stage, subbing in the orchestra pit. Other parts of his life are the pits too—including his love life. Why does he always date men who already have boyfriends?

But now Stephen has been given the chance of a lifetime: to be the music director on a brand-new, Broadway-bound show. He couldn't be happier. Trouble is, Stephen doesn't do happiness well.

"Seth Rudetsky knows every skeleton in (or out) of the closet on Broadway and his PASSION, JOY, AND ENCYCLO-PEDIC KNOWLEDGE of that Magic Kingdom inform every sentence of this book. He makes our age, this age, seem Golden, too, and he is right about that."

—**Terrence McNally,** playwright

Also by Seth Rudetsky

THE Q GUIDE TO BROADWAY

BROADWAY

NIGHTS

*A Romp of Life, Love,
& Musical Theatre*

- - - - - - - - - - - -

Seth Rudetsky

alyson books
NEW YORK

This is a work of fiction. Names, characters, places, and incidents are the product of the author's imagination or are used fictitiously. Any resemblance to actual events, locales, or persons, living or dead, is coincidental.

Manufactured in the United States of America

Published by Alyson Books
245 West 17th Street, New York, NY 10011
Distribution in the United Kingdom by Turnaround Publisher Services Ltd.
Unit 3, Olympia Trading Estate, Coburg Road, Wood Green
London N22 6TZ England

ISBN-13: 978-0-7394-8928-4

Cover design by Victor Mingovits
Interior design by Nicola Ferguson

For my parents, Ed and Sally, who took me to see my first Broadway show when I was four. (FYI, it was Hair. *They weren't big on boundaries, but they meant well.)*

Acknowledgments

$\mathcal{J}$ have so many people in my life who are wonderfully supportive, and I'm so appreciative of all of them. First off, I'd like to thank the hilarious Maria Bostick, who inspired me to write this book. One day we'll do an encore performance of our old show, *Dial M for Marjorie*, again! I want to thank Aaron Dai (a great writer), who gave me support the whole time I was writing the book.

I'd like to thank my mom, who read each chapter as it was written and always made me want to write more, and my sister Beth who would read chapters on the Long Island Rail Road and would literally underline sections she liked and quote them back to me later. Shout out to Andrea Burns to whom I gave my first chapters while backstage at *The Full Monty* and whose encouragement helped me to continue writing.

I'd also like to thank my fellow musicians who read *Broadway Nights* while in the pit: the great pianist/composer Steve Marzullo (that's really his name!), fellow sub Sue Anchutz, *Phantom* cellist Jeanne LeBlanc, as well as cellist Anike Oulianine from *Thoroughly Modern Millie*, and especially, Steve Greenfield from *The Producers*, who's not only a great reed player, but also a great guy! My good friends: the beautiful Kali Rocha, Jason Little and Robert Tatad (FYI, Jason got me obsessed with *Dreamgirls* and Robert taught me the steps to the title song). I can't give enough gratitude to my two amazing friends, Jack Plotnick and Tim Cross, who got each chapter fresh off the printer and whose critiquing was invaluable. Thanks to my sister Nancy, who read the first chapters on the Internet and gave me such positvie feedback that I had to finish the book. Thank you to my dad, who made me feel I could do anything. Mega thanks to the brilliant beltress, Anika Larsen, who should have a side job as a cheerleader. Everlasting thank-yous for the constant support and love of the sweet James Wesley. A major thank you to my editor, Joseph Pittman, who gave me the opportunity to be a published author! And finally, a lifetime of thanks to my agent Eric Myers, who worked tirelessly to get this book published and whose nonstop support, encouragement, and hocking made it possible!

Overture

As usual, I'm frustrated. I don't know how much explaining I need to do throughout this tome. Like, do I have to define what "half hour" is (the time actors have to get to the theatre, i.e., a half hour before the show)? Or how high Betty Buckley belts (an E)? It all depends on whether you (the reader) are in the business.

All right, forget it. I'd just better assume you're not, because I can already imagine the glazed look in the eye of the non-"in the business" reader as he/she reads the first paragraph muttering, "Betty Who?" and decides to promptly put it back on the shelf (please, not the "Gifts for under $5" one) at Barnes & Noble.

Or the non-"in the business" reader who, shallowly, liked the cool cover and decided to buy the book, but while waiting on line to pay for it, read the first few sentences and decided, "BE-YOND forget it!" yet didn't have the energy to walk back to where he/she got it, so just placed it near the latest John Grisham best-seller that had a good plot but an unbelievably awful ending. Or surreptitiously left it next to the Godiva chocolate collection that Barnes & Noble has inexplicably started displaying. Why are bookstores multitasking now? Stick with one thing and sell it, 'yatches. Of course, double-standard style, I do think it would be cool if my book came with a CD of my favorite Broadway belting.

OK, I know it's nervy to call it a book. It's really a diary *slash* homework assignment from (my therapist) Monikah (pronounced Monica). She suggested I start keeping a "log" ("log" is for boys, "diary" is for girls). Ugh! I hate that gender-differentiating BULLSHIT! My grandmother would always say, "boys are handsome, girls are pretty." Maybe *I* wanted to be pretty? Ever think of that, Granny? WHY CAN'T I BE PRETTY?

Answer: genetics.

I'm actually not bad-looking. Sort of good-looking-ish. Yes, that's it. A *qualified* good-looking. Hmm . . . let's just say "not ugly." Does anyone actually think of himself as good-looking? I guess models do. Actually, no.

Typical *Mademoiselle* half-page interview with model *du jour*:

Q: You're beautiful . . . how does it feel?
A: Oh my G-d! When I look in the mirror all I see is that my lips are too big and my eyes are spaced too far apart!

Really? Then why the F did you decide to pursue modeling? A career that's based *on your good looks?*

Anyhoo, about this diary/best-seller. Monikah thought it would be helpful if I would keep track of day-to-day events. Obviously, she thinks I'm going to see some pattern in my behavior once I have it written down.

She said I could choose to keep it private or read it to her each week. Well, I must admit, as soon as she suggested it, I immediately began fantasizing I would have one of those diaries that are published, either after I become totally famous ('cause the diary has delicious insights into what I was like before I hit it big) or after I commit suicide (Sylvia Plath-style, which I'm so not planning on doing).

So, I thought, why feign it's just a diary? I'm treating it like an actual book! And not a headachy Stephen King chapter-by-chapter Internet installment . . . a real (once-defunct, recently reinstated) Oprah's book club contender!

Okay, about me. My name is Stephen Sheerin. The last name sounds Irish, but I'm Jewish. My grandfather changed it from "Sherinsky" so people wouldn't know he was a Jew, but for some reason left his first name intact. How many Irishmen are named Mordechai? Oh yeah, in memory of him, my middle name is Mordechai. That statement doesn't quite have the same effect as, "My middle name is Danger." Quite the opposite.

As for my career, I work as a pianist on Broadway. At night. Hence the title, "Broadway Nights." Well, that's actually a misnomer, since there are always two matinees a week, but the title "Broadway Nights and Two Days" spelled "Gifts Under $5" to me. Also—full disclosure—not all my nights take place on Broadway; some are spent in my apartment waiting for the phone to ring. In reality, I'm a "sub." "Sub" means "substitute" in Broadway lingo. It's like being an understudy. I play piano in the pits of several Broadway shows when the regular pianist has taken off.

First, a word about "pianist." When you read it, please have the voice in your head pronounce it "piAnist," not "pee-anist." I'm always so embarrassed when people pronounce it the genitalia way. Ditto on my college degree. I make it a point to say I have a Bachelor of Music, because I'm too mortified to proudly proclaim I have a BM.

Not to brag, but I'm really a good pianist.

So why am I still a sub, you ask?

Thanks for DEPRESSING ME! That's like me asking, "If you work out, why do you have love handles?" Because people can't control the universe! God wants me to stay a sub as much as he wants you to be a little thick around the middle. Monikah says a part of me wants to stay a sub. That comment is even more annoying than the stupid "K" and "H" awkwardly added to her name! (Obviously during her college years as a way to separate herself from her New Rochelle Jewish upbringing . . . how Liberal Arts Major).

Why would I want to make unsteady money and not have the health insurance a full-time Broadway gig gives?

Monikah's reply: "Why *would* you want to make unsteady money and not have the health insurance a full-time Broadway gig gives?"

Does anyone else hate that therapist trick? Answering a question with a question? I want an answer, not another question. Actually, it's not even another question, IT'S THE SAME ONE! What chutzpah!

All right, so what are the problems I want resolved in a neat, pithy, creative, yet unexpected way at the end of this book?

PROBLEM ONE

Why *am* I still subbing? It doesn't make sense. Just to fill you in: Pit musicians are hired in any number of non-logical ways. There are no advertisements in the want ads saying, "Musicians wanted for Broadway show," or whatever. You get the job through:

a. The director. ("I like/am sleeping with that pianist and I want him to play in the pit of my next show.")
b. The conductor of the orchestra. (See quote from director.)
or
c. The contractor. The contractor is the person who officially hires (or "contracts") the musicians in the pits. Every contractor on Broadway is a man. Believe me, you have more of a chance seeing a female drummer than a female contractor. (A little pit musician humor. Trust me, that would get major belly laughs from the viola section.) The contractor can have a ton of power or very little depending on the cachet of the conductor.

The reality is, I don't just want to play piano full time for a

Broadway show; ultimately, I want to conduct one! These are the steps usually followed to attain that goal:

1. Sub
2. Piano/assistant conductor (Meaning you're no longer a sub . . . you're playing piano full time for a show and you're the second choice for conductor if the conductor is out)
3. Piano/associate conductor (You're the pianist and *first* choice to conduct if the conductor is out)
4. Conductor (You've arrived)
5. Write scathing memoirs

Almost every conductor on Broadway started out as a pianist. One exception I know of is Paul Gemignani (a great Sondheim conductor), who began by playing the drums, which I don't even consider an instrument, although I tried to do a drum roll once and I found it literally impossible . . . so, although not technically an instrument, drums are difficult to play.

PROBLEM TWO

When will Craig and I move in together? Soon? Should we wait? Hold on, I just thought of something: by the time you read this, I could be living with Craig in Vermont. *That* is so exciting! I hope Craig doesn't think I'm pressuring him by writing about this in my novel. Well, even if we don't move in together before my book tour to promote this, I bet when Craig reads it he'll think it was cute that I was fantasizing about us opening up a bed-and-breakfast in Bennington while I was sitting in my studio, writing.

However, his boyfriend won't find it so cute. Oh yeah. . .Craig is sort of dating someone else who doesn't know about me. Jeffrey. They're also kind of living together. You know, a one-bedroom loft with a rooftop terrace in the Village. I guess "kind of" should read "totally." But Jeffrey (G-d forbid you should call him Jeff . . . don't even get me started on that. I can't stand those people who refuse to let you abbreviate their name. Why is Jeffrey any more acceptable than Jeff? It's like my mother's friends who still make me call them Mrs. Jaffe or Mrs. Klein. Why not Debra and Margaret? Better yet, why not Debbie and Maggie? Honestly. They're lucky I'm even talking to them. THEY'RE 80 YEARS OLD!)

Anyway, Jeffrey often goes away for business (Banking! Talk about boring. And yet . . . Banking! Talk about an income twice mine.). Almost every weekend I stay at their fabulous loft and Craig and I always have a great time. I just don't know when Craig will ever actually leave Jeffrey for me. I mean, I never literally asked him to. I'm kind of waiting for him to offer. I don't want to seem too pushy.

All right, that's the outline of the book in a nutshell. I'll just keep writing and see what develops. So far I don't see any pattern, except an overuse of parentheses. Hmm . . . Do you think that's significant?

Do you *think that's significant?*

Monikah, SHUT UP!

ACT
ONE

ONE

*I*t's only been a week since I wrote my first journal entry and already I'm in crisis. The day started out with just a slight foreboding of doom. Woke up at 9:30 and realized it was my day for cardio, so I donned a pair of grey sweats and one of my Sweeney Todd T-shirts, (I actually have shirts from the original production in the '70s, the revival in the '80s, and the one in '06!) and quickly got Heather, my chocolate Lab mutt, ready for her walk. Even though I know global warming is melting the polar ice caps, it's not making this October any warmer. I was forced to wear a hat outside, which I was then too scared to take off at the gym because I knew my hair would be full of static electricity and look crazy. I guess I could have run a sheet of Bounce over it, but then I'd smell like a dryer for my whole workout. Since it's Saturday, the gym was extra crowded, so I couldn't snag a treadmill or elliptical machine and was forced to use one of those stair-climbing machines, which is essentially a living example of the nightmare where you're frantically running up a flight of stairs and *they never end.* Exhausting myself, I showered and headed over to Amsterdam Avenue to have brunch with Jackson and his horrible boyfriend.

Jackson and I have been friends since we both worked at Surflight Summer Theatre together. Surflight is located on the Jersey Shore and is a two-month "one-week stock," meaning that while you're performing, say, *Hello, Dolly!* at night, you're rehearsing *Evita* during the day. The next week you're doing *Evita* at night and rehearsing *Grease* during the day. Looking back, I can't believe Jackson had free time to hang out with me considering that when you're not in rehearsal, you're usually sitting and memorizing lines. We became friends immediately the first day of rehearsal when I namedropped the relatively obscure musical *Seesaw* and he immediately launched into the First Act comedy song "Holiday Inn." He was the first person I met who knew as much about musical theatre as I did *and* was in my age range. Everyone else I knew who equaled my level of obsessions could recall seeing a young upstart named Ethel Merman. We shared the exact same fixations (Patti LuPone's "Rainbow High" after the modulation) and hatreds (Barbra Streisand's version of "Tomorrow." Who told her to slow it down and make it mellow? Certainly not Andrea McArdle!)

I was the music director and Jackson was the leading man for the summer. At summer stock you have one of all the typical types for a musical: song and dance, character, belter, soprano, fierce dancer etc., plus assorted chorus types. You also usually have one of all these types: one sex addict who sleeps with everyone, one psycho/loner, one nonstop chatterer you try DESPERATELY to avoid at meals, one gay-hater who turns out to be gay at the end of the season, and one unrequited crush. Jackson and I had just graduated college, and I love thinking about how we spent that whole summer fantasizing about being on Broadway, because now we *are!* Of course, I'm still subbing, but he's actually in a show. He's covering the Prince in *The Little Mermaid,* or, as we in the business call it, *Mermaid.*

P. S. Why do Broadway people have to abbreviate everything? Does it take that much more energy to add *"-erables"* to *"Les Mis,"* or *". . . of the Opera"* to *"Phantom"*? I must admit, though, it does sound kind of cool and jaded to shorten the name of a show. I feel bad for the cast of *Rent*. How do *they* feel cool? Or what about that '70s Irish play *Da*? I guess you would sound cool if you said, "Yeah, I'm in the D show," but that actually takes longer to say than just "*Da*."

So, in conclusion, I guess coolness is not determined by how long it takes you to say the name of your show, but how sassy a nickname you come up with.

Anyway, Jackson gets to cover the hunky romantic lead in *Mermaid*. He's 6'1" and *très* good looking. Sort of a taller Tom Cruise with a Waspy nose and blue eyes. Unfortunately, he has one of those amazing upper bodies paired with twig legs. He does squats and calf-raises galore and yet his legs refuse to change. He gets away with it in shows because they costume him well, but every summer he sweats to death because he *refuses* to wear shorts. He'll wear a tank top so your eye immediately goes to his pecs and avoids his leg sticks. I'm one of those not-much-upper-body/not-much-legs types, so all I can do is distract someone with my verbosity. My nonstop stream of words implies: *Don't look anywhere below my mouth.*

Jackson has been dating Ronald for six months. Ronald's fairly rich and a pretty big agent. And a pretty big asshole. The first fifteen minutes of our brunch conversation (which he dominated) was about who is

a. Washed up
b. Not talented
c. Getting old
or
d. Oh my God, GORGEOUS!

As he was lecturing us, his eyes kept frantically roaming around the restaurant to see if there were any other "gay A-listers" (as he calls himself) around.

Ronald is one of those guys who doesn't have a lot to work

with, but tries INCREDIBLY hard to make the most of it. He's only 5'6" but wears lifts in his shoes to bring him up to 5'9" (I only know because when we went to Fire Island he couldn't get away with lifts in his flip-flops and I suddenly had a fabulous view of his bald spot). He has one of those old-school nose jobs . . . you know, sloped and turned up at the end. It's totally obvious, too, because the shape of his face demands a bigger nose. It's like looking at a fully made-up clown without the rubber ball on his schnozz. Add to that: small eyes, perfectly shaped David Gest eyebrows (waxed 2x a month), and mousy brown hair highlighted and styled at NY's top salon ("All of the *Sex and the City* girls went there." WHO CARES?!) He also has essentially no lips. Ronald is a little older than us but looks the same age thanks to a rigorous regimen of gym/facials/alpha-hydroxy peels/tanning/electrolysis/waxing/Pilates, and an apparent deal with the devil.

He was on a tear about someone. "Did you see those hideous hair plugs when he accepted his Tony?"

Boring! I tried to change the subject.

"You guys, I'm trying to decide whether I should start subbing for "*Hairspray.*"

"Why don't you play it full-time?" asked Ronald STUPIDLY.

"Because," I said as if explaining to a child . . . an overly waxed, moronic child, "someone already IS playing it full-time and he needs another sub."

Thank goodness some fresh coffee was delivered at that point. But then Ronald turned to me, put down his corn muffin (NO BUTTER! He had demanded), and said, "Steve, what are you waiting for? You're already in your mid-30s. Maybe you want to try something reliable, like piano teaching. Wouldn't it be great to have a steady paycheck?"

The audacity! I tried not to tell him to fuck off and succeeded, but in repressing my emotions did manage to spill coffee on my new overpriced Gap jeans. Yay!

Essentially, what freaked me out was Ronald homing in on

the issue that's been plaguing me for the last six years. From the time I hit 30 I've had a fear of perpetually being a sub and, because of the financial instability, finally moving back to my mom's house to teach piano to untalented Long Island children. I panicked and unfortunately spoke.

"Ronald, I happen to be very close to getting *Flowerchild!*" A lie. Background: *Flowerchild* is a new show slated to come to Broadway featuring a conglomeration of sixties songs by various pop artists inserted into a plot about a hippie commune transitioning into the '70s. You know . . . now that the decade is over, should they sell out and actually start working/making money or can they always be spacey peaceniks? It's what's called a jukebox musical. A jukebox musical is a show that features the music from one artist/group or time period. They can be revues (*Smokey Joe's Cafe*/Lieber and Stoller) the story of the actual artist(s) (*Jersey Boys*/The Four Seasons) or, like *Flowerchild*, have a plot surrounding the songs (*Mamma Mia*/Abba). There was a string of flop jukebox musicals, *Good Vibrations*, *Lennon*, and *All Shook Up* (which I loved, by the way), that, for a while, put the kibosh on the genre, but with the major success of *Jersey Boys*, they're back in vogue.

"Oh, wonderful," Ronald said with the conviction of a soap actor. "That should be a fun show to sub."

I couldn't take his low expectations! "Not as a sub," I said while dripping haughtiness, "as the *con-duc-tor.*"

Jackson dropped his fork into his brioche French toast, narrowly missing the warm fruit compote next to it.

"Stephen! That's amazing! Why didn't you tell me?"

"Well, I don't like to jinx things."

"That's ridiculous and superstitious," harrumphed Ronald.

I'd had it.

"I don't know" I said, savoring the bust that was to come, "It's kind of like the time you sent everybody a mass e-mail saying that you had signed Audra McDonald but the deal wasn't finalized and she wound up going with another agency."

Ronald studied his food with fascination.

"Remember?"

Egg whites were moved about his plate in an aimless manner.

"I mean," I glibly continued, "I personally think it's smarter to be a *little* superstitious if it lessens massive industry-wide embarrassment."

Our brunch table was silent, save for me digging into my goat cheese omelet with unusual relish.

Usually I'm not so brazenly hostile to Ronald, but I was annoyed that he had forced me to lie. I tried to lighten up the situation.

"It's not that big of a deal. I mean, Audra's already won four Tonys. There's nowhere to go but down."

"Stephen," Jackson went back to the other subject, while giving Ronald's hand a squeeze, "what do you have to do? Audition? Have a meeting with the director?"

Uh-oh.

"I'll know more later." I started craning my neck wildly. "Where's the waitress? I want more decaf." I frantically waved my coffee cup in the air, hoping it would put them in a snakelike trance.

"Actually," said Ronald slowly, "I know the director."

I put down the (still-empty) cup and waited for him to finish.

"He directed a reading for a client of mine. I'll put in the good word."

Shit! I didn't even know who the director was.

"Oh, Ronald," I sputtered, "please don't do that! You don't have to."

"It would be my pleasure!" His pleasure was my pain. "I'll find out where you fall on the list so we'll know if you have to step up your efforts. Check, please!"

Was he onto me? Or trying to impress Jackson by being kindly with a dose of namedropping? Even if he wasn't onto me, he will be after his "good word" about me is met with a "WHO?"

All of us paid and went our separate ways from 82nd Street. Jackson called me on my cell phone when I was just reaching 80th Street.

"Why do you have to be such a dick to him?"

"Dick to *him*?" I was incredulous. "Why is he always advising me to quit the business?"

"He feels bad for you. He doesn't want you to stay a sub. He thinks you deserve a nice life. "

"*I* don't want to stay a sub either! But I don't want to become a teacher! I've been working all these years towards becoming a Broadway conductor! And that's what I will be one day! What does *he* even know? HE'S A FAILED ACTOR!"

Jackson gasped. "I told you that in confidence! No one is supposed to know he was an actor!"

"He *wasn't* an actor! He was someone who went to auditions and never got called back! OPEN CALLS at that! He *wishes* he were an actor!" I wasn't so mad that I forgot to use the subjunctive.

Silence.

Or a bad cell phone connection.

Regardless, Jackson finally spoke, starting with a long sigh.

"Look, we always get into fights about Ronald. Why don't we just drop it?"

I wish *he* would drop Ronald. Or at least leave him home in his dungeon.

Jackson is one of those people who always has to bring along the person he's dating to all social outings. Like, whenever you call to make any kind of plan he'll say "What time should WE be there?" Or "What can WE bring?"

I'm not calling BOTH of them! They don't even live together! The only time I can really talk to Jackson is on the phone. We'll always call each other after 11:00 and blab. And now that cell phones exist, we have a lot of little conversations throughout the day, too.

HIM: Hi, where are you?

ME: (*whispering*) On the 104 bus. People are glaring at me because my ringer was set to *Fur Elise*.

HIM: Just quickly, should I try to go blond?

ME: No

HIM: O.K, 'bye.

Click

So, ironically, most of our most intimate moments have happened when I'm not physically with him. When we see each other, he always has some moron boyfriend with him. Oh yeah—Jackson is a serial dater. He's never been without a boyfriend. And his boyfriends are never without IDIOCY. I don't get why someone that good-looking can keep choosing horrible people. Anyway, I'm writing all this on the subway downtown and it's about to be my stop. Suffice it to say, Jackson and I called a truce on Ronald and I'm now dreading the Ronald/director conversation that is imminent. Oh, here's 42nd Street. Gotta go!

TWO

I'm on the subway again. I just went with one of the women I coach to play an audition for her. (Traci Lyn . . . fabulous belter/actress . . . unfortunately she is 5'2" . . . in heels . . . on a box. Hard type to cast.) At most auditions there are the casting people and any assortment of other theatrical types: director/producer/music director/choreographer/lead in the show who wants to see who else is being cast/various assistants, and sometimes a "reader" (someone who reads the scene along with the actor who's auditioning). Well, I walk in and suddenly see my piano-bar-audience fave, Mason Littleman. I've been playing piano bar since my early 20s and I would always love when Mason would come in with his classmates from NYU because:

1. He's not an alcoholic. (Piano bars attract a clientele of beginning, midlevel, and raging alcoholics. It's worse than a regular bar, because in a piano bar, the winos don't have the courtesy to be quiet and pass out. Instead they request *and* sing along with the entire score of *Gypsy*, including "Little Lamb"! Get OUT!)

2. He always appreciated my musical jokes. The fun part for me about playing there is the medleys I put together. (My manic/depressive medley consists of:

"Sitting on Top of the World"
into
"At Seventeen"
into
"Happy Talk"
into
"Ode to Billy Joe")

3. He was always friendly, tipped well, and had talented friends who would come up and sing obscure Broadway songs that only we would appreciate. (e.g., the mother/daughter love duet from *Carrie*, the musical . . . it's actually amazing!)

Anyway, I hadn't seen Mason for a couple of years and was really excited to see he'd somehow be involved in this project. (It was a two-week reading of a musical version of a gender-bending spin on *Whatever Happened to Baby Jane* that took place in Biblical times and was called *Whatever Happened to Baby John the Baptist*.) I quickly waved to Mason (I didn't want to waste everyone's time at the table watching us catch up), but he wound up getting up and coming over to give me a hug.

"Stephen, three years later and it turns out you look great out of the smoke-filled haze of Rose's Turn."

He looked good too, and I told him. "I don't think I've ever seen you pre-dusk." Something else was different. Aha! "Or with a beard."

He made an academia face. "That's my *Paper Chase* look. I just got out of Yale Drama School."

"I thought you went to NYU. And, P. S., *Paper Chase* was Harvard."

He laughed. "Busted. I went to NYU for my BA, but got my grad degree from Yale."

I suddenly remembered Traci Lyn and went to introduce her to Mason but when I spun around she was gone. Turns out she had stepped out of her shoes to fix her heel and was completely out of my line of vision since my line of vision doesn't look straight down. But I heard a muttered "Shit!" and finally saw her struggling with her heel.

"Mason, this is my multitalented friend Traci Lyn." I didn't want Mason to get fired his first day as a reader so I whispered to him, "I'd better play for her before the director gets pissed."

Mason mock-ran to the table and sat down.

Traci Lyn was amazing on her song. Because we were told that the score of this show was old-school musical theatre with a dash of pop, I had arranged a version of "I'm Just a Girl Who Cain't Say No" together with "Girls Just Wanna Have Fun." It sounds like an awful idea, but it rocked out and made them all laugh (in the appropriate spots). She was auditioning for the role of the rat that the Bette Davis character cooks and serves to her horrified sister at the top of Act Two, and since the dead bird has to fit on a plate during the entire number, her height could pay off.

Here's some inside scoop. After you sing at an audition there's either:

A. The devastating "Thank you very much" (the kiss of death);
B. "Good job . . . OK," combined with head-nodding;
C. Or the promising "Do you have something else?" "Can you read for us?" or "Can you come back?"

Traci Lyn finished and the casting director asked, "Are you doing anything right now?"

Good sign. Traci Lyn said no.

"Well, thanks *so much* for coming in."

Bad sign. The more emphasis on the thank you, the worse it is. Traci Lyn collected her music from the piano in a trance. "Do you mind looking at some material and coming back next week?"

Excellent! I guess the casting director didn't know the rule that every actor is devastated once they're thanked, and if you're going to call someone back do it RIGHT AWAY because the anxiety is horrible for the actor (and the accompanist)!

I waved good-bye to Mason (who I guess would read with her the next time) and Traci Lyn and I rode the elevator down. She was running off to go babysit (that's how she earned extra dough) and I was running to play a day of auditions!

Three

*H*ello from Chelsea Studios. I decided to write *while* I'm playing auditions. I know playing for auditions sounds sort of depressing, but I love it! Usually they're held in a rehearsal studio, (or, very rarely, a Broadway theatre). I sit behind the piano, and during the one minute between the actor leaving and the next one coming in I can enjoy my *Newsday*, cell phone (surreptitiously left on, but ringer off so I can see who's calling), bagel/coffee, and Maeve Binchy book (I know she's for women in their mid-50s, but I adore her!). The best is when the actor is asked to read; then I get an extra two-minute slot to enjoy my sundries. No time is wasted.

Monikah thinks I over-occupy myself so I don't have to feel my feelings. Bull. If I'm not doing anything I feel BORED!

She says boredom is a cover-up for other feelings. Hmm . . . I guess I was covering up other feelings when I saw *From Justin to Kelly*.

Well, today, added to my stockpile, is *you*, dear Diary/*New York Times* best-seller. This whole morning I'm playing a dance call for *Young Frankenstein* and this afternoon I'm playing an open call for a tour of *Les Miz*. Ooh . . . gotta play.

* * *

*O*K, right now, every fifteen minutes a group of around twenty male dancers comes in and learns a combination from the dance captain of the show. The dance captain is a person who is a dancer in the show, but is responsible for keeping the dances correct on a nightly basis. One wrong move and, even though the dance captain is "one of the gang," they suddenly have the authority to discipline you. They bear a striking similarity to the kapos (Jews working for the Germans in the concentration camps) during the Holocaust.

All right, I'm exaggerating. Actually, the dance captain is usually the normal one and everyone else is infuriating. After an actor/dancer gets a note (aka correction), they usually pull the famous, "That's the way I've been doing it since we opened." Maybe so, lady, but it's not the way you were TAUGHT TO DO IT! Just because you've changed it out of:

1. Laziness
2. Technical inability
3. Forgetfulness
4. STUPIDITY

Change it back!

Anyway, right now the dance captain is teaching a 32-count combination that includes a little ballet/tap/jazz. I love watching dancers. Especially men. I'm always so impressed by guys that can do high kicks and splits because even after a half hour of stretching at the gym, I'm as flexible as a wishbone. Here goes, gotta play.

*O*uch. After the guys danced, they were asked if they had any special skills. This can sometimes really help you get a part. Like, if you're trying out for a summer stock that's doing *Bar-*

num and they see "stilt walker" under your special skills, they'll call you back. Although, why are you trying out for *Barnum*? That's the show that gave Glenn Close two solos!

Special skills can mean anything. Sometimes people put down impressive things like "can read music" or "speaks French fluently." Often, though, they redefine the term "special." People literally put down "Can burp on cue" (what's the cue? "Please gross me out"?); "Drives stick shift" (hmm . . . I'm from New York. What would I put down? Takes cabs?); and my favorite, "Good with children."

Is that an actual marketable theatrical skill?

ACTRESS ON PHONE WITH AGENT: Did I get the lead in that new Broadway show?

AGENT: Unfortunately, it went to another actress. They were concerned that you wouldn't be good with children.

ACTRESS: But it's a one-woman play!

AGENT: Janet, I'm dropping you as a client. I suggest you become "good with children" if you ever want to make it on Broadway.

At a dance call, "special skills" refer to dance tricks and acrobatics. A couple of guys said they don't have any, and the rest said they have an array of backflips, roundoffs, back handsprings, etc. (A lot of dancers were gymnasts at one point.) Well, usually that's it, but suddenly the dance captain asked them to show what they said they could do. (Susan Stroman is notorious for doing that.) Everyone blanched. That's like me in my personal ad saying "35 yet looks 25" but never expecting to have to DEMONSTRATE IT! Well, each guy's name was called and the first four were fierce. Flips, leaps, etc. Suddenly—

"OK . . . Robert Janki."

No response.

"Robert Janki?"

He had claimed major gymnastic tricks including, but not limited to, blackflips, walkovers, Russian splits, and round-offs with a double twist.

"Um . . . his dance bag is gone," from one of the dancers.

That's right . . . he pulled the ol' skedaddle-before-you're-busticated-for-fake-acrobatics chestnut! He was obviously planning on getting hired and then when rehearsal began, since it's pretty hard to fire an ensemble member, he'd say his doctor told him he shouldn't do back handsprings eight times a week. Busted at his own game!

Now it's the afternoon and here I am at the *Les Miz* open call. The sucky thing is, right now they're auditioning the role of Gavroche, the little boy with the loud singing voice who (thankfully) gets shot in the second act. The only audition playing I don't enjoy is for kids. Auditioning is new to them and a lot of times they're less prepared than a Catholic girl on her honeymoon. (Why am I suddenly a Borscht Belt comedian?) Oops, gotta play.

Unbelievable! This kid just walked in and handed me his "music," which was typewritten words on an 8 1/2 × 11 sheet of paper. THAT'S NOT MUSIC! That's like me asking you to play this book. I passive-aggressively asked if he had music to go along with his lyrics and he stared at me blankly.

Well, fortunately it was a song I've played so many times at my piano bar that I knew by heart. Unfortunately, it was Liza Minelli's 1970s hit "Ring Them Bells." What was he thinking? "I'm 11 and I'm a boy . . . why not sing a song for a diva in her mid-30s that is only fully realized if one uses a handheld microphone and works the cord while strutting around the stage?" The song was vaguely appropriate because the casting director told the boy ("Paul Dunstein" according to his resumé, which I, at first, thought was his ballad) to take off his baseball cap, and his hat hair seemed to suggest Liza's signature hairstyle. You know, shaggy and brushed forward at the sides. He also, to my joy, had Liza's signature Broadway belt and sang the SHIT out of it. The bad part for him is that they want that role of Gavroche to be very un-showbizzy and more street urchin/ tough hood/no-vibrato-like.

In other words, ending the number in a split was a mistake. I felt bad for him, though. He reminded me of a little me. I noticed that on his resumé under "special skills" he listed piano, tap/ballet/jazz, and macramé. I could have gotten a disk of his resumé, CTRL C'd his special skills and CTRL V'd them right onto mine. I loved making macramé plant holders when I was a kid, and even though I haven't danced since I was in college (and not even well), that doesn't stop me from saying I "used to" be a dancer, implying an incredibly promising career cut short by a hamstring injury.

Well, the boy left and I caught a glimpse of his father waiting for him in the area outside the audition room as the door closed. That's going to be a depressing car ride home to Long Island or Westchester or wherever.

Uh-oh . . . here comes a young Cosette.

*O*hhhhhhhh! I'm so annoyed! OK . . . this girl came in and asked me to transpose her song (*Ave Maria*, that forever-12-year-old freakazoid Charlotte Church's specialty). You know, she wanted to sing it lower because the key that it's written in is too high. I asked her what key she wanted it in and she gave me the same blank look first displayed by Paul Dunstein nary two minutes ago. So, I then asked her what note she likes to sing up to, thinking she would say F or G or whatever. Instead she simply *demonstrated* the note, giving me:

A. A splitting headache;
B. A whiff of her Ricola (honey-lemon flavor);
C. An eyewitness account of the four fillings she has in her back two left teeth;
D. Hatred of children.

I finally figured out she wanted it down a fourth. Luckily, I can sight-transpose (meaning I can look at the music and know that where it says to play a C-major chord, I should play a G chord to make it lower; if it says E minor I should play B minor, etc.). This is fairly hard for some pianists but I've been doing it for years because I grew up playing piano for my older sister.

Circa 1982

DIANNE: Stephen, turn off the Atari! (P. S. Why couldn't I have Intellivison? Why awkward/outdated Atari?) Can you play "Theme from *Ice Castles*" for me, but make it lower?
STEPHEN: How about you just make *this* higher?
DIANNE: Mom! Stephen just gave me the finger!
MOM: Stephen, stop it and just take that awful Melissa Manchester hit down a minor third!

OK, back to now. There I am, transposing it *beautifully* for this Young Cosette wannabe and since she never practiced her song with a pianist or, I realized, sang it by herself (she probably just sang along with her CD of Charlotte), she is not quite sure of the melody and keeps hitting clam after clam. So—here's the annoying part, and I mean *annoying!*—every time she hit one, she had the nerve to glance over my way as if to imply that *my playing* was somehow cooking up the clambake coming from her yap! As she left, she picked up her music and said, "Thanks, anyway . . ."

As soon as she closed the door, the casting director looked at me sympathetically and I thought, "I'm glad someone feels bad I was blamed for that debacle." But instead he smiled wanly and whispered, "Transposing on sight is hard. Not everyone can do it." OH!!! I can't believe she flamboozled him! But if I say anything, I sound like a crazy person. (*She* was messing up! *She* was hitting wrong notes! I was amazing!)

Well, we'll see what the casting director thinks of sight-reading when he's casting a Broadway show I'm actually music directing (instead of being just the audition pianist), and I ask him to "sight-read" this sentence:

You're fired!

Four

J'm in Monikah's outer office waiting to be called in for my first appointment since I began my diary/ prequel to a National Book Tour. Hold on, my cell phone is vibrating—

*G*reat news! Traci Lyn got the canary! And turns out my friend Mason is the *director,* not the reader! One more person I started out with moving up in the world. I'm so happy for him. I always knew he had talent because of the way he'd dissect the slew of flops that hit Broadway in the '80s. Whenever I'd take a break at Rose's Turn we'd sit together and he'd tell me his theory about why *Merlin* or *Bring Back Birdie* or *A Doll's Life* crashed and burned. He was never mean. Instead, he'd make me realize that something about each show was good and that's how it got to Broadway, but other areas were overlooked and that's why the show bombed. For instance, in the '90s, *The Red Shoes* had amazing dance sequences and a classic story, but in order to get someone who could dance the lead, they had to use a ballet dancer who couldn't sing. So even though she was the lead in a musical she only sang for around fifteen uncomfortable seconds in Act

Two. He told me he thought it should have been a play with dance sequences and no singing. I just remembered it sucking. He asked Traci Lyn to make sure she invited me to the reading.

Ooh, Monikah's patient before me is leaving. Mustn't make eye contact.

There's an unspoken hope that you're not as crazy as the other patients your therapist sees. You're just there for a "tune-up." A ten-year, sometimes twice-a-week, tune-up. Looking at another patient is like admitting, "I, too, have a TON of issues dating back to my childhood and I've made scant progress. Hello, mirror."

.Ⓘread Monikah my first couple of chapters (skipping the comments about her and her "name"). I asked her what she thought and she asked me what *I* thought. My annoyance at her signature style soon turned to anxiety when I started to wonder if she had suggested the same idea to someone else and they would get their journal published first and beat me to national acclaim. *Why* didn't I start writing it when she first suggested it to me (early '99)? I decided to ask Monikah if any of her other patients were also writing a journal and hoping to publish it. She adopted her "I can't discuss other patients with you" visage, which consisted of rendering all her facial muscles immobile. She is the queen of keeping boundaries. I was positive that I saw her at Popover (an Upper West Side restaurant specializing in said popovers) as I was exiting it one day, and when I asked her at my next session if she was eating there the previous Wednesday, she became a breathing statue. Why is revealing her love of delicious popovers a boundary she can't cross? She claims that the less I know about her, the more I'll be able to project onto her so we can see what issues I project onto other people. BORING! Once therapy is over (Monikah calls it "graduating"), I'll finally be able to grill her on everything I've been wondering:

1. Does she have a dog? I'm obsessed with my own dog
   (Heather), and I can't stand those idiots who don't have
   a dog because "it's cruel to have a dog in an apartment." It's crueler to let it be gassed at the pound! And
   what dog needs an enormous house to run around in?
   Dogs rest at home and go running outside. Hence the
   term, "dog run." That apartment argument is just
   people's excuse because they don't want the responsibility of a dog or they're too uptight to deal with one
   messing up their precious, precious Pottery Barn
   couch. Anyway, I once heard her on the phone before I
   came in saying she had to pick up "Skippy" before she
   came home. Hmm . . . scruffy terrier mix stuck at the
   vet? Or vat of chunky peanut butter? It could be the
   peanut butter because I've noticed she's on a low-carb
   diet. How? I once asked her if I could keep my milk (I
   had gone shopping right before therapy) in her fridge,
   and I noticed a hamburger platter covered in Saran
   Wrap WITHOUT THE BUN! I know my Atkins.

2. *Why* is she on a low-carb diet? Is she not satisfied with
   the way she looks? Is her husband not? Is she con-
   trolled by what he thinks of her? My mother was always trying to please my father by dieting all the time
   (not Atkins—Scarsdale, circa the late '70s). She totally
   validated herself through him and he *still* left her for
   his page-turner! (He was my mom's accompanist.)
       Is Monikah cutting carbs to be healthy or because
   she just hit forty-five? Which brings me to

3. How old IS she? I'll purposefully mention things that
   were in the Zeitgeist from my childhood ("That homeless guy on the subway was way 'too close for comfort,'
   . . . and he sure didn't smell like Nancy Dussault!"), and
   she'll nod knowingly—but is it a nod of "I, too,
   watched *Too Close for Comfort* when I was a child," or "I
   remember coming home onspring break from college

and observing my little brother/sister was watching that Ted Knight vehicle." I just want to know because if she were nearer to my age she'd understand how hard it is for people in my age group to commit.

All right, know-it-alls. I know you're all smugly reading this and saying, "He's unbelievable! What sweeping judgments!"

People who don't have dogs are uptight.

People who diet have low self-esteem.

Younger people can't commit.

Fine, Monikah et al., you're right. I *do* project—THE TRUTH!

It's called *life experience*. Why call me judgmental when you can call me wise? Yes, once in a while I assume something and I am wrong (e.g., not *every* Republican is literally evil—some are simply ignorant), but I'm *usually* right.

Monikah says my judgments get in the way of me really getting to know people. They're a defense mechanism so I can avoid intimacy and retain control. Today I promised her I would try at least once not to assume something about anyone, but would ask him or her instead.

So I said, "I've been assuming I'm the only patient you've suggested should write a journal. Am I projecting?"

The silence was DEAFENING!

Five

*S*orry I haven't written all week. Nothing very interesting has happened to merit putting pen to paper (or actually, fingers to keyboard). It was a combination of me subbing (*Spamalot* Tuesday night and both shows Wednesday) and obsessively watching the *Broadway's Lost Treasures* DVD. That's a compilation of old Tony Awards telecasts, and whenever I need a lift, all I have to do is put on Dorothy Loudon pulsating her groin to "Easy Street" and I'm in a great mood. Brilliant. But tonight's gonna be special because I'm staying at Craig's. Excellent! Jeffrey's out of town till Monday morning, so Craig and I will have dinner between shows, (even though I'm not technically playing a matinee and night show today, I always consider dinner on a Saturday at 5:30 "between shows"), and then I'm subbing on his show (*The Phantom of the Opera*, aka *Phantom)* and coming over. Craig is a dancer. JUST a dancer. He doesn't sing very well. Actually, take out the words "very well." He's like the old-school Broadway dancers. Until the late '50s, there used to be a *dancing chorus* and a *singing chorus*. When that got to be too expensive, dancers were expected to be able to sing (and likewise singers to dance). Craig was in a ballet company for years (where people often stop dancing in their late twenties) and decided to move on to Broadway. He made his Broadway debut in *Movin' Out*, where the focus of the show was on dancing and no singing was required.

In *Phantom* he plays a ballet dancer in the opera sequences but is also expected to sing in the large group numbers like "Masquerade." Which he does. In his own style. A *unique* style. Blending the voices of Bea Arthur, Charles Nelson Reilley, and the woman who sang "99 Luftballons." But, luckily for him, his main job in the show is dancing and his voice hardly cuts through the chorus of classically trained opera singers in that show.

In the old days, everybody sang loud and was picked up by floor mics. Then Anna Maria Alberghetti wore a body mic during *Carnival!* (FYI, I'm not yelling at you . . . the exclamation point is part of the title), and soon it became *de rigueur* for leads to wear them. When *Les Miz* came to Broadway, the technology was so advanced, it became possible for *everybody* in the show to wear their own mic and the sound could be mixed so all the ensemble voices balanced.

Body mics are scary. There are tons of stories about them not being turned off when an actor goes offstage to do offstage things. Kaye Ballard was in *Carnival!* and still remembers doing a scene and hearing the sound of Anna Maria peeing in her dressing room. I think Anna Maria left that out of her memoirs.

Going one step further, there's a famous theatre story that ends with a Tony-Award-winning actress's booming voice being heard through the speakers muttering, "Corn? I don't remember eating corn . . ." Disgusting—and hilarious.

The sound people run the show every night and they can adjust everyone's volume. Ever notice how loud and echo-y Eponine from *Les Miz* sounds during "On My Own" when she sings "a world that's full of happiness that I have never kno-o-o-o-o-o-own!!!" That's a combination of singing from her diaphragm and the volume/reverb switch.

Sound people also turn people's mics on and off. Or in Craig's case, never actually turn it on. I found out from one of the guys who runs the sound board that the music director requested that Craig's stay forever off. Good idea. Everybody wins. Especially the ticket buyer.

I sub pretty often at *Phantom* and during intermission I go visit his dressing room. By his, I mean his plus all the other dancers in the show. Those male chorus dressing rooms can be a hotbed of bitchery. Tonight after I finished Act One, I ran upstairs and when I walked in, there was a heated dishing session about *"Miss Thing being fuh-LAT tonight . . ."*

"She sounds awful . . ."

"How did she get the gig?"

It took me a while to realize that Miss Thing was the phantom. It was an understudy *Phantom* and everybody was up in arms because he was flat on the big money note of "Music of the Night" ("Let your soul take you where you want to BE-E-E-E-E-E-E-E-E-E-E-E!)

Who can blame that poor phantom? How dare they (Andrew Lloyd Webber et al.) write a role where the high note (A flat) is on an E vowel? The hardest vowel to sing! It tightens up your whole throat. Who wouldn't be flat on it? I told everyone to stop dishing because it was understandable—it was his first night on, it's a difficult vowel, etc. Then I found out that the new understudy was an AWFUL ex-boyfriend of mine who dumped me unceremoniously and I quickly begged everyone to keep up the dishing.

Craig loves it when I come up to the dressing room. I get along great with most actors and I think Craig enjoys being around me when I'm making everyone laugh. He seems to have trouble bonding with the other dancers in the show. (I've heard they think he's an insecure snob, which is what I thought when I first met him, but in actuality, he's a really deep guy who's always thinking, so his quiet is mistaken for snobbery.)

Whenever I visit the dressing room and start holding court, Craig stands next to me. I've noticed him looking back and forth between me and the other dancers who are (usually) guffawing up a storm. It's really cute. You can tell he wants to join in, but he doesn't have the same sassy asides that I come up with (which is fair, since I don't have the pecs he was born with . . . or the calves . . . or the biceps. In other words, take any of my muscles, multiply them by three, strip away any trace of fat, and you have his body—if he didn't work out). I was deep into an imitation of Sarah Brightman as Tevye when the stage manager called "places" for Act Two, so I bid everyone, including Craig, a good rest of show.

Of course, in public I have to pretend Craig and I aren't dating because of Jeffrey. I've decided to not change their names because I'm sure that by the time this book comes out, Jeffrey will be out of the picture and I'll be in the loft! Or Craig'll be in my studio. I'd prefer the loft.

Since last Saturday, I've spoken to Jackson as often as we always do (every two hours), and I've been prepared each time for the deathblow from Ronald, but Jackson hasn't said *anything*. He probably feels bad that I felt I had to lie. But you'd think he'd at least have the courtesy to give me the benefit of the *obvious* doubt, i.e., "Ronald spoke to that director and he said he never heard of you. Do you think there's some kind of misunderstanding?" It's so much worse that he simply pities me. I'm meeting him (plus Ronald, as usual) for brunch again tomorrow and although Jackson is tactful, there's no way Ronald is going to let it slide. I'm trying to think of how I can cover up.

"I never said I knew the director . . . I said I knew of the director. You must have misheard me, Ronald . . . too many brunchtime mimosas."

There's no way they'd buy it, but at least I'd get a little dig in at Ronald's burgeoning alcoholism. He's one of those people who works out/eats right/drinks like Elaine Stritch circa 1952.

*W*hoa! That was close. I was so intent on writing/hating Ronald that I almost didn't play. Every musician has a book or mag to read during dialogue scenes, or, in the case of *Phantom*, which is pretty much all music, during the sections where you're not playing. There's some sound advice I was once given: "Don't read before a solo." It's one thing if you don't come in when everyone is playing (you'll just be a measure late and who'll notice?) but, if you miss the beginning of a solo it's a BIG, NOTICEABLE, HORRIFYING mistake and most human hearts cannot survive more than a few times the unbelievable surge in blood pumping that happens when you realize you've missed your entrance. Luckily, other musicians watch out for you when they can, and the *Phantom*'s viola player and I get along. As I was writing the Elaine Stritch analogy, said violist hit me in the back with her bow (only two measures before I was supposed to play!). I dropped the diary with a noticeable *clunk* but immediately played my beautiful "Wishing You Were Somehow Here Again" solo with full blank face, so no one suspected where the clunk came from.

P. S. Why is Christine singing about wishing her father was "here again"? Who *is* her father? He's dead before the play begins and hardly mentioned throughout. It's a blatant non sequitur. It's like me suddenly writing a whole paragraph elaborating about a crying jag I recently had because acid-washed jeans haven't come back in fashion.

Have I ever mentioned acid-washed jeans before this moment? No. Do they merit a paragraph? No. Should they ever have existed? No.

If you ever come to *Phantom*, look over the pit to the left. If I'm subbing, you'll see me wedged right behind the strings and the harp. I must admit it's such a pleasure sometimes to look around the pit and see everyone playing their instrument. Especially the strings. I'm obsessed with violins and I'm always caught staring at the violin players while they're doing some sassy phrase with fast fingering or elaborate bowing. It's so cool! They seem to appreciate someone noticing them and usually add some extra vibrato for me when I'm staring at their fingerboard.

As I write this, I realize I should clarify what instrument I play in the pits. Most shows on Broadway rarely use a real piano. *Phantom* is one of the few. Pianos aren't ideal for a pit because they take up a lot of space and the sound people say they're hard to mic. You can get a fairly realistic piano sound from a synthesizer, and another advantage is that there's no need for a mic because it goes directly into the sound system.

Also, synthesizers are used because a lot of the time you're not even playing a piano sound. Instead, you're covering other instruments. Since the '50s, Broadway show orchestras have gotten smaller. It's devastating when I compare and contrast musical theatre CDs and hear how fantastic Broadway show orchestras sounded all the way up to the early '90s and how pathetic they sound now. Broadway theatres used to have orchestra minimums, but now producers can get around that by asking the union for a "special situation" (i.e., "My musical will suffer with the sound of real strings! It's about pop music!"). So certain theatres that used to have twenty-six-member orchestras now have paltry nine-piece bands. Mamma Mia! Unfortunately, it's all about saving money and not about the artistic product. Producers feel "Why hire a harpist when there's a harp sound on the synth? Who cares if it sounds like the quality you get on a cell phone ring?"

I must admit, though, that sometimes it's fun to play all those instrument sounds. A synth player plays strings, brass, organ, etc. all on the same keyboard. So, in a cool way I sometimes feel like I'm playing every instrument in the orchestra, but it's also frustrating because while everyone is playing their primary instrument that they studied in music school, I'm not. A synth is similar to a piano, but it isn't. The touch is totally different and you don't only control the volume with how hard you play, you also control it with a volume pedal. The volume pedal sits on your left, and there are markings in the score telling you which level the pedal should be on.

One time during a show I was very nervous about playing,

the conductor was panicked because there was a crazy vibrato coming from my synth. The tech people tried in vain to figure out what it was, but there was nothing wrong with the mechanics. Around fifteen minutes into the show, I realized that I was so nervous, my leg was shaking on the volume pedal! Up and down, up and down, up and down. It made everything I played sound like Ethel Merman!

The weirdest part of playing a synth is that sometimes you're not even playing musical notes; you're making a sound effect. It's embarrassing to be sitting next to an oboist who's playing a beautiful solo while you're plunking out the baby cry (*Seussical*) or screechy cat meow (*The Producers*). And I miss those classy black, baby grand pianos I played in college. On Broadway I'm usually stuck behind a synthesizer on a metal stand. I feel like Shirley Jones when she would play those two stupid keyboards on *The Partridge Family*, except I'm not also singing backup harmonies. And I'm not sleeping with Mr. Kincaid.

But, as frustrating as some aspects are, I love Broadway music so much, I'd play an accordion so I could keep hearing it all the time.

Well, maybe not an accordion.

Now I'm at Craig's apartment, lying in Craig's (and, yes, Jeffrey's) bed, waiting for him to come out of the bathroom. I want to tell him about my anxiety with this whole Ronald/director/big lie thing, but I don't know if he'd be 100% interested. The worst thing is telling someone a story and realizing halfway through that they're not interested, but being too mortified to stop talking. So, you start rushing it, and at the end mutter, "Whatever . . . who cares . . . anyhoo." I sort of do that a lot with Craig. I think that sometimes he's really tired after the show and it's hard for him to feel supportive. Also, he likes his home to be his "quiet space," so I try not to do much talking when I'm there.

All right, don't start thinking it's some fucked-up abusive relationship. It's not like I sit there with tape over my mouth. It's just that he likes to relax at home, so if I'm going to talk about something, I make sure it's really worth it, not just idle chitchat. Ooh, he just turned off the shower, I'd better make the bed up. I'll write soon!

Six

*C*razy, crazy craziness! I'm still shaky. I'm writing this from Alice's Tea Cup, a delish café that I stepped into to calm down. I just came from Josie's where I met Jackson and Ronald for Sunday brunch. I was talking nonstop because I was petrified that as soon as Ronald saw a rest in my vocal symphony, he'd jump in with a solo in the key of bust.

"Stephen," Jackson put up his hand to silence me, "stop for a minute. What's going on with *Flowerchild*?"

"Oh, you know, stuff."

"Like what?"

"Stuff stuff."

He dismissed me. "Ronald, you'll know. You still haven't told me what the director actually said when you spoke to him."

Aha, I thought. Jackson doesn't know I've been lying. Ronald had been saving his info so he could devastate me in *front* of Jackson. What a dick!

I tried to change the subject. "Oh, wait. Quick question. What are your favorite musicals from the '60s till now? You can choose two per year. You first, Jackson."

"What are you talking about? You asked me that in an e-mail last year."

"And I had some serious issues with your choices from the mid '80s."

Jackson turned away from me. "Ronald, back to the director conversation."

What was I supposed to do? I knew Ronald would spill the beans (with glee) that not only am I not in the running for the job, but the director *literally did not know who I was!* I decided to nullify whatever Ronald would say by implying the director was crazy. "Guys! You know as well as I do that directors are flakes."

Ronald suddenly smiled while nodding and put down his latte (WITH SKIM!). "Stephen, I have to agree with you. This director could easily change his mind. He seems like an idiot."

Huh?

Ronald's smile wasn't friendly and yet he was letting me off so easily.

"Exactly." I tentatively went along with Ronald. "That stupid director's using the old 'I don't know who that is' chestnut now, but next month he could be clamoring for me!"

Silence.

"What?" Jackson and Ronald spoke/looked at me in unison.

"What?" I fired back.

Jackson looked confused. "What just happened?"

"Where?" I inquired. When stalling, just keep repeating questions.

"Stephen, repeating question syllables is only effective when people don't know it's one of your stalling tactics."

I forgot it no longer works on Jackson. Shit.

I had to come clean. "Look, guys—"

Ronald held up his hand in a "don't lecture me" way. "Stephen, you can music direct *Flowerchild* if you want, but mark my words: Mason Littleton is an avant-garde freak wannabe. A director with no future."

MASON LITTLETON IS THE DIRECTOR!!! Why was my karma suddenly so amazing?

Ronald was explaining to Jackson, "Apparently, the novice just got his MFA in directing from Yale and now he's suddenly going to direct a Broadway show." He snorted as he prepared to be insightful. "Every skyrocket has to fall back to earth."

Jackson didn't give the knowing nod Ronald expected. Instead he just motioned for him to continue. "What did Mason say about Stephen?"

I smiled. "Yeah, Ronald. What?"

"I don't remember. Something about him seeing you at some gay *Baby Jane* audition and deciding you'd be right for the project. He seemed very surprised that I knew anything about it. I told him we were friends *(We were?)* and that you had told me."

I'll bet Mason was still surprised since he hasn't actually told *me* yet.

"When did you talk to him?"

He was getting impatient with me and spoke quickly. "This morning right before I got here. Now can we please change the subject? I haven't even told you both about what my new cell phone does."

Ronald was always getting the latest/best of every needless thing there was. He went on a lengthy diatribe about his new cell phone that fit into the palm of your hand and could translate any words going into it into 143 languages. What language could Ronald possibly need his shallow blabbering translated into? I wish it would translate his words into silence.

He wouldn't shut up. "Just for fun, I called a phone booth in Mozambique, I got the number from the Internet, and spoke to a native for a half hour! It was fascinating. Unfortunately, the phone can't translate the other person's language back to English so I didn't really understand what he was saying, but I did most of the talking anyway. I was telling him about that *Will & Grace* episode, he'd never seen it, they don't get NBC in his village, or any television I guess, anyway, I was telling him about the episode where Grace tells Will he'd better shape up or ship out, and Will says, "Gladly! I always thought guys in sailor uniforms were hotties!" He thought it was hilarious, although it was hard to tell because there's a delay with the translator so whatever he laughed at I had actually spoken two to five minutes before."

Jackson was nodding and smiling. I was nodding, too. Nodding OFF! Thank G-d Ronald's cell phone went off in the middle of his babbling. It was AT&T checking to make sure he had just made a $1200 call to Africa.

It seemed like it would take him a long time to "work it out" (i.e., finally have to pay it) so I got up to leave.

Jackson gave me a hug. "Congratulations, Stephen." He grabbed my shoulders and looked in my eyes. "Don't fuck it up."

What was that supposed to mean???

Seven

SUNDAY

*S*till no word from Mason, the director. Maybe he thinks it's unprofessional to call me on a Sunday night. OH! It's been more than 24 hours since Ronald told me and I can't take the tension!

OK, to get my mind off my possibly skyrocketing career, I've decided that the reader needs to know about my childhood. In other words, I was just flipping through Elizabeth's Wurtzel's *Prozac Nation*, and in it she talks a lot about her growing-up years. I figured I should copy her format somewhat since our books are sort of similar—minus the privileged self-indulgence. All right, minus *some* of it.

I grew up on Long Island in wealthy Hewlett Harbor. My mom worked at the Met as an opera singer. She was famous-ish/not really. She'd only get cast in secondary roles at the Met but she had a successful career doing solo recitals around the country because she could always charm an audience when she'd talk between songs. She and my dad (remember? He was her accompanist) would travel for two or three days every couple of weeks and perform German Lieder or French art songs all over the country. When I was little and they would leave, I would

FREAK OUT! It was horrible for me. Every once in a while my parents would just disappear. It was like the Hitchcock movie *The Lady Vanishes*, but with two ladies vanishing—yet one is a man. I would have three-day crying sessions with Mrs. Remick, who was my governess, I guess. Wait . . . that totally sounds weird and implies that I'm a Wasp. Is there a Jewish word for a governess who's not Jewish? Goy-verness?

I'd beg Mrs. R to send me to my parents, but she'd explain that my mom needed all of her concentration when she was preparing for a concert (and apparently my dad needed time alone with Mitzi, his page turner. Mitzi. Ugh! Affairs are so pathetic! Oh, wait, except mine).

I'd promise anything. "I'll be quiet." I stuck out my chest. "I'll bet I can go without talking longer than anyone." THAT was the biggest lie I ever told.

"Little Stevey" (her nickname for me, even when I was carrying around an extra twenty pounds in my love handles/ass during a rocky adolescence), "you've got to stay here in this Nixon-loving, McGovern-fearing, homelessness-ignoring town." She was the one who instilled in me an undying love of Democrats . . . and a vicious hatred of Republicans.

"Mrs. Remick—what if I bought my own plane ticket and found out where Mommy and Daddy were staying and got my own room there, then they couldn't stop me!"

"How are you gonna pay for that, little man? You need to become successful and rich and *then* you can go stalking whomever you want. And, by the way, if you become rich one day and therefore start voting Republican, I'll smother *you* and however many kids you have." She was pro-Democrat and also a touch psychotic.

"I don't wanna wait. I wanna become rich *NOW!* NOW NOW NOW NOW!"

Sometimes it felt good to yell the same word over and over again. It would probably feel good today as well, but I don't think you can get away with monosyllabic repetitive screamature past age eight.

"One day you *could* be rich. You just have to figure out what you're good at, and then become the best you can be so people will pay you to do it. Hopefully, what you're good at is worth a lot to people. I'm good with children, but no matter how good I am at it, I'll never be rich." Her face clouded over. "I'll always be screwed by the values of this celebrity-worshiping country. Pray that what you're good at will translate into big buckage for you, and not into a life of hardship dominated by right-wing demagogues."

I alternatively felt excited for my future and horrible for her present. I didn't really know what "screwed" meant, but I knew she wasn't happy. It was partly from her angry verbiage, partly from the half-hour crying jag she succumbed to within minutes. Years later I found out that her Republican hating came not from a deep belief in her core humanitarian values, but from an affair gone awry with a Republican deputy mayor from nearby Suffolk County. Anything that party espoused she felt was coming directly from his two-timing mouth. Her anti-right message was always more vitriolic after she'd had some kind of contact with him. Said crying jag was a direct result of her reading in the *South Shore Record* about his recent marriage to a local newswoman.

I went to my room to think. When I have money, I can do *anything!* I'd started piano lessons the previous year and I was already *way* ahead of Allan Berman, who was still on John Thompson's *Teaching Little Fingers to Play*. I was up to *Easy Classics to Moderns*. Maybe I could make money playing piano. That was what my father did and he made a pretty good living. But I want to make *megabucks*. I thought of my parents arguing. I could always hear them through my bedroom wall.

The italics are where my mother would furiously spray Joy perfume on herself. "Maybe if you had a little amb*ition* you could actually con*duct* one day instead of sitting in the pit like some *und*erling!"

"Zelda, I don't ENJOY conducting and you know that!"

"Do you en*joy* living in a *dump?*"

"What are you talking about! This house is enormous! We both make more than enough money!"

"No we don't!!!!"

"Stop spraying! You smell like a tramp."

"Why don't *you* stop spraying? Spraying your lack of ambition around like a cat marking his territory!"

I suddenly heard a wet THUMP. "Zelda, your simile makes no sense. And the dog just knocked your grapefruit half onto the shag rug."

"Shit! That was my dinner!"

My mother harassed my father constantly about staying "just a piano player." Of course, now I realize she was trying to get him away from the tempting Mitzi (his page turner/humping partner) but she *refused* to be direct, so instead they would argue for hours about why he didn't want to conduct. But I didn't know then that Mitzi was the underlying cause. To me, conducting sounded like the highest job you could get. Piano playing was just a stepping-stone to the big bucks. I figured that if I conducted, I'd have all the money I'd ever need and I could buy plane ticket after plane ticket and jet-set to all the fabulous cities they would perform in. *Cleveland, Milwaukee, Fort Worth.* The possibilities were staggering.

The only problem with becoming an opera conductor was opera. BORING! I was never into it. It was always being played around the house, and although it was pretty, so were peasant skirts. In other words, I found it pleasant, but not something to dedicate my life to. From the age of five, I knew you had to have *passion* for your life's work. My mother was constantly saying during interviews "I love singing. It is . . . (she'd pause trying to find the phrase, even though she's said it in 1,000 interviews) my *passion*. I think of *nothing* else." Whenever I'd see it in print in one of the many articles done on her I would take a pencil and add "except my wonderful son, Stephen" to the last sentence.

I practiced saying those sentences. *I love conducting opera. It is my passion. I think of* nothing *else.* It always felt forced and untrue, but I thought if I said it enough it would begin to feel right.

It didn't work.

Likewise when I substituted the word "girls" for "conducting opera" . . . but that was in my teen years.

Anyway, when I was around ten, Mrs. Remick was taking care of me one weekend and my parents had bought us tickets to a special performance of some romantic art songs performed by a rising Russian soprano at Town Hall. We went to the Long Island Rail Road and there at the station was an enormous advertisement for the TV news show that Mrs. Remick's Republican ex-lover's wife was anchoring. It was a picture of the dark-haired, bushy-mustached anchor and his blonde co-anchor, otherwise known as "the whore" around my house. Mrs. Remick stood and stared at the picture. There was silence. Suddenly, she reeled back, curled her hand, and violently swiped at the poster. I realized she was literally trying to claw the woman's eyes out. The problem was there were no real eyes since it was a poster, so instead of blinding "the whore," Mrs. Remick simply broke two nails into jagged stubs and screamed, *"Fuck!"* horrifying a mother and small child on their way to a matinee/circus/art exhibit for kids in the city.

I watched Mrs. Remick run to the pay phone with a fistful of change and call his office. I ran after her and listened to her end of the conversation.

"Hi, I'm a taxpayer in your district. Are you the receptionist? OK. Do you know that you're working for a fraud? That's right, a fraud! F-R-A-U-D!" She was starting to pant like a dog. "Uh-huh! A fraud is someone who says 'I love you' but actually doesn't. That's right. ACTUALLY DOESN'T! What do you mean, 'Actually doesn't what?' *Love you!*" She was getting annoyed she had to be so literal with the receptionist. "Yes! Actually doesn't love you! What are you, a fucking idiot? No, not loves *you*, loves ME! LOVES ME!" Every word was verbally assaulted. "HE DOESN'T LOVE ME!!!" She started sobbing. "Yes, I'll hold."

The sound of oncoming police sirens made Mrs. Remick hang up frantically, grab me, and run down the stairs towards the parking lot. We hid out where they sell newspapers and gum. I don't necessarily think the cops were coming for her, but she obviously panicked and was too nervous to take a chance. I guess while we were hiding behind the Wrigley's display our train came and went, because after Mrs. Remick thought the coast was clear, we had to wait another twenty minutes on the platform for the next train to New York.

The whole train ride to New York was very tense. I think she was mortified that I saw her go Dr. Jekyl/Ms. Psycho-Ass on the phone, so she told me she was going to take a quick nap, which I assume was solely because she couldn't look at me and needed an excuse to close her eyes.

We got into Penn Station at around 1:20 and the Russian soprano concert began at 1. Mrs. Remick hailed a cab and told the driver to take us to Town Hall, pronto! The driver had a tough time, because it had started to violently snow. The kind of snow we used to get when I was a kid before Republicans/Reagan allowed the greenhouse effect to blanket the planet. Now we're lucky if it sleets once a year.

Anyway, we ran into the lobby and she thrust our tickets into the hand of the usher, who was standing guard at the door to the auditorium. He ripped them in half but didn't open up the door.

Mrs. Remick tried to maneuver her way around him, but he didn't budge.

"Sorry, Ma'am, no one can enter until the applause between songs."

We checked the program hanging in the lobby and saw that La Soprano was starting with a set of Russian folk songs.

"How long are the folk songs?" Mrs. Remick asked the usher as she started taking off her scarf.

"Around four minutes each. Depending on what tempo the pianist sets."

I laughed loudly, implying I too know what a tempo is and I can laugh about it because I am an insider as well.

Mrs. Remick checked her watch. "I guess they're just about over".

"Actually, they are over. She just started her next section."

"How long is it?"

"Well, it's a song cycle. Could take up to a half an hour."

Mrs. Remick had a little sweat on her upper lip. "It's boiling hot in this lobby."

He nodded. "That's 'cause it's so cold out. Patrons like to enter the theatre and feel a blast of hot air." He was obviously proud of the theatre's overactive heater.

Mrs. Remick started fanning herself with her ticket stub, which did nothing but look ridiculous. "I'm sure it's usually appreciated, but patrons aren't supposed to stand in the hot air for the duration of a song cycle. I'm dying with this coat on." She had on one of those long down coats that are perfect for a cold day on Long Island, stuck outside your ex-boyfriend's house while going through his garbage. "Where's your coat check?" she demanded.

He pointed with the energy of a mop. "Over there."

Mrs. Remick started lugging me and her full-body coat towards the direction of his limp finger. He added, "But it's closed until intermission." That did it. She walked right up to the ushers face.

"We are NOT going to stand here and sweat to death in this lobby while Lady Babushka sings a 20-minute snorefest!"

The usher planted himself more firmly. "Oh, really? Where are you going to stand?"

"*In-side!*" She geared up to take a running sprint forward, topple over the usher, and then push her way over his body into the theatre when unexpectedly the sounds of police sirens cut through the tense air.

She cocked her head to the side, grabbed me, covered her face with her hat, and pulled me out of the theatre, down 43rd Street, and up Broadway.

"Let's walk for a bit." She said, with a crazy fake smile, while continually looking over her shoulder, "It's beautiful out." The snow was falling completely horizontally due to the fifty-mile-an-hour winds. After ten blocks or so I finally asked if we could sit down somewhere. Right at that moment, Mrs. Remick's ears perked up to the sound of a distant siren blocks away, probably helping out some pedestrian trapped in a snowdrift. She clamped her hand on my elbow and pulled me in to the nearest doorway. We were in a lobby again, but this time it was filled with people and *tons* of kids. I was used to being the only kid in a lobby due to my parents' proclivity to buy tickets to things only the most snobbish of highbrows would attend. Mrs. Remick ran up to the ticket window.

"Two, please."

The ticket woman pointed to a seating chart. "All we have left is back balcony".

"Fine, fine. Two please and I'm paying in *cash!*" I knew that was so she could erase any trail a cop had been following since her harassing phone call to the secretary.

We took our seats and I opened up the program the usher gave me.

On the cover it said *Annie*. Hmm, I thought. Could it be Ann Von Strousberg, the Austrian spinto soprano and noted Wagner specialist? I'd never heard her referred to as "Annie" in *Opera News*. Must be a new nickname to appear younger. Pa-thetic. It was odd, though, that she opted out of her last name. I figured that she must be so famous they could put just her first name on the cover and everyone would know who she was.

I looked all the way down to the stage and saw a conductor getting on his podium in the pit. I was shocked! He wasn't wearing a tuxedo! He was in a black shirt and pants. I racked my brain for an explanation. Maybe the blizzard had something to do with it, like he was having brunch, and was too nervous to take a cab ride home (to get his tux like he normally did) because the weather had slowed traffic so much.

The lights dimmed, the conductor raised his arms, and a single trumpet started playing a melody I would later become obsessed with. Soon the whole orchestra played the overture and I remember noting it was much bouncier than the overture to The Ring Cycle. Kinda catchy. Lights up on eight girls in a seedy orphanage. One of them is scared so another one sings her a lullaby about one day finding the parents that dropped her at the orphanage.

"*Ma-ay-ay-ay-b-e-e-e-e . . .*"

What a voice! What music! What excitement! I felt like a layer of shadow lifted off me.

Just as I think it can't get better, it does! Miss Hannigan, the owner of the orphanage, walks in. She's a klutzy, hostile drunk. Hilarious! The kids sing a song about their "hard-knock life" and make fun of Miss Hannigan in the process. I actually laughed. I had never laughed in the audience before, except when the conductor of a rival opera company took the tempo of one of *Wozzeck's* final scenes at a *moderato* when it's clearly marked *andante* in the score. But that wasn't even really a laugh, more like a snicker, and only because my mother initiated it.

The show moved on. There was a dog onstage that trotted over to Annie when she called him! How did the dog know how to do that? I was so into the story, I forgot about Mrs. Remick and my parents being out of town. All I wanted was for Annie to be adopted by Daddy Warbucks! There was so much stimuli. The music, the lights, the harmony, the up-and-down emotions. This is what I wanted in my life. Singing, dancing, comedy, tension, tears, resolutions . . . BELTING! I had never heard girls sing in their chest voice. The only singing I knew was classical where everything was in that opera style, like the way Julia Child talked every day. Hmm . . . I'd better clarify the difference between chest and head voice: *chest voice/belting* is Ethel Merman,

Melissa Manchester, Whitney Houston. Opera divas don't belt. They use their head voice. *Head voice* is Charlotte Church, the end of Minnie Ripperton's "Loving You," Glinda the Good Witch. This was brassy! The conductor looked like he was having a great time. Suddenly, I had a shocking thought . . . maybe he didn't forget his tuxedo . . . maybe he wasn't wearing one because he *didn't want to*. On Broadway, you make your own rules! (I've since found out that's *completely* not true, but it *is* true that many conductors don't wear a tux—they just have to wear black.)

There was a number happening on the streets of New York. The "star-to-be" character stepped forward from the crowd and sang her brains out about how she'd just arrived that morning but would one day be living in a penthouse, her name up in lights . . .

That was me! No more opera—I'd discovered Broadway! I "just got here this morning," but one day I'd be there! Not necessarily onstage, but down in that pit waving my arms and wearing a sassy outfit instead of some stuffy-ass tuxedo. Conducting that brassy orchestra and making everyone belt like Andrea McArdle did! Thank you, Mrs. Remick, for being crazy as a loon, for, because of you, I discovered Broadway and, finally, my *passion!*

Eight

*R*ecounting that story took me out of my obsession for a while, but now it's back: Should I just call Mason Littleman? No, I should be patient. He'll call me.

OK . . . I'm calling information.

That was a mistake.

(Recorded voice) *"What city and state, please?"*

"Hi . . . Mason Littleman, residence . . . oh wait . . . that's not what you asked . . . what city, right? Sorry. New York. New York *City*. You know, Manhattan . . . *in* New York . . . State . . . how long do I have to keep babbling? Can't the operator just come on?"

(Live person) *"What city and state, please?"*

"I'm sorry. I just always get wigged out with those recordings."

Silence

"I mean, are you guys listening to it *as* I record it, or do I record it then you listen to it. For some reason, it stresses me out. I feel like I'm performing. Which is weird that it would stress me out, because I *am* a performer, sort of."

(Exact same line reading) "What city and state, please?"
Sound of me hanging up angrily and opening up a phone book.

Anyway, after all that, the number was unlisted. How can I contact him? Should I casually run into him? That always worked at college . . . you know, position yourself outside of Music Theory 2 because you know your crush will exit it at 2:05, and see him and act surprised to bump into him and say, "Hey, what's up?" and then follow him down the hall making light banter (hoping he'll ask you to meet him at Veggie Dining Hall for a romantic dinner next to the salad bar), and eventually arrive at the door to his next class with no definite date made so you somehow bump into him *again* at 3:15 when he gets out of *that* class until finally he changes his class schedule because he can't take the stalking. (OK, that happened only once but the humiliation is still fresh as a daisy.)

But can you casually run into someone in New York City? Maybe if I knew what gym he went to (Hey! I'm *also* taking the 11 o'clock Washboard Abs Samba Step Class!). Or where he got his eyebrows waxed weekly (he doesn't get them waxed into a girl style, but he told me he has to get rid of his monobrow every seven days. He's part Italian . . .'nuf said.).

All this anxiety reminds one (or me) of being in a relationship.

I know! I'll tell you some dating history so I can stop Glenn Close-ing. In high school I was in dire need of Oxy 15 (they only went up to Oxy 10) *and* I sported a large Jewish Afro, so suffice it to say my dating life began in college.

I guess the first legit *relationship* relationship I had was with Jim Cross. I'd had a few dalliances with other "coming out" freshmen during the fall, and in April met Jim in the audience of a Rodgers and Hart revue that the senior musical theatre class was doing. He was there because his ex was the tenor and I was there because I was (and still am) obsessed with musical theatre and will even suffer through a revue if I think it will have good belting at some point.

Anyway, there was a lot of looking at each other during applause, and then lingering at the coffee bar during intermission, and finally phone numbers (and later, fluids) were exchanged. He lived around 45 minutes outside of Boston (I went to New England Conservatory) and I'd see him on weekends. Lookswise, he was ke-yute! (cute in two syllables). *Very* my type. Dark Sephardic skin, short and compact, piercing green eyes. He was older by a few years but had a *much* better body. Apparently sitting on your fat ass all day practicing the piano *doesn't* give you as good of a body as running and/or lifting weights three times a week does. This was the late '80s, so he had just started doing Nautilus and wouldn't stop talking about it. Because I fancied myself a dancer, I soon became a fan of Jazzercise and got my body into relatively OK shape, not that it mattered to him. He was one of those "you're-cute-no-matter-how-you-look" type people. As opposed to Michael Klimzoch (more on this psycho later) who visibly cringed when I wore a tank top on a summer picnic with him (Jazzercise doesn't help your bicep/tricep area).

There were so many great things about the relationship with Jim. He really appreciated my sense of humor (I literally made milk come out of his nose at least twice—once when I did my impression of Carol Mayo Jenkins, who played the annoying know-it-all English teacher in the TV version of *Fame*, and once, inadvertently, when I was singing along with my CD of Whitney Houston's "The Greatest Love of All" and he turned off the volume and silenced the music right when I was hitting what I thought was a "fierce" high note) *and* he put up with my "quirks" (read: incredibly neurotic behavior). Like, he never got annoyed that I made him call me *the minute* he'd get in after he drove home from one of our dates. He knew if he left me at 11 and didn't call me by 11:45 I'd be freaking out that he was in a car accident. Sometimes I can't stop my mind from creating scenes and I'd psyche myself out seeing the accident, imagining the call from the state trooper, having to go to the hospital, getting there and having the doctor say "we did all we could" while gently closing the OR door, fighting with his family over what kind of music to play at his service, deciding to have a *separate* service for his "real" friends because his whole family was acting like such assholes, etc. But if he called me 45 minutes after leaving me (the maximum driving time it should take), my mind would relax and I could go to sleep.

Anyhoo, after things were going great with Jim for a year he got a job right in Boston and his company paid for him to have an apartment in the city. It was perfect! I had been fantasizing about moving with him to NY after I graduated, and now we'd have a chance to try out living together. I figured I could spend weekends at his new apartment, slowly move in my toothbrush/underwear/piano, and eventually segue into staying there seven nights a week.

But then, I don't know what happened. I remember that the night he officially moved in, I didn't want to stay over. I hated the sheets he had just bought (poly-cotton mix—I need 100% cotton), and I longed to be in my own bed, on my own sheets, reading a delicious book. Looking back, it seems like sleeping over would have been so much more fun than going back home alone, but I remember itching, itching, *itching* to get out.

I thought that maybe I had spent too much time with him that day (unpacking, etc.), but soon I began to dread even meeting him for dinner. I felt a panic overtake me when I'd sit with him near the Sizzler salad bar and I'd think maybe I'm nervous about my upcoming recitals. Actually, looking back, it's very similar to the panic I feel when I'm playing auditions and I've misjudged the length of my book, and I finish it too early with two hours still left to play. (Note to Monikah: If I read this to you, no smirking and saying I panic because I'm afraid to feel my feelings. Panic IS a feeling and that's what I feel!)

When he lived out of town I would get really excited about seeing him and then devastated when he had to drive home. But when home was just five minutes away, I started to dread seeing him. My therapist at the time (don't be jealous, Monikah) said it was ye olde fear of intimacy. In other words, when Jim lived in the suburbs, I knew I could be into him as much as I wanted and he would always have to leave, i.e., I'd never have to fully feel intimate with him. But why would I fear intimacy? All I fantasized about as a teenager was having a boyfriend. I craved intimacy. It still doesn't make sense to me. I'd have to repeat to myself during dinner with him, "You like Jim . . . you enjoy spending time with him" . . . but at the same time I'd be trying to think of some excuse for why I'd have to go back to my dorm room to study.

It was right around that time, I started getting a big crush on Michael Klimzoch. Now that I think of it, I had seen Michael the whole semester, but didn't become interested till Jim moved into town. Michael didn't even know who I was at the time. (I only knew his first name was Michael because of his name tag. His work-study job was serving dessert at Veggie Dining Hall, and I would always linger at the Ches-soy-peake Cheesecake so I could take a gander at him stacking the plates.) I used to sit in music theory class and fantasize about moving to NY with Jim, but by midsemester I simply replaced him in my mind with Michael, which is crazy because *I didn't even know him.* But, you know how it is when you look at someone and they seem like they're probably so much fun . . . PLUS they're cute . . . don't you want to move to New York with them? Hello? Anybody? Nobody.

Jim would show up at any recital I did and always have a bouquet of flowers for me and as I'd take them from him and hug him I'd think, "He's really sweet and cute . . . but aren't there people sweet-*er* and cute-*er*?" Some nights he'd call just to chat and even though he was really fun on the phone, I'd tune him out and think, *"I'd love to be having this same conversation with Michael Klimzoch,"* and then I'd get off with Jim and call Michael three times in a row and hang up (this was before caller ID . . . those were the days).

I'd say to myself it's "fear of intimacy," but that was no help because I couldn't force myself to want to feel intimate with him. In fact, soon I was actually grossed out by him. I would look at him in his Gap sweater and CK jeans and think, "E-yew . . . he's naked underneath those clothes." Although two months before (when he lived 45 minutes away) I was obsessed with wanting to see him naked. Is that crazy? But maybe it's different at the beginning of a relationship when you really don't know someone . . . you can see them naked and be turned on purely physically. But when you really know them, and you're not into them, your turn-on factor is clouded by your "I'm-SO-not-into-him" factor.

I finally accepted the fact that Jim wasn't the one for me and broke it off in an awful way, i.e., stopped calling him back and hoped he would eventually fade out of my life.

This was due mostly to me finally "getting together" with Michael. Our relationship was a series of late-night sex sessions where we would have to be quiet so his roommate wouldn't wake up (both during the sex and while I was sneaking out of the room to go back to mine), which were followed by days of Michael pretending like nothing happened. I'd see him at the dessert counter and he'd sort of say "Hey" and suddenly have to go into the kitchen area and not emerge until I left. Then after a period of five to seven days, he would call my room at 2 a.m.—waking up/infuriating my roommate—and ask me to come over. Even though I would vow never to degrade myself again with the late-night sex/next-week ignoring, there I'd be, hopping on my bike and pedaling across campus by the light of the New England moon.

Needless to say, I began to miss Jim. He really was great and so different from Michael, i.e.:

A. He would acknowledge me when I was near him;
B. He spoke to me during daylight hours;
C. He didn't vow after we had sex that it would "never happen again";
D. He wasn't a FUCKING ASSHOLE.

I was too scared to just call Jim because I had dropped him in such a non-explanation way. Should I write? Should I just show up at his office? Should I get one of his friends to tell him I was thinking a lot about him? Well, lo and behold, suddenly I got a letter from him in my student mailbox! It had been around six months since I stopped calling him back and I guess he figured that the best way to reach me would be through the mail. I saved his letter.

Dear Stephen,

As you may have guessed, I was very upset when you stopped returning my phone calls. I assumed that was probably your way of ending a relationship. I do not recommend you continue this technique because it is very upsetting to be on the receiving end. (*I felt awful after reading that. I was so intent on winning over Michael during that period I wasn't even thinking about what Jim was feeling. I just figured he'd get the message and move on.*)

Anyway, I'm not mad because I know you still have issues to work out that prevent you from being direct about a lot of things. (*Seeing his cute handwriting made me remember how much I had liked him. Why did I drop him, I wondered?*)

I'm essentially writing to thank you. (*I thought this was a good sign—maybe we'd get back together!*) Being with you taught me a lot. You can be with someone you think is fantastic (*he meant me!*) but if they don't think you're fantastic back, it can never work out. (*I thought: Wait! I think I loved you . . . I mean, I know I never expressed it, or felt it when you were around, but—I realized how fucked up that sounded and how sucky it must have been for Jim to be with me.*) I'm with someone now who really seems to enjoy being with me. Something you felt at the beginning but seemed to stop feeling when I moved to Boston.

Please take care of yourself and work on whatever you think you need to work on. I know you'll be in a great relationship one day if you do.

Jim

Reading that again is so fucking FRUSTRATING because I still don't know what to work on! Of course I found out through some mutual friends Jim had a commitment ceremony with his new beau around five years ago. AND THEY STILL HAVEN'T BROKEN UP! Well, at least now I'm with someone I like (a lot).

Guess who just called me??? Mr. Mason Littleton asking me to meet him at Café Edgar (delicious dessert-ery on 84th Street). I'll write when I get home.

Nine

I'm curled up in bed with Heather next to me and I'm SO EXCITED! Here's what happened: Walked into Café Edgar and ordered a decaf. Mason came in and we hugged. He ordered and since I couldn't decide, I asked the waitress to bring whatever chocolaty dessert she recommended. I immediately tuned out the beginning of Mason's small talk because I was busy obsessing that I didn't want coffee anymore; I wanted a cold skim milk. (I put a lot of sugar in coffee and I wanted something to counteract the cake's sweetness.) So I was doing a lot of nodding to Mason, but was actually looking over his shoulder for the waitress. I get *crazy* when people do that to me, but I also get compulsive about food, so I couldn't stop myself.

"Do you see someone you want to say 'hi' to?" Mason asked me, turning in his seat so he could look behind him.

Of course, I was too embarrassed to tell him it was as shallow as wanting to get a skim milk, so quick-thinkingly I said, "Oh, I'm looking over there 'cause that blond guy's an ex-boyfriend of mine and I'm dying to see who he's with now."

I should have thought my lie through because the guy I was referring to was so obviously not someone I would want Mason to think I would have ever dated. He sported a home perm and a T-shirt that proudly read "One nation *under God*, with liberty and justice for all."

Mason tried to see whom my "ex" was sitting with.

He whispered, "I guess he's with her now . . ." referring to the matronly woman holding hands with *Under God*. "Did you know he was bisexual when you dated him?"

Luckily, the waitress approached at that moment with the cakes and the decaf. I ordered my milk. I noticed the waitress for some reason had brought Mason a slice of carrot cake instead of the cheesecake that he clearly ordered.

She walked away and I motioned towards Mason's dessert.

"Didn't you order the strawberry chessecake?"

He looked at the carrot cake. "Yeah . . . but it's fine."

"But aren't you the one who once told me at Rose's Turn that you hate vegetables in your dessert."

He looked shocked. "Oh my God, you remember!" He laughed. "Yes, that's true . . ." He started feebly eating the cake. "But don't worry about it."

Huh? It's one thing to be my mother and eat 8/9ths of a meal and then send it back because "there's something not quite right about it," then proceed to order an entirely different meal, eat the whole thing, and refuse to pay because the first meal was so awful. It's another thing to blatantly get the wrong order and not have it replaced. It took all the strength I had to resist my strongly honed codependent urge to summon our vaguely accented waitress and get Mason his delicious strawberry cheesecake.

I forced myself to take a bite of my Death by ___, or Sinfully Delicious ___, or some other Cathy Guisewite-named chocolate cake and decided to get back to the business side of our meeting.

"So, Mason," I said innocently, "I'm so curious why you called."

"Stephen, don't play dumb. I'm sure Ronald told you I was going to woo you to work on *Flowerchild*."

I gave up the act and smiled. "Totally busted. He told me at brunch this morning."

He put two sugars in his latte. "The weird part is, he said you knew I was going to ask you."

I did a lot of eye rolling and shaking my head as if to imply Ronald can't be trusted/is crazy/was on one of his benders again and gracefully moved on to, "First off, congratulations for getting a big fat Broadway directing gig!"

As he impounded fat/carbs/caffeine, he filled me in. *Flowerchild* started out at Yale. Mason and his friends put it on in a coffeehouse just to get one credit in some artsy "Make-up-your-own-syllabus" course left over from the mid-70s when Yale tried to be less stodgy. The show got great word of mouth among the "I-come-from-poverty-but-studied-like-a-mofo—to-get-a-full-scholarship" students, the "my-parents-both-went-here-and-I'm-not-actually-smart-but-money-talks," and the "I'm-smart-and-have-money-but-I'm-studying-computer-science-so-essentially-I-have-no-friends" students, and even the "I-hate-you-fucking-Yale-snobs" townies that happened upon the show.

Soon word got down to New York and some producers came up and bought the rights. Ever since *Rent*, Broadway's been looking for the next young upstart to create a new gazillion-dollar-making show.

I took a long sip of my milk. By the by, I love milk with any dessert, but I hate those effing "Got milk?" ads. The "milk mustaches" are so obviously *FAKE!* It should be called *NOT* MILK. I read some article where one of the actor/models said, "The guy who mixes the mustache ingredients is *very* particular about his recipe." Why? It sucks! I get myself crazy imagining the makeup guy, all proud, painting the mustache on, taking a step back, and then putting the finishing touches on his "masterpiece." It doesn't look like milk and it's so obviously placed perfectly. Am I the only one who thinks he's a blatant charlatan? I was, of course, further infuriated when they took it to a "new level" with the *chocolate* milk mustaches. I'll bet they were thinking, "No one will expect this . . . we're hilarious!" Finally, to destroy any hope I had for a peaceful life, they had the nerve to come out with a whole book dedicated to those ads! An *entire* coffee table book with pictures of celebs and a fake gooey substance on their top lips that we're supposed to believe is milk. Here's an idea: why can't they actually USE MILK??? Why involve us in their lies? I suddenly realized Mason was still talking.

". . . so glad I spent those years hearing you at Rose's Turn. Those arrangements you used to make up are exactly the kind I want for this show. I was just telling someone about your codependent/fear-of-intimacy medley."

I combined The Beatles' needy "Got to Get You into My Life" with the emotionally void *Valley of the Dolls* ("*Gotta get off . . .*") theme song.

My cell phone rang. It was (of course) Jackson. I gave Mason the "one-minute" finger and picked up.

"Hi, Jackson. I'm meeting with Mason Littleton." I checked my watch. 9:35. "Is it still intermission?"

"Ask Mason if the *Flowerchild* has a part in it for me," he whispered conspiratorially. The Sisyphean truth for most actors is that once they get a show, they *immediately* start looking for their next one. It's a combination of trying to stay one step ahead of a show closing, wanting to get as many connections as you can so you more easily move from show to show, as well as the fact that it's considered kinda loser-ish to stay in a show too long (i.e., "Is this the *only* part you can get?")

"The desserts are delicious," I responded non sequiturially, implying, "*I'm not asking Mason that at this moment.*"

"Fine . . . I guess that is kinda tacky until you actually have the gig. Oh, P.S. Do you want to go to *Gypsy of the Year*? (I'll describe what that is later . . . basically it's a big charity event/variety show that Broadway puts on for Broadway.)

"Sure, I'll go," I responded enthusiastically. *Gypsy* (note the cool abbreviation) is always great.

"Excellent. I'm performing in it. I'll get you a seat next to Ronald."

SHIT! "OK . . . call me later."

Mason asked who that was and I told him a little about Jackson and turns out he had recently seen him in a workshop of a musical version of *Three's Company*. He played Jack, which is great for his resumé, but the music was a headache and the plot made no sense. The main story was about the competition between him and his landlord for the lead in a community theatre production of *Oklahoma*. His big comic number was called "Mr. Furley Ain't No Curley," and it brought the house down. Down into a deep depression because it wasn't funny. But it wasn't Jackson's fault—it was the material.

I was commiserating with Mason about the script problems and trying to talk Jackson up at the same time. I told Mason that whenever Jackson and I used to go to bars together, everyone would talk to Jackson and leave me standing, awkwardly holding my virgin Shirley Temple.

Mason seemed surprised. "Really? Why?"

Yay! I got to spell it out. "Well, he's much better-looking than me."

He looked quizzical. "Hmm . . . I don't agree." At that moment the waitress came over and refilled Mason's latte. What did he mean? He didn't agree that was the reason, i.e., maybe it's your awful personality? Or did he mean I'm better-looking than Jackson? That's crazy. I was too scared to ask him to clarify, because then it would look like I was interested in if he thought I was good-looking, which I wasn't. Of course, suddenly, my cell phone rang and I saw from the number displayed, it was Craig. I thought maybe it was rude to get two cell phone calls during the same meeting, so I turned it off mid-ring. I decided to find out whose job I was getting.

"What about the music director who did it at Yale? Did he die?" That came out a little blunt, but I didn't want some guy whose job I stole to appear on opening night with a subpoena and a machete.

"What music director? We all made up our own harmonies and wrote out the arrangements. Don't forget, at Yale, we're multitalented."

Even though he was sitting, he did a grand mock bow, which reminded me of my brief stint as an actor performing *The Court of King Arthur* for an outer Boston children's theatre. Maybe being a court jester was fun in the 1500s, but it's not fun at 8:30 in the morning at Jefferson Elementary when your "court" consists of hostile third graders who know a multitude of slang words for *gay* AND *untalented*. Ooh . . . he was still talking.

". . . and every couple of weeks there'd be a different band playing for us. None of the actors or musicians wanted to commit to the show for too long because there wasn't much buckage, and most people at Yale freak if they're not studying every minute. I was the one who came up with the idea for the show and wrote it and I'm the only one who stayed with it from beginning to end."

Speaking of lawsuits, I asked: "Are the people who helped put the show together sharing in the profit?"

There are countless stories about people who worked on the initial stages of a show and were shut out of revenues. One of the most recent is the original cast members of *A Chorus Line* (whose real life personalities and stories make up much of the show) not getting any royalties for the '06 revival.

Mason nodded as he tentatively ate a bite of carrot cake. "Everyone that's been involved creatively with the show," he grimaced and swallowed, "around thirty people, are getting a percentage."

By the by, that doesn't necessarily mean they're getting much. They're probably splitting one percent. Still, that could add up to a lot of moolah, if the show runs for a long time.

I gathered up the delicious crumbs from the remains of my cake and promptly downed them. "What about casting the show? Are all your Yale friends gonna be devastated if they're not used?"

He'd finally finished the cake part of his dessert and was now just eating the yummy icing. "There are only three main roles. I played one of them and I'm not gonna pull a Barbra (I assumed he meant directing and starring—not singing an ill-advised love duet with Don Johnson), and my fellow graduates aren't inter-ested in Broadway. "They want the big bucks of a TV pilot or movie." The check came. He grabbed it. "I'm paying for it. After all, this was a business meal."

He slapped down some money and looked me in the eye . . . actually both eyes.

"Stephen, you're perfect for this gig and you deserve it. Please say you'll do it."

I was so excited but didn't speak. I thought, "Let me remem-ber this moment." Ever since the *Annie* experience I've fanta-sized about conducting a Broadway Show. During all of my parents' subsequent out-of-town trips, I'd soothe myself by imagining myself on the podium. It's my favorite fantasy next to the perfect boyfriend one. The good news is, dear *dear* Diary (just kidding . . . I just always wanted to write dear *dear* Diary), I don't have to fantasize anymore, because it's coming true! What could be better?

I shook his hand. "I am *so* doing it!"

Ten

*H*ello from the pit of an unnamed show. I'm too embarrassed to say I sub here because this show represents everything I hate about Broadway. Not only does the "orchestra" consist of mainly synthesizers, but there is LIP-SYNCHING in the show! For some reason, the unions allow prerecorded vocals to play on Broadway. One of the reasons producers love it is because it allows them to hire fewer people. An ensemble gets winded singing and dancing at the same time so there needs to be a good amount of them to get a big, consistent sound. But if you play a prerecorded vocal track at the same time, you can hire fewer people. Of course, I'm concerned for my actor friends because it means fewer of them are being hired, but I'm more concerned with how Broadway shows are sounding. When you have a vocal track playing, all the imperfections that make a show sound live are gone, and instead you get a very even, boring sound. Speaking of boring, the show is starting.

I just played the overture and opening number and now there's a ten-minute scene, so I can write. OK, here's the update. I found out this morning that auditions begin next week for *Flowerchild*. They should go on for about three weeks and then we're taking off a few weeks for the holidays. Rehearsals start the second week of January, previews are the beginning of March, and then we open the show in April. Wow! I can't believe I just wrote, "*We* open the show!" I'm really doing it! I keep waiting for a Mack truck to crash into the pit and run me over. Maria DaDio (the general manager . . . in charge of payroll, etc.) called me on my cell phone and offered me a deal. I have to show the contract to my mother's agent before I sign 'cause I have no idea what to ask for. I've never negotiated a big contract before. All my actual music directing/conducting has been for regional theatres and one pretty much takes whatever deal is offered. There are so many things to negotiate for Broadway: dressing room, title page of the program billing, font size on the poster, SALARY, etc.

The matinee is over and I just had a session with Monikah. As usual she was cryptic/annoying.

ME: I have amazing news!
HER: *Silence*
ME: I've been asked to music direct a new Broadway show!
HER: (*nodding slightly*) You seem happy.
ME: (*annoyed*) Of course I'm happy—it's what I've been working towards for years. (*Here's my chance . . .*) By the way, I was thinking my last name is too Jewish. Maybe now that I'm gonna be on my first Broadway show poster, I should change it to something more Waspy. Like Adams, or . . . ATKINS.
HER: (*no sign of recognition*) Why do you think it matters if your last name is too Jewish?
ME: That's not my point . . . do you like, or should I say, are you *familiar* with the last name Atkins?

HER: Atkins is a common name.

ME: Well, it's gotten a lot of attention lately. You know, Atkins Hardware, (*what?*), Atkins Menswear (*awful*), Atkins *di-et*.

HER: *Silence*

ME: (*telepathically*) Are you on the Atkins Diet? Are you on the Atkins Diet? Are you on the Atkins Diet???

HER: (*looking concerned*) Do you have a headache?

ME: (*explosively*) ARE YOU ON THE ATKIN'S DIET??? (*breathing heavily*)

HER: (*calmly*) Is focusing on insignificant things a way for you to distract yourself from feeling a connection with someone?

ME: Um . . .

HER: Do you have trouble feeling close or intimate with other people?

ME *Shamed silence*

I changed the subject and asked her if I could just end my book on a happy note. You know, like, turns out the reason I've been only a sub all this time is because nobody really saw how talented I was. It took a young genius straight out of Yale to take a fresh look at me. The last sentence would read:

My nights

are now

. . . on Broadway.

Vivent les nuits de Broadway.

Two pages of acknowledgments, bio, and cute/professionally retouched author photo on the inside back cover and we're out.

HER: I think you should continue writing in your journal.

ME: Why? I thought it was to find out why I'm still subbing. Not only won't I be a sub, I've graduated to conductor!

HER: That was *one* of the reasons you read to me. If you'll check your opening journal entry or "chapter" (*she made quotation marks with her fingers*), it was to explore your relationship with Craig, as well. And also . . . (*searching for the right non-personality-ridden words*) I'm not sure if your summation of why you remained a sub for so many years is accurate.

ME: Why? What do you think the reason is?

HER: *Silence*

Well, obviously I've decided to keep writing. Besides the fact that it's fun, the truth is it's not long enough to be a book yet. Right now it's only the length of one of those awful *Worst-Case Scenario* handbooks. What a waste of trees. Here's a worst-case scenario: being forced to actually read that book! The piss-me-off news is that they've also turned it into a *board game!* Is there no end to idiot merchandising? And, in a similar vein, could *my* book be turned into a game? Hmm . . .

Regardless, even though things seem pretty much resolved for me, I'm gonna keep on writing. Why not?

Uh-oh. Things are SO not resolved. Craig just quit *Phantom*.

Eleven

I'm at Craig's apartment. He's taking a bath to de-stress, which gives me some time to write down what happened . . . and get ready, 'cause it's a doozy.

OK, Here's how it went down. Craig is trying to transition from dancer to actor but, like I said before, his singing voice can't seem to transition past "awful." He found out they needed a new cover for the *Phantom* male romantic lead (Raoul) and asked to audition for it. The stage manager, not being deaf, said no. Craig had his agent call and manipulate the casting director into giving Craig an audition. He prepared "All I Ask of You." (You know, the song that's a duet between Raoul and Christine that Barbra Streisand recorded and somehow managed to turn into a solo.) Craig told me he went in and sang it the best he's ever sung. (Don't be excited . . . that's like the Elephant Man saying "I walked in and I looked *fan-tastic*!!") Craig kind of has no awareness of the limitations of his voice. I think it's from grow-ing up good-looking, rich, and with a good body. In the gay community (i.e., the bar scene) he's treated like a god and he's used to assuming he can do and get away with anything. He was positive he was going to get it. He proudly proclaimed that after he sang they thanked him profusely. He doesn't yet know the equation I was talking about with Traci Lyn: amount of thanking and "great job-ing' is equal to the Amount of flat-out rejection and no way Jose-ing. (T/GJ = R/NWJ.)

OK, cut to this afternoon: he goes to sign in and on the call-board is the understudy rehearsal schedule. One afternoon a week, usually Thursday, the show is performed onstage with all the understudies. The annoying part is there's only a piano (orchestras cost $), and since union rules say only stagehands can move scenery, none of the sets are used (stagehands cost $). That means usually an understudy works with the orchestra/set for the first time during an actual performance. So, if you're an understudy on for the first time, not only are you trying to remember your lyrics, staging, and acting moments, but, in a show like *Phantom*, you also have to remember when and how far down to duck when the chandelier comes crashing down towards your noggin. Yes, you've rehearsed it many times, but it's not the same as finally doing it in front of an audience in full costume with lights in your face. It's like going to the proctologist for the first time: you're essentially prepared for what's going to happen, but it's shocking nonetheless.

Well, as Craig was signing in, he saw the new understudies listed. Next to Raoul's name was Hunter Plotnick, a dancer who was in ABT with Craig. I've actually heard Hunter sing and he really is great, but Craig was infuriated and felt they gave it to him because the stage manager was once married to Hunter's sister, Tulita. Craig barged into the stage manager's office and demanded to know why he wasn't cast. The stage manager told him the music director didn't think he had the right quality of voice for the role, which was a nice way of saying, "Please, please, PLEASE stick to dancing!" I don't know what Craig said, but it ended with him opening up his dance bag and throwing whatever was right on top (unfortunately, his dance belt) at the stage manager, giving notice, and storming upstairs. Craig was too angry to ask for his dance belt back, so he did the whole show without wearing one. I'm sure you know what male dancers look like in tights while wearing dance belts . . . imagine what they look like without one. The Japanese tourists who make up 60% of the typical *Phantom* audience now have a great story to tell their friends. Hopefully, there's a pithy Japanese idiom for "flaccid and obvious."

Craig wanted to know from me if he did the right thing. Hmm . . . when is throwing an athletic supporter at anyone the "right thing?" At an S&M bar? I told him if he didn't like being in *Phantom*, it's better to quit than to do the show while hating it. I didn't know what else to say so I tried to get his mind off *Phantom* by telling him about me getting *Flowerchild*. It's bad to brag about getting a job when someone else hates theirs, but since we're in such different fields, I figured it didn't matter. Plus, he's my boyfriend and he knows how sick I am of being a sub. He was happy for me, but felt he had to call his agent and tell him what happened. Ooh, my cellphone's ringing.

꼭hat was Mason. He wanted to get together to talk about the show. I was too embarrassed to tell him where I was. All my friends know about me and Craig, but I felt Mason would think the so-called "cheating" was sleazy. You have to understand how fucked up Craig's relationship with Jeffrey is to realize why it's OK for him to be with me. I didn't think I could fully explain it to Mason over the phone, so I told him I was on my way out of a yoga class (it made me sound at peace) but I would meet him in an hour. I can't believe a director of a Broadway musical is calling to meet with me to take my opinion seriously! I feel so grown up!

꼭ust walked Heather, and I thought I'd write before I went to sleep. Met Mason at Café Edgar again. He shaved his beard and he looks great. He had a round baby face when he used to come to Rose's Turn, but now his looks have matured. He kind of looks like a cuter version of John Cusack. Also, he's not wearing his "funky" East Village glasses that everyone at NYU wore in the mid-'90s, and it turns out he has crazily beautiful long lashes. I asked him if he was wearing mascara, 'cause if he was, he put way too much on, and he fluttered his eyelashes just to prove to me they're real. Of course, while he was fluttering them, he got an eyelash in his eye and he spent five minutes trying to get it out. We were being glared at for laughing so much by someone with a laptop at the next table. You know what? Why are you bringing serious work to a dessert cafe? "Hmm . . . I have to finish my dissertation. Should I go to the library where people are supposed to be quiet, or a public eatery where people are supposed to *TALK!*?" I did the old cough into my hand while muttering "inappropriate workspace," and Mason scurried off to the bathroom to flush out his eye with water.

We spent the night talking about different concepts for the opening. Should we include real hippie film footage from the '60s? Should we do *Forrest Gump*-style superimposing of the actors into group scenes from Woodstock, which would be really funny, as opposed to *Forrest Gump*, which was really SUCKY (not that I've seen it . . . but I'll still judge it). We hugged good-bye and I realized I could still make it over to Craig's house, but I had work I wanted to get done tomorrow morning to prepare for auditions next week, so I came home and waited an hour to call Craig until I knew it would be too late to come over. I told him more about *Flowerchild*, and this time he seemed really excited. Who knows? Maybe by the time it opens he'll have broken up with Jeffrey and we'll be able to go to the opening night party together!

Twelve

J'm meeting my mom for brunch. Even though she and my dad are divorced, they still tour together. Do the words "Codependents Anonymous" mean anything to you? Wouldn't someone normal want to let go of the past instead of recreating it in 40 cities a year? Oh yeah, not only do they still tour together, but the infamous Mitzi, who's now married to my dad, is still *turning pages!* It's like they all want to keep up the tension of their earlier touring days. My mom is 58, so her singing is not what it used to be, but she can still do lecture/demonstrations at various music schools across the country and make pretty good $. Oh yeah, they got divorced when I was 13. That was a fun conversation.

"Stephen."

I whirled around at the sound of her voice. I hated when my mom walked in on me suddenly. While most parents find their kids masturbating, mine would find me lip-synching to Patti LuPone's balcony scene in *Evita*. I would never hear her approaching 'cause she never wore shoes at home. She claimed it was because she didn't want varicose veins, but I think it's because she loved walking around the house like a diva after a triumphant performance, receiving celebs in her dressing room.

The outfit I associate her most with was her purple satin robes with feathers, hair up in a turban, and beautiful white slippers "lined with real fur . . . not the fake stuff!" For someone concerned with varicose veins, she had no problem with the fact that her slippers had four-inch heels and came to a tip as small as pencil lead. The only good part was that they prepared me for the requisite "Oh-my-G*d-I'm-totally-gonna-go-in-drag" Halloween party everyone has in college. While my dorm mates were clunking around in their first pair of Easy Spirits, I (because of my mother's many weekends out of town and my many forays into her closet) was pirouetting, prancing, and walking the catwalk better than a young Tyra Banks.

Hmm . . . my mom, usually fully made-up from sunup to sundown, didn't look like she normally did. She looked lopsided. Did a heel break? Then I realized it. She had obviously been crying and then redid her eye makeup but for some reason stopped before doing her right eye, which was matted with old mascara and liner. She was always so meticulous. What the hell was going on? And why was she crying? I had seen her with tears in her eyes at my bar mitzvah reception two weeks before, but I assumed that was the whole "my-son-is-becoming-a-man" syndrome. Uh-oh. Was it my Patti LuPone lip-synching? Was she nervous that "my son is becoming a woman?"

The truth is I didn't really want a bar mitzvah but my mom talked me into it by appealing to my inner ham (no Kosher pun intended). At that time, I not only wanted to be a Broadway conductor, but I wanted to also be Andrea McArdle. I would sing with the *Annie* record and dream of conducting *and* somehow starring in *(M)annie*, the male version. I was auditioning for lots of professional shows at that time, but kept not getting cast because I spoke like a girl (my voice hadn't changed yet) and looked like Totie Fields (I never met a Combos flavor I didn't like). When I first balked about having to learn the haftorah portion for my bar mitzvah my mom told me that since there's no accompaniment at the synagogue I could put it into any key I wanted.

"So?" I asked, bored.

"I'll bet you'd sound good belting Yerusha*la-a-a-ay*im on a B flat."

She dangled that comment like a carrot. She knew B flat was my money note, and even though her opera training meant she didn't approve of Broadway-style belting, she also couldn't deal with the community-wide shame of not having a son bar mitzvahed and was prepared to make it happen by any means necessary. It worked. I got excited at the thought of finally having a public venue to sing up a storm and said to myself, if Elvis could do Vegas, I could play a synagogue. Needless to say my haftorah performance had the most vibrato, scooping, and sustained high notes this side of a Donna Summer double CD.

"Stephen, we waited until the bar mitzvah was over, but now there are gonna be big changes around here."

"What kind of changes?"

She took a deep breath and adjusted her turban. "Have you noticed Mommy and Daddy fighting a lot lately?"

"No." How do you define "a lot"? They'd been having at least one fight a day since I was a toddler. More on holidays.

"Stephen, sit down."

We were in my room and my bed was riddled with Broadway show albums, so I had to sit on the only other available chair—my red beanbag. It always looked so cool, but in reality there was no proper way of sitting in it. Reclining? Awkwardly erect back with no support? Stomach down with no equilibrium?

I chose awkwardly erect back.

She had to kneel down to speak to me. I could smell her Anais Anais perfume. "Mommy and Daddy are going to get . . ." She started crying. I tried to finish the sentence in my head. Mommy and Daddy are going to get . . . counseling? real with each other? it together?

She stood up and fluffed her robe out so it hung correctly. "We're getting a divorce and I don't want you for one minute to think it's your fault. The tension of having two children way too early in my career had nothing to do with your father cheating on us."

"Cheating . . . how?"

"I don't want to involve you. It's between me and your father and Mitzi."

"What does Mitzi have to do with it?"

"PLEASE don't mention her name."

She turned away from me abruptly, hitting her head on my homemade plant holder in the window. "Goddamn this ugly-ass batik and goddamn your father!"

Batik? Ugly-ass? Two phrases that can't possibly *go together. Besides, it was macramé.*

"Does this mean you'll be staying home more often?" I began to get excited.

"No. I feel it's only professional to finish out our touring schedule. But after that, who knows?" She paused for effect, dreamily staring off into the distance, absentmindedly fingering a *Meteor* poster I hung up from a *Dynamite* magazine.

"*After that, who knows?*"! I now not only fantasized about having enough money to one day join them on their tours, but I added the fantasy of my mother completely stopping going on the road so she could create a world-class garden. I got the garden idea from watching a PBS *Nova* special about a family that gardened together. They seemed to spend inordinate amounts of time tilling, weeding, and planning their various plants morning, noon, and night. I started smiling.

"Stephen, you don't seem upset."

I erased the smile. I was nervous that if my mom knew what I wanted, it wouldn't come true.

"Will Daddy move out of the house?"

"Your father has already moved most of his clothing to her tacky split level. This was all done behind our back, mind you, I didn't find out about that tidbit till last night." She sighed heavily. "I assume those two will live there, and we'll keep the house."

She kneeled down again to face me. "Now, I know this is a big shock for you, as it is for me. If you want to talk about anything, anything at all"—she took my hands in hers—"Mommy will be back in two-and-a-half weeks."

She gave me a quick kiss, then rushed off to get ready for her flight to Ontario. But I wasn't upset. I knew if Mitzi really was my dad's new (woman? girlfriend? old lady?), my mom wouldn't be able to take the uncomfortableness of being on the same stage with them and it would speed up the end of her touring days. I thought about that all through that tour, her Christmas gala tour of New Mexico, her Boise Brahms recital—pretty much up until high school graduation. She'd come home from every tour raging about my dad and Mitzi not inviting her to dinner at a layover in Denver or Mitzi changing her hairstyle to the "*exact same one*" my mom had when they first married, etc. I asked my mom why she just didn't get a new accompanist and she'd laugh bitterly and say "Believe me, if I could, I would." Monikah said my mom enjoys feeling like a victim and this was the perfect way to perpetuate it. I told that to my mom recently, in a loving way, to see if she was ready to change, and she told me to tell Monikah to "take that stupid K in her name and shove it up her ass."

I have some time to kill before the matinee. I left two hours for brunch with my mom, but she had to run to get to a rehearsal for her latest gig.

"Your father is up to old tricks again." She downed the rest of her second mimosa. "Flirting right and left with Mitzi."

We were in the middle of splitting three different kinds of pancakes at Josie's. My mother was in full glam: black glittering blouse over sassy black tailored slacks. Half her lipstick was on her coffee cup, but she still looked like she had enough on to last through Passover. She hasn't changed her makeup scheme since the seventies—nor has she ever differentiated it between on- and offstage.

The topic of our meal conversations was usually my dad et al. "Flirting?" I wondered out loud. "Is it still called flirting now that he's married to her? Isn't it called being affectionate?"

"Oh, Stephen, you don't understand." She waved the conversation away and I noticed she had her nails done French Tip. "Now, *when* am I finally going to see you on Broadway?"

That was the question she always asked me. She didn't want to hear me play a show while I was still subbing. She felt she should wait until I had my own gig so she could "really see my Broadway debut." I knew where she was coming from. She wanted the initial rush of watching me and knowing I was a bigwig on Broadway. The annoying part is we've both been waiting a long time.

"Well, that's the amazing news." I was holding out the whole brunch for the proper moment. "I've actually been offered the chance . . . to conduct a new Broadway show!"

She motioned the busboy for more Sweet 'N Low. "You've conducted on Broadway before. That's not news."

Not the reaction I wanted. "No, Mom. My *own* show!"

She opened her eyes wide, splitting apart some of her Lancôme "Just Lids" shadow. "Stephen, fantastic!" She looked concerned. "Is it definitely going to open?" She shook her head. "I'm always hearing stories about shows losing their backing money and having to postpone."

"Well, so far, so good. I haven't heard about any backers . . . backing out, as it were." I never even thought about that. Most shows I knew about that actually announced their preview and opening dates opened on schedule.

She motioned for the check. "Well, let's hope it really happens. And *please* let's also hope the opening is when I'm in town. I'd hate to have to miss it." She pointed a well-manicured finger at me. "And *do not* sit me with your father and Mitzi—I couldn't bear it. Just put me in the back of the balcony. *Anywhere* so I don't have to see them."

I put down my credit card. Now that I was an adult, I liked being able to pay for my mom. "Well, we haven't gotten any ticket order forms yet, but I'm sure I can work out something. I'm just so excited."

"You sound it!" She took one last bite of the multigrain pancake with real Vermont maple syrup. "Thank you so much for brunch, and call me when you know that it's definitely happening."

Several heads turned as she exited. I don't know if it was because they're opera fans or because they saw her face and wanted to look at the pretty Monet up close. I had one more cup of coffee, then headed over to the Barnes & Noble on 66th Street. It had three floors and a music section downstairs. I always feel guilty patronizing Barnes & Noble because they've essentially put every small neighborhood bookstore out of business, but *they have a café!*

By the way, I hope you didn't feel like I'd been holding out on you when my mom said that I'd conducted on Broadway before. It's true, but like everything in my life up to this point, it was as a sub. I explained before that usually a show has two keyboard players and they're the associate and assistant conductor, respectively. But if it has only one keyboard, then either another instrumentalist (usually the drummer) is the assistant conductor, or they have someone not regularly in the pit (me) do it. So, I have had the thrill (and terror) of standing on a Broadway podium and conducting a musical a few times as an assistant, but I've never been able to think "this is my show."

Ooh, how exciting! I was just flipping through *Backstage*, (the newspaper that lists theatre news and auditions) and saw an audition announcement for *Flowerchild!* At the bottom it said *Mason Littleton, Director, Stephen Sheerin, Music Director.* If it's in print, it must be true! I really hope my mom will be in town for the opening.

* * *

I'm (as usual) in the pit (*Little Mermaid*). I got to the theatre early so I decided to go to the Starbucks by the Marriott. Around an hour before showtime, you can no doubt find a mélange of actors there, getting their caffeine on. It's always fun to run into someone I know.

"Yoo-hoo, Stephen!"

Unless it's devastating. I recognized the piercing voice of Roberta Munkel, a headache I did *Ragtime* with years ago. She's not even in a show, I thought. Why is she hanging around this neighborhood on matinee day?

She did a laborious twirl, showing me her business suit.

"I'm temping today, on a Saturday." She shook her head. "How pathetic."

I had a sudden flashback of being backstage with her in the wig room with her saying, "I'm on for Emma Goldman today. How pathetic."

Roberta was one of those people who hate whatever show they're performing in. I played her audition for *Ragtime* and she was bitter about the show by the final callback two weeks later.

She looked around. "I guess everyone's getting ready for their matinee."

I looked over by the barista and saw two guys I knew from *Spamalot* and one of the Four Seasons from *Jersey Boys* waiting for their brew.

I nodded. "Yeah . . . I'm about to play *The Little Mermaid*."

"I'm sorry for you. Kids shows are the worst." She took a sip of her coffee and grimaced. "Oh! It's always so bitter here!"

Tell me about it.

She looked me up and down. "I read you just got a Broadway show."

Please don't ask me to get you an audition.

She sighed. "I thought I'd ask you to get me in," (*I knew it!*) "but I know that first-time music directors have no power."

What?

"I might as well ask an usher to get me an audition." She

sipped and grimaced again. "Bitter!" She threw the whole cup of coffee out. "I think I know the stage manager." She rolled her eyes. "I guess I'll have to suck up to him."

The stage manager! I'm more important than him! How dare she!

"*I'll* get you an audition!" I whipped out my cell phone and promptly called the casting director. I scheduled Roberta for the following Monday at 1 p.m. I then bid her adieu, put eight sugars in my coffee, and headed for the theatre.

As I was sitting down at my keyboard in the pit, reality came back into focus. What was I thinking? She's totally wrong for *Flowerchild*, unless there's a role for a massively overweight soprano with no pop/rock style and zero sense of humor. Wait, I think someone's talking to me . . .

That was annoying. As usual, some idiot audience member leaned over the pit, dumbfounded. "Oh, I thought . . . I thought . . . isn't the orchestra on tape?"

NO, YOU DUMB-ASS! IT'S BROADWAY! NOT A BRITNEY PRERECORDED MOTHERFUCKING SPEARS CONCERT!

It happens once a week. This time I let someone else deal with it.

There is a feeling among musicians that there is very little mention made of the orchestra so that little by little the live musicians will be replaced with prerecorded music and/or all synthesizers. The musicians union has lobbied to have a picture of all the musicians put in the lobby so people will know they exist or have an announcement always made about who is conducting the orchestra as the lights dim, but so far it hasn't happened. So we have to constantly face the "I-thought-you-guys-were-on-tape" comments from ignorant audience members over the pit. And *they* have to face my constant hostile replies, which include lots of sighing, eye rolling, and aggressive pointing to instruments.

* * *

I saw Jackson during intermission. He sort of rocked my world . . . and not in a good way. He was on for the Prince so he had his own dressing room. Essentially the size of a bathroom with lots of good luck cards to the actor playing the Prince hung up around the mirror. Of course, every time Jackson goes on he brings an enormous framed photo of himself and Ronald and puts it on his dressing table. I kept trying to not look 'cause it sickened me, yet my eyes were drawn to it because I was obsessed with looking at Ronald's total lack of a top lip. How long does it take him to get through a tube of Chapstick? A decade?

Jackson broke me out of my staring. "What up with your psycho boyfriend?"

MY psycho boyfriend? *That* was the relationship addict calling the kettle addicted to love!

"Meaning what?" I said with deliberate haughty air.

"Meaning throwing his dance belt in the stage manager's face and doing the show with a dick outline."

"Oh." Meaning *that*. "He was just pissed off."

"How about crazy? No wonder his ass was fired."

"Nice try, Señor Negativo. He quit." I plopped down on the one comfortable chair in his dressing room.

"Quit? That's not what it says on Stalkin'." I plopped back up again.

There are lots of theatre Web sites and message boards (Playbill.com, Broadway.com, Theatremania.com), but the one *everyone* in the business looks at is Talkin' Broadway. (I don't know why the G is missing. I guess that makes it hip sounding. "Talking Broadway = uptight, Talk*in*' Broadway = hipmeister.") It's also the one every "ardent" (translation: beyond obsessive) fan goes to, hence the nickname "Stalkin' Broadway."

"You're gonna trust what Madame Mann (the fake name someone obviously obsessed with Terrence Mann posts under) wrote over what *I* say? Craig's boyfriend?" I stopped and clarified. "His *other* boyfriend . . ."

"It wasn't Madame Mann. *Everyone* was gossiping about it and then I read the post my friend Eliana wrote who's in *Phantom*, she always posts under the name M.Deville, oh, I guess I shouldn't have given that away." He shrugged. "Anyway, her post confirmed the story. Supposedly it's also all over some Japanese Web site, too."

"It said he was fired?"

"I can't read Japanese." He started doing a mini vocal warm-up.

"I mean the one on Stalkin'."

"Oh. Yeah . . . at intermission. They gave him back his dance belt and put on the understudy for Act Two."

I was getting very annoyed. "He was *not* fired. He gave two weeks' notice. He's at the matinee right now."

Jackson turned and looked at me. "Is he?"

I actually had no way of really knowing. Unless . . . Jackson read my mind and handed me his cell phone.

He explained, "It has caller ID blocked, so he won't see my number."

I knew Jeffrey wasn't home this weekend so I wasn't scared of having to talk to him. I dialed the number and it rang. Once, twice, three times, four times.

I felt triumphant. "Ha, Ha!"

"Hello?" It was Craig.

Shit!

I frantically hung up and threw the phone on the couch like it had just burned me. I started muttering, "I can't believe it. Craig flagrantly lied to me."

"You're right . . . he's such an honest person." *Pause for effect.* "Ask Jeffrey."

I waved him away. "Oh, that's different. He's not actually lying *to* Jeffrey. He's lying by omission." I felt slapped in the face.

"The point is he blatantly lied to me." I got annoyed about the whole *Phantom* thing. Why can't he stay a dancer? "This never would have happened if he would accept his voice sucks." I gave up. "Dating an actor is a headache."

"You know," he said in his old-biddy way that comes out whenever he talks about me and Craig, "I have *never* approved of your relationship." He reached all the way over to the couch and put the phone on his dressing table. "By the way, thanks for throwing my new Nokia."

"Does it also translate into 44 languages like your precious Ronald's phone?"

"Leave Ronald alone. He's not the one with the flying jock-strap."

I was prepped to sling another comeback but I kept hearing weird feedback from Jackson's body mic. "Hey, your mic is screwed up. I don't want this conversation broadcast around the theatre."

He tapped it. "It can't be. It's off during intermission."

"Then why do I keep hearing a voice talking that sounds muffled?"

We both stared at the phone.

He whispered, "Did you hang it up?"

"Yes! Before I threw it."

He picked it up and looked. "Stephen," he angrily whispered, "you didn't hang it up, you pushed the phone book button!"

"Well, hang it the fuck up now!" I hissed.

Jackson clicked the right button this time and before I could do any damage control it was "places" for Act Two and I had to run to the pit.

Great. Craig now knows I was checking up on him. Plus he heard Jackson say he never approved of the relationship. Maybe there was also a video feed so he was also able to actually see my disgust when I said his voice sucked.

* * *

I'm on the M104 bus going to Craig's apartment. I guess that's why he wanted to meet me there instead of at the *Phantom* stage door.

My cell phone has four missed calls from Craig's phone number. I can't believe he lied. I can't believe he heard everything. I can't believe the man's ass to my right is encroaching into my seat area.

*A*nger resolved. Craig's blow-drying his hair now. We're actually going to go to dinner and a movie! It's been unheard of before because he's always had a show on Saturday night, but Vive la Freedom! I'm so looking forward to having the whole night to hang out with him. When I got here, he buzzed me up and as soon as I walked in, he apologized. He said he just couldn't acknowledge what really happened.

"Boy, I sure was shocked that I didn't hang up the phone!" I attempted to laugh. I couldn't read Craig's face. Did he hear me say his voice sucked?

"I assumed you pushed the wrong button" (was he avoiding my eyes?) "'cause I could hear you guys still talking."

SHIT!!!

I started babbling. "Oh, you know me and Jackson." Again, a failed attempted laugh. "Sometimes we talk jive." I obviously was in a state of shock because I resorted to '70s funk slang.

He shrugged. "I couldn't actually hear you guys . . . all I heard was crackliness."

Oh! The relief. The relief of a bad cell phone connection! Thank G-d I threw the phone on the couch, away from the dressing room's good reception area. Cingular, your nonstop static has finally paid off! I was so glad I didn't have to do an awful coverup (*"I said your voice was lucky, NOT sucky"*) that I gave Craig a big hug. "You could have told me you were let go." I murmured into his hair.

He pulled away. "No, I couldn't face you."

Why? Did he think I'd judge him? I know I'm the most judgmental person ever, but didn't he know I would have put it on hold for him? "Craig, if you can't tell me, who can you tell?" I hoped he wouldn't say Jeffrey.

He sighed. "No one." *Thank God!* "I thought you'd hate me." He looked straight at me. He seemed like a little boy. "You're so funny and talented, you have so much going for you—why would you stay with someone who's been fired?" He actually looked teary eyed.

Hmm . . . he suddenly seemed very needy. That wasn't what I was used to. I knew I should speak but couldn't really think of anything to say. "Craig . . . I'm not with you because you have a *job* . . ." I was drawing a blank. I saw a picture of Craig and Jeffrey at Fire Island with their arms around each other and suddenly knew what to say. "I'm with you because I love you." When will *I* get my picture displayed?

I'd never used the word "love" with him before and it had a *great* effect. He gave me a big hug and luckily the bed was nearby. It's a little intimidating having sex with someone whose body fat percentage is equal to the number of times I've laughed at *Suddenly Susan* (0), but, boy, you get used to it!

Afterwards, we had a really great talk about *Flowerchild*. Now that he's out of *Phantom* he seems so much more interested in my career. I demand that he gets fired more often! Anyway, we're going to have a special dinner at this fabulous restaurant in midtown called Pietrasanta. Since we had the sex and smooching before dinner, I can really enjoy the garlicky Italian food and not obsess about using one of those Listerine strips between every course. I'll write later!

Thirteen

*F*irst day of auditions! We began at 10:00 and I got there at 9:45 and was about to sit at the piano when I realized that I was behind the table today!

Mason was wearing a tie-dyed *Flowerchild* shirt that they must have made at Yale. It looked great on him. He'd obviously started working out and I was jealous. I was used to him being a sort of schlubby version of John Cusack, not John Cusack with a V shape.

Staci (the *i* is for idiotic), the casting director's assistant, was there. She was in her late twenties but still hadn't found her look. She nervously scurried her waiflike body around in a tan shapeless cotton dress that miraculously made her skin look even paler. You could tell she recently got a body wave that somehow managed to lose its body and its wave. The only thing distinctive about her was her eyes. Round and moonlike, they appeared as if they were perpetually surprised or terrified. Probably both when she saw what her hair looked like and remembered what the salon charged her. She was from the same office that told me that *"transposing is hard"* at that annoying *Les Miz* kids' call. I wish Eric the casting director was there so I could have smirked triumphantly at my step up in the world.

Kris the choreographer was there too. I ran into him on the way up. Whenever I see him, I immediately untuck my shirt so my stomach's not as obvious. He's an even six feet, copper colored, and perfectly shaped. His shaven head draws even more attention to the fab bod. Why was I in the one business that has me regularly running into people whose zip code is from Mount Olympus? Kris intimidated me when I first saw him, but we get along great. He started out as a dancer, but eventually segued into choreography. He's only 33 and can dance up a storm, but the sad fact is that it's still difficult for black people to get work on Broadway. If you're a white dancer trying out for the ensemble there are usually around seven slots to fill. If you're black, there's usually just one, so the odds are against you. Ditto if you're Asian or another obvious minority. Of course, it's also hard to get work as a choreographer, but once you establish yourself you can go from job to job. Kris was nominated for a Tony for his first Broadway show two years ago, and this is his next big show. I met him when we were both in our early twenties and were doing an awful workshop production of a musical based on the *Good Times* TV show. The authors hadn't secured the rights to the title in time for the workshop so they had to call it "Great *Times*." It wasn't.

"Girl," Kris air-kissed me in the Equity lounge before we walked in. "This shit is *too* early! I'm still in the middle of my disco nap!" Kris spoke like an old-school queen whenever he was around gay people, but turned it off as soon as someone straight was within earshot. "I'm a Gemini," he once explained. "I got two of me, and you can kiss both their asses."

"Staci!" Kris went right up to her as soon as he put his stuff down. He was suddenly all business. "Tomorrow I'm going to need to have my assistant start out the day without me. I've got an appointment until noon." Appointment? An appointment with R.E.M!

The morning was going great. Lots of good people, hardly

anyone totally wrong for the show. Once in a while if someone cute came in, Kris would fan himself like a Southern matriarch so only Mason and I could see it.

At 1 p.m. in walked Roberta, squeezed into her audition outfit. There's something sort of depressing about knowing that someone actually has an "audition outfit." Especially since it's the same one she wore when she tried out for the *Bye Bye Birdie* tour in 1990. I was dying to run up and take the oversized '80s safety pin out of her skirt.

As opposed to any night backstage at *Ragtime*, she was all smiles. The bitterness wouldn't be fully in flower until the first day of rehearsal.

"Hi." She did a mock curtsey. "I don't know what kind of voice you're looking for . . ." She looked apologetically hopeful. "So, I thought I'd show you my whole range."

"That's fine, great, *fantastic!*" I was crazily overcompensating because I couldn't believe I was subjecting this eyesore to Mason et al. I noticed she was wearing the same floppy hat Molly Ringwald wore in either *The Breakfast Club* or *Fresh Horses* and I smiled nervously at Staci, feeling mortified because two days before I had *demanded* she get an audition.

She launched into the "pop" song from her repertoire. There is nothing more horrifying than hearing a soprano try to sing funky. The song was The Pussycat Dolls' "Don't Cha (Wish Your Girlfriend Was Hot Like Me)?"

That's a musical question whose answer is a simple, but firm, "NO."

Instead of ending the song in the signature pop fade-out, she held out "Me-e-e-e-e" and slid all the way up to a high C, cracking midway through.

"Can I try that ending again?" she asked, while glaring at the piano player. I knew that trick, the old "*He* screwed me up."

Why not let her hang herself? "Go ahead." I said enthusiastically. She tried it again and cracked in the same spot. This time she had no one to glare at but her larynx.

"Sorry." She rubbed her throat. "It's still early. And I've had a cold. Do you want to hear anything else?"

" I don't need anything." Mason smiled. "Do you, Stephen?"

"NO!" I said/screamed loudly. "That was fine! Great seeing you again!"

She looked over at her enormous music book. "OK, but I have a Christina Aguilera medley—"

"No, don't worry about it." *Please leave!* I tried to make a private joke to ease the tension. "See ya with a Venti!" I said with a jaunty line reading.

She stared.

"You know, a Venti coffee . . ."

Staring.

Oh, God, I had to spell it out. "'Cause we saw each other at Starbucks . . . and I was, uh, referencing it . . ."

"My decaf was a tall."

Her literalness was mind-boggling! "You're right. Great job! Excellent! Thank you *so much!*" I waved at her/waved her out.

She gathered her things and mouthed "bye" while rubbing her throat.

Mason paused before putting her picture in the NO pile. "I think her voice is too operatic for the show, don't you?"

That's it? Mason didn't make any comment about the outfit, Ringwald hat, crazy song choice, etc. He was decidedly less dishy than I normally am. I guess it's much nicer for an actor if their worst fears aren't realized . . . i.e., the people behind the desk don't start immediately making fun of you the minute you leave the room.

"Can we briefly pause?" Mason asked while pulling out his cell phone. "I've got to call Jase. We're trying to arrange going to the folks for the holidays."

Mason lived with Jason. I'd never met him, but I think they've been together forever because I once called Mason years ago when he would come into Rose's Turn and I remember hearing Jason's name on the machine. Two boyfriends with rhyming names is something that stays with you.

"*Hi, for Mason press 1, for Jason press 2, for Mason AND Jason press 3—*"

And for a splitting headache press 4! "Um, Stephen." It was Staci. She began every sentence with "um." It's like she was always apologizing for having to speak.

"I knew Roberta would be wrong for the show when you asked for the audition. I didn't mind scheduling her in, but the producers really want to get this show cast quickly and you're going to hold us up if you insist upon us seeing people who are clearly wrong."

I was so busted. What could I say? My ego made me get her the audition? I did the next best thing—I pretended my phone was vibrating and I made a "sorry, I've got to take this call" face and feigned having a conversation.

It was no surprise that the producers were trying to do the auditions quickly. They were the Geisenschlaags . . . the stingiest in the business.

The Geisenshlaags were an older married couple who should be starring in a reality series called *Lifestyles of the Rich and Cheap-ass*. Bettina was a glamorous Chinese-American who never met a nip she didn't tuck. All that work has given her the beautiful face of Gong Li but has never quite solved the fact that it sits above the body of a more squat Danny DeVito. Fritz towers over her at 5'3" and hails from Germany.

Though Bettina didn't learn English till after she emigrated here in her twenties, she speaks it perfectly, unless you're asking something she doesn't want to answer. Then there's a sudden, enormous language barrier. Fritz must be ashamed of his German accent because the only talking I've ever seen him do is into Bettina's ear. He whispers, she repeats it. He's much older, but rumor has it she just turned fifty and is suddenly terrified that he's going to leave her for someone younger. Nowadays, she rarely lets him out of her sight. When they hired me we went out for drinks.

"Sweetie, I'm Bettina and this is my husband, Fritz," she said, ignoring the fact that I've met her three times before at various functions. She was dressed in a smart brown suit. Triple E. He was in a classic Brooks Brothers. I guess Brooks Brothers does have a children's department. She smiled warmly. "We're so glad you're going to be working with us. (*whisper from him.*) There are just a few things we'd love to discuss about your contract."

That's right, the drinks excursion was used as a way to negotiate with me without my agent/lawyer.

They played good cop/bad cop. Or good cop/bad whispering cop.

I started looking for an exit. "I think I should wait to talk to my entertainment lawyer."

"Nonsense." She scoffed and opened her Kate Spade handbag. "We have the contract right here." *Whisper.* "This way you won't have to pay your lawyer. *Whisper.* "They charge by the hour, you know. Why pay the bumblebee when you can simply reach in and get the honey from the hive yourself?" She always had some folksy Chinese saying to back up her cheapness.

"But I'm paying my lawyer to protect my interests . . ."

"What?" she said, because I actually made sense. She waved my words away. "You speak English too fast for me. Sit down." She steered me towards a seat and the haranguing began.

Between her charm, his whispering, and two frozen daiquiris I agreed to cut 10% of my salary until the show ran for six months. This is why they're successful producers. People tend to think that producers put up all the money for the show, but the producer's job is to *raise* all the money for the show, and then make sure it's spent wisely. Their input into the actual show is in direct proportion to how well known the artistic staff is. Unfortunately, Mason and I are first-timers on Broadway so the Geisenshlaags have already started imposing their vision on us— and since their vision was responsible for the proposed revival of

Mame starring Shannen Doherty, I don't think it's 20/20. For one thing, they keep insisting that the show have at least one recognizable name in it. I have no problem with that if it's some big Broadway star, but the Geisenshlaags seem to think that only TV names are recognizable. They demand that we see Scott Baio. Scott Baio??? I'm sorry, but this Joanie does *not* love Chachi.

"Staci," I said as I "hung up" the phone.

"Um . . . yeah?"

"Do you know when the Geisenshlaags are coming by to auditions?"

"No, I haven't heard."

"Hopefully, not till opening night," I said with a wink. Staci didn't acknowledge the joke . . . or that she was breathing. She remained impassive and finally nodded slightly. It was going to be a fun round of auditions.

Just then the monitor knocked. He's the guy who sits outside the room and brings the actors in. He's an older character actor/Santa Claus look-alike who starred (*as* Santa Claus!) in a holiday show I did a few years back and he obviously made extra money doing this. "Why don't you guys take an early lunch? We just had a cancellation." He checked his list. "You're next appointment's not till 2:30."

"Great, Calum." Mason waved to him as he hung up. He picked up the "maybe" pile and smiled at Kris and me. "Let's take these photos to Sbarro and get grease all over them!"

"Sounds great!" Kris said, stretching his perfectly proportioned torso. He leaned over to me. "I hope Morticia's going back to the crypt."

"Um . . . I'm gonna go back to the office. Is that OK?" Staci said with a glassy-eyed stare.

What a relief. "We'll see you back here in an hour," I said as I put on my coat. I noticed the pianist was engrossed in a Sidney Sheldon book. I felt a kinship. "Hey, Marzullo!" I startled him and he threw his book down as we all do when we think we've missed a cue. "Relax!" I laughed, looking at his hands poised to play. "We're on break. See you at 2:30."

I've written all this from Sbarro while Mason went to Chase Bank to get cash. I can see him crossing the street so I'll write later.

*W*e're on a break. I tried to call Monikah because I'm having a mini-breakdown, but of course, I got her "I'm in a session" answering machine message. I hope the volume wasn't up because if it were, one of her patients heard, "Why, when I'm having a complete mental breakdown, are you with one of your annoying, whiny, Upper West Side clients! You always pick up during *my* sessions! PickuppickupPickupPickupPickupPickupPickupPickuu-u-u-u-up!!!" until the machine reached it 60-second message limit.

Maybe writing it all down will calm me. We came back at 2:30 and saw some good people. At 3:15 the door opened.

"Hey, Stevey!" Craig walked in holding his picture/resumé and music. I thought I had explained to him that the show needed four singers. SINGERS! I went into a state of shock but acted like I was expecting to see him.

He strolled over to Mason and shook his hand. "I don't know if Stephen told you about me. I'm Craig." He smiled his beatific smile and moved over to Staci. "Hi, I'm Craig Nerio." Staci took one look at his gorgeous mug and her lips moved into an involuntary smile position. I think her teeth were so unaccustomed to being hit with direct light they tried to shrink inside her gums. I looked around the room; everyone was smiling. People were always initially taken in by his good looks. Craig walked over to the piano and started to talk to Marzullo about his song. Staci leaned over, "Um . . . I assumed from his resumé he was only a dancer, but his manager called and said you've worked with him before."

"That's true . . ." I began. I could have said Craig sucked, but

I didn't want to get him in trouble; he was my boyfriend and I had to protect him. But what about my job? I was panicking because the other person I've "worked with before" (a.k.a. Horrible Roberta) sent my recommendation status plummeting. I felt like I would never be trusted again if they heard Craig's version of singing and I knew I would then have to deal with a "time is money" speech from Bettina and Herr Geisenshlaag.

Craig was taking a little time to talk through his music with Marzullo. "Um . . . even though we had that cancellation, we're like fifteen minutes behind," Staci whispered, motioning to Craig. "If we go past 5 o'clock we're going to have to pay."

I knew I had to prevent them from hearing Craig. Or at least postpone it. I had an idea! "You know what," I quickly said to Mason, "This is just the prelim audition and I've certainly heard Craig sing," implying he sounded fantastic. "Let's not waste time today and just bring him to the callback."

"That's a great idea," Mason said. "If you say he can sing, I don't need to hear him. He certainly looks right for the show."

Staci nodded.

"Um . . . Craig?" She actually got up. Staci then walked across the room, hips a-flurrying, obviously trying to "work it," but unfortunately her "it" was on unemployment.

She gingerly touched Craig's shoulder. "We're running behind, so we're just gonna have you come to the callbacks."

"Hey, that's great." A million watts shot out from his mouth. "That was the easiest callback I ever got." I laughed a little too frantically and started to cough. He looked over at me as he walked out. "Stevey," he winked, "I'll call you later."

Kris leaned over at me and clucked. "I think you just got yourself a date."

"Not likely," I said, flustered. "He's been with a banker for years." I didn't want anyone to know about us till Jeffrey was out of the picture.

"Hey," Mason was looking at his resume. "Does he live on 10th Street?"

"Yeah, between 5th and 6th." I finally started to breathe normally.

"I knew it! I've met him before at a Christmas party." He smiled proudly. "His boyfriend went to my high school."

"Oh . . . that's great." My head was swimming. What if Jeffrey suspected Craig was cheating and mentioned it to Mason? What if Mason put two and two together? *Must speak.* "What, uh, high school?"

"Dalton," he said, still looking at the resumé.

I needed more info. "How often do you see each other?" Awkward laugh. "I mean, I'm Jewish but even I know that Christmas comes but once a year."

"Well." He put the resumé down. "I just saw him recently."

Uh-oh. "How come?"

"Well, he's said he's always secretly wanted to do something artistic. And now he's put his money where his mouth is." He smiled broadly. "He's one of the main investors in the show."

SHIT!!!

"*W*hy didn't you tell me that Jeffrey invested in the show I'M CONDUCTING ON BROADWAY?" I pushed my food away. I couldn't eat. "Were you going to wait until I saw him at the opening night party and hope I had taken my heart medication?"

"Stephen." Craig stopped eating his pad Thai. We were at Dragonfly, a restaurant in the Village that I loved and knew Jeffrey would never be seen at.

"Why won't you listen to me? *I didn't know!* Jeffrey doesn't tell me what he does with his money. He loves to play with it." He took a sip of his Thai iced coffee. "He's always investing in something . . . stocks, inventions, whatever. Why does it even matter? He knows we know each other."

He was right. Jeffrey could invest in a show I was doing. It didn't mean we'd have to have a public showdown over Craig. I didn't know why I was making such a big deal out of it. I think the real reason is that I was shocked Mason is friends with him. Why would Mason associate with a banker? Monikah said to try and be less judgmental, so I'll just say that, ofttimes, bankers appear to be stiff, uptight, and bad dancers. The truth is I'd only met Jeffrey once quickly on the subway, but I could tell he was a tight-ass from his power suit. Hmm . . . I guess Mason became friends with him when they were both young, and no doubt it's hard for Mason to give him up now no matter how much they've drifted apart . . . you know, like Tenille still sticking with the Captain years after the heady success of "Muskrat Love." That relationship should have ended long before they inflicted "Do That to Me One More Time" in Spanish on us. Ooh, Craig was still talking.

" . . . for the callback, or I could do "Sittin' on the Dock of the Bay."

"Well . . ." I pretended to mull. "I think your first choice."

"*Bad Girls*? Really?" He considered it. "Do you think the accompanist will sing the 'toot, toot, aah, beep, beep' backup?"

"Bad Girls"? The only thing appropriate about that song for Craig's voice is the first word. I couldn't deal with talking about him going to the callback. By then, the Geisenshlaags would definitely be there lurking and if they thought Craig came in because of me putting in the good word, they'd think *I* had worse taste than *them*.

"Look, Craig . . ."

"Stephen." He put his hand on mine. "I don't want you to think about it. You don't need to help me for my callback." He looked at me seriously. "I'm not going to trade on the fact that I know you to get this gig. My manager manipulated our connection with the casting people but I told him no more. I don't want to use you."

He looked out the window facing the street. "That whole *Phantom* experience kind of traumatized me . . . and I'm trying to be more honest now." He took a breath and looked at me. "Listen, we need to talk."

Uh-oh. I've heard that before every breakup.

"I started seeing someone . . ." he trailed off.

I felt devastated. The boyfriend I was cheating with was cheating on me! How dare he? *And* how dare he be so cavalier? Did he think a public place would prevent a spectacle? He obviously didn't know that I looked for any opportunity to live out my fantasy of playing all of Bette Davis's dramatic roles. I glared. "Who is it?" *Damn it!* Why didn't I smoke?

"No one you know. I thought it was better that way." He paused, obviously for effect. "Her name is Gail."

WHAT! He had the nerve to have two boyfriends *and* a girlfriend? Wait a minute—isn't that the title of some bad Steve Guttenberg movie?

"Since when are you into women?" I asked incredulously.

He looked embarrassed. "I thought I could open up more to a woman."

"Why can't you open up to me?" Rampant judgment aside, I was a very good listener.

"Stephen, you're not a therapist. And I decided I needed one."

"You have two boyfriends, a girlfriend, AND a therapist? Thank God you have a Blackberry!"

"What? What girlfriend?"

I finally had a sentence I could use a Bette Davis line reading on. "I believe you said her name is Gail." How dare he try to pretend he never said it? I saw *Gaslight!*

He started laughing. "Stevey! Gail is my therapist." He laughed harder. "I started seeing a therapist! I'm not suddenly straight!"

I'm one of those classic I-can-dish-it-out-but-I-can't-take-it people, so even though the whole situation was pretty funny, I refused to laugh.

He noticed my pout. "I'm sorry I'm laughing, Stevey, but"— he nodded knowingly—"Gail says laughter is great medicine." Oh no! He wasn't going to start quoting his therapist after one session! And, P.S., was *that* the deep insight she was giving him? Why not "Absence makes the heart grow fonder," or "It takes 334 muscles to frown but only 20 to smile"? Does it? How many muscles does it take for me to give you the finger?

I decided I wasn't mad at Craig; I was just stressed from the whole day being a Space Mountain of ups and downs.

I chuckled. "It's OK to laugh . . ." I actually began to relax a little.

Craig stopped laughing and began massaging his throat. "I'd better not strain my voice before the callbacks."

Well, my relaxed state lasted a full five seconds. We got our check and, because Jeffrey was in town, Craig walked me to the Christopher Street subway, gave me a kiss, and I descended the stairs.

I just walked Heather and lit a delicious-smelling/overpriced aromatherapy candle. Hmm . . . How odd that Craig is in therapy. Him, who has never taken much responsibility for anything. I guess people can change. Or try to change. Or waste money trying to change. Well, tomorrow's another audition day. I should try to enjoy myself before the callbacks destroy what credibility I have left.

Fourteen

*T*his morning had drama. Kris's assistant was supposed to fill in for him, but never showed up. I was, of course, nervous about everyone that came to whom I had connection. If I acknowledged knowing them and they didn't do well, I felt it lowered my standing even further. So there was a lot of me being friendly, but in a distant, noncommittal way, so there was no way for Staci et al. to know how close I was to anyone. The whole morning was a headache because I was weird, Mason was weirded out because of me, and then the coffee we ordered only came with Nutrasweet and not Sweet 'N Low, which sent Staci into a tailspin. All this continued until lunch when Kris finally showed up, obviously having just woken up. We all (w/o Staci) went to Sbarro again, and Mason and I filled Kris in on what the morning auditions were like. Kris was *livid* at his no-show assistant.

"This is the *third* time she said she was gonna show up, and instead pulled a Supremes Reunion Tour!" That was an obscure reference to the fact that there was a promised "Diana, plus the originals" concert tour that never materialized. Instead, it was Miss Ross plus two women who had been

Supremes after Diana left. The point is, Kris's conversational references are bizarre.

"Did she leave you a message?" I was eating a delicious piece of Sbarro's pizza. I decided I could gain weight now, as long as I lost all of it plus an additional ten pounds by opening night.

"Yeah, on my voice mail. She said she was at the '*doctor.*'" The momentum of the finger quotes he put around *doctor* was big enough to cause a breeze.

"Well,"—I pulled off a long piece of cheese that was hanging on my chin—"even beautifully well-toned dancers/assistant choreographers get sick. Don't they?"

"True." Kris raised an eyebrow. "But should I assume that it was a nurse I heard screaming, 'All right, group two . . . 5,6,7,8' during the message?" He threw down his fork. "She should know that her awful Sprint phone picks up background noise better than it does her actual voice." He banged the table with his fist. "Missy was at a rehearsal for something she's not 'fessing up about." Her name was Claire, but "Missy" was the name he called all people he was mad at. It didn't work with that traffic cop who busted him for jaywalking.

Just then his phone rang. He checked the caller ID. "It's her!" He flipped open his phone and launched into a tirade. "I know you've been rehearsing something for the last week so don't even try it." He listened. He obviously didn't buy it. "So then what *have* you been doing? . . . What? Why?" He pursed his lips. "So that's it?" He let out a long sigh and smiled. "You are a fool in love . . . What am I gonna do?" He shook his head and laughed as he hung up. "Bon voyage."

"Well," he put his phone away. "I was half right. She wasn't at the doctor today, but—" He paused for effect. His voice got low for full dishiness. "Last month she met some guy at the Blue Fin bar who works as a captain on one of the Princess Cruise lines." He licked his lips. "Let's just say they hit it off." He made the mature choice of repeatedly pushing his right index finger through the hole his left thumb/index finger made.

I noticed two young children at the next table no longer playing their Game Boys because they were trying to re-create Kris's hand choreography. I'm sure that will go over well in third-grade show-and-tell. Mason spoke. "So she's been holed up with him in a hotel while he's on break from the boat?"

I, of course, started to sing that '70s classic, "Rock the Boat."

"Good song, but you're a little off." Hopefully he didn't mean pitch-wise. "She's spent the last week auditioning to be a dancer in one of their "I *Heart* Broadway" shows so she can be with him on the high seas."

A cruise ship show. That was worse than Six Flags. At least after you do your Country Rockin' Review you can escape to your studio apartment. On a ship you're stuck socializing with 65- to 90-year-olds and their new hips. I was incredulous. "She's going to give up working on a real Broadway show to be with a one-night-stand Captain Stubing?"

"You know her." He rolled his eyes. "She did *Cats* in Vienna for three years once because she was involved with that diplomat." Hmm . . . I did remember seeing a picture of her in a fur-covered costume hugging a seven-foot Aryan.

"So now you have no assistant?" Mason wondered.

"Exactly!" Kris shrugged. "And I'm going to have a hard time finding one. No one wants to work for the Geisenshlaags. You never know if they're gonna fire your ass."

He was right. They're notorious. I think all of us were willing to take a chance on them because we were the heads of our respective creative areas, but why just be an assistant if you feel constantly on the verge of getting fired?

"Forget it, everyone hates those cheap-asses. I'm assistant-less."

"You'll find someone," Mason said, ever the positive force.

"Well," Kris said yawning, which showed off his amazing lats. "My main problem right now is getting up at the crack of nine to make it to auditions."

"Why is it so hard for you to get up? You're not doing a Broadway show right now." Lots of Broadway actors do their show till 11:00 and then go and have dinner after the show, get home at 1:00, and go to sleep at 3:00.

"Do the words back-to-back *Golden Girls* at 1 a.m. mean anything to you?"

I nodded. What could I say? Those four ladies have fostered many addicts, and I knew there were no words that could stop him from being hooked on Dorothy Zbornak's slow burns.

We finished eating. Kris left to make some more phone calls and Mason wanted to walk off some of the meal. I feel odd now that I'm actually in the middle of putting together this show. By odd, I mean I thought I'd be happier. I mean, I am happy, but not to the level I imagined. *Shake it out*, as my Jazzercise instructor would say. I think I'm just stressed about this whole Craig/callback thing and it's superseding all the positive feelings I'm having. Oh, well, gotta run to more auditions!

Saw Monikah today instead of tomorrow. She called and graciously gave me an appointment, no doubt based on the crazy message I left her yesterday which I decided to pretend never happened.

I walked in and sat down.

"Stephen, why did you leave me that message?"

I guess it did happen.

"Well, I was freaking out and I was frustrated your machine was on and . . ." What could I say? I took a deep breath. "I'm sorry." It felt odd apologizing to my therapist. It felt odd apologizing. Hopefully that was the only one for the year.

She smiled. "That's OK. I never have the volume up on my machine. Lots of patients use it as a chance to rant." I've figured out she has lots of patients in the business (mostly by standing under the awning next door for four hours straight one day to see who came in and out every 45 minutes) and I assume her answering machine tape must be a *Who's Who* of the latest Broadway crises.

"*I deserved that Tony!*"

"So what if she can belt, *I'm* an actress!"

"She purposely kicked me in the face! *This face! The face that all the New York critics have had a love affair with since my days Off Broadway!*"

"By asking why you left that message, Stephen, I meant to ask what was upsetting you so?"

I told her the whole Craig story and she thought my quick thinking was a good short-term fix.

"But what should my long-term fix be?" I begged her.

She countered. "What *should* your long-term fix be?"

Son of a bitch! I can't believe she's still employing that trick! I *had* no long-term fix—that's why I was there! We talked about loyalties and being truthful and just when I was getting somewhere near a resolution my 45 minutes were up. It's unfair. Why can't she be like a parking meter? If I decide I need more time, why can't I just slip her a quarter and stay parked on her Macy's couch for another 15 minutes? I left more confused than ever. So many questions harassed me as I walked down Columbus Avenue. Should I be mad at Craig for possibly jeopardizing my career? Is it his fault that he can't accept he ain't no singer? What's more important: your boyfriend or your job? What if you love your job as much as your boyfriend? Should your boyfriend love *his* boyfriend as much as he loves you? Should your boyfriend *have* another boyfriend?

My dad called me tonight.

"Stephen, it's Daddy," I heard from my answering machine as I was getting out of the tub. "Is the screen on?" He still doesn't quite understand what call screening is. I picked up as I was drying off the deliciously scented Body Shop bath water. I'm probably the only guy who follows *Cosmopolitan*'s guide to how to use "private time" to relieve stress:

1. Take a bubble bath
2. Light a scented candle
3. Pamper yourself with a mud mask
4. Another idea that any four-year-old could think of, yet looks great because of the layout of the article.

"Hi, Daddy." I paused. "Hi, Mitzi." She's notorious for being on the extension and not admitting it till I've said something dishy about her.

"Hi, Stephen," she chirped. "I just picked up."

I could see them in two separate rooms in their Great Neck house that Mitzi received when she divorced her first husband (before she met my dad). Picture an artist's palette turned into a split-level. Every room was done in a different color (*"We had it hand painted!" she'd brag*), and Mitzi has a different pantsuit to go with whatever room she's going to spend the most time in each day. Powder blue for entertaining in the living room, off-white when she's with my dad in the practice room all day, lime green when she's cooking for the upcoming week, etc. Mitzi is a well-preserved baby boomer who's kept her figure *and* her wardrobe from when she was younger. She's definitely pretty but she isn't as diva-ish looking as my mom. She's more of a suburban woman with red hair ("It's still natural"), a nice body ("I walk every morning"), and a smattering of makeup ("I don't need it!").

"She looks like Gracie Allen, doesn't she, Stevey?" my dad constantly says. He refuses to realize I didn't grow up during the '50s, so I have no idea what Gracie Allen looked like. I guess I must feel the way he did when I told him one of my dance teachers resembled Pinky Tuscadero.

My dad worked out way before it was popular ("Me and Jack LaLanne"!) so he also has a nice bod, but unfortunately it is counteracted by a toupee that's as real looking as Barbara Hershey's lips in *Beaches*. He started going bald when I was around eight and immediately got a toupee that has, by now, seen six presidents. He still has a handsome face, though. He looks like Hal Linden—if Hal Linden had a ratty brown sweater on his head at all times.

"Stephen." It was my dad again. "Your mother tells me you're conducting a new Broadway show."

I felt good she was bragging about me to Dad. I've always wanted my parents to be proud of me, even though I was on Broadway and not a classical music star. I remember when I first came out. I don't mean as gay, I mean Broadway-wise. After I saw the *Annie* performance that gave me my "passion," I led a double life. Instead of reading a book by flashlight after my bedtime like many kids, I would take out the enormous headphones I hid under my bed; plug them into my stereo and blast *The Pajama Game*, *A Chorus Line*, and any other albums I bought with my allowance. I got $5 a week, so every two weeks I could buy a different album from the local Record World. I would read and memorize the album cover at the store and then throw it out so there'd be less evidence for my parents to find in the house. When I got home, I'd stick the show album in one of the many opera albums we had (there's room in the envelope sleeve if you place it correctly). I always made sure to stick it in an opera that was starring someone my mom was feuding with, so there'd be no chance of her going to listen to *Rigoletto* and by accident finding *Ain't Misbehavin'* shoved in there too.

Unfortunately, my method of not being discovered backfired because I forgot my mother was a diva onstage and off. One fateful day she was in a rage because of a visit to her dressing room by British Soprano Deena Lisner. ("*She had the nerve to come backstage and tell me that I sounded wonderful considering I hadn't warmed up. When I told her I had warmed up she said that she stood by her first statement!*") Instead of putting a moratorium on listening to those albums, as I assumed she would, she decided to form a pile of them and smash them with her "Opera Americana" award. (It was bronze plated.)

I was in the kitchen making a Fluffernutter (hence: the beginning of my fat years) when she called me downstairs and I saw her standing next to two piles: one was the greatest hits of Deena Lisner and the other was at least seven Great White Way favorites.

She brandished *Pippin* in her hand. "What is the meaning of this?"

She was wearing her version of a demolition outfit. Bedazzled overalls, hair pulled back in a ponytail (then hair sprayed), "no makeup" (meaning her regular stage makeup, but no false eyelashes), and Frye boots. She gestured (with *Pippin*) to my collection nakedly sitting on the floor.

I spoke quietly. "I bought them by mistake."

"You bought *ten* albums of "show tunes" (said with a poisonous taste in her mouth) by mistake?"

I nodded.

"Why didn't you return them?"

I was silent.

"Was the store closed?" I didn't answer.

She gestured grandly to all the albums. "I demand an explanation."

Her eyes widened suddenly with shock and/or horror. "Do you actually *like* this music?"

I couldn't speak. I'd been listening to those records for a year and a half every night, and all weekend long when they'd go out of town. I'd place the needle down and imagine myself getting up on the podium and waving my baton wildly as the audience went crazy. My parents would come to opening night and be shocked that I could command such respect from all the musicians and actors and decide right then and there that they could *never* go out of town again, they *had* to watch the magic happen every night. I'd reserve two special seats for them in row B so I could always see them out of the corner of my eye as soon as the show began. That wouldn't be hard to do, I'd think . . . after all,

I'd be so famous I could ask for *anything* in my contract, and two perpetual seats a night wasn't that much. I could see the look on their faces when I'd turn around and bow after the overture.

I couldn't explain that all to her. I knew that she'd be devastated if she knew I was listening to such unpure music. She said repeatedly that it poisoned your ear. I heard her numerous times complaining about Bernstein. "Lenny was never the same after he started writing for the musical theatre. Never!" She'd shake her head. "It's sad. He's lost it."

Of course, he went on to conduct the Philharmonic and be considered one of the world's best classical conductors, so I think her vitriol was actually because he never used her as a soloist during the one summer she was a guest artist at Tanglewood. But the point was that she was such a classical music snob that if she knew I really liked the albums she'd take them away forever and tell Mrs. Remick not to allow me to buy any more. What would I do at night? What would I do when they were out of town? I *had* to prevent her from knowing how important they were to me.

Unfortunately, I was only twelve and a half—I hadn't perfected the adolescent art of lying.

"Stephen, I asked you a question." She leaned in closer. I could see she used two different shades of lipstick on her upper and lower lips. "Why didn't you return these things?"

"Because . . . because . . ." I burst into tears. "I love them. I'm sorry, but I love them. Please don't throw them out!!!"

I couldn't stop crying. She looked shocked. I started sobbing and almost hyperventilated. She didn't know what to do. She put down her *Opera News* statuette, stepped over the pile of records ready for demolition, and hugged me. Well, almost hugged me. She put her hands on my shoulders, squeezed, and shook her head.

"I don't know what to do with you." I stopped audibly sobbing and was trying to control myself.

"Are you going to throw them out?" I didn't know what I'd

do if she did. Run away to Broadway? See if I could join the orphans of *Annie*? Live in one of their dressing rooms and finish school with a correspondence course?

She patted my head. "If these mean so much to you, of course you can keep them." She beamed. "I must tell Lenny. I'm sure he'll be pleased." She saw my expression change from relief to shock and clarified for me. "Why, just the other day I was talking to him," she coyly smiled and spoke *entre nous*. "I just found out he's given me a solo in his new *genius* choral work"—she stepped back to act out the scene—"and I said 'Lenny, how do you find time to write brilliant works like *West Side Story* and still have a full classical career?' He said the most marvelous thing." She looked dreamy eyed. "He said musicals ground him and classical music—" She spread her arms like a pterodactyl—"classical music lets him fly."

I smiled at the poetry in the words. She looked confused for a moment. "Or maybe it was the reverse." She waved it away with her hand. "I don't remember . . ." Her face clouded over as she spat out, "That Lisner hag was lurking in the background and I was so intent on looking like Lenny and I were old friends I unfortunately had to tune out everything he was saying so I could concentrate on grabbing his upper arm and throwing my head back with laughter every seven seconds."

I later found out her newfound respect for Bernstein was also because she heard a rumor that he was going to conduct and record an operatic version of *West Side Story* and she was lobbying for the role of Anita. She would kill to be on any recording conducted by Bernstein. Unfortunately for her, the role went to Tatiana Troyanos. Unfortunately for the listener, too. Have you ever heard that travesty? Anita's songs should be BELTED like Chita Rivera did on the original cast recording. Troyanos and her opera voice made Anita sound like an aging matriarch with asthma instead of the Latin spitfire she's supposed to be. Why didn't anyone consult me? I'm listed in the book.

My mom suddenly saw one of the Deena Lisner album covers

(*Debussy Tous Les Jours*) and remembered the task at hand. She picked up her statuette to start smashing the Lisner albums. "I'm so glad Lenny found his talent again." SMASH! "Of course, there's nothing *really* wrong with musicals." SMASH. "After all, everything in moderation . . ." SMASH.

I can't remember what else she said. It was hard to concentrate not only because of the ear shattering noise, but because I was still so shaken up from the thought of my beacons of hope being thrown out. Soon I calmed down and felt incredibly happy I didn't have to hide anymore. I thought my mom and I were on the brink of a new relationship . . . I could start expressing to her what I felt without fear of being contradicted/ignored/one-upped. I decided to really explain what musicals meant to me. I knew she'd be thrilled when I told her I had found my "passion."

"Mom," I said, between her panting gasps. She was completely out of breath from the physical exertion. "You know how you talk about passion?" I didn't know how I was going to phrase it but I was so excited to open up to her. "Well . . ." I took a deep breath—

She checked her watch. "Oh!" She looked around her feet. "Be a dear and clean up." Clean up, I thought? But we were about to share an incredibly intimate moment where I express my dreams with you and you look at me with newfound respect and warmth. We then make a vow to have "sharing" time each day over Celestial Seasonings tea and Tastykakes. She must have seen me look crestfallen. "Stephen, I'm sorry. Mommy has to go to work." She patted my cheeks. "Whatever you wanted to ask me about my passion will have to wait." *Her* passion? "Or better yet," she continued, "read the *Opera News* article where I talk all about it!" She picked a piece of broken LP off her boots. "I think it's the October issue. I must get ready for l'opera!" This last word was sung. Not to be cute, but to start her vocal warm-up. An hour before my mom left for the opera she would sing every conversation so her voice would be completely warmed up by curtain.

"Who spilled milk on the floor?" she'd trill.

"Has anyone seen my Arrid Ex-tra Ex-tra Dry-y-y-y?" she'd warble.

The worst was when my friends called me after 5 p.m. My mom would insist on answering the phone. I'd hear the phone ring and go running for the downstairs extension but often catch it too late. I'd pick up just in time to hear my mom vocalize all the way up the scale. "Hello-o-o-o-o!!!" Ending on a high B flat.

"Uh . . . is Stephen there?"

I'd quickly pick up the extension. "It's for *me!*" I'd whine.

Down the scale: "Good-by-y-y-ye!" She'd sometimes hold out the last note because she claimed the i/e diphthong in the last vowel of "good-bye" was a great way to clear phlegm.

"Hang up!" I'd yell and finally hear a click after a lot of mucous clearing.

"Who was the freakazoid?" was the question most commonly asked at that time. What was I supposed to say? That my mom became bored doing vocal exercises the conventional way and instead used normal conversation as a way to warm up/bring shame upon me? I would claim we had a party line (I thought of that after I saw *Pillow Talk* on the "4:30 Movie") with a dear but mentally unstable widow who thought she was still the famous soprano she was in Vienna before the Nazis invaded her village, forcing her to come to America, too traumatized to ever sing again. I said her family told us this was the first time she had sung in over thirty years and to try to stop her would mean that "the Nazis had won."

I don't think anyone bought it, but at the time I thought I was incredibly creative—even sort of believing it for a while. It all came crashing down when I got an unexpected visit from Dan Fiore (he was in chorus with me and always forced himself into the tenor section, even though he was a bass. Infuriating!). He rang the bell at 5:30 (I never made plans at that time for obvious reasons.) My mother answered the door and proceeded to sing a whole conversation, asking Dan about his PSAT scores. I was in my room hiding but I heard the whole thing (being vaguely impressed by the lilting melody she used to talk about whether the Stanley Kaplan Course helps or hinders) and I prayed he would keep his trap shut. Of course, soon everyone in school started calling my mom "The *Phantomess* of the Opera" and would specifically call my house just to try to engage my mom in a conversation/aria. Yay! It's fun to be a fat, gay teenager with a mother everyone thinks is *out of her fucking mind!*

*B*ack to tonight's conversation. "Yes, Dad, I got my dream gig! I'm sorry I haven't called." I actually rarely called once I realized every conversation on the phone was going to be a verbal ménage à trois. "Things are going great, though, and we open in about three months."

"Fantastic!" His voice got quieter. "Listen, if your mother doesn't want us to come to opening night, we understand." My mother? What about me? *I* wanted them to come. Well, I wanted *him* to come.

"Not come? I want you (there's no difference in English between the singular and the plural 'you,' but in my head I was using the singular) to be there."

Mitzi piped up. "We just didn't want to get your mom upset."

Really? Maybe you should have thought of that twenty-five years ago before suggestively turning my father's page one late night and leading him down Cheaters' Alley.

"Don't worry, Dad. It'll be fine. You (*singular*) can definitely come."

"I heard you and your mother went out to brunch." He's notorious for this. He repeats whatever info my mom tells him.

"Uh-huh. We had a great time." Who cared about brunch? I wanted to show off about my newfound job. "*That* was when I had time for brunch," I dramatically sighed. "Now I'm thick in the middle of auditions. No more brunch for a while."

"Hmm . . ." my father wondered. "Your mother never gets brunch when we're on the road,"

"Harvey!" Mitzi interrupted. "Constantly." She punched the word with her shrill voice. "She *constantly* gets brunch. She just calls it breakfast."

My father was annoyed at being contradicted. "Then it's not brunch, Mitz."

Each sentence pushed her shrillness level up. "She wakes up at 11:00 and eats an enormous amount of food at noon. Breakfast food. *At noon.*" As usual, they were having a conversation on two separate phones *in their own house.* Mitzi was still at it: "Then she doesn't eat another meal till 6:00. Dinnertime." She wrapped up her theorem. "The first meal is like two meals, breakfast and lunch—i.e., brunch." She pronounced it with two syllables. "Ba-runch."

My father sounded defeated. "Maybe you're right. But with Stephen she calls it brunch. With us she calls it breakfast."

WHO CARES?!! I had to get off this party line. "Guys, I have more auditions tomorrow. I'll call you over the weekend."

"OK, son. And don't worry if opening night doesn't work out with all of us. We won't be offended."

"OK. Bye, Dad. *(Pointedly.)* Bye, Mitzi."

It's really beginning to hit me now. I'm transitioning away from subbing to conducting! Although, doing only one show won't put me on the same level as other conductors. I've decided to conduct this show for around six months and then start working on another. *That* will feel amazing, having two shows running simultaneously that I developed. Mason asked me if I'd do everything (musical) on *Flowerchild.* I said I'd do the dance arrangements (writing/creating the music for the dance breaks), vocal arrangements (creating the sassy harmonies and vocal counterparts), and music direction (teaching/overseeing all the music). Sometimes three different people split those jobs up, but I really want the music to be totally my vision. The only thing we still needed was an orchestrator. As I was getting ready for bed I saw myself in the mirror and said, "You are a full-time Broadway Music Director." My reflection remained silent.

Fifteen

*T*hird day of auditions. Kris was actually here before any of us. "It was easier if I just pulled an all-nighter. I was too nervous I wouldn't wake up." He looked awful.

"What did you do?" I asked him, "Stay up all night drinking coffee? That's so freshman year of college."

"Didn't have to—" He suddenly looked alive. "Luckily, after the girls, there was a different *E! Hollywood True Story* on every hour. It was a *One Day at a Time* salute." *Now I was interested!* "There was an hour on Bonnie Franklin, then an hour on Mackenzie Phillips and Valerie Bertinelli, and finally Pat Harrington Jr." He growled.

I nodded. "He *was* cute." I had a big late '70s crush on him—mustache, dirty jeans, tool belt. "Why didn't he and Bonnie ever get together on the show?" I mused.

He looked shocked. "It would have ruined the sexual tension. Everyone knows if you want to stay interested in someone sexually, *don't* have sex with them!"

Hmm. Is that what my problem was with Craig last night? He called me from his cell phone while he was walking his dog. He was all lovey-dovey, saying he missed me and had a great

time with me last weekend, especially *before* we went to dinner
(i.e. *sex*) . . . and the more he spoke the more I was fascinated
watching *Project Runway* with the mute on. He's never that romantic on the phone—or actually ever. Could it be that I've lost
sexual interest in him like Schneider would have done to Ann
Romano had their obvious desire been consummated?

Forget it. As I write I realize that's crazy. First of all, it's not
as if this weekend was the first time we had sex. Second, I happen to be in the middle of a high-stress situation. *Working
Woman* magazine said stress is the number-one way to ruin sexual desire. (I flip through it every six months at the dentist's
office).

I can't believe I feel stress. The irony is palpable. I thought finally being in charge of auditions would be a breeze, but I must
say it's hard to be behind the table. There's so much pressure . . .
you want so much for your friends to be good, you're terrified
there won't be someone whom the whole creative team will
agree on, you don't want to kick someone out right away who's
wrong for the show so you have to force yourself to sit thru their
entire audition, etc. I'm sure actors are reading this and thinking
(or saying) "F.U.! What's the hard part about judging?" I feel
like those parents who beat their child and say, "This hurts me
more than it hurts you."

I noticed Kris had sat down while I was writing all of this and
promptly fell asleep. I immediately shook him awake and called
a diner on my cell phone to order him some espresso.

"Ten-dollar minimum," came the low-energy reply.

"All right—five espressos." I hate minimums. I've ordered so
many side salads and steamed vegetable dumplings I didn't want
because of them.

I clicked off and Kris asked me to sit next to him so I could
subtly wake him up if he nodded off again. Mason arrived, obviously freshly showered (hair still wet) . . . and then Marzullo and
Vampira. We all settled and Calum, the monitor, brought in the
first person. I rolled my eyes to myself. It was Nancie (last name

withheld for fear of lawsuit), the Broadway flavor of the month. She had done some obscure but deep Off-Broadway musical last year and ever since then has been featured in numerous workshops and concerts.

After standing for a minute in the center of the room with her head down as if concentrating deeply (*please* save that stance for yoga class), she started to sing and, just as I un-fondly remembered, her voice had the limited range of someone's wrist with carpal tunnel syndrome.

She finished and proudly sauntered over to the piano. "I also brought a Sondheim song—that's much more my oeuvre."

Oeuvre? She didn't really just use that pretentious word! The words *au revoir* came to mind, but I simply said I've heard all I need to and she was great, wonderful, fantastic! She put on her cloak (!) and left.

Staci dangled her picture like spun gold. "Um . . . she's a callback, right?"

I glared. "Yeah—call her back and ask her to get voice lessons."

"Um, Stephen"—Staci had her 'I'm explaining something to a child' voice on—"she's *really hot* right now."

I was getting indignant. "She doesn't sing well."

"But . . ." She sounded like she had a delicious morsel up her sleeve that would override everything. "She's a *great actress*."

I was really annoyed now. I turned and faced Staci. "The interesting thing is, we're doing a *musical!* I want someone who can do *both*."

There is a pervading theory that someone is either a singer or an actor. And, the worse someone sings, the more the myth is enlarged by certain critics/fans that they're such a wonderful actor, it doesn't matter. You know what? On Broadway, I want someone to be multitalented! We're supposed to be getting the cream of the crop, not putting one requirement over the other. That was the whole spin during *Sunset Boulevard.* Patti LuPone sounded *fantastic* but people fawned over Glenn Close and said that her acting was better. Why? I say, not because her acting *was* better, but because she didn't sing as well as Patti. Patti has it all! Need I remind you, she has an acting degree from Juilliard *and* she's able to belt a G! If you're a musical theatre star with a great voice, there is an assumption that you're not a great actor. For instance, Betty Buckley is a first-rate, top-of-the-line actress *and* brilliant singer. But I have a feeling her world-class acting will never be fully appreciated because her voice is so spectacular.

Thank goodness Mason piped up. "I'm sure we can get someone who acts just as well and can sing up a storm." He dropped her picture into the "no callback" pile. Staci stared downward sullenly. I smiled with all 31 teeth (and my one crown, in the back on the left side).

The door opened and in walked . . . Jackson! I totally forgot he was auditioning; we hadn't spoken for the last three days because I'd been so busy. I got up and gave him a big hug. I didn't care if everyone knew I was friends with him because I was sure he'd do great.

The light was hitting his hair just right to accentuate his chestnut highlights. He also wore ratty jeans and a Rolling Stones shirt that showed off his blue eyes. It was a little '60s *radical* meets *Chelsea boy*. He stood center and sang one of my favorite songs from that time: "The Worst That Could Happen" ("Girl, I heard you're getting married . . ."). He sounded great, and during it I noticed Staci narrowing her eyes at me. I assumed she was thinking. "Stephen's friends are all going to be good singers and Sofia Coppola-style actors." Who knows if I was projecting, but I decided to prove her wrong. I wrote Mason a note asking him to ask Jackson for a monologue.

"Jackson, you sound wonderful." Mason smiled—he had his schmooze on. "I know we didn't ask you to prepare one, but do you possibly have a monologue?" I knew Jackson had just done a regional show about The Mamas and the Papas, and he had a great monologue in it that explained why the group had no choice but to break up. It was a total metaphor for having to leave the '60s—i.e., our show.

He launched into the monologue and when he finished there was that tension-filled silence that happens when an audience is so transported they don't want to come back to reality.

Jackson stood there. "Uh . . . anything else?" He finally asked.

"No," said Mason quietly. "That was very effective."

Jackson walked out and I plucked his picture out of Staci's hand and held it up.

"Wow, Stephen!" Mason said with a smile. "Definite callback."

Into the callback pile.

"Um . . . he seems kind of young for the lead," said naysayer Staci.

"What about for Sonny?" I asked Mason, pointedly ignoring the downer. Sonny was the comic relief. He essentially became a hippie just to meet chicks.

"Hmm," said Mason. "I've always thought of Sonny as a little more character looking." (Read: fat.) "Let me see his resumé." I picked up his resume and was about to hand it to Kris so he'd pass it to Mason when I saw unmistakable deep breathing and fully shut eyes. I couldn't nudge him because I was holding the picture so . . . "ACHOO!" I let out the fakest sneeze this side of Adelaide, but I knew it would wake Kris up. Staci and Mason looked over at me and gave me mutual "Gesundheits," which allowed Kris to wipe the smidgeon of drool from his mouth and pass the 8 × 10 to Mason.

"Hey!" Mason liked what he saw. "He did lots of comic roles before. Maybe I should rethink what Sonny looks like."

"Um . . . we have more people waiting." Staci looked more withdrawn than usual. I guess she missed the comfort of her casket.

"Sorry, Staci." Mason was polite to everyone, even casting cadavers. "Send 'em in."

* * *

We saw a ton more people and decided not to take lunch so we could bring in some non-Equity people (Equity is the actors union) who were waiting. There are all these union rules which I don't really understand; you can't get an audition for an Equity (union) play unless you're Equity, but you essentially can't get your Equity card unless you get cast in an Equity play. So, one of the techniques to get around this is to show up at an Equity call and see if the casting people will let you come in during downtime. All of the people we had seen so far were prescreened by Staci last week, and they were from an initial Equity call. I remember when all my friends were nonunion, so I asked Staci if we could see some today, because it was the last day before callbacks began next week.

She looked devastated (aka normal) and went out into the hall to ask all the non-Eqs for the picture/resumé. We saw around 15 people, and for the most part, there was a reason these people were still non-Equity. Ouch.

"Hi, I'm Tyler!" said one perky 21-year-old.

Didn't he read the casting breakdown which stated every role was someone in his/her 30's? He probably did, but figured this was a chance to get seen by Staci, and if he were right for another show she was casting, she'd call him in.

Manipulative, but smart.

At auditions, sometimes it's smart to sing a song intended for the opposite sex so the people behind the table are familiar with the song, but not bored by it because there's a new spin. Usually, all you have to do is change a few he's to she's and whatever else is gender specific. Tyler pushed it, though, by singing "There Are Worse Things I Could Do," which required *way* too many fullout lyric changes. The bridge is where I drew the line:

"I could flirt with all the girls . . .
Smile at them and toss their curls . . ."

Toss their curls? The last time that was a come-on was in a

Jane Austen book. AND the girl always tosses her own curls. Not vice versa.

Of course, we thanked him profusely and after he left, I was waiting for a sassy comment from Mason.

He put Tyler's picture in the "no callback" pile. "Oh, well. He's not right for the show."

Shocked again! I can't believe his lack of needing to dish about other people. Maybe that's why he was more relaxed than I was. He wasn't constantly thinking of cutting comments to make later on.

After a couple of other people sang who made me envy Beethoven's deafness, this guy named Vince sauntered in. He looked like a combination of every race: dark curly hair, exotically shaped yet hazel eyes, pouty lips, barrel chest. Aka CUTE!

"I don't really have a lot on my resumé." He said after he handed it to us.

"That's OK," Mason said as he scanned it.

"I've been in LA for a while."

Mason looked horrified. "Were you doing musicals out there?" he sputtered.

Musicals are respected by LA people as much as earthquakes are. Doing theatre in LA is like performing a drag show for the Southern Baptist convention.

"No!" Vince was adamant. "I got a record deal and spent most of my time doing albums no one bought." He shrugged.

I—codependently—immediately felt bad. "Oh, wait . . . I think I heard of you," I said to make him feel better. Kris rolled his eyes at me. He knows I haven't bought a pop record since the *Flashdance* album.

"Um." Staci glared at his resume. "So you're *still* non-Equity?"

"Yeah, I know." Vince smiled sheepishly. "I got that recording contract right around the time all my friends were getting into Equity and I stopped pursuing theatre. Then my label dropped me—"

Ouch. That's what happened.

"—and I decided to quit the arts and got my massage license."

Kris leaned in and whispered, "Maybe that's where you know him from." He started to hum "*Please* release *me . . .*"

"Why did you move to New York?" Mason asked.

"My first love was musicals. I don't think I wanted to quit the arts; I think I wanted to just quit the recording business."

"Um, you might as well sing, then." Staci wanly gestured towards the piano.

He gave his music to Marzullo and came back to the center of the room.

He was *fantastic*.

Even though much of what the judges on *American Idol* spew is bull, their point that people have to be individual to become stars is incredibly accurate. Vince had a type of voice that was great but different from the standard musical theatre voice. Velvety, yet with an "I-haven't-totally-cleared-my-throat" undercurrent. Yet, just when you thought his voice was on the brink of cracking, he suddenly would sing a higher note with total control. So exciting!

AND, not only did he sing great, but his acting was spot on. While he crooned "Young Girl (Get Out of Mind)" you could totally feel his longing for the girl countered by his revulsion with himself. Maybe I was projecting my own weeklong crush on a 21-year-old trainer at my gym, but by the end of his song, I actually wiped away a tear.

And subtly shook Kris awake.

As soon as he left, we all (minus Staci, whose head was buried in his resume) decided we had to call him back.

How weird! What would have happened if we had gone to Sbarro instead of seeing the non-Eq's? It's kind of frightening to me how arbitrary the business is. I always thought people were born to play certain roles, but often it's some weird happenstance that facilitates their stardom. Here's a side story: Rebecca

Luker wanted to be seen for the role of Marian the Librarian in the revival of *The Music Man*, but she was told by the casting people that the artistic staff thought she was wrong for the part. She asked her agent to let her audition as a courtesy and they did. She went in knowing that the people in the room didn't want to see her, yet she didn't let that stop her from giving her full sass. She wound up getting the part *and* getting a Tony nomination. What if she had accepted that they didn't want to see her? What if she hadn't pushed? The randomness gives me a headache.

After Vince left, Staci said she needed a break and quickly walked out of the room. She was obviously in a foul mood. Well, more foul than usual. I understood. A casting person wants to be able to see a final cast and know that they were responsible for bringing those people in. She must have been royally pissed off that the most likely contender for the lead was not someone she had prescreened and brought to us, but some guy who just wandered in from non-Equity land. HA HA!

Sixteen

*S*orry I haven't written since last Wednesday. First of all, I've spent the last couple of days listening to tapes of all the different versions of the show that Mason gave me. They did *Flowerchild* at Yale over such a long period of time that it kept evolving—and not always for the better. It's obvious some of the cast just got bored and decided to change things that were great. (Why add a harmonica solo to "California Dreamin'"? Are you dreamin' of a bluegrass band? Or did someone in the band take a one-credit course in harmonica and think it would be "so cool if I actually got to play in front of an audience, man!"?) There were also some musical moments that never worked, no matter what version, so I'm trying to figure out which arrangements to keep, which to tweak, and which to totally rewrite. Not to mention the new songs we're thinking of adding.

Today was a two-part disaster. The first part was the "Gypsy of the Year Competition," where I acted like an ASS. Every year, basically all of the Broadway, Off-Broadway, and touring shows spend six weeks collecting money for Broadway Cares/Equity Fights AIDS. They stand at the back of the house and collect cash as people exit, as well as sell autographed posters, programs, and "specialty items." Like you could pay a couple of hundred bucks and have tea with Whoopi Goldberg in her dressing room, or have Harvey Fierstein record your answering machine outgoing message, etc. You can even do a walk-on in a show, or conduct the orchestra for the exit music! A lot of the fundraising is really fun and creative.

Anyway, at the end of all that, there is a big variety type show where each play puts on a sketch or song (usually dishing some aspect of themselves or another show/star/producer) and at the end there is an award for best presentation as well as awards for shows that have raised the most money.

Well, if you remember, Jackson got me a ticket, and since my seat was next to Ronald, I was trying to avoid sitting down for as long as possible. As I'm standing near the concession stand, who do I see in the audience but Mason standing next to a good-looking guy in a suit. I had never met Jason before but I immediately saw why Mason stayed with him all these years. Cute! Plus, narcissistically, he looked a little like Mason too. They say dogs grow to resemble their owners and, apparently, so do boyfriends.

I suddenly felt a smidgeon of weirdness seeing Mason and his rhyming named boy toy. I'd been spending so much time with him over this whole audition period and I guess I feel a little territorial. I smiled at both of them, but my subtext was, "How dare Jason come along and think he's closer to Mason than I am?" I know he didn't really just "come along," but it was the first time I actually saw his mug. Of course, because I was so tense, I crazily overcompensated by being extra friendly.

"Stephen!" They both came over. "This is Jason, my—"

Lover? Partner? I couldn't quite bear it. I started babbling. "I know who Jason is." I bared my teeth/smiled and shook Jason's hand frantically. "I've heard your name on the machine a lot and I can't believe I'm finally meeting you. Mason's told me a lot about you." Which was a lie. He's actually told me nothing about him. I think he once mentioned that he was a lawyer.

Mason looked at me. "Jason's never seen *Gypsy of the Year* and I thought—"

"You're gonna love it!" I couldn't stop talking/interrupting/ speaking way too loud.

"Well," Jason finally got a word in. "Mason and I don't really have the same taste—"

"You know what they say!" Why couldn't I shut the f*ck up? "Opposites attract!"

"What?" they both said, in unison.

I laughed crazily and then waved to an usherette like I knew her. "I'll see you guys later." The usherette started backing away, perhaps based on the look in my eyes, but I doggedly pursued her. She finally backed herself into a wall and, even though she was frantically seeking means of escape, could go no further.

I knew I was acting bizarre and had to speak. "I simply want a program," I hissed.

"You're holding one," she whispered, terrified.

"Fine. That's all you had to say."

I turned on my heels and slunk back to my seat, being careful to avoid the section with Mason and Crazy Jase-y. (I'm having a hard time coming up with a mean nickname for him—give me some time.)

"*OK,*" I started talking to myself, "*it's stupid that I resent Mason's boyfriend . . . it's not like I have a crush on Mason. I mean I think he's cute and really smart, but I'm literally dating an Adonis. There's no comparison. And even if there were, Mason already has a boyfriend. Well, so does Craig, but I'm not getting involved with two people with boyfriends.*"

"Who has a boyfriend?" SHIT! Of course, Ronald *had* to hear me muttering.

I covered. "Who *doesn't* have a boyfriend? It's the holiday season!!"

Of course he took me literally. "I know plenty of people without boyfriends." Thankfully, he was distracted by Chita Rivera walking by. His starfucker-ness overrode any interest in me.

"Hi, Chita!" He waved like a ten-year-old. She looked at him quizzically and then quickly proceeded down the aisle to row B. Ronald looked at me nervously. "She can't see very well without her glasses."

"She was wearing her glasses."

He shook his head. "I think those are her reading glasses." Either Chita didn't know who he was, or she did know who he was. Both reasons were appropriate for glaring and ignoring him.

He looked at me smugly. "I hear you're interested in my client Vince Rocha for *Flowerchild.*

His client? I made my eyes into slits. "Ronald, if Vince is your client, why didn't he have an actual appointment? He sat outside the audition room the whole morning hoping to get in."

"Well, I just started representing him on a freelance basis."

MOTHERFUCKER! Jackson's ass was grass! Right after Vince's audition I had called Jackson on my cell phone and told him the whole Vince audition story. I'm sure he then told Ronald (because, like an idiot, he actually speaks to him), and Ronald saw a potential windfall. Ronald is essentially a theatrical ambulance chaser. He keeps each pic/resumé that struggling actors send in and he has spies at every casting agency. Whenever he hears that someone who doesn't have representation is close to getting a part, he calls them for an interview and magnanimously decides to represent them on a trial basis. If they get the part, they wind up paying him 10% to show what a good client they would be if he signed them, and if they don't get the gig, he just drops them. I found out about this scheme because I used to date Ronald's assistant, Wesley, but I never told Jackson because I didn't want to get Wesley in trouble for giving me the dish. And also, Wesley (who works out at my gym) made me swear not to tell or he would tell people what I listen to while on the treadmill. Everyone at my gym is listening to the latest house music and I would be mortified if they knew the CD in my player that I carefully put a "Gwen Stefani" sticker on was actually Barbra Streisand's 1977 *Superman* album.

I tried to get Ronald to admit it. "It seems you always seem to represent someone on the brink of their first big job." I stared him down.

He looked more cocky than usual. "Yeah. I have what they call 'the eye.'"

"Lazy eye?"

"I don't have lazy—"

"SHH! It's beginning!"

The lights in the audience started dimming so I was able to let my last comment resonate.

The show was great as usual, and as the curtain was coming down I was awkwardly stepping over Ronald so I wouldn't have to talk to him anymore.

"See you later, Ronald. I'm in a rush." Of course, as I was running up the aisle I ran into M/Jason. Immediately my mouth became a babbling brook.

"Hey, guys? Did you like the show? I know I did. What's not to like?"

Mason spoke while I was taking a breath. "Stephen, do you want to go get something to eat?"

The thought of hanging out with the two of them was completely *not* appealing. Would they hold hands? Would Mason have one arm draped casually over Jason's shoulder throughout the meal? Wait a minute! Would they be the type that actually made out in public? I was on the number 2 train *last week* and I saw a man in a suit with a briefcase and quite possibly his secretary standing in the middle of the subway car, holding on to a pole and kissing—*with tongue!* And even if I hadn't been completely captivated and watching closely I would have seen the tongue action . . . *and heard it!* I thought people stopped doing that kind of stuff around the same time they stop studying for the SATs. But apparently you don't have to be 16 and an idiot to make people uncomfortable in public, you can be mid to late 30s as well and wearing sneakers 'cause your heels are in your bag. The point is I said no to Mason's offer. Luckily, I had a good excuse, which is the other reason why I haven't been writing:

"I can't, I have to sub *Smile Out* for the first time tomorrow. See you at callbacks!" I fled the theatre and ran for the number 1 train.

Yes, I'm still subbing. Even though I have this new Broadway show, I decided to go ahead with *Smile Out* because I committed to playing it a while ago. I also didn't feel like giving up some extra bucks, especially right before Chanukah/Christmas. What the hell was I going to get Craig? We met last year at a New Year's Party so I haven't had to deal with getting him a Xmas present yet. I'm sure Mr. Midas (Jeffrey) is getting him something fabulously expensive so I obviously have to do the same, yet somehow one-up him. The pressure is enormous. I also have to make sure it doesn't look like it's from his mistress (is there a male equivalent? "mister-stress"?). For his birthday I got him front-row tix to a Kelly Clarkson concert. Yes, he's a big fan. I pretended I went along only to indulge him, but secretly I love her voice! At the concert, I totally got in touch with my inner child and apparently mine is a night-brace-wearing ten-year-old girl who screams "I love you, Kelly," once every two minutes. Anyway, now I've got to top that, and I figure the more extra money I have, the better.

Then there's my mother, who always claims, "Jews only give Chanukah presents because they're jealous of Christmas!" but it doesn't stop her from reluctantly accepting/expecting an extravagant present from me, Dianne, and my dad every year.

I'll definitely be making lots of moolah this month. The holidays are a big time for subs. On Broadway, actors have a certain number of "personal days" (weddings, funerals, etc.) that they can take off. But you can't just miss shows whenever you feel like it. However, a musician can miss up to 50% of their shows (four shows out of an eight show week). That's one of the great things our union negotiated for us. It sounds scandalous, but as long as there are good subs, the orchestra sounds the same. And although there's a different standard applied to the actor, it's just about customer satisfaction. If one of the leads is out of a Broadway show, the audience is usually PO'd, but I've never heard of an audience member wondering where that fabulous piccolo player was that they've heard so much about. Anyway, like most people, musicians like to take off major holidays, so I've subbed many a show on Christmas Eve, Easter Sunday, etc.

I told Phil, the pianist for *Smile Out*, that I would play the last week in December because he was taking his lady friend and her kids to Disneyland for Xmas vacation. Yes, there are straight musicians. As a matter of fact, the vast majority of the pit is straight. Although I will admit, most of the pianists are gay. Phil is actually a woman. Just kidding.

So a while ago, I began the subbing process. I showed up at the theatre wearing my "blacks." Musicians always have to wear black in the pit. Some are stricter than others. In certain pits, all that mattered is my shirt and pants are black (*Grease*). In others, the shoes *and* socks must be black (*Phantom*), or shirts must have no visible logos (*The Producers*), or shirts can have a logo but must have a collar (*Thoroughly Modern Millie*), etc. Each pit is different.

Anyhoo, I went straight to the musicians' locker area to put my knapsack away. Of course, I took my tape recorder out. When you're a sub, you never get a chance to rehearse with the orchestra, so the only way to learn a show is to play your part along with a tape. Phil walked over and started to hang up his coat. He saw my tape recorder and stealthily looked around the locker area.

"Hey," he whispered, "if your tape doesn't come out well, I just got a great video last week."

"Video?" I was confused. "Of the show on stage?" Bootleg videotapes are totally illegal, and even though I own quite a few, they don't actually help you learn your part because the way an orchestra sounds in the pit is totally different once it's put through the sound system

"No." He grinned. "A new sub came in and surreptitiously videotaped the conductor so you can practice along and actually see what it looks like when you're in my seat!"

I was thrilled! Usually, you have to come and watch the show in the pit at least three times so you can get used to how the conductor looks cueing certain sections. But now, thanks to law-breaking, I'd have it on video so I could rewind whenever I needed to and practice up a storm!

"Where can I get a copy?" I was panting like Heather after a half hour at the dog run.

He closed his locker door. "Call Françoise Smith. She made the original."

GASP! I recoiled. Françoise! My archrival! (for the last five months).

OK, here's the background about my bitterness. I didn't sub my first Broadway show till I was 26 (*Grease*), yet Françoise has the nerve to be subbing up a storm while *still in college!*

Her father is a Broadway contractor (the guy who hires the musicians), and he easily got her connected with every pit in town. Since no Broadway pianist wants to piss off a potential future employer, Françoise can sub any show she wants. She doesn't have a full-time position yet because it "conflicts with my heavy workload. I'm a double major."

Yes, Françoise, you've told me a hundred f*cking times. "Classsical piano and"—she always bows her head slightly—"my first love, harpsichord." I'll bet that harpsichord degree will get her incredibly far—if she can time travel back 300 years. To be even more annoying she also insists on saying "harp-see-chord," which she claims is the original pronunciation.

P. S. It's not only that I'm jealous she's 1,000 years younger than I am and already playing on Broadway. I'm also pissed because lately there were at least *two* shows I wanted to sub on, but she got there before me and the sub list filled up. Plus, because her Francophile mother named her Françoise, she thinks she can pepper every conversation with French phrases, even though the only Left Bank she's ever been to is a Chase on the left side of 73rd St. and Broadway. Her personality drives me up the *rampart*!

And the icing on the cake: she's beautiful. Angelina Jolie with 50% less lip. So, of course, she's always a big hit in the pit with the abundance of straight players. Ergo, color me green.

Well, we went into the pit and Phil set me up a chair next to the keyboard. I sat there with my copy of the score open and watched the conductor's style and the score (and simmered about *la jeune fille*).

I got home that night and reluctantly called her.

It rang once. "*Salut?*"

I glared at the phone and pretended to not understand. "No, it's Stephen."

What an idiot! French people don't even answer the phone with *Salut*. She wasn't even namedropping the proper French!

"Oh Stephen! I hear we're both subbing for *Smile Out*."

I had no interest in *petit* talk. "Uh-huh. Can I have a video?"

"*Mais oui!* It really comes in handy! I've cut my practice time in half so I have much more time to dedicate myself to classical piano and my first love, harpseechord."

"I know what you mean—I used to be in love with my Betamax."

"What?"

"Nothing. Can I pick one up?"

"You don't have to travel all the way to my apartment. Why don't I leave it at your gym? It's right around the corner from me."

That's another thing. She was always really pleasant to me, so I couldn't even revel in my disliking her.

I sighed. "Thanks, Françoise."

"I'll leave it there tomorrow. *A bientôt!*"

That was around a month ago, and tonight was the night I had to play.

It went downhill from the beginning. As soon as I got to the theatre I saw Phil putting his stuff in his locker. He was there because he was the assistant conductor, and the reason I was subbing for him was because he was conducting. As I came closer I saw him talking to Françoise. I quickly bent down to tie my shoe, and when I looked back up she had disappeared. I was positive I caught just a glimpse of her exiting through the door that leads to the audience. How obvious! She was going to watch the show and listen to see if I made any mistakes! The nerve! It was my first time and I was already being judged by Phil. Oh yeah, the first time you sub is essentially your audition. If you don't do well, you're not asked back. You don't have a couple of shows to ease into it. You pretty much have to ace it the first time, so the pressure is enormous! If Phil didn't think I was up to snuff, he would have to cancel his trip or find another sub for the week I was subbing for him (i.e., Françoise!). I *knew* she was just as competitive as I was. She was champing at the bit for a chance to rake in my bucks!

I got into the pit at half hour (*for definition: See Page One*). I quickly played through all the trouble spots. Like I mentioned before, when you play synth for a show there are usually a lot of difficult things besides the actual notes. *Smile Out* had three really quick sound changes (organ to harp to Fender Rhodes) in a row. I got used to the distance between the two pedals so I didn't miss my mark and wind up hitting the floor instead. Since there was only one beat between each sound change, I kept practicing moving my foot from the sustain pedal to the change pedal as quick as I could and nailed it every time. If you ever play pit keyboard, the main thing to remember is to always check the window on the top of the synthesizer to make sure you're on the right sound. Elizabeth Slatton (went to college with her) played *A Christmas Carol* and was supposed to play an organ sound and then quickly change to a dulcet harp, but she panicked, hit the foot switch twice, and wound up playing the "Scary Ghost" sound instead. In the middle of a poignant romantic scene, the audience suddenly heard an old man's voice moaning "Whoo-oo-oo." The conductor (and the crying ten-year-olds in the audience) were not amused.

Anyway, I gave the whole score a once-over and waited for the houselights to go down and the conductor to raise his baton. *Smile Out* starts with a drum roll and then the whole orchestra starts playing the overture. There is an amazing moment the first time one subs when, instead of doubling the keyboard part on a tape, you're suddenly the one playing it. It's like you've been sitting outside the machine, and suddenly you're in it. I always get a rush. There was a difficult scale I had to play at the end of the overture, but I saw Françoise's face in my mind and I *nailed* it! The cellists to my left banged their bows on their music stands, which is a string player's version of applause. Knowing that the regular musicians approved gave me all the confidence I needed to stick it to Françoise. Every time I approached a difficult passage or exposed solo I thought of her smug (yet stunning) little *visage* and I attacked each note with an incredibly precise yet painful stroke that left both hands so sore I could barely open up Phil's locker after the show.

"You did great!" Phil shook my hand.

"Ow!" I recoiled. Phil looked concerned. "What's wrong with your hand?"

"Oh . . . ha ha." I did my signature cover-up laugh which, upon usage actually calls more attention to my lying. "My hands are all sore from pottery class." It was the first thing I thought of. I had just watched "The Egyptians and Pottery" on The Discovery Channel.

"My girlfriend does pottery! What kind of clay do you use?"

How the f*ck would I know? I had to change course. "I meant

Pottery *Barn*." There was silence. "I carried one of their signature country chairs back to my apartment 'cause I couldn't get a cab."

Phil stared at me.

"I hurt my hands on all that wicker."

Phil looked thoughtful. "Oh. Will you be able to play Christmas week? I don't want you to injure yourself more. I can always call Fran—"

"No!!!" My shriek caused several sax players to turn from their lockers and look concerned. "I'll be fine, Phil. That is"— I put on my humble face—"if I was accepted."

"Of course you were!" *Yes!* Phil went to shake my hand again and instead patted me on the back. "You were great! Such focus." He reflected. "And determination."

"Thanks a lot, and thanks for the gig!" Phil buttoned his coat and waved. I called to him, "Have a great trip if I don't see you before!"

Just as Phil turned the corner to go to the stage door, my cell phone rang. It was from Françoise's home number.

"Hello?"

"Oh, Stephen, I'm so glad I caught you. *C'est* Françoise. I left my sweater in Phil's locker and he's not answering his cell. Can you leave it with the stage doorman?"

How did she get home so quick? It didn't make sense. "Why didn't you come backstage after you watched the show?"

"Watched what show? I have classes every Monday night at 8:00. You know I'm studying piano and my first love—"

"Harp-see-chord." I beat her to the pretentious second syllable. "Fine, Françoise, I'll leave it at the door."

I was stunned. I can't believe I completely bruised my hands/arms and she was in class *the whole time*. If I tell this story to Monikah, she'll say it's because of my issue with projecting. I had no actual proof Françoise was going to watch the show, it was all based on assumption, blah blah blah. She'll try to get in touch with my need to project and tie it to when I was a child, always having to figure out what my mother's next mood swing would be. As usual, the session will end up with me teary-eyed. We've been through it a thousand times before, and if I ask her why I haven't changed yet she'll say, "*Why* haven't *you changed yet*?"

I have a better question: "Why haven't I changed *therapists* yet?"

Seventeen

*T*he whole Gypsy of the Year/subbing debacle helped distract me from the fact that today is the first day of callbacks starring Craig. I'm writing in the morning because *Men's Health* suggests it's a way to focus before beginning your day. Actually, I'll admit that I read it in *Seventeen* while I was on line at Gristedes, but I think the advice is age- and genderless. I don't even know what I'm supposed to focus on. I can't make Craig not come to the callback. The only one I felt I could confide in was Kris. He had asked for a wake-up call for this morning. He picked up on the first ring.

"Did you pull another all-nighter?" I asked.

"No, even more drastic. I got rid of my TV. Gave it to Housing Works." It sounded like he was drinking something, which reminded me that he still owed me for those five espressos!

I heard him put down his cup. "If I don't have an assistant who's going to get there early and cover for me, I knew I had to eliminate all risk factors. The Geisenshlaags have never fired a choreographer, and I don't want to be the first one.

I couldn't hold back anymore and launched into the whole callback story. Kris did a lot of "You go, girl" when I told him Craig and I were secretly dating and proceeded into whoops and

"No, he didn't" during the *Phantom* dance belt story. When I told him that Craig was coming to callbacks today complete with tin ear, Kris offered a "Bitch, you're screwed." I told Kris to keep his trap shut about me and Craig and he promised he would. He then told me a phenomenally dishy story about a mutual friend who just got cast in *Legally Blonde* and insisted he needed his costume washed after the matinee (It's usually done after the night show). The dressers at the show refused until the guy finally 'fessed up that he had crabs. He made me promise not to tell anyone because he was sworn to secrecy.

Hmm, I thought, just like I swore him to secrecy about Craig and me.

CALLBACKS (LUNCH BREAK, 12:00)

It's lunch break and so far we've seen half of the guys called back for the two main roles. The show will have an ensemble of dancers, but we were curious to see how the leads could dance because if some of them were fierce, we'd reconceive certain numbers to feature them. All the guys (around twenty altogether) had to do a combination Kris taught them and then improv for 16 beats. There is nothing more horrifying than seeing people who've only played leading men (i.e., stood center stage and sung) "funking out." There was one guy who was really heavy but had sassy moves on him. I fondly remembered Rerun from *What's Happening!!* Craig, of course, looked great during the regular combination and then during the freestyle he looked *amazing!* He was trained only in ballet but was such a natural dancer he could do any style. Each person did it a couple of times, and Craig did a totally different freestyle combo each time he went. He thought of some amazing steps that I hope Kris steals for the actual show! If only I could get Craig into the chorus and skip his callback for the lead. But there's no way he'd miss out on his chance to "impress" Mason and Staci. I've finally accepted there's nothing I can do, and when Craig auditions I'm just going to pull the Nazi Big Lie technique. Apparently if you keep repeating something that's not true—"He's in *great* voice today! He's the new sound of Broadway"—the nonstop repetition eventually makes people believe you. What choice do I have? Eventually, I'll just let out a big sigh and chalk it up to different taste.

"Well, I thought we weren't going for the traditional Broadway Sound" (I'll shake my head to imply I'm stuck with people locked in the past) ". . . but if you all feel strongly that he's not right, I'll reluctantly go along with you."

They'll think I'm eccentric, and a part of them will think they're not hip or astute enough to hear what I hear. It should work out great.

Or else the Geisenshlaags could fire me.

I'm hiding in the bathroom to collect myself. Me, Kris, Mason, and Craig (!) are about to go out to lunch. Kris pointedly asked Craig to come along. Whatever happens, I lose:

Option A: Kris is going to let slip (in front of Mason) that Craig and I are an item because he cannot keep a secret, or

Option B: Because Kris also fancies himself a matchmaker, he's going to try to talk Craig into breaking up with Jeffrey and dating me exclusively. That should be an amazing conversation because Mason will love finding out that his music director is cheating with his high school friend/investor's boyfriend.

Why did I say anything to Kris, who has the impulse control of a drunk Mel Gibson? What the hell am I going to do? If I don't go with them, anything can happen. If I do, I'll get to see Mason's look of shock/disappointment/disapproval when he discovers my illicit affair.

I'd better go. At least if I'm there I can try to control the situation.

* * *

Very, very strange. I'm going to try to write this all down before the afternoon session begins. We all went to the West Side Cottage on Ninth Avenue and I had my water glass poised in the air for the first ten minutes of the meal in case I had to smash it to the ground to create a diversion. But nothing happened. We spent the whole lunch just talking. It almost seemed like Kris was into Craig because he wouldn't stop asking Craig questions. It was very *Glamour* magazine's "Tips on how to make *him* fall in love with you": *Ask him about himself. Guys love to hear themselves speak!*

I finally got bored listening to Craig talk about his dance training since I'd heard it all before (I used the same trick on our first date), and Mason and I wound up talking.

"Stephen, do you know of any sublets?" he asked while eating the deep-fried deep fried-ness that all New York Chinese restaurants put out on the table with duck sauce.

"Why? Are you and Jason breaking up?"

He laughed. "I think we may have to move. We've been renting from the same woman for years and she's only raised our rent $100 each year." He took a bite of his cold sesame noodles. Aka peanut butter, oil, and spaghetti.

"Anyway." He had a ten-foot strand to suck up. "When she found out I was doing a Broadway show she raised it $800!"

"What! That's so eff-ing rude!"

"Well, it's her right. It's her apartment."

What did rights have to do with it? It was still asshole-ish. "Mason, she can't screw you like that. What does Jason think. Can he afford it?"

He looked embarrassed. "Well, it doesn't really affect him."

"Why? Doesn't he have to cough up another $400 a month?"

"Actually," he was trying to phrase something. "He doesn't pay half the rent." I knew he had more to say. "Or any of it." He sighed. "I do."

I was speechless. But got out, "How come?"

Mason started talking really fast. "Well, when we got the apartment I was at NYU, but I was making money doing commercials and he was in law school not earning anything, so I didn't think it was fair for us to split it. And"—he shrugged—"it just kind of stayed that way."

It didn't make sense. "But isn't he working as a lawyer now?"

He laughed. "I know, I know. I'm just sort of used to taking care of him. Let's get back to the sublet." He suddenly plunged into his sesame noodles with wild abandon.

"Uh, I don't know about any. But I'll ask around." I signaled for more tea. "Are you gong to confront your landlord?"

"No. It's OK." He smiled. What was with him? *I* was constantly in a rage about nothing, *he* was constantly at peace about horrific events.

I realized I'd spent the whole lunch talking to Mason and looked over at Kris and Craig. They were whispering. Whispering!

I don't know which was worse: Kris revealing to Mason I'm cheating with Craig or Kris revealing to me that *he's* about to cheat with Craig!

I didn't want to cause a scene à la *Dynasty*, so I promptly dropped a twenty on the table and said I had to go to the bank. I can't believe Kris is so shifty as to work it in front of me. And I can't believe Mason is so spineless as to support his boyfriend who is a blatant lawyer. Why is everyone fucked up but me?

*H*ow do I describe what just happened?

I watched the second group of women in a daze. I had no one I could talk to. Mason was (thankfully) oblivious to my distress. I couldn't get him to cancel the callback without admitting why I was so insistent to go out on a limb for Craig. I couldn't confide in Kris—as soon as I told him that Craig and I were an item, he moved in for the kill. And I couldn't confide in Staci because it's hard to be comforted by a mummy.

Well, before I knew it the women were done and Staci went shambling out.

"Uh, we start the rest of the callbacks in five minutes."

Mason and I were just getting out of our chairs behind the audition table. We slowly sat back down when we saw them. The Geisenshlaags.

I know I've made them sound like the craziest producers ever, but truth be known, there were worse. David Merrick, who produced *Hello, Dolly* and *42nd Street*, was so annoyed at getting bad reviews for *Subways Are for Sleeping* that he looked in the phone book for people with identical names as the biggest reviewers in town, bought them tix to the show, and over a sumptuous dinner asked them what they thought of the show. The next day he took out a big newspaper ad that read: "One of the few great musical comedies of the last thirty years . . ." —Howard Taubman; "A knockout, from start to finish."—Richard Watts, and five other over-the-top praises.

Nowhere did it say that Howard, Richard, and the rest of the "critics" quoted weren't critics at all, but plain old New Yorkers who simply shared the same names! So the Geisenshlaags were just another in a long line of eccentrics.

They strode into the studio like royalty. She was wearing a mink that, because of her kooky body, was as long as it was wide. A matching mink hat was firmly ensconced over her stylishly short, jet black hair, and her tight face seemed to be pulled higher than last time (could she have gotten another face-lift in the last week?) He was in a double-breasted suit (brown tweed) with his signature ascot (cranberry) tied neatly around his neck. Impeccably dressed, unbearably annoying.

Of course, only Bettina spoke. "Hello, Stephen, Hello Jeremy!" I looked around the room and there was no Jeremy. There was, however, a red-faced Mason.

Mr. Geisenshlaag whispered something that got a loud "Who cares?" from the Mrs.

That was their charm. They never stood on ceremony. They were rude to everybody.

There was an awkward silence. I piped up, "*Mason* and I are glad to see you again."

She ignored me and looked at Mason. "Did you get our message?"

He looked uncomfortable. "Yes, and, quite frankly, I don't see how it will work."

"What?" She asked, with bad acting. "Your English is too full of idioms." She started looking for something in her bag.

Mason was speaking very softly. "Well, we agreed on three weeks of previews and—"

"Is it actually *in* your contract?" Bettina was able to spit this in Mason's face since she had found what she was looking for. Her red Elizabeth Arden lipstick. It was almost empty. Not surprising since she applies it liberally to her lips and, apparently, her teeth.

"No, it's not, but—"

She held up her hand to stop him. "Listen, Garrett, a chicken's a chicken." Who's Garrett? And who ever heard of that expression? She continued, "We *cannot* open the same night as the new Lincoln Center show." She said this all while applying her lipstick.

I figured out what was going on. Broadway shows always want to open on a Thursday so they can get the review into all the Friday papers, which are usually the most popular. If two shows open the same night, usually only one gets the front page of the *Times'* Arts and Leisure section and one is relegated to the inside. It's very tense trying to secure an opening night with no competition and apparently Bettina was nervous the Lincoln Center show could overshadow us. The *Times* has a history of not liking the Geisenshlaags (see article titled "Geisenshlaags running out of B stars for C shows" 5/21/05), and this would be a perfect excuse for the *Times* to give *Flowerchild* less visibility.

I looked at Mason. He was looking at the floor. I suddenly thought of something and piped up. "What about opening up a week later? That would give us extra time."

Bettina cut me off with a glare. "*And* cost us extra money! This show will not start really selling tickets until we get the reviews. Another week of preview ticket sales will lower our projected intake."

Why couldn't she see the big picture? Why couldn't Mason show it to her? I kept talking. "Bettina, if the show's not ready, and it therefore gets bad reviews, there won't *be* any ticket sales."

There was whispering from Mr. G.

"Well, there's one way we could open the show a week later and not lose money . . ."

Mason was visibly relieved.

Bettina was casual. "We just won't pay you for the last week of previews."

What? How much would they really save? Mason was probably making three grand a week at most since he was a first-time director *and* this was a Geisenshlaag show. They'd save very little, but Mason would lose a whole week's salary. And now with his rent going up! I knew he'd have to say no.

"Sure! No problem. Thanks a lot, guys!" I was flabbergasted. He suddenly was speaking in his normal voice, yet he was selling himself down the river. He didn't even try to compromise with them. The whole thing seemed fishy. While they kept talking, I called my friend Shawn Spamarro, who worked in their office.

He picked up after one ring.

"Shawn, it's Steve."

"Hey, are the vipers there yet?"

"Yes, and their fangs are dripping poison." Down to business. "Puzzle me this—" Shawn and I went up to Provincetown a few years ago and were repulsed by/obsessed with the name of the local toy store: Puzzle Me This. Now, whenever we have a question for each other, we always preface it with Riddle or Puzzle me this.

I riddled him: "Have you sent out any press releases yet?"

"No—but they put one in my out pile before they left. I haven't even looked at it yet." I heard a shuffling of papers. "Oh, yeah. It says they're going to postpone the opening to a week later. I'm supposed to get it to all the newspapers so they put it in their listings."

I knew it! They were "playing" (a word I learned from the WB network) Mason! They weren't stupid. They never intended to open the show a week early; they knew it wouldn't be ready. They just wanted to see if he'd go along with a salary cut, but either way the show was going to open a week after the intended opening night. They'd decided before they even came by.

You can't blame them for trying to cheat him out of money. Well, I guess you can, because it's a cheap and underhanded thing to do, but it didn't matter because I was going to stop Mason from agreeing.

I rushed back in to find the Geisenshlaags talking to Marzullo, who was saying something and shaking his head "no" (no doubt refusing to part with some aspect of his salary). Bettina countered that with her signature "You talk too fast. English is my second language." I walked past them and over to Mason, who was sitting at the audition table eating an apple.

I whispered to him what I had just found out and told him he'd better get to his agent before the Geisenshlaags do. For some reason he kept eating.

He finally swallowed. "Stephen, I know I shouldn't let this happen, but I feel sometimes it's better to leave things alone."

Was I missing something? "Mason, you don't have to refuse to the Geisenshlaags' faces—that's what agents are for."

He wasn't looking me in the eye. Or anywhere near my face. "I already told him it was OK."

"So call him back!"

He shook his head languidly. "I'd rather just focus on the show." And with that he walked out to go to the bathroom.

What was with him? He seemed to let people walk all over him. Seemed? He essentially had the heel prints from Bettina's six-inch Manolo Blahnik's on his sternum.

The Geisenshlaags came and sat next to me. I smelled her

Joy perfume and the pastrami sandwich he must have had for lunch.

"Stephen, why couldn't we have callbacks tomorrow?" Bettina looked annoyed. "I *always* have my hair colored at 5 o'clock on Tuesdays and Pierre nearly had a conniption when I said I had to reschedule."

Why was I stuck having this conversation? Where was Mason?

"Well, Bettina," I said, patiently, "as I understand it, the studio was only 'available' until the end of this week." Translation: "available" meaning that's all you f*cking cheapskates would rent it for. "And I think Mason was nervous we wouldn't have enough time to see everyone if we waited until tomorrow."

"Well, everyone had *better* be good." She seemed to narrow her eyes at me. Or was it my imagination?

"Um, they will be," said Staci, who had suddenly materialized at the table. "Everyone we called back has a fantastic voice, right Stephen?"

"Well," I began. Was I being set up? "How do you define fantastic? Fantastical? Like science fiction?"

Thank goodness Mason and Kris both came back at that moment.

"Hey guys, sit over here!" I said, fervently. Where else would they sit? There was only one table in the room. I suddenly remembered Mason's spinelessness and Kris's double-crossing. I adopted a combination hurt/judgmental look that could work for both situations. Apparently I was Medusa because both refused to look me in the eye. I glared at Kris. I couldn't wait to kick his ass after callbacks. Verbally kick his ass, that is. I'd wind up with a broken third metatarsal if I actually kicked those Tae-Boed cheeks of granite

I looked down at the list of people who were coming. We were seeing two men and two women. Craig was last, so I could be a nervous wreck the whole time.

The first two women were fairly established Broadway

actresses who wouldn't come in to audition unless they could immediately skip to the callback. I didn't blame them. We'd all seen plenty of their work and there was no need for an initial look.

Well, I felt awful for the first girl, Rachel-Sarah. Not just because she had a hyphenated first name, but because she had started out years ago as a fierce chorus dancer and moved her way up to featured actress in two mid-90s musicals, earning a Tony nomination and Drama Desk Award. She was trying out for Andrea (pronounced Ahn-DRAY-a), the romantic lead character: a girl who lived on the beach for years as a hippie, yet was suddenly fiercely determined to make something of her life now that the '60s were ending. The beach living is why she appears in a bikini in almost every scene. Tacky, yes, but there's got to be some way to make straight men come to the theatre.

Unfortunately, recently Rachel-Sarah was all set to do her first leading role in a new show when the funding fell through due to it being financed by someone who worked for one of the companies on Wall Street that was busted for insider trading. Sadly, the role was to be Bridget from a musical version of *Bridget Jones's Diary*. Rachel-Sarah had gained the requisite twenty pounds Bridget is always trying to lose and hadn't lost it herself.

I knew she could lose it all by the time the show opened, but while she was singing, Bettina got out a marker and furiously started scrawling something on Rachel-Sarah's 8 × 10. She passed it to all of us so we could see her tactful "She's fat, no way" in bright, red ink. During Rachel-Sarah's ballad, I scribbled back, "She can lose it by opening," which is when Bettina got sick of writing and instead whispered LOUDLY, "Publicity shots begin in three weeks!"

Rachel-Sarah looked towards the table and I quickly plastered a fake smile on my face but then realized her song was "Losing My Mind," which is supposed to be phenomenally depressing. I turned my smile upside down and Rachel-Sarah finished her song looking miffed. Mason covered up Bettina's outburst by saying "Rachel-Sarah, publicity shots begin in three weeks. Are you available?" Why wouldn't she be available? "You're not going on vacation, are you?" Good save, Mason!

"No. If I leave town it'll be Christmas week." She laughed. "I'm not one of those people who go on vacation at the beginning of January just to save some money!" We all laughed. All except the Geisenshlaags who, as far as I knew, had always left town for the first two weeks of January since '83.

Rachel-Sarah then gave a great reading, but we all knew it was a lost cause. Mason, of course, thanked her very kindly, and as soon as she walked out, in walked Anike Burns. Pronounced A-neek, translated from the Norwegian to mean Psycho Diva with no morals.

She was the critics' darling after doing a concert version of *Sweet Charity* where she played the Gwen Verdon role with a mixture of sass, sweetness, and Broadway Star quality. She then landed a great role on a soap and became nationally known due to her torrid love affair with a certain married son of a never-convicted Mob boss. She had a reputation for being late to rehearsals, press events, *and* actual performances. Before she did *Charity* (insider abbreviation), she did lots of Broadway chorus work and was constantly late not only for the beginning of Act One ("Taxi problems" was her common excuse), but Act Two! She'd literally sneak out of the theatre during intermission, go down the block to a Starbucks, and come back 25 minutes later. I was subbing in the pit and many times heard "Ladies and Gentlemen, for Act Two the role usually played by Anike Burns will be played by Mary Lee Kamioner." Since she was sleeping with the stage manager (among others), she always managed to not get fired.

Regardless, around a year ago she quit her soap, moved to LA, married her Mafioso hunk, divorced him a month later, was dropped by the tabloids, and was here auditioning for *Flower-child*, apparently trying to revive her career. She was a name and extremely talented. However, we wanted someone who would perform *both* acts. She walked in looking better than I'd ever seen her. Her hair now had gold highlights, either from the LA sun or salon, and her signature grey eyes were shining. She was wearing a fitted dress so we could totally imagine what she'd look like in a bikini—fierce! With her heels on she was over six feet, but she didn't look like a giant, she looked like a bombshell. She scanned the table and saw me. I knew she vaguely recognized me but probably didn't know from where. She must have figured out I was somewhat important because, even though we'd barely spoken a word when I subbed the show she was in (and the word was usually "move" when she walked by me), she ran over to the table and gave me a *big* long-lost-friend hug.

She stood back to admire me. "How *are* you?" She asked with real concern. I was torn between being annoyed she was being friendly only to get ahead and wanting to show off for knowing a famous person. I responded in a cross between both feelings.

"I'm doing great, Anike. I haven't seen you since . . ." I trailed off because I wanted to put her on the spot. I knew she wouldn't remember.

"Um, didn't you sub on *42nd Street* when Anike was in it?" Staci blurted. The one time she comes out of her coma is to ruin my putting someone on the spot-ness!

Anike feigned being insulted. "Of *course* Steve subbed there. I've never forgotten. He was the best sub we had!" Again, torn between her obvious bullshit yet loving being complimented.

"Why don't you sing?" Mason was not into the fakeness any longer.

Anike walked to the piano, gave Marzullo her music, and launched into her song. I couldn't help it—she was amazing! A combination of sexy and hot, yet a girl you totally want to be best friends with. She then read the scene and actually made me laugh on certain lines I hadn't thought were that funny. Change was in the air. Five minutes before, I never would have considered casting her because of her psycho behavior, but suddenly I was thinking it would be worth it because of the performance we'd be getting. Had she stopped acting out? Was she now reliable? *The Star* had recently said in a "Celebs Clean Up" article that she did 30 days in rehab. Maybe she got herself together. I mean, she did get to the audition on time . . . and she did think I was the best sub on *42nd Street*. What? She said it!

She thanked us all as she left and I knew everyone was thinking what I was thinking. Is she worth the risk? We couldn't even discuss it because in walked Vince. Staci handed his picture and resumé to the Geisenshlaags. He had changed out of his dance togs (sweatpants and a tank top—the better to show his biceps!) and into a pair of Levi's and a flannel shirt. Simple yet sexy! He started to sing and immediately Bettina passed a note around with a scrawled NO CREDITS! NO WAY! The last time I wrote back to her she wound up just blurting out her response so this time I pretended to not see the note when she passed it to me. Bettina started gesticulating wildly towards it and I feigned I was so focused that I didn't see her. I knew she'd frustratingly have to wait till he left to start dishing on him. Obviously I didn't know her.

When she saw I wouldn't respond to her exhortations she couldn't take it and blurted out, "Stephen, *the note!!!*"

It was so loud that Marzullo abruptly quit playing. He must have thought that someone was yelling from the table for him to stop.

Vince quizzically looked at us and said, "What note?"

I glared at Bettina and then said with aplomb, "The G sharp! Our producer here loves your voice and said to me she doesn't need to hear any more of your song. She just wants to make sure you can hit Glen's big note at the end of Act One."

"Well, actually," I couldn't tell if Vince knew I was lying or not, "my song ends on a G sharp. Why don't I just skip to the end?"

"Perfect!"

As he started singing, I scribbled, "Give him a chance."

She shook her head.

I wrote NO CREDITS=CHEAP SALARY.

Mother's milk. She and Fritz smiled throughout the rest of Vince's audition.

Vince finished and left. I looked at my watch and tried a last-ditch effort to prevent the Craig debacle. "You know, it's 5:45, we're not going to have enough time to do the next audition. Let's just postpone it!" I started gathering my things.

Bettina grabbed me by the arm and sat me back down. "If you think I cancelled my raven highlights to see three measly callbacks, you're mistaken." She yelled to the monitor. "Send in the next one."

Staci tapped Bettina on the shoulder. "Um, this is Stephen's friend coming in. He recommends him highly." Was she setting me up? Was she trying to be supportive? Who cares! I was sunk.

"Well," I stammered, "by 'friend,' I think Staci means I know of him. And by recommend, I think she means I . . ." I what? How could I twist that to save myself?

"Um, by 'recommend,' I mean that Stephen specifically told me that he has a great voice."

Yay! By trying to save myself, I gave Staci a setup to finalize my ruination.

Staci was smiling. Yowtch. Maybe I'll get her some Crest white strips for opening night.

Craig walked in.

I tried to disassociate. If I wasn't feeling anything, it wasn't happening.

He looked at Kris.

"Yes." He said, nodding.

"Excellent." Kris got up and gave him a hug.

I dis-disassociated. What the hell was going on? They hadn't even had a date yet. Were they going to announce their engagement?

"We have an announcement to make." Craig smiled at me

AHHH! They were!

Kris took a step forward. "I've asked Craig—"

To move to Vermont? That's where we were going to move once he broke up with Jeffrey. How dare they steal my state?

"—to be the assistant choreographer—"

"And I said yes!" Craig blurted out.

How do I describe the feeling? Shock mixed with getting off the hook-ness, mixed with dreading the therapy session where Monikah silently judges me for projecting?

"What the hell does this have to do with callbacks?" Bettina's voice cut through the air like a man on a flying trapeze. An angry, overly made-up, squat man on a flying trapeze.

"Bettina, I'm sorry." Kris walked over to her. "You see, I lost my assistant and was having a hard time finding someone who would fit all the requirements you laid out (i.e., take your pennies that you call a salary and deal with the constant risk of being fired). Craig was called back for the lead, but when I saw his dancing and obvious choreographic skill, I asked him to assist, and he said yes!"

Halfway through this conversation Bettina had picked up her cell phone and was frantically dialing. "I can be there in five minutes. Start getting the foil wraps ready."

She muttered something in Chinese, put on her fur, and ran out of the room, closely followed by Fritz.

Craig's cell phone rang and he went to a corner to answer it. Kris immediately ran up to me. "I'm sorry, Stephen. I didn't want Craig to think you were influencing my decision, so I kept you out of the loop."

"Don't worry," I lied. "I was so happy to see you two getting along, I didn't care that I didn't quite know what was going on." I pulled him closer and whispered, "Did you do it just to save my ass?"

He hugged me. "Child, that was just a fringe benefit. Your two-timing boyfriend is a fierce dancer and I was des-pe-rate."

I was giddy. "I can't believe you talked him into it!"

"It *did* take a lot of convincing on my part. He didn't want to give up the 'great chance' he had to star in the show." Kris rolled his eyes—both ways. "But he also said he always had a secret desire to choreograph."

Secret was right. He never mentioned it to me. "Why didn't he ever try to pursue it?"

Kris explained. "Look, he has no concept of singing, so he has no way of knowing that he *sucks* . . ."

I shushed him. "Keep your voice down!" Thank goodness Craig was still on his cell. Wait a minute, I thought. With whom? Jeffrey! What nerve! *We* should be sharing this moment together.

I relaxed and thought, forget it. Let Jeffrey have his bone. Soon Craig and I will be working together every day. Oops, Kris was still talking.

Kris continued, ". . . thinks he's a great singer. However, he really knows dance, so he's super aware that there are certain things he can't do as a choreographer yet, and that intimidated him."

I focused back on the conversation. "It totally makes sense. Craig's been good at everything he's tried right away."

"Save the sex details for later . . ." I looked around the room and thankfully no one heard Kris's big mouth. He blithely kept talking. "I told him he's got to take a chance and be willing to make mistakes. He said Gail had recently told him the same thing."

Again with the Gail! *I'd* been saying that to him forever. Well, maybe not forever, and maybe not actually saying it, but I was *thinking* it. I bought him a watercolor set for Valentine's Day because he's always wanted to paint, but he refuses to open it up because he's afraid he might suck. I've been meaning to tell him that, of course, he might suck *at first* but he would progress. People can get better at things. I just haven't said it because I've learned he doesn't take well to advice. E.g., the last time I suggested he might want to think twice about getting a tattoo that said "Brit and K-Fed 4ever" he kept canceling dates ("I have a sinus infection." Please! That was my excuse in seventh grade before every gym class) until I relented. Now, I keep my mouth shut and hope he figures things out. Apparently, though, his precious Gail is getting through to him. Yes, I'm happy he's progressing, but I'm PO'd he's listening to anyone but me!

Craig was now standing next to us with a wall-to-wall grin. "Did Kris tell you that he thinks I have *a lot* of potential?"

Kris patted him on the back and looked at me. "All he needs is experience and he could be our next Michael Bennett!"

Craig frantically shook his head "no." I was glad to finally see some modesty from him. "I think I'd be more like Jerome Robbins. Michael was limited."

Oy.

I pulled Craig into a corner, looked him in the eyes, and put my arms on his shoulders. "You know, I had nothing to do with this."

He nodded.

"I mean"—I pretended to keep looking in his eyes when actually I was now blurring my vision—"I thought you had a *great* shot at the lead."

He looked concerned. "Really? Do you think I should come to the callback tomorrow just to see what happens?"

Why do I always have to push it?

Kris was eavesdropping and intervened. He rushed over. "Craig, I need you. And if this show goes on national tour you could be in charge of setting the company. That would look great for your resumé and bring in *a lot* of bucks." He reconsidered. "Well, Geisenshlaag-style bucks."

Craig wasn't convinced. "But the lead role would pay a lot of money, too."

"Craig," Kris looked serious. "I've learned this the hard way from my own struggle to be a performer. You'll have a much longer career as a choreographer than as an actor."

"Even an actor who sings as well as I do?" He asked.

What a setup!

Kris launched into one of his stories from the trenches. "OK, look at Scott Wise."

Craig stared blankly. He lived in such a little world (i.e., his own), he'd never heard of him. "He's a dancer," I said. "A kind of famous Broadway dancer."

Kris nodded. "Stephen is right, but he's more than that. He won a Best Featured Actor Tony award for playing Riff and other roles in *Jerome Robbins' Broadway*."

Craig perked up. "So you're saying I could win a Tony?" Craig's innocence made him always bring everything back to himself.

Kris was thrown off track. "Well, maybe . . . but do you know what Scott's next job was after his Tony win?"

Craig and I both shook our heads.

Kris sadly smiled. "A Ninja Turtle at a Teenage Mutant Ninja Turtle-themed birthday party."

Craig was confused. "Was that on Broadway?"

He was obviously not getting the point.

Kris adopted his speaking-to-a-ten-year-old voice. "No, Craig, it wasn't. It was in Westchester at a wealthy couples' house for their son's eleventh birthday. Scott told me it paid $100 an hour and it was an hour long." Ouch! $100 for a Tony winner. Well . . . maybe he got a tip. $110?

Kris tried to make his point as clear as possible. "He had a Tony and he was still pounding the pavement." Craig finally got it and looked panicked. Kris continued. "As an actor you're at the mercy of a lot of elements. But once you make it to Broadway on the artistic staff, you'll always get work."

Even though he was exaggerating on both ends, he was essentially right. There were a lot of sucky directors and choreographers who worked all the time even though they weren't that good. They got hired again and again just because they were in "The Broadway Show Club." Once you've got a Broadway show on your resumé, whether it's a hit or not, you're set. On the flip side, there were a lot of actors who do a great Broadway show and are then unemployed for a long time. Of course, Scott Wise went on to do a ton of Broadway shows after his low-point Ninja-Turtle debacle, but hopefully Craig didn't know that.

Craig smiled broadly/looked gorgeous. "Kris, you've convinced me." They shook hands. "It's a good career move, and financially, it just makes sense," he added. We all smiled and Craig gave me a hug. He whispered in my ear, "And I'm gonna need money if you and I are going to buy an apartment together one day."

Huh? He never mentioned that before. I went into a slight trance. I wanted to be overjoyed, but after the events of the day, I felt vaguely numb. I hugged him back and said I had to go to the bathroom but instead snuck out and jumped on the bus. This whole audition period has had too many ups and downs, and I need to go home and take a bath. *Working Mother* recommends it!

Eighteen

his is it—final callback day. Mason called me at 9:00.
"Are you up yet? It's Mason . . . pick up."

I had actually gone to the gym early so I was up,
but I was taking a post-step-class shower. I heard his voice on my
machine, ran out of the shower with Finesse conditioner not yet
rinsed out (leave it in a full two minutes!), and, of course, picked
it up right when he hung up.

I rinsed my hair out, toweled off, applied my Banana Republic moisturizing body lotion liberally (smells fantastico!), and
called back Mason.

Jason answered.

I considered hanging up because I didn't feel like dealing
with the Mrs., but I realized my caller ID would be displayed because I hadn't disabled it.

I was flustered. "Hello Jason . . . uh, I think Mason just called
me." Why did I say I think? I knew he just called me. I guess I was
trying to be polite—but why does politeness equal unsureness?

"Hey, Stephen. You guys have sure been talking a lot lately."
He lowered his voice to a growl. "I'm beginning to think you're
becoming an item!"

I let out a manic laugh at such a high pitch level that it set off my fax machine.

"Hold on!" I was yelling as I ran across the room to my three-in-one printer/fax/scanner. By the time I turned it off and got back to the phone, Mason was on.

"Stephen, just ignore Jason. That's always his big joke. He thinks I'm having a secret affair with everyone."

"Don't worry." I tried to diffuse the awkwardness I was feeling. "My friend Jackson is always accusing me of having secret affairs."

Not exactly. He's always *asking* me about my *actual* secret affair. I guess there's a little difference.

"Oh yeah, that's what I was calling about." Mason said.

Fuck! He knows about me and Craig! He hates me because I've ruined his best friend's relationship!

He sounded tentative. "I know we're seeing Jackson for the role of Sonny today, but do you think he'd be an understudy?

"Of course!" I was so relieved I wasn't being outed that I responded without thinking. Upon reflection, I don't know if Jackson would leave a long-running show just to understudy in another show that may not run. But I didn't say anything because Mason immediately started talking about the Geisenshlaags.

"Look, no matter what, Stephen, let's make a vow that we're not going to cast any of the cheesy TV stars they might recommend at the last minute."

"Don't worry about me giving in—*Grease* was the first Broadway show I played for!"

The mid-90s revival of *Grease* had a parade of TV stars coming through it every few months. Mackenzie Phillips, Micky Dolenz, Sally Struthers, Linda Blair, ad infinitum. Even though a lot of them were extremely talented, the musical took on a freak-show element. Every night was like an episode of VH1's *Where Are They Now?*

"Also," he added, "I've been asking around. Anike is still certifiably koo-koo. Let's just go with Juli James unless she's awful today."

I've always been obsessed with the missing "e" at the end of her name. Maybe she left it where Monikah got her annoying "k." Oh yeah, for you non-theatre people, Juli is a sassy redhead who's been the queen of understudying (three Broadway shows, three leading ladies she understudied), and this would be her first big lead on Broadway.

Sometimes, it's not good to do more than one understudy job because people (i.e., casting directors, producers, and directors) start thinking that's all you can do. They assume you're just not good enough for the lead. Obviously, that's not always true. Sutton Foster was cast as the understudy in *Thoroughly Modern Millie* while it was out of town. The scoop is that during the last few days of rehearsals Sutton was asked to go on for the title role in order to give the girl who was playing it a little rest. Sutton played Millie in the "tech" rehearsals (where they set all the technical cues) and had a ball—she got to feel like she was the star of a brand new show! Suddenly, for reasons only the director knows, on the day of the first preview, as she was mentally preparing herself to get back to the chorus, she got a call asking her to take over the role! She did the part out of town, took it to Broadway, and then won the Tony Award for Best Actress! So obviously, being an understudy doesn't mean being untalented. The time was right for Juli's big break and we could give it to her!

"Juli it is," I said. "We're going to have too much to worry about without constantly policing Psycho McBoobs."

He laughed.

"Hey," I suddenly remembered, "what's going on with your apartment?"

He suddenly sounded uncomfortable. "Oh, right. It all worked out." He got more awkward. "We found a place . . ." He paused. It seemed like it was extremely hard for him to form the words. " . . . in New Jersey."

Holy sh*t! I had to say something. I don't know why, but I'd been really anxious for the last day or so every time I thought about Mason being taken advantage of by his landlady/price gouger.

"Listen, Mason. Why don't you first ask your landlady to not raise your rent the full $800 before you actually go ahead with moving." I knew he'd protest, so I kept talking. "It's called *negotiating*. I'm sure she didn't expect you to just accept the full rent raise."

"Stephen, she's gonna be pissed off at me if I say something and I don't want to deal with that." So what? What's wrong with having someone be pissed off at you? Especially if you're right! Especially *especially* if it prevents a move to Jersey!

He sounded frazzled. "I gotta go. Jason needs the phone. I'll see you at 10:00."

A click and then silence. Hmm . . . that was annoying.

Oh, no. I've been writing this while eating breakfast (Zabar's coffee, whole wheat toast with soy ham and melted soy cheese. It sounds vile, but it's delish!), and now these pages have two coffee stains on them. I'll write during a break.

FIRST BREAK

I tried to speak to Mason again but we've been auditioning all morning and he immediately ran to his cell phone as soon as the break began.

Callbacks are going well. Each role has two people up for it and once we've chosen between them we're going to have them come back this afternoon and show them to the Geisenshlaags. If they approve, the offers should go out tonight! It's very exciting.

Mason just came over to me to thank me. Apparently, talking to me this morning reminded him that he hadn't yet told his landlady that he was moving out at the end of his lease. When he first got the rent increase letter, he hadn't responded—he just started looking for a new place. This morning he finally called her to say that they weren't going to renew because he was moving to Jersey, she panicked and said she'd only raise his rent $200. Of course he accepted. He was jumping around the room saying he couldn't thank me enough, which was idiotic, because actually my advice was to ask his landlady not to raise his rent $800, which he did not do. He simply called her and she offered the lower rent increase, but I was feeling so great being thanked by him that I didn't offer my clarification. He gave me a hug. A sort of long hug which wigged me out a little because now that Craig was the assistant he was sitting right across the room. I disengaged myself and Mason immediately said he wanted to take me out to dinner to celebrate.

"And no talking about the show!" he added.

I assumed it was going to be one of those "bring along the boyfriend" routines that Jackson always pulls, so I asked what time Jason got off work, mentally deciding I would demur on the night in question by claiming I had forgotten a training appointment at my gym that I couldn't get out of.

"Why does it matter when Jason gets off work? I'm a free agent."

"Well, I assumed he'd be coming . . ." I trailed off.

He shook his head and smiled. "Are you crazy? We just live together—we're not attached at the hip." He stepped a little closer. "I'd rather spend time alone with you."

Was that a come-on? It felt like one, but how could it be? There was nothing overtly sexual in what he was saying . . . maybe I was projecting à la what Monikah's always accusing me of. Projecting what, though? I'm not interested in Mason, so I can't be projecting that. Maybe I'm projecting my life experience. I just assume anyone with a boyfriend is interested in me because Craig is.

The thought of dinner was appealing. I definitely have been enjoying our little lunches out, discussing auditions, etc. I thought it would be nice to hang out with him without Kris's nonstop, "Child . . . I have a sto-ry!"

I finally answered. "Sure!"

"How about next Friday?" he quickly asked.

I brightened up. "Perfect timing. Casting will be over and we can just relax."

"Eight o'clock. Hudson Corner Café." He held out his hand.

I shook it. "I'll be there!" He walked away and I started whistling (!). I immediately walked into Craig.

He pointed to my puckered lips. "You seem happy." Uh-oh. Did he think I was just asked out on a date? He smiled bashfully. "I'm glad that my being an assistant has cheered you up so much."

Phew! His bringing everything back to himself paid off. I scurried off because I wanted to write all this down while it was fresh. I'm sitting in the Equity lounge now, writing furiously. Uh-oh . . . I see dead people . . . aka Staci looking for me because the break is over. Write later!

1:30 P.M.

We've got our cast! I knew Vince was going to get the lead as soon as he came in from non-Equity land. Three weeks later, I was proven right. Ha ha, Staci! Juli gave a *great* audition, so we don't have to use crazy-ass Anike.

As for Jackson, Mason decided (and I agreed) that he's not exactly right for either of the leads. He's not quite goofy enough looking for the comic lead (Sonny) and, in terms of playing the leading man, he doesn't give off the maturity/been-through-the-mill-ness that Vince does. The good news is that Mason loves his acting/voice and, even though Jackson isn't perfect for either role, Mason thinks he'd be a great standby for Vince. Being a standby is not the same thing as understudying. When you understudy, you perform a certain part every night in the show and understudy a bigger one. (In *Wicked*, the woman who sings, "No one cries 'They won't return'" in the song "No One Mourns the Wicked" is the Elphaba understudy.) When you stand by, the only thing you do is go on for the part or parts you stand by for. You don't even have to be at the theatre during the show! Many standbys are just required to have a beeper and be near the theatre. Janine LaManna stood by for Chita Rivera in the National Tour of *Kiss of the Spider Woman*. On opening night, in the middle of Act One, Chita hurt herself so they beeped Janine, who was hanging out in her hotel room wearing sweatpants sans makeup. She called the stage manager who told her that they were stopping the show till she got there. Janine rushed into a cab, told the driver to step on it, and started getting ready in the backseat. The cab driver asked if it was an emergency and she screamed, "YES! It's an emergency!" Janine told me once that she's sure that the cabbie didn't know what to make of a crazed woman in his backseat screaming "It's an emergency!" while curling her eyelashes and liberally applying foundation.

I really hoped Jackson would accept standby because we'd finally be working on the same show!

Sonny is gonna be played by Jesse Fitstone. He was definitely the best guy for the role (5'7", 170 lbs., round face, BIG smile), but I've noticed he's also one of those people who insults you under the guise of a friendly conversation.

When he came to the callback, he told me how he was telling some friends last night how excited he was about the project.

"I mean, I *really feel* excited." Yeah? Why the emphasizing?

"Maybe I'm crazy," he ran his fingers through his (lack of) hair, "but I'm not one of those actors who refuse to work with a director just because he has no experience." He shook his finger at Mason. "You just might be chock full of great ideas!"

"Thanks . . ." Mason said complimented/miffed. "I hope I am."

"You know what," Jesse shrugged, "so what if you're not? The sun'll keep rising!" Was that sun comment supposed to make Mason feel better? "Hey, Mason, even if you're not talented, plants will still be able to photosynthesize." I guess that's good to know . . .

"And you!" Jesse pointed to me. "I've always wanted to work with you ever since you played piano bar."

"Wow!" I was flattered. Maybe he's not so bad. "You remember!" I said, coyly.

"Who can forget? You still have that piano bar style when you play!" He mimed playing an exuberant piano. "Who cares if it's appropriate or not, I love it!"

Rehearsals should be "fun."

The good part: the show is cast and this part is over.

1:45

Apparently it's *not* over. I'll tell you later

3:30

OK . . . The Geisenshlaags arrived and we showed them who we wanted for our leads. Each one sang a song from the show that they had learned, and then they all read a scene together. Of course, they were brilliant. We still hadn't actually told them that they had the roles, but I'm sure they knew that since there was only one person for each part, they were cast and this was just a formality. The relaxed attitude from Mason, Kris, and me buoyed them with confidence, and there was electricity in the room when they read the scene.

Mason got up and shook each of their hands. "You guys are terrific and you'll be hearing from us *very* soon!"

They walked out and Mason turned to face us, smiling triumphantly. Bettina turned to Staci and said, "When do the meetings start?"

"Um . . . in around ten minutes."

Mason was confused. "What meetings?" he asked as he walked back to the table. "We're meeting with the design staff?"

"Jason." Bettina turned toward "Jason." "I told you we needed some star talent. I have two big stars coming here for a meeting."

"Staci, why didn't you tell me?" Mason looked really annoyed.

"Um, I just set them up during the break." Staci was looking down at her olive-colored blouse. When I was in elementary school, we called that color "vomitocious."

I could tell Mason was seething. Staci was blatantly lying! Obviously, she knew that Mason would be annoyed that sitcom stars were coming in, so she lied by omission. On the other hand, I guess it is possible that over a ten-minute break she contacted two television stars and set them up with auditions. Just like it's possible to break the time/space continuum. Suddenly, Calum the monitor was at the door. "Shall I send in Mr. Cortale?"

My heart was palpitating. There's only one Mr. Cortale I know of! I was about to see Miguel Cortale in the flesh! The taut, muscular, hairy-in-the-right-places flesh! I was obsessed with *Viva Italy!* Surely you remember that "hilarious" show where two guys from Italy come to stay with their relatives in Cleveland. I watched that show for the reason everyone else did: Miguel was CUTE and his temp job on the show as a diving instructor provided me comfort on many lonely evenings. After seeing him on a talk show, I finally realized that the reason he pretty much kept repeating his signature line (Mamma Mia Pizza!) was because he couldn't really be understood very well on any other lines. His accent was thicker than his biceps. Apparently, he was plucked from medical school in Palermo and "learned" English on the set. I was devastated when the show was cancelled a few years back and I guess Miguel was, too, because, even though he claimed he'd use his newfound job freedom to make movies, he's been having major trouble getting a break because of his accento.

He strolled in and was really friendly, but I could tell Mason was in shock. Vince was perfect for the role, but the Geisenshlaags *were* the producers. That's just the hierarchy of a show. If Mason and the Geisenshlaags disagreed on anything, the Geisenshlaags got the final say. All Mason could do was quit.

Miguel gave his music to Marzullo (a fellow Italian, but from Connecticut) and launched into his song.

After around two minutes I realized he was singing in English. All I heard were vowels and rolled R's. He had a nice voice, but the character of Vince is from California! His big songs are "California Dreamin'" and "I Wish They All Could Be California Girls." We couldn't rewrite the whole script and make his big song "Arrivaderci, Roma!" Besides, even if we did, who would understand him? Except for the title, that song is in English. Miguel would need a total accent overhaul and the show opens in three months! Mason was speechless after the song, so I asked Miguel if he wanted to read the scene. He nodded yes (with an accent, somehow) and Staci told him she had the new version.

Mason looked at Staci because there *was* no new version. The script hadn't changed in months. Staci opened her folder and slipped out a sheet of paper. I was curious/annoyed. Did Staci think she could rewrite the script? I knew Mason wouldn't do anything to find out what was going on, so I grabbed the paper and saw that it was covered with typewritten words from some other language. Was it Pig Latin?

Iht's bihn groo-vee bee-ing thah ohn-lee ghi sah-rown-dihd bi ah buhnch uhf chihcks

I suddenly realized it was Vince's big scene with the words spelled phonetically!

She snatched it out of my hands, glared at me, and sauntered over to Miguel with her customary "there's a cute guy in the room" sashay. Her hips bumped side to side with a rocking most closely matched by the boat in *The Perfect Storm*. Miguel was gracious but obviously taken aback by her walk. "Your heeps? Re-plach-ment?"

Thankfully, his accent made Staci think he was flirting back instead of asking whether she had hip replacement surgery. She giggled, checked her nonexistent bun of hair, and murmured, "Let's get to the scene."

It was a tour de force. If "tour" means *big, fat,* and "de force" means *fucking nightmare.* He read the scene with her, and for every hollow-voiced line reading of hers there was an unintelligible one from him. Back and forth it went with slight variety. Blandness, then gibberish, then deadness, then crazy accentness. Even though it was written phonetically, each syllable was filtered through a sieve of wide Italian vowels and weird Italian versions of English consonants.

Bettina smiled through the whole thing. Fritz, being from Europe himself, beamed with pride. Mason was just the shade of white I want for my living room that I can't seem to find at Janovic Plaza.

Finally we knew it was over. Not because we heard the last line we were used to, but because there was suddenly silence. Bettina said to Mason, "So, do you need to see anything else? I'm sure Miguel is a busy man."

Mason regained control of himself and allowed some blood to flow to his face. "No, thank you very much. And thank you for coming in. Thanks!" Three thank-you's in a row. Kiss of death.

As soon as he opened the door and exited, I spied the next person coming in and my mouth fell to the floor. It was *Mariah.* Still missing a last name, although newly married. She was as beautiful in real life as on the cover of *Allure.* Lo-o-o-ong blonde hair, the biggest green eyes ever, and one of the few supermodels that's STACKED. I could tell Fritz (the only straight guy in the room) was mentally calculating the cost of divorcing Bettina.

Mason greeted her and introduced us all. She was really pleasant. "You know," she said in her Marilyn Monroe/helium-ingested voice. "My new hubby works on Wall Street, and I'd love to spend some time working in New York instead of shooting at some exotic locale."

"That's great for us!" Mason said, cordially. "So . . ." We both noticed at the same time that she wasn't carrying any music. All she had was one of those pretentious purses that you wear as a backpack.

He continued tentatively, "Would you like to sing something for us?"

She looked a little panicked and immediately glanced at Bettina.

"Sweetie," Bettina said, addressing Mason. "Mariah graciously agreed to *meet* us." She smiled at Mariah. "Of course there'll be no singing." She let loose with one of her parables. "Why ask a falcon to fly when we know it can soar?"

"Oh . . ." Mason seemed tongue-tied. "Do you want to come back another time to sing?"

"Pardon us, Mariah." Bettina flashed her bonded teeth. "He's new to the business." She wrote down "She *will not* audition!"

Mason wrote "Ever???"

Bettina whispered, "She's world famous!" Then in her regular voice, she said, "We so appreciate you coming in today. Do you have any questions for us?"

Mariah thought for a second. "I don't know how rehearsals work. Would I have enough time to practice with the recording?"

What the hell? "What recording, sweetie?" Bettina was her fake, sweet self.

"You know. My singing. I'm nervous that when I sing in the show, I won't know the recording well enough and I'll get off with it."

I didn't know what she was talking about. "I've done a lot of conducting," I said. "If you get off with the orchestra, we can find you."

Now she looked perplexed. "Orchestra? Isn't that prerecorded?"

I forced myself to laugh. "That's a common misconception. The orchestra is live on Broadway."

"Oh." She nodded. "Only the singing is taped."

"No," I said slowly. "It's a *live Broadway show*. The singing is live."

"Wow!" She looked intrigued. "I thought it was like those awards shows where the singer just sings along with a tape they made."

"No."

"This could be exciting. I've never done this sort of thing before."

"You've never sang live?"

"No!" She laughed. "I've never performed. But I've always wanted to."

"Did you do musicals in high school" Mason asked.

"No."

"Have you seen a lot of musicals?" Kris asked hopefully.

"No. Never." She swelled up with pride. "I want the first musical I see to be the one I'm in."

That doesn't even make sense. She's going to be in the audience while she's onstage?

Everyone had reached their breaking point, and thankfully her cell phone rang. She checked the number and said, "I've got to take this!"

"No problem!" Mason said, visibly relieved. "Thanks for coming in! Thank you! Thank you! Thank you!"

She left.

Silence.

Silence.

"Well," Bettina said. "We've got a tough choice."

"Choice?" Kris had *had* it. "What choice? There's no choice." He got up and began pacing. "You want us to choose between a man who can't speak the language *at all* and someone who's never sung . . . excuse me, never *even performed*, yet she expects to be cast in a *lead* role on Broadway without us knowing whether or not she can even be on pitch. Or act! Or speak in a normal voice! These aren't small roles—they're the leads, Bettina! The leads!"

Fritz whispered. Bettina spoke. "If we cast two nobodies, no ticket buyer in his right mind is gonna fork over a fin and a shark tooth!" What? Was that a Chinese expression for money? Was it Old New York? Gangster? Gang*sta*?

Mason was, of course, quietly calm. "How are we going to cast her if she won't audition?"

Fritz kept the whispering flowing. Bettina looked triumphant. "Renée Zellwegger wouldn't audition for the *Chicago* film and she was brilliant. Brilliant."

I was pissed now and started yelling. "But Renée was a working actress! She had a body of work!"

"As opposed to Mariah, who just has a body!" Kris interjected. Good one!

"Listen, everybody!" Bettina pointed to the seat next to her and Kris sat back down. When Bettina directs, you follow. "We're on a limited budget here. We have to weigh who would draw an audience versus who will do it for the salary we're offering. We're *not* going to produce this show without a star as a lead."

"Um . . ." Staci was still alive. Apparently they hadn't discontinued the feeding tube. "There's one star who'd do it for the salary you're offering. And who'd be great."

"Who?" We all asked in unison, as we sealed our fate.

"Um . . . Anike."

We had no choice.

INTERMISSION

Nineteen

SUNDAY . . . JANUARY!

*S*ORRY! I've spent these last few weeks auditioning the ensemble, preparing for rehearsals, and essentially taking a break from my writing. I felt entitled because Monikah was on vacation so I had no one to show it to. Of course, P. S., I was dying to know where she was going. I figured out it's either France or Germany because I saw a Fodor's *Let's Go Europe* sitting next to her chair with a page dog-eared at the end of the first third of the book (i.e., near the letters F or G.) I also considered Finland but who the hell goes there? I couldn't think of any other F or G countries. I began to obsess and try different namedrops during my session to see her facial reaction.

"You know, *Flowerchild* may one day go on tour." I casually started listing countries. "The U.S. . . . South America . . . *Germany*." Nothing.

Then "Mmm . . . I always have *French* toast Xmas morning. Can't wait! *French* toast . . . developed in France."

Staring.

Finally I said weakly, "Do you think Finland's pretty this time of year?"

She put down her pad. "Is this somehow related to your Atkins Diet obsession?"

Silence on my part.

And abrupt subject change.

All right, everybody, UPDATES:

I had the "is it a date" dinner with Mason and it *wasn't* a date, thank goodness, but it was totally fun. He's hilarious *and* laughs at all my jokes/side comments. It's rare to find both qualities in a person. I've noticed that usually people are either a good audience to humor *or* they themselves are a riot. The other option is that they're like Ronald/Staci: neither of the above *and* a downer to boot. Anyway, we had a great time. It's so nice to have a new friend to hang out with who doesn't drag their boyfriend to every get-together (like Jackson).

Let's see, what else. Oh yeah, I spent Xmas with my family. My sister Dianne came in from Michigan. I know I've hardly mentioned her. She's six years older and we only see/speak to each other on the big holidays (Xmas and Passover). Background info on her is she's a lawyer, divorced, and looks like me in drag. My mom has always criticized Dianne for everything. I think she was personally offended that Dianne had no musical talent—my mom saw it as a reflection on herself (I know that's shocking). She kept trying to force Dianne to be an opera singer until her teacher sent a letter to my mom saying that sending Dianne to voice lessons essentially amounted to torture—for Dianne, the teacher, and for various dead composers whose spirits were no doubt being disturbed from eternal slumber.

I've grown to dread our family time together (aka who screams louder), but this visit was different. Dianne didn't have the big "I hate you" fight with my mom that was always their signature. It never failed to happen right when the main course was about to be served so Dianne would always have to sneak down to the kitchen at midnight and eat the cold version of the meal that my mom put in the fridge for her. This year, though, Dianne seemed much more "in one ear and out the other" towards my mother.

"Dianne, dear," my mother said, carrying the turkey. "I don't know why you're wearing that." She put the turkey down and gestured to Dianne's '50s vintage dress. (P. S. I thought it was cool.) "I'm sure that's considered fashionable in Michigan, but in New York," she look Dianne up and down, "it's tragicomic." She then clarified that bizarre adjective: "Funny for us to look at, but *so* sad for you."

Then she finished with her old chestnut, "I'm only trying to help you, dear."

I braced myself for the hostile-retort-leading-to-the-storming-away-from-the-table-finale, but instead of "You always criticize me, you witch! Etc." Dianne looked at her frock and said, "I don't know, I like it . . ." She then rubbed her hands together. "Mmm, let me at the turkey." Dianne started carving the turkey as my mother stood slack-jawed.

My mom tried a different tack. "You know, the dark meat *is* more fattening," she said, deciding to be more direct. "Maybe"— she patted her own slim hips—"you should avoid it."

I winced, waiting for the inevitable, "Don't tell me what to do! I'm a grown woman!" Instead Dianne turned to me and said, "Hey! Congrats on your new Broadway show, Stephen!"

What the hell was going on? The dinner conversation then turned to stories about the audition process for my show, Dianne's big legal win over an evil corporate giant, and my mom's confusing/no-actual-ending story about getting the wrong dressing room while on tour. ("I couldn't find my lashes any-where! *A-ny-where!*")

I queried Dianne in her old room after dinner. "Dianne," I said, fingering the worn poster of Leif Garret from *Dynamite* magazine hanging on her wall. "You seem . . . different."

"Oh, don't beat around the bush." She laughed. She was al-ready in bed, reading *Starring Sally J. Friedman as Herself* (we al-ways reread books from our childhood when sleeping over at my mom's. I was halfway through *Bridge to Terabithia* and looking forward to my expected crying jag at the end). "You mean, why aren't I eating cold stuffing right now."

I nodded vigorously. "Yeah—what gives? Are you medicated? 'Cause if that's what Prozac does, split it with me!" I sat down on her bed.

"No, no Prozac." She put down her book. "It was Dr. Phil."

"Oh no!" I said, annoyed. "Even his moniker gives me a headache. Either I call you your first name, or 'Doctor' plus your last name. You can't have it both ways."

"I agree, but what can you do?" I guess she didn't feel like making fun of him for a half hour, which is what I was about to launch into.

"Anyway," she continued, "this mother and daughter that fought all the time came on the show. It totally gave me the willies because it was so Mom and me."

"What did Dr. Phil say? Some down-home expression about a possum and some okra?" That show makes me crazy. I cannot identify with his verbiage. I didn't grow up on a f*cking plantation!

I started pontificating. "It's 50% annoying accent and 50% namedropping of southern animals/food/locales. The problem is I don't know what three-quarters of the things he mentions are, so all I take away from that show is that I hate the South."

"I hear ya." She wasn't going to let me go into one of my rants. Rats!

"The point is," she said, "even though every other word was 'y'all'"—I nodded in triumph—"for some reason the show helped me to accept that Mom . . ." She faded out for a minute. ". . . Mom is never going to be the mother I want her to be."

I wanted to immediately say, "That's not true! There's always hope!" I contained myself. I slowly said, "Why would you think that?"

"Well," she perked up, "I tried it as an experiment. I thought to myself, 'What if Mom is this way forever?' You know, unsupportive and bitchy."

Two accurate adjectives.

"And I found that it took a lot less energy to accept *that* than it's taken trying to change her for the last twenty years."

She looked happy. But I felt sad. I also didn't understand. "You don't love her anymore?"

She smiled. "Actually, quite the opposite. Now I love *her*. *Not* whom I want her to be."

Huh?

That sounded phenomenally depressing to me. How can you be happy knowing your mother is always going to criticize you?

For some reason, though, it made Dianne much more fun to have around the house. There was no big Mom/her showdown, and she only called me MF twice (My childhood nickname. No, not motherfucker—"Mom's Favorite"). I even invited her to my opening night, and she's gonna come!

What else? Oh yeah, all that subbing paid off Xmas present-wise. I showed up at Craig's apartment when Jeffrey was away and whisked him into a waiting rental car. While blasting all of *The Mystery of Edwin Drood* CD (Betty Buckley sounds AMAZ-ING!), I drove him (with Heather panting out the window) to a cabin I rented in the Poconos. It had a fireplace *and* a hot tub and was totally relaxing. I spent the whole time reading Bette Davis's autobiography *This 'N That*. Her denial is delicious. She talks about how she's had ten different cooks in the last two months and how they all had one thing in common: "*They can't cook!*" She then said that one snuck out of her house in the middle of the night.

So, Bette, ten professional cooks "couldn't cook"? You don't think that maybe *you're* the missing link in why they didn't work out? It didn't cross your mind that perhaps sneaking out of the house was maybe the only way to avoid your crazy-ass wrath?

Anyway, Craig skied up a storm while I stayed in the cabin. I'm always too nervous about breaking some part of my body. Whenever people ski, they seem to fall on their ass and break their coccyx. I'm too embarrassed to even say the word. See chapter 1, section: pronunciation of pianist.

The whole time was so romantic. Broken only by Jeffrey

calling him on his cell phone and me having to be quiet because Craig was supposedly on a yoga retreat.

I thought I totally outdid myself present-wise, but then I felt bad getting him such an elaborate gift because all he got me was a book of affirmations. He said Gail thinks daily affirmations help you achieve what you may think is unachievable. I wished I'd achieved a nice gift certificate to Banana Republic from him. Well, today is the first day of rehearsal. Will the vocal arrangements I wrote sound like they do in my head? How will the cast and passive-aggressive Jesse get along? Will the Geisenshlaags show up and try to make changes all the time? Will Craig and I get to make out when no one is looking? And how soon before Anike acts like a f*cking lunatic? I guess I'll find out soon!

ACT
TWO

Twenty

*T*his morning, right when I got out of the 59th Street station, I saw Jackson hugging Ronald goodbye. I, of course, hid behind a newspaper kiosk and emerged when the coast was clear. I immediately started doing the choreography from the opening number of *A Chorus Line* until Jackson noticed me. This is what we always do when one of us sees the other one first. It was only embarrassing once when I was deep into the dance, giving it my all, and finally realized that the reason Jackson wasn't joining in was because "Jackson" was actually a construction worker who had the same faded Levis jacket as the real Jackson. Needless to say, my legs stopped dancing and started running.

As soon as we saw each other this morning we grabbed hands and started skipping in a circle singing "We're doing a Broadway sho-ow! We're doing a Broadway sho-ow!" It's something we'd been dreaming about since summer stock and now it was happening!

We hoofed it over to City Center on 56th Street where rehearsals are, and there was a big table set up with food (a first rehearsal day tradition on Broadway) and it was a good spread! The Geisenshlaags sprung for H & H bagels, (the best!) and all kinds of fattening cream cheeses. Every time I looked at Mason or Kris I could tell they were thinking what I was thinking: *When will Anike arrive?* Or more specifically: *Will Anike arrive?*

As I was standing eating my second sesame bagel, Jesse, coffee in hand, walked over and greeted me with a big pat on the back and a passive-aggressive start to my New Year. "Hey, you look great!" he said, looking me up and down. "A little extra holiday weight agrees with you!"

Thank you? Fuck you? I can never tell with him.

I didn't want to risk another "supportive' comment so I waved to a phantom someone on my far left, feigning I needed to talk to whoever they were, and made a quick getaway. Unfortunately the only person to my far left was Staci. I was forced to have a conversation with her.

I tried to get it over as quickly as possible. "Hi, Staci. How was your Christmas?" I asked, with no conviction.

"Um . . . pretty bad. I had to break up with my boyfriend."

She had a BOYFRIEND? Maybe that's where the expression "lifeless in bed" comes from.

"Oh, that's too bad," I said, trying to hide my shock over her once couplehood.

"He cheated on me," she bluntly said.

Ooh. I suddenly felt a pang of something. Was it guilt? I guess it could have been even though what I'm doing with Craig is not technically cheating. I mean, *he's* cheating on Jeffrey, but I don't have a boyfriend to cheat on. So the only cheating being done is by Craig.

Right?

"Well," I offered, "was it a just a one night drunken slip? I think we've all had those." I added a wink.

"Slip?" She put her hands on her hips. She suddenly had energy. "For months. He was cheating on me for months." She suddenly lost all energy as quickly as it had come and began to skulk away.

She was muttering to herself, "I don't understand how someone can do that."

Ask Craig?

All right, yes, I felt guilty. Although I don't know why. I mean, it's not like *I* was the one cheating with Staci's boyfriend. But for all my justified reasoning, I was feeling very other-womanish.

I tried to find Craig for some comforting and saw him holding court with the stage managers. It looked odd to me because he's usually pretty shy with people. Or, as they've called it, stand-off-ish. I then annoyingly remembered that Gail was trying to get him to be more outgoing. Gail this, Gail that. I walked up just as he was saying ". . . all it does is make me hate the South!" They all laughed.

Hey! That's my Dr. Phil line! Did Gail also tell him to plagiarize? Well, at least I knew it got a laugh.

Craig saw me and gave me a big hug from which I disengaged promptly. We wouldn't want Mason getting the wrong idea and telling Jeffrey. Or, actually, getting the right idea and telling Jeffrey.

All eyes turned to the front of the room at the same time.

She arrived.

The clock said 9:58 as the door slowly swung open and she entered talking on her cell phone, head thrown back in laughter. She radiated "star."

And "time bomb."

Let's hope the former has more radiation.

That was our cue and we all suddenly convened at once and sat around a BIG table with requisite bottles of water next to each actor. Going clockwise, we introduced ourselves by first name and said what our job/role was. There were a *lot* of people there. Besides the actors, there was the Geisenshlaags, the set, lighting, and costume designers, the general manager, company manager, press person, orchestrator, and contractor. Oh yeah, here's what I also didn't write about last month. My archrival

Françoise's father was our contractor. I got a call on my cell phone from the Geisenshlaags while I was on vacation.

"Listen, sweetie, do you know Gordon Smith?" She didn't let me answer. "Anyway, he's contracting the orchestra and giving us a huge discount. Huge!"

I smelled trouble.

"Yeah?" I said, with trepidation. The only relief I had was the knowledge that, even if Bettina asked me to use her, Françoise couldn't be my assistant. I knew that her annoying "Harp-see-chord" classes would conflict with our daily rehearsals.

"Well, his daughter Françoise is a wonderful musician." I knew it! Thank G-d her classes would get in the way of where this conversation was heading.

"What would you think—" she proposed "—of her being your assistant?"

I turned on the sweet talk. Might as well not insult the contractor's daughter. "Bettina, I'd love to work with her. *Love to!*" Why not push it a little? "Unfortunately, I don't know if her father said anything, but she's in college right now so it would conflict with our rehearsal schedule." I fake laughed. "I'm sure you wouldn't want to pay someone who couldn't be there every day!" Money is always a way to get your point made the Geisenshlaags.

"Well, actually—" I could tell Bettina was applying lipstick from the diction change. "That wouldn't be an issue because her father said she gets an extended break from school to do a winter project each year."

"Uh . . . when does it begin?"

PLEASE let there be a conflict.

"I've had Tiffany (the blonde former dancer/model she used as an assistant) check the date and it fits right into the window of our rehearsal period." SHIT! "Stephen, I'm glad to hear you'd love to work with her! It makes it much less difficult if I don't have to force you."

click

I can't even blame myself. I know if I argued the Geisensh-laags would have still won. If they were getting a discount from Françoise's father based on this arrangement, they'd sooner fire me than miss lining their pockets with a few extra "fins and shark teeth."

Anyway, after Gordon the contractor introduced himself I had the "pleasure" of hearing:

"I'm Françoise, the assistant music director." She bowed her head. "*Bon matin!*"

I rolled *mes yeux* in Jackson's direction and received a sympathetic look.

Mason stood up. "I want to welcome you all and say I'm incredibly excited about our cast."

Françoise leaned in and whispered, "I know you like to do the vocal arrangements by hand. Whenever you're done, I'll pick them up and transfer them into a computer program."

I whispered back. "*I know*, Françoise. You told me!"

Just then everyone laughed at something Mason said. Ugh! Françoise makes me crazy! She's one of those people who whispers to you so you're forced to answer, and when you do you wind up missing a much more interesting conversation! Damn her!

Everyone then got a script from the stage manager and read through the show. I sat at the piano and played the songs when we got to them. Mason and I sang them because each of the leads had learned only one song for their callback and we didn't want to put them on the spot by making them sing it in front of the whole cast. Craig looked adorable in his chair doing small versions of dance steps he was thinking of. I had a quick fantasy of taking him back to my apartment during lunch for some private rehearsing.

When we got to Act Two and Anike's big song (the Bacharach/David classic "Anyone Who Had a Heart"), she suddenly looked up and said, "Hey, guys! I learned this for the callback."

She put down her script. "Let me give it a shot."

Mason and I looked at each other and shrugged. I started the intro and she launched into it. All I can say is, if Miss Lady performs it like that on opening night, she'd be a Tony award shoo-in! She belted it, acted it, and blew everyone away.

As soon as she let go of the last note, the whole cast burst into spontaneous applause. I was at the piano and scanned the room to see if anyone was being bitchy and not applauding. Everyone was beaming, including Anike. I relaxed a little. Maybe we'd really get away problem free with her after all. Just as I finished scanning, I saw a subtle wink and clandestine kissing motion come her way. The sort of thing I'd do to Craig when I'd think no one else was looking. Anike saw it, too, and blushed.

I don't think anyone else noticed. Including the winker's wife . . . *Bettina!!!*

MONDAY NIGHT

Phew! I'm home.

I'm lying on my new "Laytner's Linens" quilt (got a whole new bed set . . . after-holiday sale, 40% off!), and Heather is noisily eating her IAMS. It's the end of my first day as a Broadway Music Director.

After the read-through, Craig, two dancers, and I went to lunch. Jackson opted out because he's not a fan of Craig, to the tune of, "You can go to lunch yourself with that two-timing narcissist."

Anyway, we decided to go to the Carnegie Deli. That place is very extreme. Their idea of a sandwich is to take an entire cow and put it between two pieces of bread. I, of course, selected the vegetarian option (grilled cheese).

Craig sat next to me and Jay and Elaine were across the table from us. Both Filipino-American and both *great* singer/dancers. Craig was friends with them because they all did *Movin' Out* together and I knew them from when I used to play ballet classes. Jaylaine, as everyone calls them (started during the Ben-nifer/Vaughniston/Brangelina/TomKat craze) have been cast in lots of shows together, which is lucky since they've been engaged for ten years. ("We're waiting till we have more money!") Ten years is a long-ass time. They work all the time. How much more money do they need? Everyone thinks it's kooky but nobody says anything (to their faces).

Well, I guess traditions *can* be broken because during lunch Craig suddenly piped up, "You know, you two . . . maybe your avoidance of getting married is not about money, but about *avoiding commitment*." He said the last two words really slowly, for emphasis. Jay stopped removing the bread from the pastrami sandwich he was about to eat (of course, he was a low carber) and looked up quizzically. Elaine was oblivious and said, "We're just waiting till we have a nice-sized nest egg."

Craig shook his head. "I don't think so. My therapist says you should look at the thing you're avoiding and really examine the reasons why you're avoiding it." Jaylaine eyed each other uncomfortably. Craig kept talking. "You may find out you've been lying to yourself." He leaned forward for the final comment. "Or to each other."

He took a long swig of his water with two lemons. "Do you want Gail's number?" he asked breezily.

There is nothing more annoying than someone who has just discovered therapy and won't stop spouting off to people who are fine living in denial.

Craig started writing down Gail's number on a napkin and I looked at Jaylaine's ashen faces and shrugged helplessly.

Craig passed them the napkin, put down a twenty dollar bill, and said, "I'm gonna go for a walk." He took a deep breath. "I've found that meditating while walking really helps center me." Really? He's found this out after three therapy sessions? If his glutes didn't look so amazing while he was walking away, I would have thrown my diet Cel-Ray soda can at him.

I awkwardly changed the subject and we all chatted about

whether or not Anike had a boob job. Jay voted no while Elaine and I were a maybe leaning towards yes. Later, I noticed Jay blowing his nose into Gail's phone number.

Afternoon rehearsal began at three and everyone was on time (including L'Anike). I was in charge because I had two enormous group numbers to teach: the finale of Act One and the "megamix" at the end of Act Two. Megamixes really became popular with *Joseph and the Amazing Technicolor Dreamcoat* in the early '90s. After the bows, the megamix is a five-minute medley of the hit songs of the show. Lots of shows copied that idea including *Mamma Mia!* and *Footloose*. *Saturday Night Fever* used to have what I called the "amnesia megamix." The real show would end and you'd think, "This show sucked!" Then a medley of "Night Fever," "Disco Inferno," and "Stayin' Alive" would happen and the music would take over your body . . . you'd sway, you'd clap, you'd sing along, and you'd leave the theatre thinking that you *loved* the show. The last five minutes of the show would create amnesia about the first two hours.

Back to rehearsal. I divided the cast into sopranos, altos, tenors, and basses (there are ten men and ten women in the ensemble plus the three leads).

Everyone started taking out their recordable MP3 players (though some old-schoolers still used their little tape recorders from yesteryear) so they could record their harmony parts. I plunked out everybody's part on the piano in their respective sections. What I always find annoying is that some Broadway singers read music and some don't. In the opera world, all singers read music—it's part of their training. However, there is no official training for Broadway and some singers never learn. It's one thing if all you ever sing are solos, which are relatively easy to learn (except Sondheim ones), but it's much more necessary if you're in the chorus and singing a crazy harmony line. Wouldn't you rather read a speech and memorize it instead of me reading a speech to you and asking you to memorize it? Once, when I was still at summer stock with Jackson, one of the dancers defended her lack of music reading by defiantly saying that Barbra Streisand never learned to read music. That's true, but Streisand makes up for her lack of music reading with incredibly brilliant musicality and incredibly dumb taste in boyfriends. Well, she doesn't actually "make up" for it with bad taste in boyfriends; I just wanted people to remember when we all had to put up with her dating Jon Peters and Don Johnson.

All right. The first thing I taught was the end of Act One. It was a medley consisting of the song "Windy" (because everyone at the commune might be moving on, like the wind) into "Happy Together" (because they realize they don't want to separate, they'll only be "happy together"). Everyone picked up their parts pretty quickly, and after going through each section of the song over and over again, we got to the amazing moment of putting it all together. I got up and Françoise went to the piano so I could conduct it. I have to say, for all of her harp-seechord training, she was able to funk out on the piano part.

As soon as it began I got chills. It sounded GREAT! In the Yale production, the melody was sung by the guys, like it is on the record, but Mason asked if I could include Anike and some of the women so they could be featured in the finale. I did it by transposing the keys of certain parts of the song, or putting Vince on melody while Anike sang a harmony at the same time. I'd only heard my arrangement in my head, so when I finally heard all the harmony working out just like I wanted, and all the voices sounding so great together, I was so overjoyed I started to get teary eyed.

The cast had so much fun grooving to the '60s beat that they were dancing around their chairs as they sang. We got to the last chord, which was at the top of everybody's range, and I had them hold it forever: *Happy To-ge-the-e-e-e-e-e-e-e-e-r!!!*

As soon as everyone cut off, they started cheering. It's so nice when a cast is excited about what they're singing. Mason ran up to me and gave me a *big* hug.

"It sounds better than it ever did at Yale!" he said, with a huge smile. "I *love* your arrangement!"

I felt so flattered. I had been nervous that by changing the arrangement, I could be ruining something that already worked well. I felt so relieved and happy about him liking it that I lost my head and sort of kissed him.

Well, not sort of, *kind of*.

Actually, more like, *did*.

On the lips.

I snapped out of my reverie and was mortified that my random smooch looked like I was coming on to him, which I wasn't, so I decided to act like that's what I do to everyone when I'm happy. I quickly turned around to hug/kiss the next person and, devastatingly, found myself with my lips firmly planted on the cold, thin lips of Staci.

It was like kissing two strands of spaghetti after they've been in the fridge for a week.

I disengaged and left her staggering to the left of me while I frantically searched for an available mouth. I knew I had to do one more to make it look normal. Thank goodness Craig was standing there next to Kris, the choreographer. I gave Craig a hug and was about to do a quick peck, when he suddenly dipped me and planted a wet one on my kisser.

Everyone laughed and applauded. (I'm sure partly because while being dipped, I made sure to maintain my line yet arch my back . . . I haven't forgotten my dance training. Maybe after this book propels me to fame I can be on "Dancing with the Stars"!) We both took a small bow and I noticed that Mason was not laughing. He was just looking at me. I couldn't tell if he was wondering what was up with me and Craig or what was up with my inappropriate smackeroo with him.

We all took a ten-minute break and Craig and I went over to the coffee area.

"I have some big news for you!" He smiled. "But," he held up his hand to stop me, "I have to clear it."

"With Jeffrey?" I said, while trying not to sneer.

"Of course not!" He laughed. "With Gail." He started pouring milk into his coffee.

OH! I couldn't take it! Gail, Gail, Gail. She was like his Svengali. Maybe *I* want a Svengali! Let's see how Craig likes that one! I told him to hold on a sec and I defiantly dialed Monikah on my cell phone, but found I had nothing to say when her machine came on.

"Hey, Monikah," I muttered. "Uh . . . hope you're having a nice day—"

"Stephen?"

She picked up.

SHE PICKED UP!

The *one time* she picks up while I'm leaving a message is the one time I have no message to leave her!

"Oh, hi!" I tried to sound cheery 'cause I saw Craig was watching me. "I just wanted to *clear with you*"—I glanced over—"the fact that I may see Craig this weekend."

She paused. "Would that conflict with an appointment?"

"Uh . . . no." I started to fade out. "Just wanted to clear it." Softer still. ". . . glad it's OK."

I heard a "What?" coming from my cell phone as I hung up and looked over at Craig.

He pierced me with his eyes. "Are you jealous of Gail, Stephen?"

"No!" His directness flustered me. "She's a girl." I babbled. "I mean, a woman. Not even, she's a doctor." I wasn't making sense. "I mean she's not a guy that's gonna steal you. I can't be jealous." I threw my head back with fake laughter and my gum went down the wrong way.

While Craig was hitting my back he said, "You know, you shouldn't be jealous. She likes you." He walked away after I put the gum into a tissue.

After the break, we reviewed the end of Act One again, (it still sounded fab) and sent everyone home.

Well, as soon as I walked into my apartment, Mason called. I decided to broach the uncomfortable subject right away.

"Sorry I kissed you at rehearsal," I said right after I said hello. "That's just what I do when I'm happy, as I'm sure you saw because I kissed two other people after you." I guess that was spelling it out, but there was a slight chance that he'd missed it.

"Oh don't apologize about the kissing part, I liked it."

That sounded flirty.

"It showed the cast that we got along," he went on. "It's nice to have a unified front."

Oh, *that* kind of liking it. Very director-like of him.

"Of course," he laughed, "now there'll be rumors of us dating."

I laughed.

"Just like there're rumors of you dating Craig," he said.

I stopped laughing.

"That's *crazy!*" I said with enough overacting to land me a starring role in the Yiddish theatre. "I would *never* date anyone I worked with. That's rule number one on Broadway." Actually, tons of people date each other while doing the same show, but I was hoping the fact that Mason's inexperience with actually doing a Broadway show would support my statement. Uh-oh. What about Jay and Elaine?

"I mean," I continued, "Jalaine were engaged before they ever worked on a show together, so they don't count." I had to make sure he'd never suspect me and Craig. "In my opinion, workplace romances are unprofessional *and* evil."

Evil? That seemed sort of crazy and severe, but I couldn't think of another adjective. I hoped that didn't push me into the "methinks the lady doth protest too much" realm.

He laughed. "Calm down. I know you guys aren't dating. I went to school with Craig's boyfriend, remember?"

"Oh right. Good ol' Jeff."

"Jeffrey." He quickly corrected me. "He hates being called Jeff."

"Oops, sorry," I said, quickly. "I wouldn't want to offend an investor."

"Don't worry, I don't know what the big deal is. People call me Mase and I don't have a breakdown."

That got me started on my whole issue about people who refuse to let you call them by a diminutive of their name (see page two) and we somehow segued into talking about politics (he's as left as I am, AND left-handed like me, too!), then a blow-by-blow of today's rehearsal, and by the time we finished, he had forgotten why he had called. I saw on my caller ID that Craig was calling me, but I didn't want to click over in the middle of a conversation (actually: I was right at the climax of telling Mason the Fritz winking at Anike story and I didn't want to ruin my dénouement).

After we hung up, I figured it was too late to call over to Craig and Jeff(rey)'s apartment, so I walked Heather and as soon as she finishes eating, we're both going to bed.

She's winding down the chomping . . . OK, she's doing her final lick of the food bowl. I've got to rest up for the second day of rehearsal, so good night, and Laytner's flannel sheets, here I come!

Twenty-One

*H*i . . . it's the ten-minute break that Equity actors get every hour and a half (or five minutes every hour).

Anyway, this morning Kris started to choreograph the Act One finale I taught yesterday and I started going through the leads' solo songs. We had two studios: the big one that Kris was using and the smaller one down the hall that I was in.

At 9:59, in walked Anike, cell phone to ear, head thrown back in laughter. I looked close and saw she was only wearing a little lip gloss, yet she looked *stunning!* Hair pulled back to show off her fresh Ivory-girl skin, sweat pants that were meant to be casual but accented the phenomenal gams, and a loose T-shirt that implied an impressive set of knockers.

Don't worry, I'm not suddenly straight—I was just appreciating. Like a woman does. I've noticed they're always talking about each other's looks/body parts:

"She has an incredibly lifted butt."

"Those aren't lips, they're pillows! So sexy!"

"Could her stomach be more toned? She's a goddess!"

Yet straight guys are never saying:

"*He is such a stud! Great ass and a* nice *package in the front!*"

If you ask a typical male if another someone is handsome, he'll sputter "*I don't know! He looks like a guy!*" Being asked to describe the looks of another man makes them suddenly become a post-blind Mary Ingalls.

Anyway, I played through her songs and we picked keys. She wanted to do one of them in a really high key which she sounded great in, but I reminded her that just cause she could squeeze it out now, it didn't mean that she could do it, plus all of her other songs, eight times a week.

Suddenly, I got nervous. After all, Anike had very little experience doing *any* show eight times a week. Normally, she'd do a few performances, show up for Act One of the next show, and then take off the rest of the week.

As if she read my mind she said, "I probably shouldn't push myself. This is the first time I'm planning on doing all eight performances."

I wasn't sure what to say. "What do you mean, Anike?"

"Oh please, Stephen, everyone knows. I was notorious for missing Act Two, or not showing up at all.

"Oh . . ." I timidly said, not wanting to embarrass her, "I guess I heard something about that."

"Honey, keep playing piano 'cause your acting sucks."

I turned the shade of an apple.

"Don't worry though," she said. "This time I'm going to be notorious for never letting my understudy go on!"

She looked so fervent that I felt excited for her. "Why the change of heart?"

"Well," she stated, "I'm no longer friends with Johnny and I've accepted that I'm friends with Bill."

What the fuck?

"Johnny who?" I wondered out loud. "Johnny Whitaker who played Tom Sawyer in the '70s?" I assumed she knew a lot of celebs from her time in LA. Though why the first name that came to my mind was an actor who last made a film in 1977 simply proves that first crushes last a lifetime.

"Johnny *Walker*, Pollyanna!" She looked at me like I was a moron. "I was a big, glamorous drunk! And being a friend of Bill W. is AA talk for being in recovery."

So that rehab story was true.

She went on. "Didn't you know I was constantly soused? I figured most people in the business did."

"Well, not for sure. I just thought you were—"

"A bitch." She finished the sentence for me.

I laughed. "Sort of."

"Well, I was. And a drunk." She took a big gulp . . . of water, thankfully. "It's the same old story. My parents were lushes and I've been one ever since I was a teenager. I was always able to get by because of my talent or looks," she flashed her Ford model smile and cupped her boobs, "but I had a bit of a nervous breakdown in L.A after I beat up my husband."

She beat up her mob-related husband? "Wasn't he"—how did they say it—"in 'the family'?" I lowered my voice. "What about Omertà?" I didn't quite know what that meant, but I think it was the title of a Mario Puzo book about honor. "Aren't you worried about being wracked?"

"Hon, you mean 'whacked.' And the answer is no. It would make him less of a man to admit to having his ass kicked by a chick. And by the way," she smiled, "I *literally* kicked his ass." She demonstrated a phenomenally beautiful yet ass-cheek numbing kick in the air. "All those years of ballet and my gym's morning kickboxing class paid off." She did a couple more in succession. "Five of those while wearing pointy-toed Kenneth Cole's taught him that cheating on me has consequences." Again with the cheating! Can't people stay out of my business?!

"Anyway," she sat back down, "even though he deserved it, while he was in the ER, I thought back on the last ten years of my behavior on Broadway and the soap, which all led up to the ass kicking, and I thought, 'Anike, you're fucked up.'"

I made a face to suggest "No, you aren't" while praying my inner feeling of YES, YOU ARE wasn't showing through.

"I drove home, threw out all my hidden bottles of hooch, and checked into Betty Ford that night." She winked. "Using his credit card."

Wow. So she did get it together. I stood and shook her hand. "Congratulations!"

"That was six months ago. Only sober behavior now!" Her cell phone rang.

She checked the number. "Sorry! It's my new guy!" She picked it up and walked away from the piano to talk. There was a lot of giggling and suddenly she ran up to me with her hand muzzling the phone. "Stephen," she whispered, "do you know how to say 'I love you' in German?"

"*Ich liebe dich.*" Anyone who had to fulfill a music degree requirement and spend a semester playing Schubert and Strauss songs for badly dressed voice majors in powder blue eyeliner would know that answer.

I heard her whisper the phrase into the phone, employing a voice usually heard on late-night phone-sex ads, and I suddenly thought of a dreaded equation:

Ich liebe dich
plus *one German old man winking*
plus *an angry wife who is coproducing*
can equal the *sheisse* hitting the fan.

Twenty-Two

*A*fternoon rehearsal doesn't start for ten minutes, so I'm sitting at the piano, writing. Had lunch at a greasy but yummy Middle Eastern place with Kris, Craig, and Mason. Oh, yeah, Karen, our amazing stage manager, came with us. She's done six Broadway shows and is completely no nonsense. Even though she's in her 40s and should have some fashion sense, she literally wears her long (starting to) grey hair in a bun with pencils stuck in. ("I constantly need one!") I've also never seen her in anything but black jeans and a black sweater. Even in the summer. And her wide, round face has never seen a stitch of makeup. ("Only on my wedding day, and it was just lipstick!")

She and her team watch every rehearsal and take notes on all the direction so that when the show is running, they can run the understudy rehearsals and give notes to the leads. During the show, they'll all be backstage wearing headphones connected to all the lighting and sound people. Stand backstage at a show and you'll constantly hear "light cue 311 . . . GO! . . . sound cue 14 . . . GO!" There's a famous story about a certain celeb who was cast as a replacement in *The Will Rogers Follies* even though she had no stage experience. On her debut night, she was nervously waiting backstage before her first entrance. She suddenly heard the stage manager say GO to a light cue, but thought it was referring to *her!* Terrified she was about to miss her cue, she quickly and awkwardly ran out onstage. Unfortunately it was a good ten minutes before she was due and, when she finally realized it, she *slowly* slunk offstage.

That must have been charming for the actors onstage who were trying to do a scene. It's always fun to have a six-foot former model appear for no reason while you're acting and then steal focus as she tiptoes offstage.

I notice that stunt casting seems to happen most in Broadway musicals and not in classy Shakespeare shows.

JULIET: Romeo, Romeo, wherefore art thou Romeo?
ROMEO: I'll answer the question as soon as Iman has finished slinking off stage left . . .

Anyway, Karen was doing the schedule for the rest of the week. We all told her the different things we wanted taught and how long each of them would take to teach and she immediately began to figure out how to juggle the schedule so everyone would be satisfied.

While she was writing, the rest of us started sharing the sampler platter (hummus, pita, tabouli, etc.) and the day's gossip.

"All right, first things first," Kris said, looking us all over with a sly smile. "Any crushes yet?"

"No."

"No."

"No."

Mason, Craig, and I answered in succession. I mean, even if I had a crush, I wouldn't admit it in front of Craig, and I would assume Craig would have the courtesy to not admit it in front of me. I knew Mason was (codependently) in love with Jason so Kris's question was a conversation stopper.

"Well, *I* have a crush!" Or a monologue starter.

He proceeded. "I have had my eye on a certain dancer for some time and I think now he's finally noticing me. You all know I haven't been the settling-down type . . ." Kris has always said career first and boys second. And third, fourth, and fifth. "But," he continued, "I could totally see myself settling down with this guy."

"What's your version of settling down?" I asked. "A third date?"

"People in glass houses . . ." he began, while throwing a subtle glance at Craig.

"All right!" I interrupted. "Go on,"

"He's total *husband material* for me," he said loud enough for the mother at the next table to eye her toddler nervously.

"First of all," he continued, "he's smart as a whip and second of all, a talented motherfucker—"

The nervous eyeing turned into prompt leaving.

"—and most of all, gor-gee-ostic!"

"All right, all right." I couldn't take the lack of a reveal. "Who the hell is it?" There were plenty of gay guys in the ensemble, but I assumed it was probably Clay because I knew he had just broken up with his doctor boyfriend and Kris and Clay hadn't ever slept together. I.e., a conquest is always desirable to a self-proclaimed slut.

Kris moved his seat back so the reveal would be more dramatic. "Are you ready?" he asked us. We waited.

"Well?" he demanded.

"Of course we are!" I spat back. "We thought it was rhetorical!"

He narrowed his eyes. "Jay."

Jay? The only Jay in the chorus was engaged to Elaine. Maybe there was a Jay on the technical crew I didn't know about.

"Jay who?" asked Craig.

"What do you mean Jay who?" Kris was annoyed. "From Jay-laine!"

Mason was shocked. "What are you talking about? Even *I* know they've been engaged for ten years!"

"Exactly!" said Kris. "Why do you think they haven't gotten married?"

"Because he's in love with you?" I asked, sarcastically. Kris was a little bit of ye olde narcissist.

"No, you idiot," he said. "Because he's gay but doesn't know it. I mean he obviously knows something's not right. That's why he's been putting off getting hitched, but he doesn't know he's gay yet."

Craig piped up. "I knew I was on to something at that lunch."

I ignored him. Mason looked concerned. "What are you gonna do about it?"

"I have a plan . . ." Kris said, mysteriously.

"You wouldn't date him during the run of this show, would you?" Mason seemed concerned.

"Hopefully!" Kris shot back, with confidence.

"But you can't . . ." Mason said and then turned towards me, "Right Stephen?"

Why would I care who Kris dates? Maybe Mason was concerned about Elaine being devastated and ruining the morale of the ensemble. I wasn't sure, though, why Mason directed the question to me.

"Uh . . . why can't he, Mason?" I asked.

"Because!" He was exasperated. "What's the number-one rule on Broadway?"

Hmm . . . Always give 100%? Remember no matter how bored you are, there's an audience filled with people who've never seen the show before? Play to the balcony?

I was taking so long thinking, that Mason blurted out, "Never date anyone you're doing a show with!"

I stared.

He waved his hands at me, in exasperation. "You told me that last night!"

Shit! I had forgotten I made up that lie to cover up my smooch with Craig.

"Oh! Of course!" I bad-actingily said. "I got confused when you said 'number-one' rule. That's the *only* rule for me!" I saluted. Who was I saluting?

"It is?" asked Kris.

"It sure is!" I manically replied, "Which reminds me . . ." The subject was changed to prevent further inquiries. "I'm almost positive Anike is getting some bratwurst from Fritz."

"Oh please, child," Kris said, dismissively. "You're always assuming something and then you're always totally wrong."

He had a valid point. But this time I was sure. I told them all the little clues.

"Hmm . . ." Craig mulled. "You could be right. After all, just because an alcoholic is sober from booze doesn't mean that he or she is making other sober decisions."

He put down his Diet Coke and continued his lecture. "Many alcoholics stop drinking, but then their gambling or their spending, or, in this case, romantic addiction gets out of control."

There was silence. And on my part, annoyed silence.

"How do you know so much, Craig?" Mason asked, admiringly.

"Well," Craig was trying not to brag, "I've been in therapy."

FOR A FUCKING MONTH! How dare it be working so well!

"So, everyone," Mason looked at us. "What should we do about it?"

"We can't do anything about it," Kris said while taking the last drop of baba ghanoush I had been eyeing. Bastard! "We just have to make sure Bettina doesn't find out. If the Geisenshlaags split up, it could affect the whole show."

I looked at Kris with disbelief. "Prevent the nosiest wife in the world from finding out her husband is on the prowl? That's like saying we have to make sure Paris Hilton gains weight." My awful joke was met with uncomfortable chewing. "My point is, it's not gonna happen," I explained.

"Well, we can try to keep her in the dark." Craig said. I guess he would know how to do that since Jeffrey is still no wiser about our coupling d'amour.

"Don't worry," said Karen, who was apparently listening the whole time while scheduling. "I'll be in charge of Bettina. I've dealt with her on two different shows."

"And knowing Anike," Mason said, "she'll probably dump Fritz in a week and he and Bettina will continue the relationship that makes Broadway squirm."

We all visibly relaxed.

"Well, gentlemen," said Karen with efficiency. "The schedule is done. We should head back to rehearsal."

We all paid and put on our coats.

"And by the way, Kris." She touched his arm. "Don't cause any disruption in the ensemble."

"Meaning what?" he asked, annoyed.

"Meaning stay the hell away from Jay until this show closes."

She walked out the door and we followed.

I told you she was no-nonsense.

Twenty-Three

irst day off after a long week! I'm at my gym about to get a facial. That's right, I'm a metrosexual. Just replace the word "metro" with "homo."

I love facials. They're relaxing (except for the crazy pore squeezing which feels like someone taking pliers to your T zone) and they make your skin look fantastic (for around three days and then it's back to haggy-ass).

I want to look extra good because I'm meeting Craig tonight for his big announcement. You know, the one he had to clear with Gail first. (Grrrr)

After much mulling, I'm thinking the big news is that he's finally going to invite me to their country house. Jeffrey, the banker boyfriend, has a beautiful manor in Connecticut that's been in his family for years and Craig has always thought it was wrong to bring me up there since, even though they share it, it's really Jeffrey's. I've always tried to convince Craig that it's no big deal, but lately I've been feeling guilty about even dating him and I haven't brought up the manor. I'm hoping Gail has finally convinced him it's no big deal, which would alleviate my guilt, and we can start making plans to go once the show opens and I can take vacation days. Or better yet, on our next day off! We can go up Saturday night, stay Sunday, and drive back early Monday morning. I can just imagine the warm fire at night, Heather running around the estate and chasing squirrels while we eat a delish brunch with country-fresh eggs.

Yay! *I'm in love, I'm in love, I'm in love, I'm in love, I'm in love with a wonderful assistant choreographer!*

The most exciting thing right now is that OUR FULL PAGE AD IS IN *THE NEW YORK TIMES!* I was happy to see that the Geisenshlaags hired a great ad company to do the logo. Most Broadway posters don't just have the show title anymore. It's important to get a logo that the international community can recognize. *Phantom* has the mask, *Cats* has the cat eyes, *Wicked* has the whispering witches etc . . . Ours was a big photo mosaic of *1969*. The individual photos that make it up feature all the key icons and events of the '60s: JFK, Kent State, The Beatles, Barbra Streisand, Fidel Castro, etc., and the 1969 itself has a crack down the middle. Tip o' the hat to *Follies*. The ad was so exciting also because everybody's name is listed. I ran out yesterday morning, bought five copies, and called my mother as soon as I got home.

"It's Stephen. Open up the Arts and Leisure section and go to page four." I knew she got it delivered.

She sounded annoyed. "It'd better not be an article about your father and Mitzi."

Why would there be an article about my father and Mitzi? My mother always thought everyone in the world had on their mind what was on her mind. She was constantly shocked MTV didn't play more opera videos. They don't play *any* opera videos!

I heard pages rustling, then "Oh! Is this your show?"

"Yes!"

"Hmm . . . why isn't your name on the ad?"

"It is! Look near the bottom. It's on the same line as the orchestrator and the contractor."

"Hold on . . . let me get my glasses on." Awkward pause. "Oh, there it is. I can hardly see it." My good mood quickly dissipated. "You know, when I did my last Wagner recital I had full-page ad with my picture in the *Cleveland Plain Dealer*."

She had told me that before. I ignored it and said, "Don't forget about opening night, Mom."

"Don't worry. Nothing's going to stop me from seeing my only son make his debut on Broadway!"

I got excited again.

"Except if this tri-city tour comes through. Then I'd be out of town for the month."

What?

"Ooh, Stephen, it's call waiting, ta ta!"

I wanted to cheer myself up again so I called Mason to see if he saw the ad. He picked up on the first ring.

"Is this my *New York Times* costar?"

I laughed. "I forgot you had caller ID."

"How are you, Mr. Music Director?"

"My mother just made me feel awful about the size font used for my name."

"Excellent!" he exclaimed. "Mine is pissed off I'm not using her maiden name as my middle name!"

Wow! That was even kookier. I felt a little better. I told him about my mom's possible tour and how anxious it made me. The more I talked, the more I sounded like a baby.

"She's *always* going on these tours," I said, with a whine. "I don't know why she can't miss this one. The only reason I'm doing this show is so she'll see me!"

"What?"

I suddenly realized how crazy that sounded. "Oh, you know what I mean. One of the things I was looking forward to is her finally seeing me on Broadway. It's something I've always looked forward to, ever since I was a kid."

"Well," he began, "even if she can't come on the literal opening night, she can still see it another night, right?"

I knew what he was saying was true, but I felt like staying annoyed. Reality wasn't matching up to the fantasy I'd always had in my head and it was a downer.

"By the way, Stephen, I also want to say you're doing a great job." Mason was always so supportive. "The arrangements are totally creative and you work so well with the actors."

I work well with the actors?

He was Mother Teresa. This past week, every time an actor would get a "note" (theatre talk for "correction") from Mason and then not do it, Mason would talk like a calming father to them. *"I'm sorry. Maybe I wasn't clear . . . do you understand the note?"* Or *"Do you not agree? Tell me what you think." Always followed by "How can we make it work? Etc."* I would just make a sassy comment that would make the person laugh/feel busted and usually the note was taken the next time.

"Mason, *you* work great, *I'm* a bee-yatch."

"Yeah, but your bitchiness is so funny, everyone loves it."

"Even so," I said, trying to be complimentary, "maybe I should be a little more like you."

"No! I love you the way you are!"

Love? That word always a wigs me out a little.

I suddenly got nervous that Jason would overhear and think that Mason loved me *that way.*

"Oops, that's my call waiting!" I sounded frantic. "Talk to ya tommorow!"

I can't believe I used the same idiotic expression my mother uses for call waiting. I just got so flustered. The last thing I need is *another* guy thinking I'm cheating with his boyfriend. Not that Jeffrey knows about Craig and me, it's just something I've been much more worried about lately ever since teary-eyed Staci showed me the (white, pasty) face of the cheated-on.

At least the show is going great and I've been in a really good mood for the last few days.

Unfortunately, I've found out that since 50% of my usual conversations are me complaining, I didn't have that much to say at brunch today with Ronald and Jackson. So, devastatingly,

I had to cede the floor to Ronald, who did a twenty-minute monologue about his pride in being a gay Republican.

Even if Mrs. Remick hadn't taught me to hate the party that spawned Nixon, McCarthy, and the overused (yet never actually applied to their policies) expression "kinder, gentler," simply having Ronald as a party member would have made me condemn it.

We were all at Niko's, which is this Greek restaurant on 76th Street whose menu is as long as *Crime and Punishment* in the original Russian and has as many words I don't understand. But the food is delish!

"You should both come to a Log Cabin meeting with me," Ronald said after telling us that people on unemployment simply don't want to work *and* sending back his order for the second time. ("These eggs are still a little runny," he said, while holding a plate of eggs dryer than a Noel Coward one-liner.)

I couldn't take it anymore, so I feigned suddenly remembering my facial was for 1:00 (it was for 4:00), dropped a twenty, and fled. I know Jackson is even more liberal than I am (he voted for Nader). I don't know how he puts up with dating Newt Ging-bitch.

Right after Niko's I decided to kill some time by getting coffee and I ran into non-Equity, but now Equity Vince, who's been doing a great job as our lead.

As soon as I got my cappuccino, I saw him pouring skim milk into his coffee at the fixin's bar. (I know that's what Roy Rogers restaurants used to call their tomato/lettuce etc. bar, but it's what I call any food establishment condiment area.)

"Hey, Vince!" I said as I walked up behind him. "Save me some milk, mofo!" It seemed like he had been pouring it forever.

"Stephen!" He put down his cup and gave me a hug. "I'm sorry." He laughed. "Starbucks coffee is so effing dark I have to make it at least 50% milk in order to drink it."

I concurred, then said, "Speaking of percents, did you sign

with your agent yet?" I hoped something had happened that made him not sign with Ronald.

He nodded. "I'm with Ronald Silverstein at Artistic Associates."
Shit!

He went on. "At first it was weird with him, but, you know, when I told him I was a straight dude, it was fine."
Huh?

"What do you mean weird?"

And what do you mean "dude"? Are you Ashton Kutcher?

He looked reluctant to speak but said, "Well, I don't like to talk shit about people, but . . ." He took a quick sip of his java. "He gave me this address to go to for signing my contract and it turned out"—he lowered his voice—"it was his digs."

I had put seven Sweet 'N Lows in my coffee because I was *freaking out.*

"You mean his apartment?" I slowly clarified.

"Yeah. It's a fancy-ass crib." The MTV lingo was just adding to my head spinning. "I walked in and he had the lights low and candles lit and he said he was wearing a bathrobe 'cause he was about to get in his Jacuzzi."

EYU!

"And," he sipped more of his coffee/milk, "he asked me to join him."

I couldn't believe it! I knew he was sleazy (he was an agent, after all), but he and Jackson supposedly have a committed relationship. Then I thought, how many other struggling actors has Ronald tried that on? And how many more will he?

If I told Jackson the story he would say I'm exaggerating because I've never liked Ronald, and I don't want to put Vince in a phenomenally awkward position by making him repeat it. I told Vince I'd see him at rehearsal and skedaddled. I have to think of a way to out this whole thing to Ronald's boss *and* Jackson! That Motherf*cker's gone too far!

All right, back to *Flowerchild*. All the music is taught and Act

One has been mostly staged. Also, no one seems that scared of Anike anymore. She was such a raging hostile ass during her last shows, most people had learned to stay the hell away from her because you never knew when she'd attack. But things are definitely different now. During a run-through of the opening number, Elaine (one-half of Jaylaine) did a leap at the wrong time and wound up tripping Anike who loudly fell on her ass. Everyone was terrified of what was next, but Anike just got up, walked to her coat, pulled out her cell phone, and started talking to "Guido" in a bad stage whisper.

"Hi, Guido the Gun, it's Anike." It sounded like she was talking to one of her supposed mob connections. We didn't know if she was crazy or putting us on. "I need you to put a hit on Elaine Marcas. She blatantly just made me fall on my butt implant. The one I denied having in *The National Enquirer*."

The cast exhaled as one.

"Yeah," Anike continued, "the left one. The one Blue Cross didn't cover."

Turns out, she has a sense of humor. Everyone laughed and I obsessed over whether or not she really did have an implant and if so, do they cut a hole on the top or bottom of each ass cheek?

Anike hung up with a Bettina flourish, looked at Elaine, and at that moment Françoise leaned in and whispered something to me.

"What?" I asked as I cupped my ear.

Françoise spoke even quieter. "I want to know if it's OK if I'm five minutes late after our *déjeuner* break" (even while whispering she's still an annoying French wench), "because I have to drop my dog at the vet."

"Fine . . ." I said and looked up as everyone laughed uproariously at whatever it was Anike said during the Françoise whisper. *Damn* her and her impeccable timing!

That wasn't the only Anike experience. We had one close call with Bettina almost finding out about her and Fritz.

Me, Mason, Karen, Kris, and Craig ate lunch in on Friday to

talk about some Act Two problems and suddenly the overwhelming scent of Joy and hairspray hit me.

It was Bettina in a white fur coat with a white fur *purse*. "Have any of you fellows" (said while glaring at Karen, whom Bettina told us she thinks is a lesbian because she wears no makeup) seen Fritz?"

We all froze. All of us. Kris with his sassy mouth, Mason with his years of improv training, me with my supposed gift for verbiage, Karen with her "I'll handle Bettina" attitude, the sum of us, were silent.

Bettina ignored us and kept talking. "He was supposed to return some of my Xmas presents to Bloomingdale's and he forgot the *awful* knit sweater my daughter bought me, so I sent Tiffany with it to find him." Her assistant Tiffany was not the brightest, but all Bettina ever wanted in an assistant was beauty to help charm investors now that hers was fading (Tiffany looked like a live Barbie doll) and an ability to put up with nonstop subtle yet debilitating verbal abuse.

She unbuttoned her fur coat to reveal a white fur *vest!* "Tiffany said she's been all over the Bloomie's return area and he's not there *nor* is he answering his cell phone."

The five of us looked at each other. We were all thinking that no doubt he and Anike had rented a hotel room for a quickie during lunch.

Karen finally broke her wall of silence. "Bettina, there's a *big* cell phone reception problem on the East Side today because of sunspots." Hmm . . . I read online that sunspots could affect cell phones this week, but not that it would hit only the Waspy side of Manhattan. It was a good save, though, on Karen's part. It's very easy to confuse an older person by mentioning electronics. It's simply not in their DNA to understand the marvels of the late 20th/early 21st century. My mother stills believes the XXX video she found in 1990 sticking out of my VCR was sent by accident from someone else's VCR.

Karen kept talking with a big understanding smile. "And you can't expect Tiffany to find Fritz in as big a store as Bloomies, can you?"

Bettina sighed. "You're right . . . I'm just on edge because he's been disappearing a lot lately."

All five of us gave each other a veiled, but terrified look.

Bettina slapped her hand on the table. "He needs to be focusing on this show and *not* on drinking with his buddies . . . or whatever he's doing."

Or *whom*ever he's doing.

Karen started ushering Bettina out in case Anike came back with him on her arm.

"Bettina, if we see him, we'll tell him to call you ASAP." She pushed Bettina out the door.

Bettina stuck her head back in. "On the yacht phone!"

Who has ever said *or* heard that expression in their life?

Everyone in the cast soon filed back in after lunch. Anike looked refreshed, but there was no way of knowing if she had had a Fritz blitz. So far, though, crisis diverted.

Oops . . . Magda just beckoned me to the inner sanctum of the spa. I'll write later!

LATER

Craig met me at Village Natural (a health food restaurant in the Village that is still the same way it must have been in the 1970s—wood paneling, alfalfa sprouts, hippie waiters. I love it!).

When I got there, Craig was already seated, drinking some wheat grass juice, which actually tastes *more* disgusting than it sounds. I was very anxious/excited. This whole "big news" thing had been building up all week and I couldn't take it anymore, so I ran to the table, sat down, folded my hands, and said, "Spill it."

"No, no, no," he said, while waving his finger. "You have to order first. I don't want you to be distracted looking for the waiter while I talk to you."

How dare he know me so well! I beckoned our be-bearded waiter over and inwardly marveled over his pleather sandals (with socks). I quickly ordered my soy patty parmigiana and tapped my fingers while Craig decided between his favorite fish entrée, Organic Salmon Teriyaki, or its veggie twin, Organic Soy-mon Teriyaki.

He ordered the real salmon and I leaned forward to catch every upcoming word.

"Stephen, you can lean back. It's only another two inches, you'll still be able to hear me."

I couldn't take it. "Come on! Out with it!"

He smiled. I was immediately transfixed looking between his dimples and his uncapped, yet white as snow, teeth.

"OK. After working all this time with Gail (All this time? Is he living in *A Wrinkle in Time*, where two years his time is equal to one minute ours?), I've been reassessing things . . . and I decided it's time to break up."

Another smile. Not mine.

What the fuck? He's breaking up with me at Village Natural. Did he think there wouldn't be a scene because it's a health food restaurant? I can angrily pull off a tablecloth whether or not it's made of hemp.

Of course, to make things more awkward, the waiter appeared and put down our salads. I stared at their delicious carrot ginger dressing on the side, which I had been looking forward to all day. Why couldn't Craig have waited till after the meal so I could have enjoyed it?

I suddenly felt purposeless. I'd been working so hard on making Craig fall in love with me over the last year, I felt like a big chunk had been taken out of me.

I stared at him. He was silent. "What am I supposed to say?" I asked with no energy.

"How about 'congratulations'?" he asked with no irony.

"You want to be congratulated for breaking up with me?" People had always said he was an asshole, but I had never realized how much.

I started to get up to leave. He could pay for my parmigiana.

"Stephen, you're crazy!" he said as he bolted up and lunged to my side of the table and hugged me. "You idiot!" He held both sides of my head in his hands. "I broke up with Jeffrey!"

I didn't respond. I had to reassess everything I just felt. My head was spinning.

"Where . . ." I couldn't speak. "Where are you gonna live?"

"In Orville's apartment!" Orville and he were both in NYCB and Orville was now in another dance company that was always touring, so he was constantly subletting. "He's going on the road tomorrow and his subletter flaked out on him."

I remembered that Orville lived on Avenue A. Ouch. How was I gonna visit? Going from the Upper West Side to the East Village is like watching *Charles in Charge*: It's only 25 minutes long, but it feels like an eternity. And what about my fantasy of a bed and breakfast? I suddenly got a burst of energy. Why not start living some of the fantasy now?

"Did you give Orville your deposit?" I asked, all businesslike.

"No, when I drop off my stuff tomorrow I'm—"

"Craig." I held both of his hands. "Move in with me! It's something . . ." I decided to admit it. Jackson was always telling me I couldn't be vulnerable with Craig. "It's something I've always fantasized about."

He looked shocked/overjoyed. "Stephen, me too! I just didn't want to ask."

"Well, I'm asking you!"

"I'll do it!" We both got up and hugged again. "And listen," he said while I finally started to eat my salad. "I know how hard you are on yourself. I don't want you to feel bad that your apartment doesn't match up to what I'm used to."

I shrugged it off. "I know it's a lot smaller, but it's cozy."

"I mean the way you've decorated it."

I shrugged it on. "Oh . . ."

"Don't worry." He laughed. "We have plenty of time to look for new stuff. And we can borrow a car to get rid of your old stuff. I'm sure Housing Works would take some of it."

Housing Works takes anything because it's a thrift store whose profits go to homeless people with AIDS.

I didn't really care, though. Craig has great taste, and I'd love to have him help me buy some new stuff, especially since now I have some steady money coming in.

"How did Jeffrey take it?" I suddenly remembered to ask. I really hoped he was breaking up with Jeffrey because the relationship wasn't working, and not because of me. I didn't want Jeffrey to tell Mason that I was a home wrecker.

"He wasn't too shocked. He thought I had found out about him and his male secretary."

"People still call them 'male secretaries'?" That was a new wrinkle on an old chestnut. "What's the guy's name—Miss Jones?"

He ignored the question. "They've been together for years." He took a bite of his sourdough roll. "It's never really bothered me."

Huh? I thought the reason Craig never left him for me is because Jeffrey was so madly in love with him he didn't want to break his heart.

I had to find out. "If you knew he was cheating on you, why did we have to sneak around so much?" They obviously had an "open" relationship.

He was putting soy sauce on his salmon. "The truth is, he was a lot easier to control because he felt guilty all the time."

Control? Like a dog on a leash?

He must have seen my facial expression because he stopped pouring the soy sauce and said, "I know it's tacky. Gail helped me realize that it's not the kind of relationship I want . . . where one party lets the other one walk all over him because they're hiding something."

"Is that the only reason you decided to end it?" I asked, while trying to look as hunky as possible, hoping he would say it was also because he couldn't stand not being able to be with me 24/7.

"Well, Gail also made me realize I'm much happier with you." Bingo! "You're calm and not judgmental, and I really needed someone who doesn't chatter all the time, like Jeffrey does."

Huh? Was he describing me? I suddenly remembered that I've always modified my personality a little when I'm with him because I know what he likes.

And no judging me from the other side of the page! Relationships are about compromise! I'm sure Craig's modified things about himself to make himself more appealing to me, not that he needs to because I'd love him no matter what.

Ooh . . . I can't wait to tell Jackson! He who was always so insulting about Craig—calling him self-centered and boorish. I think I'll call Jackson right after I call Mason about rehearsal tomorrow . . . shit, MASON! Jeffrey's best friend! He can't know that Craig is living with me. I don't want him to think I'm a cheat . . . even though I guess I am, technically. But not anymore. And I don't want to be judged by the old me!

OK . . . He's obviously gonna find out that Craig and Jeffrey broke up, but Craig will have to lie for the time being and tell Jeffrey he's living with Orville. Craig and I will then pretend after a respectable period of time that we struck a romance due to working together so closely . . . SHIT! I made that big stink about never dating anyone I work with!

Ow! Now I have a headache.

OK. I'll cross each hurdle when I get to it. The important thing is, Craig is right now in *my* shower and about to get into *my* bed and will be doing so from now on! Dreams do come true!

Twenty-Four

*S*aw Monikah today and she asked how the diary was coming along. I told her that maybe it's done its duty because Craig and I are now . . . (I paused for effect) *living to-ge-ther*!

Jackpot!

She yelped with joy, ran over, hugged me, and started jumping up and down.

Oh, I'm sorry.

I mean she was blank faced.

And silent.

I rightly assumed it was up to me to fill the void. "You know, I've always wanted to live with Craig." I said, wondering if she misheard me.

"You have." Question? Statement? She's indecipherable!

"Yes." I kept plodding on. "It's pretty amazing. I feel like I've gotten my life together. I'm music directing a Broadway show and Craig is finally all mine."

"And you're happy." Again: Question? Statement?

I spelled it out. "Well, when one gets the things one wants, one is happy. It's obvious."

"And you're happy."

Mother f*cker! It was a trick question. She knew me too well. The truth is, I didn't feel completely comfortable saying I was happy. I've actually been feeling very anxious all day. But who wouldn't be being in charge of a big Broadway show? It's only the first day of the second week of rehearsals and I don't think I'm totally used to it yet.

I spent the rest of the session blithely telling her about rehearsals and in-cast gossip, yet secretly annoyed that she made me aware of how high-strung I'd been feeling.

Anyhoo, tonight I subbed *The Lion King*, or as we in the business call it, *"Lion King."* I know I've supposedly moved on, but I don't want to give up my sub work just yet. I mean, what if *Flowerchild* closes after a month? I'll be out of the sub loop and have to start again. I mentioned this to Jackson and he said once you music direct a Broadway show you have a lot more opportunities (regional theatres, new Broadway shows), and he's right but, regardless, I don't feel comfortable giving up my sub work right now.

I can't believe it's the second week of rehearsals, though! Previews are getting closer each day. Scary yet thrilling! In the middle of the first act of *Lion King* tonight, I began to think about the opening of *Flowerchild* and, more importantly, the party. Hopefully, by then my relationship with Craig will be public knowledge and we can go to the party arm in arm. Actually, arm in arm in arm because I want my mother to enter with us. I can tell she's been feeling a little over the hill lately ("I walked in for dinner at Le Cirque and not *one person* applauded my entrance . . . is the lighting that dark there?"), and the flashing of photographers at Tavern on the Green should make her feel a little famous again.

I began to think through the one or two possible outfits she could wear that wouldn't embarrass me. I prayed that she's thrown out the faux leopard print pantsuit with matching long dangly leopard print earrings.

"From Strawberry! On sale!!! *Can you believe it?"*

I guess if she wants to tour the African jungle in camouflage, it's *perfect*.

I started thinking about opening night at the beginning of Simba's big number and suddenly realized it was over. I thought back . . . I remembered playing the intro, but I had no memory of playing past the third measure. I know it's *Twilight Zone*-y, but actually it's happened to me many times. I'll be in the pit and see music in front of me that's obviously been played because we're at the next scene but I've been so disassociated that I remember nothing. It happens to most musicians when they've been doing the same show for such a long time that their body is able to play while their mind focuses on something completely different. I'm sure I wasn't the only one in the pit whom it happened to tonight. I've subbed *Lion King* only off and on, but most of the musicians have been there since the show opened. That's an average of eight shows a week for more than ten years! At this point, they'd be able to drive on the Autobahn and flawlessly play "Hakuna Matata" at the same time.

Playing a show for a long time brings out bizarre behavior. When the original *Grease* was on Broadway, my friend David Friedman was the conductor. He told me that the electric bass player knew the show so well after so many years that he got an extra long extension cord for his bass so he could walk around the whole backstage area *while playing*. He would leave the pit and go watch the ball game on TV in the wardrobe room or hang out in the hair room ('cause they always had cookies) while blatantly in the middle of "Summer Nights" or "There Are Worse Things I Could Do."

I witnessed one event firsthand. When I was sitting in the pit learning the piano book for *A Chorus Line*, the show was about to start and the upright bass player suddenly realized that he forgot his bow. You know, the bow that makes all the sound from the bass. It's essentially like showing up at work if you're a typist and forgetting your hands. Well, he had been with the show for MANY years and was very laid back at this point, so he just shrugged and played the whole show with a coat hanger he found on one of the costume racks and straightened out. That's right, a wire coat hanger. I'll leave the unfunny Joan Crawford jokes for my gay male readers over 55.

LATER

$\mathscr{I}$ got home and noticed Craig was writing something.

"What's that?" I asked. "Notes from rehearsal today?"

"No . . ." he gently closed the cover. "Gail thought it would be a good idea if I kept a journal."

WHAT?!?!

What a copytherapist! I casually asked him what his projected publishing date was (thinking that it had BETTER not be before mine), and he looked confused. I then realized that not everybody wants to turn their diary into a Book-of-the-Month Club main selection. When I first began, I'd decided to keep my desire for a best-seller secret from Craig until I was ready to show him a first draft. I tried to cover up by making a joke about diaries that featured Anne Frank, and in the silence that followed realized most comics have discovered that she's not a great subject to riff on. The ringing phone broke through the heavy air and I ran to get it. It was Mason with our nightly phone call.

"Hey, Mase!"

"Ooh, Stephen. I have some delicious dish!"

I was all ears. "Spoon it on, sister!"

"I just heard that Jeffrey 'Don't-call-me-Jeff' and Craig are done! Broken up!"

How should I react? "Yeah . . . I sort of heard that too," I said, wondering what else he knew.

He went on. "I always sort of thought they had a fucked-up relationship." His voice dropped, "You know, Jeffrey's been seeing someone on the side forever."

I was surprised at how dishy he sounded. "I thought you guys were best friends?"

"Me and Jeffrey? No!" He sounded horrified. "We went to high school together. I just stay connected to him because he likes to invest in the arts. Please," he chuckled, "he's been up-tight ever since we first met in our school's quote unquote *cafetorium.*"

I laughed. "Wait! I'm *obsessed* with the etymology of the word 'cafetorium.' First of all, why does cafeteria trump auditorium? Why isn't it called the 'auditeria'?"

He started laughing. "Or why can't they mix and match each syllable? Like . . ." He slowly sounded it out, "Ca-di-to-ri-a?"

We both cackled at the phenomenal not-rolling-off-the-tongue-ness.

Craig waved his arms from the bed where he was sitting. "Stephen! *Please* use your indoor voice."

I couldn't even react because Mason immediately asked, "Who was that?"

"When?"

That's right, the ol' answer-a-question-with-a-question technique I had perfected.

I used it because I couldn't focus enough to come up with one of my signature lies. I was still reeling from being reprimanded in the style of a mother to a four-year-old.

Mason clarified. "I heard someone say something in your apartment."

"Oh . . . it was the TV." I glared at the direction of the bed. "I'm watching *Boyfriend's Most Outrageous Comments* on Fox."

"Really? Isn't a *Seinfeld* rerun on now?"

Why do I always have to give so many details? "I Tivo'ed it." I didn't have Tivo, but Mason had never been to my apartment. "Anyway," I said pointedly. "Now comes the part where the other boyfriend has a fit, so I'd better go."

"OK, have fun watching!"

I hung up and decided I was going to be mature and not "have a fi'" and/or give him the silent treatment.

"Craig . . ." I asked gingerly. "Did you just ask me to use my inside voice?"

He looked up from his journal. "No."

Phew! I *knew* he wasn't that condescending!

"Your in*door* voice. Your in*side* voice is another word for your inner child, according to Gail." He went back to writing.

Essentially every word in that sentence infuriated me.

I spoke very calmly. "Well, if we're going to be living together, I would rather you not use that expression with me. It makes me feel like a child."

He put pen and journal down. "Actually, Gail says we can't 'make' anyone feel anything."

1-2-3-4-5-6-7-8-9-10.

That seemed to relax me. "Nonetheless," I said in my "let's-work-it-out" voice, "I think we just have to adjust to this new living situation. So, I'll try to be more considerate when you're writing in your diary—"

"Journal!" he cut in.

"Sure, journal." Gender-differentiating *bullshit*. "And I'd like *you* to realize that I enjoy unwinding with a phone conversation or two at the end of the day."

He looked at me with a half smile, then got up and hugged me. "I understand. I unwind with alone time and you do it differently."

I hugged him back. His neck smelled like that great moisturizer from Banana Republic and I *loved* it! "Thank you."

He looked at me with soulful eyes. "Gail said I can't expect everyone to be on the same level as I."

1-2-3-4-5-6-

"By the way," he continued, "who were you talking to?"

I was about to tell him when he added, "I've never heard you laugh so hard."

I suddenly felt guilty and wondered if he was hurt that he doesn't make me laugh as much as Mason.

"It was Jackson," I lied. "He was trying out some stand-up material. It was hilarious."

"I didn't know Jackson, did stand-up."

"Well, he certainly should start."

That didn't even make sense to me. If I'm saying that Jackson should one day "start" to do stand-up, why would he already be trying out material on me? Shouldn't it be in reverse?

Thankfully, the phone rang. I quickly picked it up and said, "Hello."

"Hey, Stephen."

I covered the mouthpiece and looked over at Craig. "It's Jackson."

I quickly added, "Again."

I got back on the phone. "Hey, Jackson."

"Why are you whispering?" he asked.

"I'm not," I whispered.

"Whatever. Listen, I'm sort of freaking 'cause Ronald was supposed to come over tonight and he's two hours late."

This happened all the time. Now, of course, I knew why. He was probably going over some actor's resumé . . . with his tongue!

All right, I couldn't come up with a good metaphor.

I decided to broach the subject with Jackson. "Do you think maybe Ronald has someone else on the—"

Jackson cut me off. "Please! Ronald knows I would kill him if he ever cheated on me. Of course, I'm obsessing that he's been in an accident, but I'm sure he's just working late and has his cell phone turned off."

I knew Jackson would never believe me if I told him about Ronald and his clients. I needed to present him with proof.

"By the way," Jackson said while obviously chewing something, "how's Mr. Pretty Boy faring in your studio?"

"Fabulously!" I lied.

"Great!" he lied. "Ooh, I think that's Ronald coming down the hall. Talk tomorrow!"

He hung up. I looked over and saw that Craig was asleep with his journal on his chest. I was sort of relieved. I was just too tired for hanky-panky. Well, maybe not tired, but I wasn't in the mood. He did look very cute in my bed, though. I went into the bathroom and sat on the bathtub rim to write all of this. Reading it over again is making me smile. My jealousy over Craig's new journal . . . how funny Mason is . . . the little fight I had with Craig. Actually, I think I'm smiling just thinking about Mason. He is really funny.

Twenty-Five

I saw Jesse for the first hour today to go over his music and braced myself for his compliment/insults.

"Wow," he said while sipping the coffee he always carried in a Starbucks thermos. "I have to say Anike is really talented."

I agreed.

He went on. "I don't care if she screwed every stage manager on her way to the top." He lowered his voice, "Man and woman, by the way." He took another long sip. "She deserves to be there."

What do I say? If I agree with the fact that she deserves to be on top, I'm also agreeing she slept with everyone. He was such a tricky mother.

I doubled-talked him. "I *completely* agree with half of what you're saying!"

He ignored me and added, "I ran into her over the weekend down in the Village at Tea & Sympathy." I started salivating thinking about their delicious treacle pudding. It was my favorite dessert place. "I met her new man slave who, by the way, is decidedly *not* attractive." He took another sip. "But I think that's great—she obviously likes him for his mind."

HUH???

As far as I knew (aka assumed with very little factual basis) she was dating/screwing Fritz. Could she be dating one person in the open and Fritz behind closed doors? Did we pull that elaborate cover-up on Bettina for no reason? Hmm . . . I had to find out somehow.

I put it out of my mind for the time being and started rehearsing Jesse's song. It happens when his character is out in the backyard of the commune, photographing nature, and his cat gets caught in a tree and starts to fall. He's terrified his kitty might fall and die, so he frantically takes all these pictures while it's teetering at the end of the branch. Of course, the theatrical device is that his cat's name is Sloopy, so it gives Jesse the reason to fervently sing "Hang On, Sloopy." Remember that tuner?

The joke is, at the end of the show, he's the one able to save the hippie commune because he winds up making millions by licensing one of the pictures of the cat desperately clinging on the branch and turning it into that ubiquitous "Hang in there!" poster.

It's totally stupid humor, but those audiences at Yale always applauded wildly when the poster was revealed. Audiences unanimously love when they're able to go "Oh my God, I remember that/know that reference!" In *Wicked*, which is the backstory of the Wicked Witch of the West, two characters at a party say:

"What's in the punch?"

"Lemons and melons and pears."

"Oh, my!"

The audience takes a second and then always laughs knowingly at the "Lions and tigers and bears, oh my!" callback.

Jesse and I decided that in order for the song to get laughs, he had to play it totally seriously. I also thought of a funny idea for a stop-time section. In some musical comedy songs, after the song has been sung once through, a part of it is repeated. The singer dances during it and it's called a dance break. "Stop-time" is usually done during a tap dance break and means that the accompaniment drops out (or "stops") so you can hear the taps.

I thought it would be funny if, during the second time through Jesse's song, instead of tapping during the stop-time dance break, Jesse cried.

I rehearsed him singing "Sloopy, hang on!" and then the music stopped and he cried/sobbed in rhythm for eight counts.

Jesse made it really funny because his crying almost sounded like the tap rhythm you'd hear during an upbeat dance break. And even though the rhythm was sassy, his face remained devastated.

We finished up and Vince, our lead, walked in, followed by Anike, who was wearing her hair pulled back in a bun and no makeup.

"Hey, Anike," Jesse said, gathering his music. "It's so great to see you without all that soap opera makeup."

She flashed her winning smile. "It feels great! They would slather that stuff on me starting at 6 a.m. on most days."

"Well, keep it off!" he said as she smiled demurely. "Be proud of your wrinkles!"

He exited the room.

Her extended middle finger entered the room.

"What a dick," she said.

I forced myself to be mature and not say anything about another cast member, so I pretended I was too busy looking through my music to hear. I was struggling to be like Mason was at auditions, i.e., non-dishy.

"Anike, man," said Vince. "Do you want me to kick his comic-relief ass?"

She gave him a little hug. I was so thankful that they both got along. There has been many a show with two leads who despise each other. *I Hate Hamlet* was a Broadway play that starred Nicol Williamson (famous Brit) and Evan Handler (from *Sex and the City*). They did *not* get along, and one night Nicol took the sword he used in one of the scenes and blatantly hit Evan with it! On stage! Evan left the show mid-performance and never came back.

Anybody?

Vince and Anike caught up while I was getting their music together.

"How's the long-distance lady?" Anike asked.

I had heard that Vince was still dating his live-in girlfriend from LA.

He sighed. "I thought about our rap session and I think I am gonna cool it for a while."

She laughed. "Believe me, I wasn't trying to give you advice last week. I'm a novice at healthy relationships."

Ooh! Relationships? With Fritz? This was my opening and I piped up, eager for info. "Hey Anike! I heard you ran into Jesse with your current beau."

She shuddered. "*That* almost ruined the date. He made some stupid comment about my guy's slight paunch. 'Healthy appetite means healthy mind.'" She gave the finger again towards the door of the room.

"So, uh . . ." I pushily continued. "Are you a one-woman man?"

She looked thoughtful. "I am, but he doesn't know it." I waited for more. "AA says you're not supposed to get into relationships the first year, so I feel as long as I don't tell him I love him, it's not a relationship yet."

Now I was really confused. "But didn't you tell him you loved him last week?

She looked at me blank faced and then said, "Oh! I forgot you were there when he called. My trick around it is that I say it in other languages so it doesn't count."

That's why the "Ich liebe dich" murmuring. I'm sure her AA sponsor could find holes in that logic, but that wasn't my concern at the time. I tried to surmise whether she could be cheating with Fritz because she didn't consider her other relationship "real." It's possible, but she does seem into her new beau. Even though I hope Anike and Fritz aren't having an affair, I also dread having to tell everyone that I jumped to a conclusion as usual. Which is worse? The ruination of our show? Or yet again hearing someone make that speech to me about "When you assume you make an ass out of u and me?" At least come up with a new one! Like "When you jump to a *conclusion*, you're *con*ning without a *clu*, *son*." Wait, I've still got an "i" left over—

I realized Vince and Anike were staring at me while I was in a trance. I covered up by saying, "Yes! That's it!"

What's it? Uh . . . "I've figured out how to make the Act Two songs work." They looked at me expectantly. I thought fast. "Combine them!"

Background: Mason and I thought that Act Two always ran a little long, but we loved the way Anike and Vince sounded on their separate songs and didn't want to cut one of them. Her character is about to get married to her hometown sweetheart, whom she doesn't really love, and as she writes in her diary about Vince (whose character name is Bill) she sings "Wedding Bell Blues" (*"C'mon and marry me, Bill!"*). In the next scene Vince (Bill) sings "The Worst That Could Happen" (*"Girl, I'm never getting married . . ."*).

Recently Mason suggested that we cut part of each song, but it wound up taking the meat out of them, so this morning he asked if we could somehow go from one song to another without applause. He felt that it would save a little time, plus give the illusion of Act Two being shorter because both songs with no break would feel like one long song. I didn't fully support the idea because I felt that cheating Anike or Vince out of their applause would:

A. Lead to an angry phone call from one of their agents ("My client *deserves* their 11 o'clock number applause!); and

B. Leave the audience feeling annoyed. When you're watching a show and you hear a song done well, one of the great things about theatre is to be able to show your appreciation to the performer by applauding.

When an audience is denied that, it almost feels like coitus interruptus. (That's Latin for the phone ringing in the middle of a major sex session.)

Just to cover my lie, I immediately got out both songs and started making up one of my piano bar arrangements, aka going back and forth from one to another. Well, even though I was pulling it out of my ass to disguise the fact that I was obsessing about Anike's personal life, it started to sound great! I just had to slow down "Wedding Bell Blues" to match the tempo of the other song, which actually made it more poignant (*"I love you so . . . I always will . . ."*). Plus having them both singing opposite sentiments at the *same time*, instead of following each other made for great theatre. I was so excited that we asked Karen, our no-nonsense stage manager, to ask Kris, Mason, and Craig to come in so we could try it out on them.

As soon as we finished, Mason ran to the piano, hugged me, and said, "I can't believe you didn't tell me you had this up your sleeve the whole time."

Kris muttered, "He's got a couple of things up his sleeve he hasn't revealed yet." Kris and Jackson were the only ones who knew Craig and I were living together. I glared at Kris and said something to Mason about wanting to make sure it sounded good before I told anyone.

It's weird, though, how something great can be created so arbitrarily. For instance, the end of the musical *Triumph of Love* leaves the two older characters (Betty Buckley and F. Murray Abraham) devastated when they realize the person they've both been in love with (a princess who pretended to be a boy to make Betty Buckley's character fall in love with her) has been fooling them and is about to get married to someone else. It was a very depressing ending for a lighthearted show. Everyone on the creative team didn't know what to do, and suddenly the lighting designer softly said, half joking, "Maybe they'll meet somebody at the wedding . . ." The director perked up and said, "That's it!"

and from then on Betty and F. Murray would end the show sitting in these elaborate, foolish clothes they'd assumed they'd be wearing at their own weddings. They'd stare at each other, deserted and embarrassed, and after some silence Betty would look at F. Murray and slowly say, "Maybe we'll meet somebody at the wedding." The audience would go wild as the curtain fell. Who knows how the show would have ended if that lighting designer had censored himself!

Mason patted Anike and Vince on the back. "OK," he announced, "I'm treating at lunch today!" We all cheered.

"Oh, no!" Anike suddenly said. "I have lunch plans."

All the air was sucked out of the room as Kris, Craig, Karen, Mason, and I looked at each other out of the sides of our eyes. It was like one of those bad close-ups right before a commercial break on *Murder She Wrote*.

I had to be the one to say it. "Are you meeting your new guy?" An audible gasp came from the direction of Kris.

"Yeah . . ." Anike said to me. She turned to Kris. "Why the gasping?"

"Oh, don't mind him!" I brightly said. "We all saw some silly article online saying you were back together with your ex-Mafia Man and we were nervous."

"Oh, no way!" She laughed. "This one is above board." She waved to us as she walked out.

No-nonsense Karen watched Anike walk out and then barked, "Vince, take a break!"

Vince walked out looking miffed, and suddenly everyone started throwing questions at me.

"Calm down, everyone! She's not dating Fritz." I explained the whole German love talk.

"What about the winking on the first day?" Karen asked me pointedly. I had forgotten about that.

"Uh . . . I never asked," I lamely explained. But I then told them about Jesse's encounter with her in the Village and her "decidedly unattractive" new beau.

"Please!" Karen spewed. "Jesse's as big of a drunk as Anike was! Who knows what he actually saw?"

"And "decidedly unattractive" sure describes Fritz," added Kris.

"Look," said Mason, taking control. "Let's just give her the benefit of the doubt and move on to more pressing matters. I want to run the show from the top starting this afternoon. Has everything been taught?"

"Well," Kris said tentatively. "I think Jay is having a little trouble on his dance solo, so maybe I should have an hour with him alone . . ." I'd forgotten Kris was hoping to break up Jaylaine and claim Jay as his own.

"Nice try, Romeo," Karen interjected. "Any private coaching with Jay will be run by Craig."

"But—" Kris began.

"I have my eye on you," finished Karen.

Kris walked away fretting and Karen looked in our direction. "Sometimes I hate it," she said. "But being a stage manager is like being a mother." She let out a big, frustrated sigh as she walked over to the stage manager table and started angrily sharpening pencils. "I have to be with this cast eight shows a week, handling whatever issues come up." *Sharpen!* "I do *not* have the energy to be dealing with an Elaine who is constantly weeping about her boyfriend being stolen by the show's own choreographer." *Sharpen!* "It's *bad* for the morale of the show, it's *bad* professionally, and it's *bad* for my digestion." She suddenly brightened and said "Speaking of which, let's go to lunch!" I noticed the pencil she was holding had a crazy five-inch point.

"You pick the place," Mason said, gathering his things. Just then Françoise came in the room, wearing a Betsey Johnson dress that highlighted her figure and eyes at the same time. Her beauty was in direct opposite proportion to her personality.

"Monsieur Mason," she sing-songed. "I've brought some of the music I've been composing."

I knew she had been hounding Mason to direct a reading of

the show she'd been writing. Françoise knew that if *Flowerchild* were a hit, Mason would become one of the new hot directors, and she was obviously using her "in" with him before he became too big. Unfortunately, her show was about an 80-year-old dowager (*"It's a perfect role for* Facts of Life's *Charlotte Rae's triumphant return to Broadway!"*) who travels to France after she is widowed. At night, she hears strange sounds coming from the bowels of the manor she's staying in and wakes to discover the ghosts of three brothers. (*"Hansen, anyone?"*) The brothers were murdered in 10th-century France, and soon we discover that they all play the harpsichord, which is pretty much the only instrument in the orchestra. (*"Sixteen harp-see-chords and a drummer!"*) The brothers introduce the dowager to the town baker and teach her to love again (*". . . perhaps a hot tub scene à la Kathy Bates?"*) and she, in turn, helps them ascend to heaven where they "turn things on their head." (The Act Two closing number lyrics start with *"Angel harps make us bored/from now on let's play harp-see-chord!"*) The best part is that the show is it's half in English, half in French.

In other words, a surefire hit. On opposite day.

"Oh, yeah, Françoise," said a flustered Mason. "I'd be glad to listen."

"How about during lunch today?" she asked happily.

He looked at us. "Uh . . .sure."

I unhappily saw that nothing had changed since his landlord's rent-raising debacle.

I pulled him aside. "Mason," I implored. "What happened to paying for my veggie burger?"

"Stephen," he sighed. "I know that you want me to be different, but I'm not."

I laid it on the line. "When will you learn to stand up for yourself?"

He looked at me intensely. "Believe me, it frustrates me, too." He moved me further away from everyone, toward the piano. "But I was taught that it's rude to put your foot down, or . . ." He searched for the expression. ". . . or make a demand, and I don't think I'm going to change."

I felt so frustrated from his dichotomy. He's so powerful and sure when he directs but is such a wimp as a person. Where is his backbone?

"Mason, it's *not* rude. It's what being an adult is about." I grabbed his shoulders. "Be true to yourself."

I got those clichéd, yet accurate sentences by thinking WWDPSMSH. *What would Dr. Phil say minus Southern headachiness?* Ever since he cured my sister Dianne of her mother-hating, I'd been taping his show daily. He actually has a lot of good things to say if you can completely tune out his accent, homespun expressions, and hairline.

Mason walked back towards Françoise. I knew my words wouldn't produce any magical result, but I felt at least I gave him some cud to chew on.

Wait! That sounded Southern! OK. I'm leaving that sentence in as a warning to myself to cut down my viewing.

Twenty-Six

oday Jackson and I had a life-changing brunch. And it wasn't just the delicious *delicious* food. We met at Good Enough to Eat on 84th and Amsterdam, where we each had an omelet and split a side of banana/ chocolate chip pancakes. Yum! The best part was, Ronald was supposed to come, too, but (miracles happen) he had a meeting with an interior designer about his new condo. He decided to purchase a one bedroom in one of those awful new apartment buildings that overlook the Hudson, have none of the flavor of a New York apartment building, yet convey all of the cookie-cutter ugliness of a high rise hotel in some random Midwestern city.

"Stephen," he haughtily explained last week when he met Jackson after rehearsal. "Judge it all you want, but it has a private gym and a 24-hour concierge."

"Really? Does the apartment have a *Jacuzzi?*" I asked, infusing the end of the sentence with hidden meaning and raising my eyebrow to new heights. Ever since the "Come join me in my Jacuzzi, Vince" story, I've been dropping hints that I know what he's been up to but, of course, Ronald's too self-absorbed to take in a double meaning or, for that matter, someone else's part of a conversation. He simply talks and waits until it's his turn to talk again. Jackson told me that all of Ronald's savings went into the down payment.

"Isn't that sort of risky?" I asked both of them.

Ronald chuckled. "I don't quite think you know how the big boys play with real money." *Ihateyoulhateyoulhateyou.* "Yes, I'm paying an enormous monthly maintenance, and a *huge* mortgage, but when you command a big salary," he smiled mirthlessly, "sometimes it's nice to spend it." He waved me away. "I don't expect you to understand it."

I got so angry that I regressed and said incredibly quickly, "A douche bag says 'what'" just so I could hear him say "What?"

Ah, the satisfaction of him admitting that he's a douche bag. It was nice to know that what worked in seventh grade still works today.

Anyway, I was glad I got a chance to talk to Jackson alone because, as much as I hate to admit it, I've been having major problems with Craig. Ever since he moved in, essentially everything about him has been driving me crazy. E-ve-ry-thing. From the 25-minute long showers for "pore opening" to the constant telling me he needs quiet time whenever I want to talk on the phone to, finally, watching him apparently *enjoy* listening to Madonna. No, not the fun pop Madonna we all love, but the miscast Madonna "singing" *Evita.* Never have my emotions changed so fast as that fateful day, years ago, when I first heard the news on *Access Hollywood*:

"Tinseltown is finally making a film of *Evita*." *Pure joy.*

"It's starring Madonna." *Begin immediate search for earplugs.*

I spent the last few days telling myself that my issue with Craig is the "fear of intimacy" I've supposedly had since my first relationship in college and that I should not give in. As much as I've wanted to call my landlord and report Craig as a squatter, I haven't.

But this morning pushed me over the edge. It was our day off and, naturally, I was looking forward to sleeping late, but instead of a delicious Sunday morning where I wake up at noon to the smell of coffee that Craig is brewing, he put in an exercise video at 8 a.m.!

WE LIVE IN A STUDIO!

And, by the way, it wasn't a deliciously relaxing yoga tape that maybe I could have slept through, it was *Tae Bo House Jam!* I was confronted with the pounding beat of house music coupled with the constant panting of an idiot.

"Craig," I said, with the covers over my head to block out the glaring light of the TV. "I beg you to turn that off and let me sleep for a while."

"Stephen," he said, in rhythm with the music. "As a dancer, my body is my instrument. My instrument needs constant tuning. Have I ever told you not to tune your piano?"

I threw the covers off my head. "Have I ever tuned my piano while you're obviously trying to sleep?"

"Look," he said, while working his abductors. "Gail said sometimes I need to put *my* needs first."

SOMETIMES!!! When have his needs ever NOT been first? She probably said "ONLY sometimes should you put your needs first," but he tuned out the first word!

I told Jackson the story.

"You know, Stephen," Jackson finally said after a lengthy pause. "He's always been this way."

I doubled the length of Jackson's pause.

"In a way," I said, finally.

He put sugar in his coffee and kept talking. "You also know, I hope, that this is your pattern."

I narrowed my eyes. "What is?"

"You set your sights on somebody who's unattainable in some way, e.g., has another boyfriend, and once you win them, you drop them."

How dare he???

I remembered Jim Cross from college. "Jim wasn't unattainable!" I retorted. "He was totally into me from day one!"

"Stephen," Jackson paused as he looked at me like I was an

idiot, "he lived *fifty miles away*. As soon as he moved into your area code, he made you sick."

Why did I ever tell him that story?!?

"What about Marc Tuminells?" I said haughtily, bringing up the guy I dated before Craig. "I never lost interest in him!"

Jackson waved his arms. "Hello! He broke up with you!"

"What's your point?"

"Stephen, you have to grow up! You revel in the *hope* of a relationship, not the actual relationship."

Hmm . . . I reflected on the last year with Craig. I used to get such a high every time I thought about us finally being together. I would fantasize all the time about our bed-and-breakfast in Vermont as I fell asleep. It's not that I want to "drop him"—I just think it's not possible for two people to live in such close quarters and not get on each other's nerves. If I had at least a one-bedroom, the morning probably would have ended up with us having breakfast in bed. Maybe if I rented the studio next door and knocked down the connecting wall . . . Oy, I was at a loss.

"Well, what am I supposed to do?" I asked, hopelessly.

"Do you"—he couldn't keep the joy out of his voice—"want to break up?"

"No!" I shot back. Jackson had a lot of nerve! I'm not about to throw all I've worked on in the garbage. There are plenty of things I still like about Craig. Plenty of things.

"Maybe," I said as I thought it out, "we just moved in together too soon." That sounded right. "You know," I continued, "we never got the chance to date without the specter of Jeffrey hanging over us."

"Well, you can't go backwards, you're living together now." He took the second-to-last bite of our shared syrup-drenched pancakes. "You can't ask him to move back in with Jeffrey."

"No," I said tentatively, as I took the last bite and had an idea. "But maybe he could start looking for another apartment. Just until the show opens and I can relax a little." NY rents were crazily expensive, but he was making money as Kris's assistant. Hmm . . . I began to get excited. "Then we could ease into living together." Now that I thought about it, the whole moving in together thing was just too sudden. I went from eating a soy patty parmigian entrée with Craig downtown at that momentous dinner to observing quiet time within minutes.

Jackson looked skeptical. "I don't know . . . it's not so easy to look for an apartment when you're rehearsing from ten to six every day."

My joy completely dissipated. I couldn't take three more months of being forced to whisper at night and being woken up to Tae Bo at dawn!

"*Why* did I ask him to move in?" I lamented as I put my head in my hands. I must have looked really depressed because suddenly Jackson said—

"I can't believe I'm suggesting this, but . . ." He let out a "what-am-I-getting-myself-into" sigh. "Last week I moved with Ronald into his new Trump co-op, but I haven't really had time to find a subletter, so—"

"Craig can move in today!" I quickly paid for Jackson and me, gave him a hug, and ran home.

LATER

I found Craig at my desk, writing in his rip-off journal. I decided to tackle it right away.

"Craig, I felt like I was really cramping your style this morning."

He looked relieved. "I was going to say the same thing." He looked around my 15 × 20 place. "I wish this place had another room."

"Yeah . . . it seems, maybe, that living together may not be the best idea when we're also working together."

He looked confused. "You want to move out?"

"N-o-o-o," I said slowly. "I just thought, maybe, until the show opened we should each have our own place."

He closed his journal. "What do you mean?"

I told him Jackson's situation and explained that having separate places could make it be like we were courting each other for the first time, with sleepovers and late-night phone calls and all the fun that comes with initial dating.

Craig said that sounded like fun and that he secretly had been hoping for his own place for a while, since he was just coming off of living with Jeffrey. We packed up his clothes and hightailed it over to Jackson's on 85th Street. I ordered in Chinese for both of us from the place that has green vegetable dumplings. I know it's just green food coloring added to regular vegetable dumplings, but it makes me feel healthier. Maybe the food coloring has antioxidant-rich spinach in it . . . and/or green dye no. 387.

Most of Jackson's stuff was still there, and in his white Ikea bookshelf, I found a videotape of Jackson and me from late '80s summer stock. I can't believe I actually used to wear boxer shorts as shorts. Was that an '80s thing or was I just a fashion accident?

Around 10 o'clock I realized I had to go home and walk Heather. Craig turned off the VCR and we hugged. The hug felt melancholy. I realize that our relationship is at a new point. I want it to feel like a new beginning, but it almost feels like an ending. I think I'm feeling guilty for "kicking him out," even though he loves Jackson's apartment and now there'll be so much less stress between us. I have to remember: we definitely did the right thing. Our relationship can only get stronger.

I got home two hours ago and just got off the phone with Mason, who told me a hilarious story about his aunt who was visiting today and kept calling her menopause hot flashes, "hot *flushes*." He refused to correct her just so he could surreptitiously tape her on his mini tape recorder and play it for me later. He rewound it for me like four times on the phone because I was obsessed with not only the mispronunciation but also her midwestern accent. "Whoo! That hot *flush* went from my hand right up my *ehrm*."

It was so nice to laugh and not worry I was encroaching on Craig's "quiet time." Oh! It's 12:30! I totally lost track of time, and now it's too late to call Craig. Oh, well, I'll see him tomorrow. Heather's already asleep on the bed and soon I will be too! Good night!

Twenty-Seven

*Y*es. The good news is we're finally out of the rehearsal rooms and in the theatre because previews start next week. The bad news is we're just at the beginning of what we theatre insiders call "Hell Week," so-named because it *SUCKS!!*

Sorry I haven't written in a while, but all I've been doing for the last two weeks is rehearsing during the day and working with the orchestrator at night. I gave him the final arrangements of each song a week and a half ago, and he's been orchestrating about a song a day.

His name is Joe Thalkoun. An orchestrator arranges the music for all the instruments in the orchestra. *Flowerchild* has a twenty-three person orchestra, which is exceedingly rare on Broadway these days, but certain artists would only give rights to their songs if there would be a full orchestra playing them, not just a rhythm section and three synthesizers. When did a wedding band become a Broadway orchestra?

Joe is totally different from me. He's married and in his early forties with a Waspy face and completely bald pate. He also towers over me by around a foot. His six-foot-five-ness combined with his demeanor makes him what is commonly called a "gentle giant." I've never seen him get mad and he only talks when necessary. He's been orchestrating for years (Off-Broadway, concerts, CDs), but has never done a Broadway show. He orchestrated a benefit I worked on a couple of years ago for free and did such a GREAT job I had to repay the favor. By the way, when I say "he talks only when necessary," I mean he's quiet most of the time but once in a while will say a scathingly pointed barb so that only I can hear.

When I first introduced him to Bettina, she glared and said, "I read your resumé and you have no real credits." She then smiled and graciously/fakely offered, "But every lotus flower was new when it first bloomed." I never know if she's translating these expressions directly from the Chinese and that's why they never quite make sense, or if she just makes them up on the spot using a recipe of one part Asian imagery with two parts proverb sentence structure.

She noticed our confused faces and clarified. "I'm always willing to work with new blood." Aka: pay you minimum.

Joe nodded, and as she and her assistant Tiffany looked for his contract, he muttered to me, "Of course she wants new blood—all she circulates is embalming fluid." I mimed him a tip o' the hat.

In the old days, an orchestrator would scribble out his arrangement on sheets of paper and a copyist would write each part out beautifully by hand. Now we have computer programs (most notably *Finale*) that will do it for you. Copyists had to learn how to use the computer or be out of a career. It's definitely made things *much* easier.

During the Broadway production of *Starmites* the "deluge curtain" came down by accident. That's a wall of water meant to prevent a fire from the audience spreading to the stage, or vice versa. Well, the stage was raked (sloped forward) so all the water ran into the pit and soaked the music! This happened in the late '80s before computer music printing was commonplace, so they had to cancel performances while the whole score was written out by hand again!

So Joe orchestrates on extra-long sheets of paper that have room for twenty-three instruments, and the copyist enters it into a computer. An electronic piano keyboard attaches to the computer, the computer sounds a steady beat, and whatever the copyist plays on the piano gets written on the screen. The copyist then adds all the music-type notation (fortes, pianissimos, crescendos, sharps, flats, ritards, etc.) by using the computer keyboard.

The best thing is, the copyist (Peter Miller) is able to e-mail me the orchestration and I can print it from my computer, then play it on the piano. Of course, the computer also has a function that will play the music and give you the gist of all the parts together, but essentially every instrument sounds like an electronic munchkin.

We got into the theatre this morning and it was a phenomenal feeling. The cast and I had only seen a model of the set and suddenly, there it was! The first set was the commune's backyard. It was beautiful! There was an enormous staircase from the back that supposedly came from the commune's kitchen, and the stage had real-looking pink and red rosebushes and trees (including one for Sloopy, the cat) all around. Instead of a painted backdrop, there was an actual photo of a sky projected on the back wall that made it look like a gorgeous sunny day with a few clouds. All I wanted to do was get a lounge chair and put on a Speedo (although with the "holidays" weight gain, a pair of cut off sweats and a long sleeved shirt would be more apropos).

The cast got there around 10:00 and went to their dressing rooms first. We're in one of the smaller theatres on Broadway so dressing rooms are at a premium, but Anike, Vince, and Jesse all have pretty nice ones. They're situated on the second floor, and on the floor above them are two rooms for the male and female ensembles. Because their agents negotiated for them, Jackson and Sharon (Anike's standby) don't have to share with the chorus and each have their own. But even by dressing room standards, they are *petit*. Picture a closet, add a makeup mirror, and you're in Jackson's new home away from home. I volunteered to take one on the fourth floor and discovered that because I was willing to walk up an extra flight, mine wasn't as bad as Jackson's—less closet, more walk-in closet. At first, I did feel a little like I was in a solitary confinement episode of *Oz*, but then I thought, "Who cares! I have my very own Broadway dressing room!" I immediately put up a framed pic of Heather and one of me and Mom on her opening night of *Carmen* when I was 13 (in a royal blue tux that was out of style even then). There's a black sign on the door to my room with white lettering that says: STEPHEN SHEERIN, MUSIC DIRECTOR. I want to take it off and wear it around my neck. It's so cool!

At 11:00 we started a run-through, and I was all set to get tears in my eyes because I'd finally be seeing the show on the actual stage, but the only tears I had in my eyes were because it looked and sounded awful! All day it's pretty much been about the actors getting used to the set, with performance level at 2%. In the rehearsal studio there was colored tape on the floor that indicated the two staircases and all the levels of the set, but now the cast actually has the set to work on, and because of that they've suddenly become more awkward than my father at my bar mitzvah dancing to Chaka Khan's "I Feel for You."

Also there are all these grooves in the floor of the stage that the set slides on and off on, and the women in the cast are constantly catching their heels in them. And by women, I also mean Kris the choreographer, who insisted on wearing his new Italian boots with pointy heels to impress Jay. I, however, do not think Jay was impressed by Kris's heel snapping off at 11:15 in the morning and Kris then spending the rest of the day with shoes of two different heights that forced him to limp like Captain Ahab.

The thing that is giving me a breakdown is that while everyone is learning to navigate around, they've forgotten *everything* I've taught them.

We've run six songs already and, first of all, no one is cutting off at the same time; second, all the beautiful dynamics I've drilled now have the non-range of Ali McGraw's acting; and, third, even though I've written elaborate harmony for all the group numbers, suddenly everyone's a communist and singing the exact same thing.

I'm waiting one more day and then we're going to have a *major* music brush-up.

Right now I'm sitting at the big piano that's set up in the audience near the third row. This is how most Broadway rehearsals are run since there usually isn't an orchestra during rehearsal (too much $), and I'd be too out of touch sitting at a piano in the pit. Françoise was sitting next to me, giving me a headache talking about the ending to her play (*"A half-hour megamix of French folk music from 1860 to 1871!"*), so I told her she should take the rest of the morning off to call her collaborator.

I noticed Jackson sitting by himself in the back row. Since he's the standby for both leads, he's not actually rehearsing, just observing. I called him over.

"The show's gonna be great!" he said, obviously reading the frustration on my face.

"Thanks, Jackson." I really did appreciate his support. "And thanks again for letting Craig move in."

"Isn't it kind of a trek from your place up to 85th?" he asked.

Ouch. It was, but Craig and I hadn't actually had plans in a while. I've been so busy since he moved out, I've pretty much only seen him at rehearsals. After a long day rehearsing, I haven't had the energy to trek over. Besides, most nights I've been meeting with Mason discussing the changes we made during the day.

"Oh, it's not a big deal," I said and changed the subject. "How's your new manse?"

A cloud seemed to pass over his face for a second. "Oh, it's great."

Maybe Jackson was onto Ronald, the Jacuzzi floozy.

"Is anything wrong?" I asked, as innocently as I could.
He laughed. "Oh, it's nothing. It's just that I was cleaning up
and I found the picture and resumé of some cute guy that had
his home phone number scribbled on it and I got all jealous."
"Really?" I wanted more details.
"It was stupid of me, really. It's Ronald's job. He gets pictures
and resumés all the time. I was just a little wigged out because it
wasn't in his home office."
"Where was it?"
"Next to the Jacuzzi."
I held my tongue. My all-knowing/all-judging tongue. My
one positive thought was that Ronald was going to slip up soon
and when he did, his downfall would be mind-boggling!

Twenty-Eight

*T*oday was the "costume parade." I'm sitting in my dressing room trying to digest the end of the Act One debacle that just happened. OK, starting at around 1 p.m. every single costume, beginning at the top of the show, was modeled by the performer for Mason, the costume designer, and the Geisenshlaags (more on them later). Everyone had to agree that what was at first just a costume rendering now looked good on the actor and would work with the set, lights, and particular dance moves that said actor had to execute. During *Seussical*, the costume designer was fired in the *middle* of the costume parade (!), and the cast played the first previews wearing clothes that were brought in from the local mall until a new designer could make the costumes! Even though the audience didn't get to see elaborate Seuss-ian costumes for those first previews, I guess the good part was if they liked what they saw onstage, they could run out and buy it at the local Chess King.

Well, as soon as the costumes started filing out, Elaine had a problem. Her halter top was so loose and frilly on the top that when she demonstrated one of her fierce triple pirouettes, the top popped down and her boobs popped out—as did Fritz's eyes.

Juanita charged up at that stage with her assistant and immediately figured out how to make it work. Our costume designer is Juanita Vargas. She had been a dancer in her native Argentina, came here to get on Broadway, and when that didn't work out, became a dress designer for some of New York's highest society ladies. She started doing Broadway on the side and now costumes all of the Geisenshlaags' shows. Not because she'll work for cheap, but because she designs exclusive opening-night dresses for Bettina as part of her contract. Not everyone is willing to figure out a way to fit a square into a round hole. Or in Bettina's case, a rectangle into a beaded gown.

Juanita looks like a darker version of Chita Rivera (with the same *Kiss of the Spider Woman* pageboy) and maintains a fierce figure, though she has to be in her late 60s. Also, she's been here for 40 years, but has never gotten rid of her thick Spanish accent and always called me "E-Stephen."

After an hour of costumes Bettina suddenly stood up and pronounced, "That's it! We're *not* moving on till he's sitting next to me."

I suddenly realized that Fritz had gotten up to go to the bathroom halfway through Act One and not come back. We were now up to the finale.

"Bettina, e-seet down," Juanita said, soothingly. "Let's fee-neesh out dee act and *den* look for chore Frrrritzi." Bettina sighed and slowly sat down.

Mason took this opportunity to call for the next costume but the stage remained bare. He waited another minute and then called for Karen, the stage manager, who was talking frantically to her assistant near the stage.

"Uh, Mason, why don't you come over here," Karen said, nervously.

I went over with Mason. "Listen," Karen said. "Anike is supposed to be in her finale costume and she can't be found anywhere."

Anike and Fritz missing? Again? What happened to her new guy? And was this a recurrence of the psycho behavior we knew so well from yesteryear?

"OK, let's search," said Mason, ever the pragmatist.

"I'll cover downstairs," Karen said. "Mason, you check the local Starbucks, and Stephen, you look upstairs."

We each went to our respective areas. The last thing I wanted to find was Anike and Fritz in a compromising position. He was so short and she so statuesque I would voluntarily take 1950s-style shock therapy if it would erase the image that would be burned in my memory.

I thought it was idiotic to look in her dressing room since it had obviously already been looked in, but as I stuck my head in I smelled smoke. Not "the curtains are on fire" smoke, but "you've come a long way, baby" smoke. I walked in past her dressing area and followed the smell to the window. I stuck my head out and there, and on the fire escape, was Anike in her Act One finale itsy-bitsy-yellow-polka-dot bikini costume (for real, we do that song!) with a coat over her. Thank goodness it was an unseasonably mild February.

"Uh, Anike," I said with half my body in her dressing room still. "I think you're wanted onstage."

She blew out a long stream of smoke without looking at me. "You know," she said, half to herself. "I gave up marriage, I gave up drinking—the least I could do is smoke!"

I climbed out. "No one is saying you can't smoke." *P. S. I had been saying to her all through rehearsal that she shouldn't smoke . . . it's terrible for your voice!* "But why don't you wait till you have an actual break?"

She swung her head around, blond tresses flying, and stared at me. "*He* wants to take a break."

He? He who? Did Fritz just break up with her?

"Do you mean . . . Fritz?" I offered, tentatively.

She looked confused. "Fritz? Fritz Geisenshlaag?" She threw

her cigarette on the grating and jabbed her heel into it. "What would Fritz want a break from?"

"Aren't you . . ." What was the word? " . . . dating?"

She started to laugh. Softly, then raucously. "*Why* the fuck would I date Fritz?"

"Well," I began, feeling stupid. "I saw him wink at you at rehearsal and . . ." That was it. That was pretty much all I had besides the "*Ich liebe dich*," which she explained.

"Yeah." She snorted. "I also saw him wink and throw that kiss at me too and during the next break told him, in no uncertain terms, to cut the crap!" She looked at me like I was crazy. "He's half my height and twice my age. Besides, I had my fill of married men while in my twenties." She shook her head and looked like she was reminiscing . . . not fondly. Then she asked, "Did you honestly think I was screwing Fritz?"

How do I answer? "Let's just say . . . yes."

She looked hurt. "I thought we were becoming friends, Stephen."

"We were! We are!" I offered.

"Then why wouldn't you just ask me if I . . ." she trailed off. "Oh." She nodded. "Because of my reputation as a psycho."

I was silent.

She started prancing around and talking singsongy. "Don't want to get psycho going! Who knows what she'll do!"

She grabbed the railing of the fire escape. "It's not fair!!!" she yelled to the patch of grey sky visible between our theatre and the theatre next door.

She was making me very nervous. Her behavior was so weird and we were two flights up.

"Anike," I said, taking her hands off the railing and walking her nearer the window. "What's going on?"

She took a deep breath and let it out. "The guy I'm dating is not 'in the business' so he didn't know much about me and, just for fun, he Googled me and . . ." she faded out.

I finished the sentence. "He found out you used to be a fucking nutjob."

She gave me a comic stare. "Thank you."

"So," I said, as I began to figure it out, "he asked to take a break and now you're having your own break. As in break*down*."

"Essentially, yes," she said with a laugh.

"Do you like this guy?" I asked.

She stared off in thought. "Oh, Stephen, he's not really cute or rich or anything, but I feel so good with him." She laughed. "It's true! I adore a balding man! And . . ." Her voice got softer. "It's been two-and-a-half months and we haven't even . . . you know . . ."

"Done it?"

She blushed. "Yes! I can't believe it! I mean we've done other stuff, but we've been waiting."

"Why?" I asked, even though it was hard to move my jaw because it was agape.

"My AA sponsor thought I should get to know a guy before"—she made big quote marks with her fingers—"'getting to know' him."

Wow. That takes willpower.

Or a chronic yeast infection.

All right, sometimes I still go borscht belt with ye olde humor.

"But," I concluded, "those articles in the *Star* and everything have freaked him out."

"Yes! He thinks I'm suddenly gonna turn on him." She patted her coat pockets, looking for another cigarette.

"Are you?"

She didn't answer.

She found her cigarette, lit it, and appeared to be thinking as she inhaled.

"Stephen, I hope not." She hugged herself. She was, after all, just wearing a bikini underneath her coat. "I really hope not. I've been working so hard on myself in therapy and AA." She looked at me like a little girl. "Can't people change?"

"Yes!" I said, immediately. "Yes, they can! I've been in therapy for—" Better not admit it. "Well, for a while, but I feel like I'm finally changing."

I pretty much said that just to cheer her up, but I realized it was true. I feel different. Like I'm ready to meet a challenge and actually make the smart choice.

"What do I do?" she asked me.

"He's just scared, Anike," I said as I gingerly took the cigarette out of her hand and stomped it out. I was not having my lead singer have a smoker's hack during previews. "He probably thinks you're gonna drop him when you find someone better. Tell him you're not the same person you used to be and tell him how much you care for him."

"I guess maybe I should have done that instead of hanging up immediately."

"Probably."

"And I guess, professionally, instead of pretending nothing happened, I should go and apologize to Mason for missing the finale."

"Yes." I nodded sagely and added, "I also guess you should stop smoking."

"Nice try." She stuck the pack from her coat in her bikini top. "But for now no booze means double the smokes."

What could I do?

We both climbed back in the window. "Help me take off these impossible boots." She was supposed to be barefoot in the show, but had put on her enormous winter boots for the fire escape.

I got down on my knees and was having difficulty unlacing her boot because the sun had gone down while we were outside and it was dark in the dressing room.

"Oh, my God!" Bettina suddenly screamed from the door.

She obviously thought the short figure crotch level with Anike was the short figure she had married.

"Bettina!" I waved. "It's not Fritz! It's Stephen."

She looked at me, annoyed. "Why would it be Fritz?" She asked, flicking the light switch on. "I was just startled to see people in the dark."

"So was I!" I echoed. Huh? Hopefully, that threw her. "Anike will be down in one minute to start the finale." I said, kindly waving her out.

Bettina tottered off on her five-inch mint-green heels.

Anike had her cell phone out and was about to dial. She looked at me, guiltily. "I guess I should wait until my next break to call my guy, huh?" I finished yanking her boots off.

"Yeah," I said, standing up.

She gave me a hug. "Thanks, Stephen. You're a good friend."

"You're welcome." I said, walking out to find Mason and the gang.

"And Stephen," she said as I was halfway down the stairs. "You really were the best sub at *42nd Street*."

I smiled and waved. I didn't care if she was bullshitting—I liked her a lot.

Twenty-Nine

*H*ello from the backseat of an "I'm-exhausted-and-I'm-splurging-for-a" cab. Today was the first orchestra rehearsal! Since Françoise and I had to be with the orchestra at a rehearsal studio, the whole cast did a dry run-through at the theatre without music just to get used to the costumes and fix the lights. Also, the dancers are finalizing their onstage numbers. Not their musical numbers, but the numbers where they dance. Every Broadway stage has the number 0 written on the center part of the stage and then every foot or so, the numbers 1, 2, 3, 4, 5, 6, 7, 8 are put on the stage (in both directions) so when dancers dance without a mirror they can look down to make sure, for instance, that they're on 3 so they don't block the dancer in back of them. Or they know to do their big leap on 5 and land on 7 so they'll stay in the light. Of course, there were numbers on the floor of the rehearsal studio, but things always change once you get onstage because the space is a little different.

One of the coolest things I've ever seen is a video of Laurie Gamache, who was the final Cassie in the original *A Chorus Line*. She was demonstrating how to do the Cassie dance for the upcoming Australian production. As she is flying through the difficult dance, she's calling out all of her numbers so the new Cassie can learn them. She pirouettes and lands: "three and a half!" She does a jazz run across the stage: "Nine!" As the dance builds momentum, it becomes more and more frantic. "Six! Two and a half! Left of four! Seven of nine!" Wait . . . isn't that a Star Trek character? Regardless, it's amazing to watch.

Anyway, the orchestra started assembling around 9:45 a.m. I knew almost everyone from different shows I'd subbed. I noticed that at least two people had left their long-running shows to do this gig. That either meant they couldn't bear doing another performance of their show, or they thought *Flowerchild* was gonna be a hit and run even longer than the show they were doing! I hoped the latter, though it was probably a combination.

At 10:00 I asked Jorge, my concertmaster (1st violinist) to tune everyone. He nodded to Ella, the oboe player, who played an A. First the strings tuned, and then the winds and brass (it's done that way so there aren't 23 people tuning at once).

The sound of instruments tuning gives me such a feeling of "Ooh . . . a Broadway show is about to begin." Except for the aforementioned *A Chorus Line*: when that show opened in the '70s, it was notorious because instrumentalists had to tune their instruments outside the pit so the audience couldn't hear anything. The director, Michael Bennett, wanted the audience to feel they were really watching an audition. That's why the whole show begins with that rickety-rackety rehearsal piano and the orchestra sneaks in later.

I introduced myself, got a smattering of applause from two friends in the cello section, and said we would begin with song number 19, the Act One finale.

Orchestra players refer to the songs not by the title, but by the number. I've always found it sort of separatist. For instance, when I was playing *Beauty and the Beast* and the conductor would give me a correction, I always wanted him to say "Measure 5 of 'Be Our Guest,'" not "measure 5 of number 13." First of all, I don't know offhand what the numbers are of every song, and second, it seemed dehumanizing to the song. Or de-musical-izing.

On a related note, I'm going to make sure my orchestra feels part of this show by inviting them to the final run-through we do with just piano so they can see it from the audience. It's always so weird to me that there are players in orchestra pits who've never seen the show they're doing and don't know what's happening during the songs they're playing. I feel that it keeps them isolated from the show, instead of feeling that it's all one big machine and they're part of it.

I had decided to start with the finale of Act One because it was such an exciting song. The opening number of the show is very sweet but stays fairly low-key, so it would have been anticlimactic. I wanted to have the first song I heard the orchestra play be the most memorable.

Suffice it to say, IT WAS! It was so cool to hear what had only been played on the piano suddenly played by 23 instruments. In one section, it got really quiet and just the rhythm section played (piano, bass, guitar, drums). Then the lower strings started sustaining the chord changes while the French horn played a countermelody. Suddenly, the violins played an enormous scale and the whole orchestra joined in. The brass were wailing on crazy high notes, the winds were doing staccato eighth notes, and the strings were playing the melody in octaves. There's something really beautiful and unique about hearing an orchestra play without the voices on top. Somehow, hearing a song that's missing an element makes you realize how much goes into making it: the composer, the lyricist, the orchestrator, the orchestra, the conductor, and the performers.

At the end of it, the orchestra held a low note, crescendoed, and then I gave a big downbeat and everyone played the last note double *forte*, which will coincide with the Act One curtain falling. As soon as it ended, all the musicians started clapping towards Joe, who gave a meek little bow. I ran up to him and, since he was sitting and our upper bodies matched up, I was able to give him a giant bear hug. I was so proud of him, and I couldn't wait to conduct his orchestrations every night!

LATER

I'm lying in bed exhausted, but I have to write.

I got home right as the phone was ringing.

"Hello!" I yelled, leaping over Heather and picking up the phone.

"Hi, Stephen, it's Tiffany, Bettina and Fritz Geisenshlaags assistant."

"Tiffany," I said, miffed. "I see you almost every day; I know who you are."

She suddenly dropped her voice to a whisper. "She makes me start every conversation like that."

"Oh," I whispered back.

"Anyway," she said in her normal "I'm blonde, young, and beautiful" voice, "Bettina wanted me to remind you that she needs back a signed copy of the contract she gave you for the cast party."

The Geisenshlaags wanted me to be the pianist at my own cast party so they could get out of hiring one. How much money would they be saving? Two hundred bucks? I don't know why they thought I would say yes.

"Tiffany, I'm not doing it. I'll be celebrating the show opening. I don't want to be working."

"OK," she said, "I'll tell her you're not doing it."

Suddenly I heard the click of another extension.

"Tiffany," said the nasal voice of Bettina. "I'm taking over. Off the phone. Now."

I heard an embarrassed click. Well, I assumed it was embarrassed.

"Stephen, we need you to play at the cast party. It's only for a half hour. Case closed."

"No, Bettina," I said, trying to sound jovial. "Case still open. I'm not doing it."

"OK." She said, chipper-ly.

That was easy.

"And by the way, Stephen, I can only get you two tickets to opening night. I'm terribly sorry."

That *bitch!* She knew I wanted six tickets. Two for my mom and whomever she brought with her, two for my dad and Mitzi, and two for my sister and her boyfriend. Unfortunately, I only had a two-ticket guarantee in my contract, but Bettina had assured me there wouldn't be a problem. Now she made her ultimatum: I could play at the cast party for free, or I'd have to choose which two from my family came to opening night.

"All right, Bettina—" I began. She wasn't listening because I heard her yelling:

"Tiffany, right now—go back to my apartment and get me lip gloss!"

I heard Tiffany say something, followed by Bettina's shrill, "Yes, I still have some left, but I'm nervous I might run out. Go, now! You don't need a coat! Go!"

It was a mild February, but people still wore coats at night. Why did Tiffany stay in this hellish job?

"Stephen," Bettina said, coming back on the line. "No need to finish your sentence. I'll have the contract brought to rehearsal tomorrow and then we'll see about those tickets."

She clicked off.

She was such a manipulative dick!

Again my phone rang. I picked it up and said "Hello?" in a fury.

"Hey, it's Craig!" I heard.

I thought it was good timing. I usually kept him out of the loop when I was feeling upset about something, but I really needed someone to talk to. I told him the whole story.

"Go back a few sentences," he said after I was done. "You already asked for your tickets for opening night? I haven't ordered mine. Do you think that's bad?"

"No, I'm sure you have time," I said quickly.

He didn't say anything. Where was the "I'm sorry Bettina sucks and everything will be OK" comment I wanted?

"What about everything else I said?" I prodded.

"Well," he paused and I could hear him eating something. "Gail says we give others permission to abuse us."

I was really annoyed. "Craig, I'm not asking for a robotic platitude. I wanted some comfort."

His voice got higher. "Well, Stephen, it's hard to give *you* comfort when *I'm* freaking out."

"About what?"

He paused. "Well, now I'm nervous I won't be able to get good seats for my family when we open."

Craig is really close to his parents (do the words "Golden Child" mean anything to you?), and I guess he was stressed that they would have crappy back-of-the-balcony seats on opening night. I told him to check his contract because I was pretty sure it said he got two tickets. I held on while he looked through it and he finally found the section that said he was guaranteed two orchestra seats for opening night. He calmed down and we wound up talking about what we were going to wear to the opening night party (I think I'm totally buying a new suit.) My food delivery buzzed from downstairs, so I told Craig I'd see him at rehearsal tomorrow.

We hung up, and even though I was happy I had relaxed Craig, I still felt completely stressed. I called Jackson. I told him about Bettina's bitchery and about Craig's non-helpfulness.

"Stephen, why are you dating Craig?" he asked point blank.

My back went up. "What do you mean? We've been together for more than a year!" I said, which wasn't really an answer.

"Well," he said, "your version of together seems like you do all the accommodating and comforting and he does whatever he wants."

"That's not true!" I said defensively. "He's really grown over the last year."

"Yeah, Stephen." He paused. "But so have you."

How dare he throw my healthiness in my face?

I changed the subject and we chatted about the show. After we hung up I decided to take a tip from *Essence*'s "Is he the one 4 U, or 4 a U-haul?"

It said to think about your life in five years and imagine yourself with "him." That wasn't hard. I'd been doing that every day for the last year or so.

I imagined the bed-and-breakfast in Vermont that we would live in for six months out of every year and then the fabulous apartment we'd share in NY for the other half while we'd work on a new Broadway show. While in New York, we'd have intense rehearsals during the day and nights spent giving each other mutual massages. Vermont would feature low-carb/high-delish lunches spent exchanging creative ideas, nights hotly analyzing the latest art films, and mornings at 6 a.m. making breakfast for our diverse, yet gay-leaning, guests.

I smiled and felt great.

Suddenly, Jackson's voice. "*Yeah, Stephen, but so have you.*" His annoying words rang in my ears over and over again like a bad Mariah Carey chorus. Have I changed? I thought back to who I was when I first started dating Craig. Yes, I thought decidedly. I've certainly changed, or am in the process of. I forced myself to rethink my fantasy, but add reality to it. Weird . . . it felt like a haze lifting. I suddenly couldn't put Craig into any of it. Well, not the Craig I really knew. I sat on my bed petting Heather and realized that the person I fantasized about all these months wasn't Craig. I mean, it was Craig's face and fabulous pecs, but it wasn't *really* him. It was what I hoped Craig would be.

What was I thinking? In Vermont and up at 6 a.m. cooking? Together? Exchanging ideas? That isn't the type of person he is. And he probably never will be. He's always going to bring things back to himself and demand "quiet time."

I suddenly thought, though, that he *could* change. After all, he left Jeffrey. I started to get excited planning how to exact the changes I wanted and then remembered what Jackson said at Good Enough to Eat. You know, about me enjoying the hope of the relationship more than the actual relationship. I guess it's sort of true. I got such a great feeling going to sleep at night thinking how great it would one day be with Craig. All my happiness would happen *one day*. But now that I'm aware that I do that, it's hard to fully enjoy it anymore. How dare Jackson take the fun out of my fantasy life?

But, now that I think about it, I kinda would rather go to sleep thinking how great things actually *are* instead of *will be*.

But how? Will Craig change if I give him an ultimatum? Do I dare give up all I've worked on for the last year? Can I at least still impress people by showing them pictures of Craig and saying that he dated me?

$\mathscr{I}$ just got off the phone with Craig. I decided to clear what was fantasy and what wasn't.

"Craig, have you noticed we haven't seen that much of each other lately?" I asked.

He sounded peeved. "Stephen, I see you six days a week at rehearsal."

"I meant dating-wise."

He was silent

"Well, yeah," he muttered. "Sometimes, we have lunch," he added, positively.

That was feeble. "It just seems that ever since you broke up with Jeffrey, we haven't been getting along as well."

"Well, Stephen," he blurted. "I just feel like you've changed."

Excellent! That's what Jackson said!

He went on. "For the worse."

That's *not* what Jackson said.

"What do you mean?" I asked, bracing myself. I couldn't take him not liking me. Maybe I could change back.

"I always loved how gregarious you were in public," he said.

"But when we were alone, you never used to talk so much. You were such a great listener."

Hmm . . . that was double talk. By great listener he meant I'd always let him tell me all about *his* day and *his* wants and *his* whatever and I would agree with everything he'd say. That wasn't really me. That was what I pretended to be because I knew he wanted it.

Wow. I thought about how much energy it took to keep the real me down and decided, you know what? I didn't want to change back! I liked being me (except for the love handles).

"*Now*, Stephen," he unfortunately continued. "You always have things to say and"—he seemed disgusted—"*stories* to tell."

That's what I was being busted for?

He was right: I had changed. Instead of being a complacent geisha with a sublimated personality, I was trying to treat Craig more like I treat my other friends. Almost every night for the last month, I'd call Mason and we'd tell each other about our day, laughing up a storm, and when I'd try to repeat those same stories to Craig, he'd either tune out in the middle, relate some obscure detail back to himself, or hush me because of his patented "Quiet Time." I suddenly thought, I *couldn't* go back to the way I was. I *wouldn't* go back to the way I was! I wished there were one more word that ended in "ouldn't" so I could use it in a really triumphant last sentence, but there isn't. I wanly thought I could use "shouldn't," but what would the sentence be? "I shouldn't go back to the way I was"? I decided it didn't really have the *oomph* of the first two sentences. Oh wait, he was still talking—

". . . painful for my inner, outer, and middle child."

"Exactly!" I said. Agreeing to psychobabble was usually the easiest route to take.

I had to say it. I wasn't gonna pull a fade-out like I did with Jim Cross. "Craig, I think we should end this part of our relationship."

He sighed.

"I agree, Stephen."

He concurred rather quickly. I wouldn't have minded hysterical sobbing from him, but apparently, I wasn't gonna get it.

Suddenly:

"But Stephen, even though we're breaking up—"

I braced myself for the ol' "I still want us to be friends" line.

"I still want to work on *Flowerchild*," he finished, slightly panicked.

Of *course*, he immediately worried about his career.

I made the decision to be professional. "Don't worry about that, Craig," I said, maintaining my composure. "Kris is really happy with your work."

"Oh, good."

Now what? Do we hang up?

He sighed. "I'm sorry it didn't work out between us, Stephen. I guess we're both still finding ourselves."

It was a Gail-ish comment, but true.

"I'm sorry, too." Was I? Well, I guess I was sorry I wasted my time.

We talked a little bit about the show and said we'd see each other at rehearsal.

It was over. After we hung up I got nervous that I was pulling the same thing I did in college when I dropped Jim Cross. But when I thought it through, I realized it was different. I ran away from Jim because he cared for me. If I were the same way I was in college, I would *stay* with Craig because there wasn't any hope of a real relationship. I guess I'm feeling ready for someone who's the A word ("available"). Of course, I don't know how I'll handle it if it happens, but I'm going to start by making this vow: NO MORE UNAVAILBALE PEOPLE!

Thirty

*I*t's Sunday night and I'm trying to write this in the bath. It's very hard not to get Body Shop Dewberry Bath Bubbles all over the pages, but I'm taking the risk because I need to soak my tired back.

Here's a summation of the last three days:

Friday was what we in the biz call the Sitzprobe. That's right, Sitz-probe . . . and I ain't talkin' about a visit to a German proctologist (I've got a *million* of 'em—that's right, a million unfunny jokes).

Anyhoo, Sitzprobe *is* a German word and it means sit and rehearse. It's usually held at a rehearsal studio, and although all the actors are there, they don't do any staging, they just "sit and rehearse" (sing) with the orchestra. It's the most exciting rehearsal there is because it's the first time anyone is hearing the songs the way they're going to sound. There's a thrilling rawness to it because everyone's crammed into one space and it's just about the music. We started at noon. In the front of the room facing the orchestra stood the three leads, who had their own microphones (so they could be heard above the orchestra), and the ensemble stood behind the orchestra clumped around two mics.

Like the first orchestra rehearsal, I decided we should do the finale of Act One first so we could start with a bang.

As soon as Vince began the first part of the finale, you could feel the excitement ripple through the room. Vince looked très sexy in just jeans and a peace symbol T-shirt and it was cool to watch the orchestra, who had no idea who he was, start to smile when they heard his throaty, yet full voice. It reminded me of the first time we sang it through with all the harmony, but 50 times more exciting because we had the orchestra. The dancers were grooving to the sassy electric guitar and drums, and you could tell the leads were having rock star fantasies because they each took their mic out of its stand and started strutting around.

All the men in the orchestra who had been transfixed with beautiful Françoise during the initial rehearsal dropped her like a hot *pomme frite* for Anike. Anike was not only beautiful, but she was a star they had seen on Broadway and TV. Either on her soap or on an oft-repeated *ET* clip that featured her knee and a paparazzo's groin.

Some orchestra members had played in other shows with her and were too nervous to make eye contact at first. But she ingratiated herself by getting everyone into a '60s mode by passing out her version of "pot" brownies. Meaning Duncan Hines brownies carried in a big Crock-Pot. It was a lame joke, but everyone appreciated the effort, if not the obviously-made-two-days-ago blatant staleness.

During the first break, I told Kris what went down with Craig. He gave me a big grin and said, "Girl, thank goodness you dropped that albatross! He was Debbie Matenopolous to your Barbara Walters!" Always an obscure reference. He then lowered his voice and said, "He may be cute, but every time he was around you, you were more tense than *this!*" He put my hand on his stomach, where I felt his tight six-pack delineation. It was a creative way on his part to support me *and* show off at the same time.

Craig and I met up at the coffeemaker. It was the first time we had seen each other since the phone call. Of course, he looked gorgeous in a J. Crew sweater and cords.

I adjusted my hair so it wasn't receding as much.

"How are you doing?" I requisitely asked.

"Good," he said, while looking nervous. "The orchestra sounds great!" He then scurried off.

Hmm . . . obviously guilt ridden. I started to think of possible guilt-inducing scenarios . . . might he have gone right back to Jeffrey? I could totally see him wanting to be back in that fabulous apartment. How dare he? Maybe if he got a dose of ye olde silent treatment from me and Kris (whom I'd convince to go along), he'd learn to regret being so comfortable moving on from me so quickly.

After ten seconds I stopped myself. One of my new vows is no more assuming. I don't want a repeat of the whole Anike/Fritz song and dance. That was like a wacky episode of *Here's Lucy*—*without* the laugh track.

Aka: "Viv!"

silence

The Geisenshlaags stopped by during the Sitzprobe as well. Her hair (and face) was pulled back and she was wearing a black pantsuit that was made out of some extremely glittery material. His ascot was made of the same. Where do they shop? Liza's closet? It was impossible to look directly at them because whenever they moved slightly, light would hit another section of the shininess and blind you from a different area.

I noticed she was clinging to Fritz's arm as they entered the rehearsal room. It had the essence of "we're just two kooky lovebirds" mixed with "I WILL NOT LET YOU OUT OF MY SIGHT!"

They got up in front of the room. Fritz whispered something. "Welcome, everyone!" Bettina said.

Fritz whispered again. "We just want to say," Bettina began. Here comes the requisite "we're getting closer to previews and we're so excited about this show" speech, I thought. " . . . that no matter what, we're stopping after four hours because we're *not* paying overtime."

Fritz whispered again.

"No overtime," Bettina added. After around 20 minutes of rehearsal I noticed Fritz scurry out brandishing a quarter to go put in the meter.

"Why pay for a garage?" Bettina once asked.

Why? Because you're *MILLIONAIRES, YOU CHEAP F*CKS!!!*

Around half an hour later I heard Bettina yelling at her assistant, Tiffany. (Of course, she waited until we were doing a quiet, reflective song so her yelling could be completely rude.)

"*The sound . . .*" Anike softly sang.

"Start searching for the old man, Tiffany!" Bettina hissed as she shoved Tiffany out through the string section.

"*. . . of silence.*"

"Check the men's room first!" she yelled down the hall. Then louder, "He's notorious for being in there for an hour!"

It seems that the amount of money they have is in inverse proportion to the amount of boundaries. And, suffice it to say, they're *loaded*.

We finished the Sitzprobe at 3:58 (we couldn't risk getting Bettina angrier . . . Fritz was still MIA), and the cast went to the theatre for a "cue to cue." That's when we start at the beginning and do the first light/set cue and whatever dialogue there is until the next light/set cue. It's really boring, especially for me, because we were mostly just doing the beginnings and endings of songs. Jackson sat down next to me at the piano.

I told him the whole Craig story and that his comments really helped me.

"That's what friends are for," he said, quoting Dionne, Elton, and Stevie. "I have big news, also!"

Please let them be breaking up.

"I had a little bit of a fight with Ronald after I found that card by his Jacuzzi, which, by the way, he explained was just a big mix-up . . ."

Liar!

"And . . . we're going to have a commitment ceremony!" He smiled at me expectantly.

Thank God it was dark where we were sitting, or he would have seen devastation mixed with revulsion on my mug.

"When?" I choked out.

"After we open!" He snorted. "I want to do it right before my sister's wedding to Mr. Hotshot doctor."

Was that why he stayed with Ronald? Sibling rivalry?

"Wow! That's news!" I said with the same line reading of "That sure is exciting news."

"I know! I'm so excited."

I had to play the intro to Anike's song, so Jackson walked away.

Poor Jackson! Just when I extricated myself from a sucky relationship, he got into his deeper. I *had* to save him. Hmm . . . can someone drown in a Jacuzzi, and would my fingerprints show up in water?

OK . . . on to Saturday. At around noon we started to slowly run the show from the top with costumes and lights and orchestra. I wanted to sit in the audience with the soundman, so I had Françoise conduct (she had a sub sit with her during the last two rehearsals, who then played her part while she was at the podium). She would do it once and I would set the levels with Scott Staffer, our sound designer, then I would run to the pit and we'd do it again with me conducting.

Here's the thing that drives me crazy about Broadway: a show can have a great-sounding orchestra, but ultimately it's the sound person who controls everything. In the old days, neither the singers nor the orchestras were mic'd (like at the opera) and it was up to the conductors to control all the dynamics of the orchestra. But nowadays, the orchestra has to be mic'd not only because the singers are, but also because the acoustics in theatres have been compromised because most stages have been built out toward the audience and they block the top of the pit and muffle the orchestra. So, as a conductor, even though you could be conducting the string section to play their line extra loud, the sound guy who controls their mic levels may have them turned way down and the brass turned way up, so all the audience hears are trumpets. It's obviously very frustrating for conductors.

The same with actors. You may be belting out a high note, but the sound guy could have the orchestra turned way up so you're not even heard.

My friend David Friedman, the conductor, told me that when he was conducting a famous Lloyd Webber show, the sound guy put a "leveler" on the leading lady, meaning that no matter how loud she sang, it wouldn't go past a certain level.

During intermission she called him to her dressing room and asked, why, if she was belting her brains out, she sounded only medium loud.

The sound guy explained that he put her on a leveler because he didn't want her to overpower the backup chorus.

She screamed, "I don't give a FUCK about the chorus!"

Unfortunately she was wearing her body mic, and even though the sound was off in the audience, it was on backstage . . . and was broadcast to *every dressing room*. Dressing rooms filled to the brim with chorus people she, apparently, didn't "give a fuck" about. Suffice it to say, her popularity diminished amongst the ensemble.

Back to the first run-through. During tech rehearsals there is a huge table that's put over a row of seats and everyone sits behind it. There are tons of laptops in front of everyone that hold all the cues for the lights and the mechanized set. I sat next to Mason and Scott (the sound designer) for the opening number.

"Stevey!" Mason said with a smile as I sat down. I only let Mrs. Remick call me that, but I sort of liked Mason using it.

"Mason, we start previews any minute!" I said, excited/tense.

"Shh!" "No-nonsense" Karen said towards us. "We're starting!"

Mason and I had only one armrest between us.

"Can I use this?" I whispered.

"Sure" he said, but when I put my arm on it, he didn't move his away, so they were touching. Was he trying to share it with me or was it something else? It seemed very first date-ish and reminiscent of Barbra's "He Touched Me," but I was trying not to assume so I just left my arm where it was and stopped thinking about it.

Françoise started the opening number and did a nice job conducting, except that the first time we had to stop she screamed, "Arrêtez! Arrêtez, mes amis!" No one in the orchestra knew the French word for "stop" and instead thought she was calling out some obscure musical term. Half of them got louder and half slowed down before there was a massive fade-out. I ran down to the pit and informed Françoise that there was a strict musicians union "English Only" rule. It was a total lie, of course, but I was trying to save her from an angry trumpet player punching her in the *bouche*.

During the second number, Anike stopped singing and put her hands on her hips. "Hello! Sound!" she screamed to the darkened audience. "I can't hear myself!"

There are speakers that face the stage that the sound person puts the orchestra and the vocals through. It's a totally different mix from what the audience hears. Usually, it's mostly just the rhythm section that's piped through it because that's what a singer has to hear the most of to keep their pitch and to stay in time. I don't know of any Broadway show where singers haven't complained either that they can't hear themselves, or that they can't hear the orchestra. It's a constant battle. What's even more annoying is that the level that's adjusted during tech will change once there are bodies in all the seats absorbing the sound.

Scott bumped up Anike's voice through the stage monitor and, despite a total blackout in the middle of Act Two due to a faulty computer, which took a half hour to fix, we finished running the whole show at 10:00. It looked like a big mess, which we all expected, but we knew that it would be a lot smoother the next day.

This afternoon (Sunday) we were about to run the show again when Vince ran to the pit to ask if he could mark (not sing full out) because he was worried about losing his voice. One of the worst things that can happen is when an actor has to miss a show during previews because usually there hasn't been enough time to rehearse the understudies. During *Thoroughly Modern Millie*, the fabulous Sutton Foster had to miss a performance during previews and they wound up having to cancel the show (!) because there was no way her understudy could go on. Instead, they used the time to rehearse and the understudy went on the next night.

The most bizarre story I know happened during *Jekyll and Hyde* previews. The female star, Linda Eder, lost her voice, but her brilliant understudy, Emily Skinner, was too nervous to go on with no rehearsal. Not because she didn't know the lines/songs, but because the stage had so much fake London fog that Emily was scared she wouldn't be able to navigate it and would wind up falling in the pit. So, Linda Eder went on and did the dialogue as best she could and every time a song came, Emily Skinner sang it backstage into a mic and Linda Eder lip-synched it!!! For a paying audience!

I gave Vince the OK and as soon as he left, I saw my light blink.

I have a big red lightbulb to the right of my podium that Karen, our trusty stage manager, blinks when she wants to talk to me. I can talk to her or the sound department on the headset that's to my left. I put it on (careful not to ruin my tousled—but extremely styled—hair) and pushed the listen button and she asked if we were ready to go. We were going to try to do a "stop only if somebody dies" run-through. I told her my orchestra was tuned, she told me to break a leg, and the houselights dimmed.

My red light went on, which meant we were about to begin. There was the requisite "No photographing or taping" announcement, and my red light went off, which meant I should start the opening number.

We got through the whole show with only a few mess-ups (one of the female ensemble members' wigs fell off and landed right at the edge of the stage. I, of course, put it on and conducted the rest of Act One in half drag).

Right after the bows, Mason and Kris ran up to the pit and asked if we could have a quick dinner. I hadn't had a chance to really dish with them since before the Sitzprobe.

We went to a sushi place on Eight Avenue and 45th.

"Forget the show," Kris said to me, breaking apart his wooden chopsticks. "What's the gossip?"

Mason rolled his eyes, but didn't stop me. He was Mr. "*We Are All God's Children*" but loves a good *scandale* once in a while.

"Well," I said, double-dipping my avocado sushi into my low sodium soy sauce. "Tiffany told me that Fritz couldn't be found all Friday afternoon. He later claimed he was looking for a better parking space."

"For an hour and a half?" Kris said, with the line reading of Jackee from *227*. "He was parking *something*, but it wasn't his car, OK???" he sassed.

I frowned. "B plus," I said, ranking his joke, and then asked him, "Any dish from you?"

"Well," he dropped his voice and leaned in towards us. "If you look to your left, you'll notice Elaine eating with Naomi and Nandita, but," he over-dictionized, "*no Jay.*"

I looked and saw all three ensemble girls sitting together still wearing full stage makeup, which is never appropriate outside a Broadway theatre. Onstage: gorgeous. Offstage: Bozo the whore.

Mason also looked at Elaine. "So?" he asked, blowing on his Miso soup/liquid salt lick.

"So Jaylaine don't spend so much time together anymore."

He raised one eyebrow. "Methinks he is preparing her for an ixnay."

"And you think *you're* the cause of this?" Why was every dancer I knew so crazily confident?

"Child," he said with lips pursed to the side, "all I can say is he told me he wanted some time to talk to me, *alone*, after last night's rehearsal, OK???"

Wow. Maybe Kris *was* making headway. "So, did you have the private chat?"

He got annoyed. "I *can't* with ol' eagle eye making me feel like Richard Jewell!"

It took me a minute to get that reference. Then I remembered. He was the guy who was accused by the FBI of setting the bomb at the Atlanta Olympics but later exonerated. Phew! Being with Kris requires me to constantly mentally scan through every CNN broadcast in my memory bank.

Kris tilted his head to the right, and sure enough, Karen was sitting there with her stage management team.

I began to think, though, why didn't Kris just meet Jay after rehearsal? I doubt Karen's following him home, and the more I thought about it, they would make a cute couple, yet . . . as I was thinking I suddenly felt Karen's eyes boring into me from two tables away. Was my mind being read? I turned away and tried to make it blank. I stole a glance to my right and, sure enough, Karen locked eyes with me. I feebly waved and started coughing. It was a combination of wasabi and terror. Wow. No wonder Kris is policing himself so thoroughly. No one wants to deal with the wrath of an angry stage manager.

We got back to the theatre for the Gypsy run-through. Usually, before the first preview, there is a run-through for all the other casts on Broadway.

I got into the pit, and you could feel the energy from the audience.

"Stephen, you Broadway bitch, good luck!" I turned around

in the pit toward the voice but didn't see anybody sitting in back of me.

"Stephen! Down here!" I looked down towards the seat cushion and there she was, Traci Lyn! The 4'10" belter I played for when I first reconnected with Mason at the *Whatever Happened to John the Baptist?* audition.

"I'm so glad you came!" I said, leaning over the pit and giving her a kiss.

"Mason invited me! I can't wait!"

"Stephen! *Attention!*" I shuddered as I heard Françoise's voice.

I turned back around. "What?"

She pointed to the red light. "La lumière rouge!"

"Françoise," I said, threateningly, "do you want me to report your language infraction to the union?"

She paled. "I thought that was only towards the other musicians . . ."

"No, Françoise! All the time, tous les temps!" *Tous les temps?*

"Great, now I have to write *myself* up."

I picked up the headset.

"Ready?" Karen asked.

"Let's go!" I said.

The houselights dimmed and the audience roared. That's the best thing about a Gypsy run-through. The crowd always goes crazy, even if the show sucks.

Vince did great in the opening number, holding the last note the longest he ever has. During the applause, I could hear lots of people murmuring, "Who is he? Where's he from?"

Then Anike "drove" on in her pink convertible and got entrance applause. I could tell she loved it! Passive-aggressive Jesse got loud and long laughs after every comic bit, and each number got rousing applause. Conducting is so much fun, because even though I have to look down a lot to cue my orchestra, I also get to watch the show! It was certainly very different from being in the rehearsal studio. The lights and costumes make each number *so* much more exciting. At the beginning of "(I wish They All Could Be) California Girls" a giant map of the U.S. hangs in the back. When Vince starts the song by singing about "the East Coast girls," a light hits the right side of the map from Maine to Florida and suddenly you can see through it! Naomi and Nandita (on a hidden platform) are in fall coats, brushing out their hair in rhythm, and then their light switches off. Then, going with the lyrics, the same thing happens for the South (Rachel and Sarah in cotillion dresses with sandy hair), and the Midwest (Elaine and Tammy in polka-dot dresses with red hair).

When it gets to the actual "I wish they all could be California Girls" lyric, the map of the U.S. is replaced by a giant map just of California and all the girls, who quickly changed their wigs to long blonde ones, and their outfits to wild '60s bikinis, do the watusi with Anike in the middle.

I had tried to imagine what it would look like while we were in the rehearsal studio, but I had no idea until I saw it with the set, costumes, wigs, and lights. That's the skill that Mason, Kris, and Craig have. They're able to visualize a creative idea in their head and then work with the artistic staff to make it happen.

The coolest part was, when the map changed to California and all the girls appeared in their multicolored bikinis, the audience applauded! In the middle of the number!

At intermission, Mason ran up to the pit.

"It's going great!" I said.

"Yeah, but it's a Gypsy run-through. We're never going to have this good an audience again."

He was right. Theatre people are just naturally more expressive, plus pretty much the whole audience was friends with the cast.

I didn't care. It was so great to do songs and actually get a real response, instead of ending every number to Karen saying, "OK . . . applause, applause, applause a-a-a-and lights back up."

The second act went even better than the first, and the audience went crazy during the megamix.

Everyone was exhausted backstage and rushed to leave since tomorrow was the first preview.

I changed quickly and was one of the first to hightail it out of the theatre.

I was waiting for my train when I unavoidably came face-to-face with . . . Staci!

I hadn't seen that icicle since the beginning of rehearsal. Now that the show was cast, she was able to move on to new projects, until we had to replace people in our cast.

She was wearing a long, puffy down coat. And a long, puffy, downcast face.

"Um . . . I saw the run-through," she quietly intoned.

"Great!" I said, praying for a train to come.

"Um . . . I thought you did a good job," she said wanly.

"Thanks!"

There was silence

"So . . . great casting!" I offered.

"It's my job," she said, shrugging.

Maybe I should take a downtown train just to avoid her, I thought.

"Are you . . ." What could I talk about with her??? ". . . casting anything else?"

She nodded. "Uh . . . a musical version of *Dude, Where's My Car?*

She waited for my reaction.

Thankfully an express train roared through so I didn't have to enthusiastically lie.

"So, who's the Ashton Kutcher part?" I asked, acting like I had already praised the project.

"Um . . . he's new. Owen Berman."

I shrugged. "Never heard of him."

She went on. "Someone told me that he's the nephew of someone but I don't know who."

What interesting details she had.

Thankfully the train arrived.

We had to stand, and as we exited the station, she started droning on and on about trying to cast the offstage voice of the car. Does the car talk in the movie?

"He's gotta be super masculine. The composer keeps saying that when he says 'Vroom Vroom,' you have to want to go boom boom."

I didn't respond.

"Uh . . . you know. Have sex with him."

The train stopped and even though it was 59th Street (twelve blocks away from my apartment), I impulsively dashed off.

"Don't you live uptown?" Staci asked as the train doors closed.

I pointed to my ears to imply "I can't hear you" even though I had just exited and was probably only ten inches away from her. The doors closed. I breathed a sigh of relief, ran upstairs, and hailed a cab at Columbus Circle.

So that's it. Hell Week is over.

And now, since my body is a prune, let me moisturize and go to sleep, because Tuesday is the FIRST PREVIEW!!!

Thirty-One

I'm in my dressing room getting into my "blacks." I don't wear a tuxedo to conduct because it seems too uptight for a rock show. I have a sassy black blazer I bought on sale at J. Crew and these great black trousers that the Vince Fontaine character wore in *Grease* and one of the wardrobe people gave me after that show closed. I look dressed up but not tight-ass-y.

Anyhoo, I can't believe there is a paying audience filling up the theatre right now! Well, not really filling up. It's only the first preview, so the show doesn't have any buzz yet. It's probably only going to be two-thirds full. And not really paying. At least not all of them. I'm sure half the audience is being comped. There are insider industry people whom the publicist and marketing team offer free tickets to, so the people who are paying can think the show is selling well and the cast can have a nice-size audience.

There are also those people who love going to first previews. Whether it's a flop or a hit, it's always cool to say you were there. People still talk about the first preview of *Titanic* when the show was four hours long. Yowtch! That boat must have sunk slo-o-owly.

And, of course, there are Anike's fans. Fans of the soap, fans of her Broadway days, and fans of *The National Enquirer*.

Karen just called half hour over the loudspeaker.

"Half hour, please, the call is half hour. Half hour, please."

I've always wondered, who is the stage manager saying "please" to? The half hour itself? To the cast? Doesn't there have to be the command form of a verb? Asking us to observe or acknowledge something, *that* would merit a "please." Like, "*Observe* the fact that it's half hour, please." A whole sentence can't just be two nouns and the word please.

Half hour call is also when the stage manager announces if any understudies will be on. Shockingly, tonight she said, "Heads up, everyone. Tonight Whitney Blair will be on for Elaine Marcas."

Why would Elaine miss the first preview? Was she sick? Whitney had rehearsed a couple of the numbers when the different ensemble girls had costume fittings, but she had never gone through the whole show. I'm going to go visit her in the dressing room and wish her luck.

15-MINUTE CALL

Wow! I went upstairs and walked past the stage manager's office and heard Karen in a *rage*.

"I'm going to fucking *kill* him!" I heard her stamping around the office. "He *has* to hook up with Jay before the first preview! I warned him to keep his hands on his own dance belt!"

I had to get the scoop! "What happened?" I asked as I walked in.

Karen's face was all red. "Well, I got this message at 7:15 tonight."

She pushed play on the answering machine. There was an odd sound that I soon realized was sobbing. Karen pushed fast forward. Finally:

"*Sorry. It's Elaine. I c-can't come in tonight . . . Jay and I broke . . . broke—*" More sobbing. Then a clattering of the phone receiver and finally, a click.

I assumed that the ellipse contained the word "up."

"Did you talk to Jay?" I asked.

"No." Karen said, her eyes blazing as she dialed the phone. "Kris is the one I want to talk to. *He's* on the artistic staff and has a responsibility to the show." She slammed down the receiver. "Of course, he's not answering his cell phone."

I didn't want to bear the brunt of her pissed off-ness, so I backed out of her office and ran right into awkward Craig.

He looked left and right. "Show's about to start. I'm gonna watch from out front." He quickly scurried past me.

He radiated guilt and I radiated nosiness. I *must* find out what he's up to! Is he back together with Jeffrey? Did he steal something from my apartment when he moved out? Come to think of it, I haven't seen my DVD of Streisand's *A Star Is Born* in a while. But if he stole that, he did me a favor. I never want to see Barbra rocking out while shaking her perm ever again. It's literally an antidote to Viagra.

OK, Karen just announced five minutes. I've gotta run to the pit!

INTERMISSION

The show's going great. Passive-aggressive Jesse is driving me crazy, though. At the beginning of his song I'm conducting a vamp, meaning I'm repeating the same measure of music over and over again. When he says a certain line, it's my cue to go on and then we start the song together. The vamp I'm playing is four beats long, and I told him if he says his line on beat one, it times out perfectly. When the sentence begins on the first beat, it's over by beat four and we can start the song right away. But lately he's been starting the line around beat two, so by the time he's done, I'm back on beat one and have to go all the way to beat four before we can start the song. Yesterday he told me he couldn't hear where the first beat was so I told him to watch me in the pit and he'd see me conduct it.

Of course, he missed it again today. I saw him backstage right when intermission began.

"Hey, Stephen, sorry it didn't work out again." *P.S. He didn't sound sorry.* "But you know when I say that line, I'm looking out towards the horizon, so," he shrugged, "I can't see you."

I was *très* annoyed. "Jesse, if you look closer, you'll notice that the 'horizon' has a monitor!" Throughout the whole show, there's a video camera aimed at me. There's a monitor backstage that the cast can watch me on when they have to sing offstage. I'm also broadcast to two video monitors that hang in front of the balcony so the onstage actors don't always have to look at me in the pit for cues. When you go to a Broadway show, look for the monitors and watch the conductor. Although, don't judge the conductor by his black-and-white video image. I've seen the way I look in them and it highlights all my worst features. You've heard that television adds ten pounds? Well, Broadway video monitors add 40% ugliness.

He nodded. "Oh, the monitors. I never thought of that."

That was easy!

He added with his signature smile, "Have you always made the singers follow you on your other Broadway shows?"

I started to answer, but he cut me off with, "I apologize."

Finally! An apology.

He continued. "I forgot this was your first one . . ." He whistled as he walked off to his dressing room.

Mofo!

I'm now making him a list of the parts where I follow the singer:

The ending of Vince's song (I watch him till he's ready to cut off)

Anike's Act One ballad (she slows down the middle if she's really feeling it)

Wait a minute. This is so junior high! I feel like I'm making him a list of the times he ignored me during lunch and then taping it to his locker (me and Kevin Gerber, circa 1983). I can't believe I'm letting his dickery get to me. There are certain moments of the show that have to be set to keep it flowing smoothly, and he's just embarrassed that he keeps screwing it up.

That's it—I'm conducting his Act Two song with my middle finger.

Oh yeah, Karen dropped off a note saying we're having a meeting after the show. She called Kris's cell phone and told him that it was about changing the finale, but she's actually going to lambaste him for the Jay liaison. She wants me and Mason there supposedly for support, but I think it's because she wants us to get scared seeing her in action so *we'll* never cross her.

TWO A.M.

OK, here goes. I should go to sleep, but I have to write.

Me, Kris, and Mason filed into the stage manager's office after the show. Karen was still with the backstage crew going over some notes.

"Mase," Kris said as he took off his coat. "The finale is great. There's nothing to change."

Mason looked at me with eyes that read, *"What do I say?"*

"Oh, and guess what?" Kris asked, sitting down.

"Uh . . .what?" I offered, after a lengthy silence.

"Jay and I finally had our 'little talk.'" He laughed and shook his head.

"Yeah, Kris," I said, getting annoyed at his avoidance of the obvious. "We know."

"How do you know?" he asked as Karen walked in. Mason and I sat up straight. Obviously, we both had scary teachers in elementary school.

"OK, Kris." She said as she shut the door. "Before we get into your blatant disregard for the good of the show, I'd like to know where you were tonight."

"Huh?" He looked at me and Mason. "What's going on?"

"Answer the question," Karen said.

"Karen, I told you last week that I had to miss the first preview because of my cousin's baby shower."

Karen blinked. "Oh. That's right."

"Craig took notes for me tonight." He looked around the office. "Why isn't he at this meeting, by the way?" he asked.

"He wasn't invited," Karen said quickly and then started lecturing. "Listen, Kris, I warned you about the danger of Jay and—"

"Oh, stop already with the danger warnings. I'm not your Will Robinson." I think I was the only one in the room who knew he was referring to the *Lost in Space* classic line "*Danger, Will Robinson.*"

"I never said you were my Will Rogers." *Huh?* "I specifically advised you not to get involved with Jay, even going so far as to have your assistant run any private rehearsals and—"

"Yeah, exactly. It's your fault," Kris said, confusing us all.

"Pardon?" Karen asked haughtily.

"Well," Kris began, "what I started to say before you walked in and vacuum-sealed all joy outside"—*ooh, nice metaphor*—"is that Jay called me at home last night."

"Aha!" Karen said.

Kris waved her away and continued, looking at me and Mason. "He said he had been meaning to speak to me about the show."

"That old excuse . . ." I muttered. I did that in college when I had a crush on my Ear Training teacher.

"*Hi, Mr. Meyers, I'm sorry to call you at home, but (giggle) I forgot what the homework is.*"

"There is no homework, Stephen."

"So, I guess I'm free tonight for . . . whatever."

The rest of the conversation essentially consisted of him saying "I guess" and "good-bye."

Ooh, Kris was still talking.

". . . finally asked me what it was like having an assistant. It seemed out of left field, but I told him that it was helpful and that Craig does a great job, blah blah blah, but the more I tried to steer the conversation towards gently nudging him out of the closet slash inviting him to spend the night—"

"Aha!" Sherlock Holmes, I mean Karen, said again.

"—the more he brought the conversation back to having an assistant. I thought maybe he was asking to assist me on my next show, but I was not interested in talking business. I quickly told him that I'm not looking for a new assistant because Craig is *such* a great guy, etc., etc., etc., and then I started dropping some major hints. You know, 'I have a great DVD I'd love to show you,' 'I sure could use a massage tonight,' 'I'm *so* not in the mood to go to sleep,' etc."

I nodded, having tried all those lines (unsuccessfully) in my day.

"Finally, he said he was real happy to hear that I thought Craig was a good guy because it helped make up his mind."

"Make up his mind? He wants Craig as *his* assistant?" asked Mason.

"No, Innocent Millicent!" Kris made his hands into a megaphone. "He wants Craig as his LOVER!"

"What?!" I screamed.

Kris ignored me. "He said they had fooled around a month ago (*we were still going out!*) and Craig was pushing him towards something more serious, and," Kris suddenly turned towards Karen, "thanks to the *private rehearsal time they spent together"*—Karen pretended to adjust the pencils in her bun so she could look away from Kris—"Jay was really getting to know and like Craig. He just needed the final push to make it official."

"And you gave him the push," I said, halfheartedly.

"And he gave Elaine the shove," Mason concluded.

"Jay broke up with Elaine?" Kris asked.

We filled him in.

"That's why that motherfucker's been looking so guilty towards me," I said to myself/out loud . . .

"Why?" asked Mason.

Shit. I forgot he didn't know.

"You know," I started. "I, uh . . . used to go out with him. A long time ago."

"So, Karen," Kris said bitterly/triumphantly, "how does it feel to be Yente the Matchmaker?"

"*You* gave the final push in the bush!" Karen added, sixth-grader style.

Mason broke it up. "Children, I think we're all tired." He turned towards Karen. "Karen, you tried your best, but I guess you can't control everything."

"Stop comforting her!" Kris wailed. "I'm the one with the broken heart!"

"Kris," Mason said, "you can take comfort in knowing that your gaydar is more powerful than any other mortal's."

Kris smirked. "Actually, I've been thinking . . . our adorable lead Vince recently broke up with his girlfriend—"

"Don't even try it," Karen warned.

"Well, a girl can hope," Kris said as he put his leather coat back on.

We all left and Mason and I went uptown together.

I was feeling really depressed. I thought that Craig cheated on Jeffrey to be with me because I was special, but I guess I should have realized if he could do it to Jeffrey, he would probably do it to me. I felt like an idiot.

Mason got out at my stop with me. "I don't know what's going on, Stephen, but you look too depressed to walk home from the subway alone."

I thought that was sweet of him and invited him up because I wanted someone to talk to. I knew Jackson would be asleep by now.

"Stephen, are you upset about the show?" Mason asked me as I unlocked my apartment door. "I think it went pretty well."

"No." I decided to be honest without revealing everything. "I guess . . . I know it's stupid, but, I guess it hurts me to think of an ex-boyfriend pursuing someone besides me."

I started to make hot chocolate for us, i.e., put the Swiss Miss (*with* marshmallows) into a mug with microwaved water.

Mason was petting Heather. "But if he's your ex, why does it matter? Did you care when he was with Jeffrey?"

I decided to not answer the question directly and brought the mugs to my little breakfast table next to my piano.

I sighed and finally said, "I feel like there's something wrong with me."

Mason laughed and said, "There is, but it's great! It's what makes you who you are."

I smiled and shook my head. "I think it's what keeps me alone."

Mason looked at me. "Haven't you chosen to be alone?"

"No!" I said, quickly. "I want to be with somebody! Somebody who loves me . . . besides my dog." I motioned towards Heather, who was lying on top of my quilt and pawing the air, trying to get Mason to pet her again.

"Well," Mason said. "My experience is that a lot of my friends choose to be alone without realizing it."

"Do you think I've 'chosen to be alone'?" I asked.

"Do you?" he asked, Monikah style.

"I don't know," I said, taking the marshmallows out of the hot chocolate with a spoon and eating them. "I don't think so. I just don't think I've found the right guy yet."

He looked at me over his mug with his piercing brown eyes. "Maybe you have found him, but you don't know it's him yet."

Have I? Who? I mean, whom?

I took a long sip and finally said, "I just don't understand why so many people can have relationships and I can't."

Mason stopped drinking and put down his mug.

"Stephen, I think you can." Suddenly, he walked to my side of the table. What's happening? Was he after my last remaining marshmallow in my *Ragtime* mug? Wait, he wasn't going for my mug. He was going for my *mug* (à la forties slang)! My eyes opened wide as he puckered up and kissed me. On the lips! On the chocolaty lips.

He sat back down and we stared at each other.

I had never really thought of Mason as a boyfriend. I mean, I got along with him really great and I certainly thought he was cute, but I had been focusing on Craig for the last year. All right, if you're gonna force me to be honest, I do remember a *few* times I considered what it would be like to have Mason as "more than a friend," but it was followed by incredible guilt. I couldn't betray Craig.

I know, the irony is palpable.

OK, I decided to consider this development. What would it be like to have Mason as a boyfriend? He wasn't moody *and* he made me laugh. And he was talented. I gave him a once-over. He looked so cute with his messy hat hair and his plaid shirt sticking out of the bottom of his sweater.

I suddenly remembered what I thought when I was with Anike on that fire escape. I had felt I was ready to meet a challenge and actually make the smart choice. I thought it through: Did I want another Craig who had a Jeffrey waiting at home? Did I want to spend my time trying to tear Mason away from Jason? Also, as much as I kept saying that *Craig* was the one who was cheating on Jeffrey and I was just an innocent bystander, I know I played an equal part. Seeing Staci's awful-looking face (not her regular one, the one after her boyfriend cheated on her) was the last straw. No matter what part you play, cheating sucks. Do I want to cause that kind of pain again?

No.

As much as I like Mason, which I admit I do *a little*, I'm making a vow I am not going to repeat the same mistakes. I had just told Mason that I want someone who loves me. And that meant, *just* me and not me and their other boyfriend.

I smiled and shook my head. "Mason, we can't do this."

Mason looked mortified. "Stephen, I know! It's wrong!"

He pushed his chair back and started to get up.

"Mason," I said, getting up too.

"I'm so sorry!" he said as he scrambled, trying to find his coat.

"Don't be sorry," I said, leading him back to the table. "It actually made me feel great!" It was true. Mason was a wonderful guy. And it felt great to be liked by a guy like him.

"Wow," Mason said, calming down. He drank some more cocoa. "I can't believe I did that." He shook his head and laughed. "This has been a freaky day."

"Yeah," I said, but I didn't feel so bad anymore. As fucked up as I've been in the past, I know things are gonna change for me as long as I hold up my end of the bargain.

"Listen, Mason," I said. "I love this show and I love working with you." He nodded. "And being friends with you." I stuck out my hand to shake. "No weirdness."

He shook it. "No weirdness."

"Let's do what I did after I saw *Showgirls*." He looked quizzical. "Pretend it never happened," I explained.

He laughed and we hugged. Of course Heather immediately ran over and jumped on us.

"I love your dog," Mason said, as he bent down to kiss her.

I looked at him. Perfect boyfriend material.

For Jason.

It was OK. Because I'm becoming perfect boyfriend material, too!

Thirty-Two

I'm sitting at my table eating a balanced breakfast (whole wheat toast, Egg Beaters, and soy cheese) because I need my strength. This is the most important week for the show. All the cuts and finagling that Mason, Kris, and I have been doing over the last few weeks of previews are done and the show is now frozen, meaning that no more changes can be made. The most famous use of that expression was uttered by Ethel Merman during previews of *Gypsy*. Arthur Laurents, Jerome Robbins, and Stephen Sondheim had been tinkering throughout the whole preview process, and finally Ethel decided that she'd had it and proclaimed, "Call me Miss Birdseye, this show is frozen!" Sassy!

I can't believe that the show opens this Thursday! It used to be that the reviewers all came on opening night, and then scrambled to write their reviews so they could get in the next day's paper. It also put an incredible amount of pressure on the performers because everything depended on that night. Now, the four or so performances before opening are deemed "critics' nights" and the critics come to those so they have time to write their reviews. Opening night has gone from being the most pressurized of all, to having no critics at it! It's more a night for friends/family and stars to come and then go to the party.

Well, the day after the Swiss Miss kiss, I began to look at Mason differently. I tried to treat him the same, but it's like that kiss knocked down a Berlin Wall inside me and all my feelings for him were East Germany. They're finally free to mill around my head, and, as much as I try to deport them, they refuse to get exit visas.

Wow. That was a long headachy metaphor to say, I think I'm falling in love with another unavailable man. We've been seeing more and more of each other and I can't stop thinking about him "that way."

We'll meet for brunch and both reach for the sugar (not the regular white kind, the Sugar in the Raw brand that I love. It's supposed to be healthier because it's not processed . . . so I can feel healthy while being unhealthy), and our hands will touch and I'll feel a crazy jolt of electricity. I don't think it's because I sit too close to the TV (my mother's stupid theory: *You're two inches away from that screen! You're body's becoming electrified!*). I think it's because we're both in a perpetual state of tension. The good news is we haven't done *anything* about it. Or even discussed it. It just seems like we're a couple . . . except we don't have sex. It's like Parts One and Two of *The Thorn Birds* before Richard Chamberlain smooches her on the beach. I don't dare bring up Jason's name, but I keep hoping Mason's going to tell me that they broke up.

The good news is that this whole thing is very different from my affair with Craig. Even though I think Mason is a cutie, that's not the only reason I'm into him. I kinda like everything about him, not just his perpetually messy hair and intense eyes. Well, everything but the severe lack of backbone, which still comes up. Two days ago, a cashier at Fairway blatantly gave him change for a five even though I saw him give her a ten. He thought I didn't notice, but when we left I confronted him and said, "Mason, when you have respect for yourself, people have respect for you." I also told him "honesty is the best policy" and "every cloud has a silver lining" because I realized how trite my first statement sounded. But the reason certain things are trite is because they're true! He said he was frustrated as well. He also said he didn't know what it would take to make him change, but he was working on it. Probably the same way I'm working on retiling my bathroom . . . aka every two weeks I flip through a Braun Catalog and then fade out.

But speaking of working on yourself, I'm proud to say I haven't been trying to trick him into anything. We always say good night with an (electrified) handshake, and I haven't attempted to lure him to my lair. (*Can you help me one night to put together this IKEA table?*)

Oh yeah. More updates. Craig has moved in with his new dancer lover, Jay (!) but, oddly enough, I don't seem to care. Elaine's come back to the show and there's always some backstage ignoring/telling off/crying happening. I've noticed Craig always has to have some drama in his life and it's delicious not to be starring in it! Jay mentioned to Kris that he thought it was too soon for Craig and him to move in together, but Craig had nowhere to live. Evil Ronald is doing more renovations at his Trump castle, and Jackson was sick of being woken up at 8 a.m. by pounding hammers, so he moved back to his place for the time being and kicked Craig out.

Oh yeah, my mom called me this morning.

"Stephen, you'll be happy to know I can go to the opening of your little show." I heard her grinding coffee in the background.

"I guess your tour was cancelled," I said, trying to hide my glee.

"Actually, I got the date wrong," she said. "It starts next week. Oops, I've got to brew this or else some of the flavor is lost. Ciao!"

I held the receiver in my hand for a minute and then slowly hung up. I seemed to be in a slight state of shock that she was still going on tour. It's weird, but I felt like a rock had been placed on my shoulders. I guess I'd always had a fantasy that once I was making enough money on Broadway, she wouldn't have to tour anymore and we'd have more time to do things. Not that I'd literally support her, but between her investments and in-town gigs, I could spot her the difference of whatever she'd make on the road.

Wait, the phone's ringing.

LATER

Jeez, Louise! What a crazy phone call.

"Stephen, it's Jackson. We have to talk and you can't be judgmental."

"Yes to the first, no to the second."

"I'm not joking!" he said, sounding frantic.

"What's the matter?" I asked, pushing aside my egg whites and opening the bag that held my almond croissant purchased from the French bakery on 74th. I figured I could have 5/8ths healthy breakfast and 3/8ths breakfast that tasted good.

"Listen, I haven't told you the reason I moved back to my apartment."

"Yes, you have," I said, between bites. "Ronald's apartment is getting more renovation."

"No. That's not it."

Hmm . . . this could be good.

He sighed. "Well, normally I've been staying in the theatre after the matinees to go over my blocking, but I'm feeling secure now, so I decided to come home between shows." I took a bite of the French almondy goodness and thought how bizarre it was that people put butter on croissants. Butter is essentially the only ingredient! It's like putting a stick of Hotel Bar on a slab of Land O'Lakes. It's redundant, people. Oh, he was still talking.

". . . so, I walked into the apartment and I was tidying up, you know what a slob Ronald is, when I thought I heard shouting from upstairs. I ran up to see what was going on, but by the time

I navigated the crazy spiral staircase that Ronald had put in, the shouting stopped."

That was the story? A poltergeist in his apartment? "Is that the end?" I asked.

"Let me go on," he said, annoyed. "Ronald was supposed to be at work, but instead he was standing there in a *towel!*"

Hmm . . . seeing that profusion of back hair would certainly make *me* move out.

"So," I said, trying not to be too hopeful, "maybe he was arguing with one of the construction people."

"Stephen, there *were* no construction people!" he yelled. "I opened the upstairs door to the hallway and saw a young guy getting onto the elevator."

"Huh. Maybe he was visiting someone else . . ." I offered, trying to see how much he knew.

"Please!" Jackson snorted. "When I popped my head out the apartment door, he looked at me and yelled 'Your friend is a sex sicko.'"

I guess someone didn't respond that kindly to the Jacuzzi offer.

"Jackson, I'm really sorry." I was. As much as I loved Ronald getting busted, I felt bad for Jackson. I also felt bad that Jackson heard me say that with my mouth full. I knew I should stop eating because the story was so serious, but I can't resist any form of oil, carbs, and sugar. I discreetly swallowed.

He went on. "Ronald assured me this was the first time he'd ever done anything like that . . ."

"Did you believe him?" I knew he did.

"I did at first, and then I noticed . . ." he paused and his voice got small, "he was holding a picture and resumé."

Finally. I didn't have to keep the secret any longer.

"Stephen, this is his little scam. He gets young actors to come over somehow—"

I filled Jackson in on what I knew.

"Why didn't you tell me?" he raged.

"Would you have listened?" I asked

He didn't respond.

I helped him out. "It's not you. Everyone's the same. Did *I* listen when you told me to dump Craig?"

He laughed a little. "No, and it drove me crazy."

I was smooshing my finger on the plate to get stray crumbs. "Listen, Jackson. We each realize things when we're ready. You can beg and plead all you want, but a boll weevil stays in its cocoon till it's ready to come out. That little critter won't open its eyes until—"

Damn Dr. Phil! How dare he infiltrate my personal conversations! I curtailed my analogy and asked Jackson why he was finally telling me if this all happened last week.

"Well, I moved back to my apartment because I was so angry. But I didn't want to end everything on terrible terms. So, a couple of minutes ago I decided to call him at work to see if we could meet for lunch, and they said he doesn't work at the agency anymore!" He sounded hysterical. "Do you think he did something drastic?"

No way. Ronald would never harm what he loved most: himself.

"Jackson," I said calmly, "Did you try him at home?"

"Oh." He snapped out of it. "I didn't think of that."

"Look, I have three-way calling. I'll try right now."

I was smart enough to block my number so Ronald wouldn't know it was me.

It rang once.

"Hello?" said Ronald's impatient voice. "Hello?" I was hanging up when I heard, "Owen? Let's be reasonable . . ."

I clicked the off button and called Jackson back.

"Who's Owen?" I asked.

"I don't know. Maybe the guy," Jackson said. "I guess I'm glad he's still alive, though."

"Yeah, so am I," I said, praying that you can't see eye rolling over the phone.

"Stephen, I'm gonna call him. I hate loose ends."

"OK, and . . ." I had to ask. "Did I keep the judgmental-ness down?"

He laughed. "Shockingly, yes. Thumbs up to Dr. Phil!"

He hung up.

Actually, Mason really deserved the credit. You could tell him anything and he was understanding. I'm glad he was rubbing off on me. Even though he's not actually "rubbing off" on me, if you get my drift. All right, I'm a little horny! It's been a while, folks.

Wow. A lot has happened since I started writing this diary five months ago. Once opening night is over, I'll officially be a Broadway conductor. The funny part is that some people don't know I'm doing the show and are still calling me to sub! Phil, from *Smile Out*, left me a message asking me to play this Wednesday before opening, but I have it in my contract that I can't miss any shows during the week before opening. But the more I think about it, the Geisenshlaags only put that there so I wouldn't miss any critics' performances. It makes sense. No actor wants to be reviewed unless they feel 100% comfortable. In truth, Françoise has conducted a few shows during this preview period, so I was able to watch from the audience to hear what the show really sounds like. She's very clear when she conducts, but the actors have made it known that they prefer me. Here's the thing: when you conduct, you're leading the pace of the show in a lot of ways. If your cue to start a song is after a laugh line that happens to get a small laugh one night, you have to be ready to come in earlier. Françoise was very literal. She always had the same timing. On certain nights, some songs got extra big applause and she would cut it off by starting the scene change music. She didn't understand that each performance is different. Also, she spent most of the time looking at her score. Even though most musicians know when they should enter after they've had a few measures rest, it makes them feel more a part of the show when they're cued back in by the conductor. And actors appreciate looking down from the stage and seeing the conductor connect with them. I've given her some notes on all these things and she's definitely making an effort to be less rigid. The best news is, she's never made a mistake and she's keeping her multilingual "gifts" to a minimum.

I decided to call Karen. She picked up after several rings.

"Karen, it's Stephen. Sorry to call you at home, but—"

"Who's having an affair now?" she asked.

I laughed. "No one. I just wanted to know the critics' schedule for this week."

"Hmm . . ." she seemed to think. "I'll tell you, but you can't let anyone in the cast know. It freaks them out to know when certain critics will be there."

"Don't worry," I said. "As the Go-Go's once said, 'our lips are sealed.'"

"Who are the GoGo's?" she asked, annoyed. "And what do you mean 'our'? I just told you not to tell anyone. Is there someone else on the line?"

She was obviously heavily into stage managing during the '80s and had little time for pop FM radio.

"Forget it, Karen, I won't tell anyone."

She gave me the list, and turns out, no critics were coming Wednesday matinee, so I *could* sub *Smile Time!* I called Phil back and told him I was in. It only makes sense to do it. What if *Flowerchild* closes the weekend after we open, like *Rags* or *Carrie?* I've got to keep up my connections. Besides, it'll be the same as when Françoise conducts and I'm in the audience, but this time, I just won't be in the audience. I know it won't make any difference, and once the show opens, she'll definitely be subbing for me. Might as well get the cast and the orchestra used to it now.

Hey! Stop thinking I'm full of justifications! It's all very logical. Anyhoo, tonight some of the second-string critics are coming so I'm excited. I'll write soon!

Thirty-Three

*M*y sister Dianne is staying with me through opening. She thought it would be a lot calmer for her than staying with our mom. I agreed, and I didn't mind the company. Plus I appreciate her traveling all the way in from Michigan.

We had breakfast at the Utopia diner on Amsterdam and 72nd.

She looked good. Her face looked refreshed and her bod had a little more curve than I remembered at Christmas. She said it was 'cause she was doing Pilates. I find that mode of exercise way too subtle. I took one class: "*Focus on your inner ab muscles . . . in a few months you'll definitely see a result.*" First of all, I want results *now*. Second, I don't want to waste my focus on inner muscles—I want to focus on the muscles that *count* in a gay bar. Aka biceps and pecs.

"Stephen," she said, after we ordered. "I'm really proud of you."

"Thanks," I said, trying to sound excited.

She looked at me. "What's with you? You're more low energy than when you had mono in tenth grade."

That was a fun memory. A month sitting home playing Clue with the maid. At least I had my show albums then. I memorized the Broadway *and* Spanish versions of *Evita* ("No me plurio, Argentina!").

She was right. I just wasn't looking forward to the opening as much as I used to. Maybe I was tired from previews and all the typing I've been doing. I've transferred all my diary into one file on my computer. I figured once this show opens, this book is *done*. I'm finally working full time on Broadway, ergo: happy ending. Tag Line: *I am . . . a sub . . . no more!* I decided to tell Dianne all about what I've been writing.

"Ooh! I wanna read it!"

"You'll have to wait till it's published!" I singsonged.

"OK." She opened up two Nutrasweets for her coffee.

Wait! Where was the begging? This was not the Dianne I grew up with. This was the new Dr. Phil/Pilates Dianne and it was throwing me for a loop. I actually *wanted* her to read it. And then tell me it was fabulous. I needed some positive feedback. The only feedback I've gotten is from Monikah, which had the hollow ring of silence. Essentially because it was silence.

"OK," I said, conceding to Dianne. "I can't argue with you."

Obviously, because she wasn't arguing. "It's in 'My Documents' under 'Bestselling Diary,'" I informed her, putting ketchup on my home fries but *not* my eggs. Eggs with ketchup always seems very straight man to me.

"I'll read it while you're at the matinee," she said with a mouthful of pancakes *sans* syrup. That wasn't 'cause she was on a diet. It was the way she always ate them. I think it was to spite my mother, who always bragged about bringing home "pure Vermont maple syrup" whenever she'd tour through any area in Vermont.

My cell phone rang. I saw Mason's number on caller ID.

"Hello," I said in my *"I'm in a restaurant"* voice.

"Stephen, I have great news! The buzz is that we're getting

good reviews from at least two of the bigger critics who've come so far!"

"That's great!" I said, not feeling it 100%.

"A-a-a-and . . ." he said slowly and then blurted, "the Geisenshlaags read the straight play I wrote and want to option it! They're actually giving me a non-Geisenshlaags-style high price because they think it could also be a great movie!"

I actually *was* happy now.

"Mason, that's great!" I said in my *"I'm in the privacy of my own home"* voice. I, of course, got shushed by an elderly couple at the counter. Have you noticed that the older people get, the fewer social traditions they follow? They obviously figure that they've spent their whole lives being polite and now, finally, comes the honesty years. I'm constantly being told to "Get out of the aisle" or "You are a *very* rude young man" by those past retirement. It doesn't really bother me because I plan on being the same way. The only thing about elders that gets my goat is when they say, "I'm 86 years *young*." OK, people, here's the thing. If you had just said I'm 86 years old, I'd have taken it in without much notice. But don't you realize that replacing *old* with *young* actually focuses *more* attention on your advancing years? Your intention may be to sass yourself up, but actually all you're doing is *emphasizing* your complete discomfort with aging.

Oh, he was still talking!

". . . meet after the matinee to celebrate. I'll look for you in the pit."

"Oh, Mason," I said, remembering. "I'm subbing *Smile Time* this afternoon."

"You're still subbing?" Mason asked, sounding incredulous.

"You're still subbing?" Dianne asked one second later.

That was stereophonically annoying. "Yes and yes!" I said to both. "However," I said broadly, not wishing to discuss my subbing further. "I can still meet you after the matinee. *Smile Time* gets out a half hour before *Flowerchild*, so I'll walk back and meet you in my dressing room, OK?"

"Oh . . ." He could tell I curtailed the subbing talk. "OK . . . see you this afternoon."

I hung up.

"Wait a minute, Stephen," said Dianne. Here it comes, I thought. "I thought the whole point of your book was to spend your 'nights on Broadway'."

"That's why I'm subbing a matinee."

"That's not what I mean and you know it."

"Dianne," I said, loudly. "One day you may write a whole book against Pilates, but . . ." *where was this going?* "I wouldn't bother you if you still took classes!"

"What?" she asked.

Wow. That didn't even make sense to me.

"Look, I can't explain it," I said, with finality. "But I want to sub *Smile Time* today and I've already said yes, so I'm doing it."

She was quiet.

"OK, I can't stop you."

Hmm . . . that was what Jackson said right before I started dating Craig.

I'm in the pit of *Smile Time*. There's plenty of dialogue to write during.

I decided to check in at the theatre before I came over. I went upstairs to say hi to Anike. Her door was closed so I knocked.

"He's not here!" Anike called, from inside.

"Anike, it's Stephen!" I said, not understanding.

She opened the door and gave me a kiss on the cheek. Even with her hair in a wig cap she looked great.

"I'm sorry, Stephen, sit down." She motioned to one of her plush chairs that she got "antiquing one weekend with Hugh" (her new guy . . . they were back on again!).

She went to her makeup mirror. Contrary to doing a movie, everyone on Broadway does their own makeup, unless it requires something extra special. Like the Phantom. He has to get to the theatre at least an hour early to get his makeup person to attach all of the scars and grossness to his face. I was recently told that the reason it *only* takes an hour is because of all the advances in makeup. When the show first opened, Michael Crawford had to be there *three* hours early!

Anike was applying mascara. "Bettina is on a rampage because Fritz is missing again. She's combing the theatre."

Ooh! The cat was out of the bag. "We were trying to keep that secret from the cast," I said.

"Oh, please!" she said. "Everyone knows. She's been yelling into her cell phone at Tiffany nonstop." She launched into a great Bettina impression. "Tiffany, check the *boys* department at Bloomie's. We both know he's the height of a twelve-year-old."

I laughed. "How are things with you and Hugh?" I asked, looking at the picture of them on her dressing table. They were wearing winter coats and he had his arms around her from the back.

"Really great!" She held the picture and gave it a little kiss. "You'll meet him at the cast party."

I knew she had to get ready so I said good-bye, and just as I was closing her door I ran into Staci in the hallway.

"Um . . . hi," she said. For some reason, I suddenly remembered I wanted to buy the DVD of *28 Days Later.*

"Hi" I said, searching for an escape route, but she was blocking the only path to the staircase. I guess I could have run back in to Anike's room, but that would have meant subjecting Anike to Zombina.

"So . . ." I said, trying to make conversation. "How's *Dude?*" I decided to be nice and abbreviate the title of her new show, making it legit.

"Um...it's great."

Silence.

"Oh yeah," she said, "I remembered who our lead is related to."

"What?" I asked, nonplussed. What the hell was she talking about? "Oh yeah . . ." I said, remembering vaguely. During our torturous time underground, she said she had cast someone who was related to somebody but she forgot. I couldn't believe she remembered the boring conversation we had on the subway. I was tuning it out as I was listening to it.

She went on "Um . . . he's the nephew of Lou Fleishman. I forgot 'cause he never talks about it. He doesn't want people to treat him differently."

I wouldn't treat him differently because I didn't know who Lou Fleishman was.

She knew I wasn't impressed. "Um . . . he's very important," she said, adopting the condescending tone I knew so well from auditions. "He's the head of Artistic Associates . . ." she half smiled, "which is funny because Owen didn't have an agent when he auditioned."

I stood there. *Owen, Owen, Owen.*

I knew that name, I thought.

Owen, be reasonable, I heard in my head.

It suddenly hit me! Owen was the name Ronald said on the phone when Jackson and I called him! Holy sh*t! It all suddenly made sense to me! Owen must have been about to be offered the lead in *Dude*, and then someone tipped off Ronald, who must have called Owen and offered to be his agent. Ronald invited him to sign a contract, which, of course, led to the Jacuzzi rejection/ Jackson and Ronald breakup. An obviously angry Owen must have immediately told his uncle, aka *Ronald's boss! That's* why Ronald wasn't at work anymore! His ass was fired!!! I knew his scheme would eventually backfire!

"Staci, I gotta go!" I said, as I physically moved her out of the way.

I ran outside and called Jackson on his cell phone. "Jackson, I just found out who Owen is," I said, getting ready to savor telling him the delicious story.

"You mean Lou Fleishman's nephew?" he asked, changing all the barometric pressure to deflate whatever wind was in my sail.

"Well . . . yeah," I said.

"Stephen, Ronald told me everything, and if this weren't happening to me, I would think it's as juicy as you do."

"I don't think it's juicy," I said, with 0% conviction.

"Look, it's over between me and Ronald—"

Oh, joy of joys! I wanted to set off firecrackers, but couldn't because the mayor made them illegal, plus I didn't have any.

"—but I still don't want him evicted."

"Huh?" Why did Jackson say evicted? "What are you talking about?"

"Ronald sunk everything he had into his condo and now that he doesn't have a job, he can't pay his monthly mortgage."

"Let him use his savings." I said.

"He doesn't have any! He literally spent everything on this place!"

Wow. I was torn between enjoying Ronald eating his words (*"You don't understand how the big boys play with money")* and feeling bad for Jackson. He obviously still cared about him.

"Can't he get another job?" I asked.

"Everyone knows the Jacuzzi story. No agency will ever hire him."

I suddenly noticed it was 1:45. "Jackson, I have to play a matinee. But I'll try to think of something."

I started to consider solutions. I certainly didn't have enough money to lend him. Besides, he has to pay that mortgage monthly. He needed a new career. Oh! I gotta play the Act Two ballad! I'll write later!

WEDNESDAY, 7:30

I'm in my dressing room before the night show. I'm trying to remain calm. I finished playing the matinee of *Smile Time* and as I was walking out I passed by the stage manager's office.

"Stephen!" I heard. I couldn't believe it. I stopped in my tracks and turned to the open door of the office.

"Hi, Bettina."

I had forgotten that the Geisenshlaags also produced *Smile Time*. She must have been skulking around the theatre, looking for Fritz. She looked at me through angry eyes. "Did you just play this show?"

"No," I lied, immediately. She looked at her Rolex for Women watch.

"It's 4:30 and *Flowerchild* doesn't get out 'til 4:55."

"Oh!" I said while trying to smile/escape. "I guess you're right." I didn't have the energy for one of my signature yet useless lies. "Look, Bettina, I had Françoise conduct because there were no critics coming this afternoon—I checked."

She started pointing at me. "Your contract specifically states—"

I cut her off. "Françoise does a fine job, so I didn't think it mattered!"

I started to briskly walk out, but she was following me.

"Stephen, slow down."

I felt like The Fugitive, if the Tommy Lee Jones part was played by a walking facelift.

I pretended I couldn't hear her. "I'll see you at the show," I said, waving.

The theatre was just a block away. That was the cool thing about Broadway. Most theatres are within a ten-block radius. It's like a small town within a big city.

I hurried into the stage door and heard the beginning of the finale. There were 15 minutes left to the show. I said hi to Charlie the stage doorman and started looking for the key to my dressing room.

Then I remembered that Françoise must have taken it. Whenever she conducts, she has the use of my dressing room, but it drives me crazy because she always forgets to lock the door. You never know who really is walking around backstage and I don't want some hoodlum stealing my complete CD collection of the musicals of Jerry Herman! I hoped that she remembered to lock it.

"Can I have the extra key?" I asked Roy, who found it in his desk. As soon as I left, I heard the stage door open and Bettina calling my name. I thought if I could make it to my room in time, I'd be safe.

I shoved the key in the lock and started to throw open the door just as Bettina rounded the corner.

The first thing I noticed was that my scented candle was lit. Why would Françoise leave it on during the show? I thought. Then I heard a shrill sound. It was Bettina screaming.

As my eyes adjusted to the candlelight, I saw what she saw.

Fritz. On my couch. In the raw.

Not alone.

Apparently Tiffany had found him, and had *been* finding him. Her blonde hair framed her black lace bra and she had pulled my Pottery Barn couch throw over her lower half.

After Bettina screamed, she stood next to me in the doorway with her manicured hands in little fists. She took a deep breath and started verbally lacing into them.

"So!" Bettina said, as she stormed in. "I guess he wasn't at Bloomingdale's!" She ran right up to Tiffany. "I guess I should have looked *in Tiffany's!*"

Wow. She had enough control to make a pun in her most humiliating hour. Well, not really a pun. More like ironic wordplay.

"What an idiot I've been," she said to herself. "It's so obvious . . . He would disappear, I'd send *that* one off to go find him, and then they'd spend the whole afternoon together while I'd be calling each of their cell phones."

It *is* ingenious, I thought.

"What?" Bettina yelled, as she whirled around to face me.

Shit! I guess I not only thought it, I said it!

Thankfully, Fritz whispered into Tiffany's ear.

"Bettina," Tiffany repeated, pulling the blanket up over her bra. "He says it's all his fault . . ."

Bettina blanched.

"How dare you! That's *my* job!" I guess it was one thing to bed her husband, but Tiffany had now crossed the line. Bettina was sputtering.

"You're not his mouthpiece! *I* am! You're just his . . . you're . . . you're *fired!*" she screamed.

Then she turned around and pointed at me. "And," she said with the line reading of the Wicked Witch of the West talking to Dorothy, "if it weren't for you, this *never* would have happened."

I was speechless. This was *my* fault? Talk about blaming the messenger. And I wasn't even the messenger. I was just the door opener!

"I won't forget this!" she said as she vanished in a puff of green smoke (essentially).

By the time I turned back to my room, the lovebirds had flown the coop.

I saw Mason waiting at the stage door and told him I couldn't celebrate with him because I didn't feel well, which was actually true. I had a terrible foreboding of danger. I went out to dinner by myself and got back for half hour.

Wait, someone's knocking.

♪ hit.

That was Françoise. As soon as I opened the door, she pointed to her face, saying, "Je suis désolée! Je suis désolée!"

"You're what? You're desolate?"

"Oh, Stephen," she said, closing the door behind her. "I'm *sorry*. The Geisenshlaags . . . they want me to take over the show!"

Take over? "What are you talking about?"

She was talking faster than I'd ever heard her. "They just

came to the pit and told me that you breached your contract and after opening night, they want me to be the conductor." She really did start crying. "I told them I can't! *You're* the conductor! But they just said that if that's the way I feel, they'd find someone else!"

Wow. That was pretty loyal of Françoise.

"Stephen, they told me not to tell you because they want the opening to go smoothly, but I couldn't keep it a secret!" She sounded hysterical.

I put my arm around her, told her not to worry about it right now, and ushered her out.

I can hardly move the pen to write. I'm sort of in a state of shock.

Well, the Geisenshlaags are right. I did breach my contract, and I guess this is Bettina's way of getting revenge on me. It's odd, but I don't really feel surprised. I think I sort of expected this to happen ever since I called Phil back and said I would sub for him. But why? *Why* did I do it?

Shit. It's "Places."

I ran right out of the theatre without saying good-bye to anyone. I just wanted to be alone. I walked upstairs to my apartment and was shocked because I could see light coming from under my apartment door.

As I unlocked the door I heard a soft, "Hey, Stephen."

Oh, no! Don't tell me Fritz and Tiffany were now using my apartment!

I opened the door and saw Dianne sitting cross-legged on the fold-out couch. I totally forgot she was staying with me. There goes my alone time.

"Hey! How was your night?" I asked with my "everything's great" smile.

She immediately got up and walked over. "What happened? What's wrong?"

Shit! When you grow up with somebody, they're onto your tricks. "Nothing . . . I just . . ."

I couldn't talk. I suddenly started crying. A lot. "Oh, God, I screwed everything up," I said through sobs. "I've sabotaged everything." Dianne took off my coat, led me to the table, and I sat down.

"Stephen, I'm making you hot chocolate, and I want you to tell me everything."

As she heated up the milk and got out the unsweetened cocoa (she was doing it the old-fashioned way . . . she always had more patience than I did), I told her what had happened. Then I realized she didn't know who any of these people were. I started to explain, but she cut me off with—

"Stephen. I know about crazy Bettina and short-ass Fritz. I had the whole day to read your diary, remember?"

She carried over two mugs with hot chocolate. They were the same ones that Mason and I used the night of the kiss. The kiss! Why did he have to have a boyfriend? I started to cry again.

"OK," Dianne said. "Drink first, cry later."

I took a few sips. It really is better her way than with Swiss Miss packets. It was hard to drink, though, while sobbing.

"Stephen," she said with a big sigh, "Mom's not gonna change."

Huh? Where did that come from? I thought that maybe she based it on the theory that you can stop someone from having the hiccups by scaring them. I guess she thought she could stop me from crying by saying a non sequitur. It did sort of work, though.

"What does that mean?" I asked, blowing my nose.

"Well," she said after patting her lips with a napkin. "Once I accepted that, I stopped sabotaging my life—I told you that at Christmas."

That had nothing to do with me. "I remember, but you and Mom always fought. I don't have that issue with her." Now I really was confused. "And even if I did, what does this have to do with the Geisenshlaags?"

"Stephen, you're scared to be a full-time Broadway musician."
Now she was just throwing things out to see what stuck.
"Dianne, that's all I've been working towards my whole life."
She sat back and folded her arms. "Why?"
"Because I've always wanted to do it."
"Again, why?" She said, challengingly.
"Because," I said (with a subtext of "Duh!"). "I love it."
She shook her head. "I believe that you love it and that you
want it, but I think what you want most is for mom to love you."
I felt slapped in the face. "She *does* love me!"
She smiled. "Calm down, Stephen. She loves both of us. But
not the way we want her to. And"—she made an "I-hate-to-say-
it" smile—"she loves herself more than she loves anyone else."
I shrugged. "I guess."
"Well, it's true, and I think we both realized it at the same
time. I was 16 and you were 10."
I laughed. "That was the year I won all those piano awards,"
I said. I entered every music competition I could. I kept hoping
Mom would be able to see me win, but it was always Mrs.
Remick who came.
Dianne nodded. "That was also the year I first told Mom that
she sucked."
I remember that also. Dianne had waited for my mom to pick
her up after band practice and finally had to call a taxi. She ran
up to my mom's room, threw open the door and said "You . . .
suck" really slowly, like she had been practicing the whole time
she was waiting in the band room. My mom was so devastated
that she took to her bed and had to miss that evening's performance. She got an enormous fruit basket from the conductor the
next day.
"Well," Dianne said, matter-of-factly. "I think you're still
waiting to be number one in Mom's life and, according to your
diary, you think that when you finally conduct a show, that'll be
the ticket."

I waved her away. "Well, it obviously won't happen. You said she'll always love herself the most."

"*I* think that's pretty obvious, but a part of you doesn't want to face it."

"This part?" I asked, giving her the finger.

"Yes, that part," she said, staring at me till I retracted it. She finally began again. "The part that would rather lose your job than face it."

Just because she had one Christmas vacation that didn't end with having laryngitis from cursing my mother out, she thought she was Dr. Phyllis.

"You think I purposely lost my job? Are you crazy?" Of course, that's what I had been thinking, but how dare *she*?

She took a long sip of hot chocolate. "Yes, I do. Because now you can go back to walking around thinking (she put on a baby voice), "Well, when I get my next show, *then* things will be great. When blah blah blah happens, *then* things will be great. Why be in a real relationship when I can waste my time hoping for a better one?"

Now I was getting annoyed.

"All right, Dianne, enough with the theories. I'm going to bed." I stood up.

"Stephen, will you always be a sub?" she asked.

Always a sub?

My mind began whirling. I saw myself conducting a big splashy musical with my whole family in the front row applauding. My mom cutting her tour short to see me on Broadway. Craig and me living in a bed and breakfast. All the fantasies I always had. I had to hold onto the chair as it hit me. That's all they were: fantasies!

My fantasies were the only things that made me feel good when I was kid. And I guess I figured out a way to live my life with them intact. One day my mother will make me the center of everything. One day a boyfriend will make my life perfect.

Was I afraid to face that they would never come true the way I envisioned them? Is that why I never got to the end of anything? Would I remain a perpetual sub? Always playing someone else's piano part on Broadway and always with a boyfriend who had another boyfriend? I was in my FUCKING THIRTIES!!!

"No!" I yelled. "No more!"

I started pacing. "This is BULLSHIT!"

Dianne recoiled and said calmly while drinking, "Less yelling, more doing something."

"All right," I said, forming a plan. "I'm going to force those Geisenshlaags fuckers to give me my job back or else Page Six is gonna have a great item featuring Fritz, Bettina, and Tiffany!"

Just then the phone rang.

"Hello?" I said, picking it up after one ring.

"*C'est* Françoise."

"Say, Françoise . . ." I said, just because of the symmetry.

"Stephen, let me speak *premier*. The Geisenshlaags have decided—you're keeping your job!" She giggled with glee.

"Françoise, are you sure?" I asked.

"*Oui! Certainement!* My father just told me." I forgot her father was the contractor! I felt a wave of relief wash over me.

"Did your father say why they changed their mind?"

"No, they never give him details about anything."

Well, I don't need to know the reason. I just want to keep conducting the show.

"Françoise, thank you so much for telling me."

"*De rien.*" I could tell that she did a little curtsey.

"And," I added sincerely, "thank you for all the work you've done."

"Ah, Stephen, it is a pleasure to be working on this show with you."

"Thanks . . ." I decided to throw her a bone. "Sorry there's no harpsichord."

"Actually, it's pronounced 'harp-see-chord'—"

That did it.

"OK, that's my call waiting. Thanks again."

I hung up.

Dianne was finishing up her cocoa.

"Well, I guess I don't have to go to the papers." I told her what Françoise said.

She got up and hugged me. "Stephen, that's wonderful!"

"Dianne, thank you for opening my eyes."

"Oh, Stephen," she waved me away, "you were almost there. You just needed a little push." She went in the bathroom to get ready, and I've been sitting on the bed writing.

What a night. I feel determined about tomorrow. I'm going to do the show with no other expectation than just doing a good show. No more hoping my mother will change. No more living in the future. No more unavailable boyfriends.

Oh, no.

Mason.

Is that why I've been so interested in him? Because I know he's unavailable? Would I not like him if he didn't have Jason in the wings?

I began to think about it. All the time I've spent with him I could have spent with someone who's not involved with someone else.

That was the last bit of housecleaning I needed to do. It's time to grow up completely. I have to break up our non-relationship relationship.

ACT TWO
FINALE

Thirty-Four

I'm in my dressing room. Opening night shows are usually at 6:30. This is left over from the days that reviewers all came on the same night and the early curtain gave them enough time after the show ended to write a review and get it in by deadline. The tradition stayed, and it's nice because the opening night party can start at 9 p.m. (instead of 11:00). I'm finishing up writing everyone a card and sorting through my gifts that I'm giving. I got each person in the cast a framed 45 record of "California Dreamin'" with the date of opening night written in tie-dyed letters in the little hole in the center.

This morning I went to the gym and then had a nice breakfast with Dianne. I so appreciated all her help last night that I told her magnanimously *I'd* leave the tip. Just kidding—I bought her a fantastico breakfast (challah French toast . . . yum!) and thanked her profusely for de-clouding my head and saving my career.

After getting a massage from Greg "Get the Knots Out" Miele (painful during, but delicious after), I stopped by the Geisenshlaags' office under the guise of confirming my tickets for tonight, but really to see what the vibe was. Not surprisingly,

Tiffany was no longer employed and Bettina was having a very hard time. Not only because she didn't have an assistant, but because she had no one to hurl abuse at, which she needs to do at fifteen-minute intervals. As soon as I walked in though, Bettina brightened up.

"Stephen, great to see you," she said, beaming from behind her desk. "We're so excited about the show tonight!"

I was taken aback. I wasn't sure what to expect when I entered, but extreme friendliness didn't make the top ten.

"Uh, yeah . . ." I said after literally stepping back a few inches. "I'm excited, too."

Fritz whispered.

"Oh, yes," Bettina said, nodding to him, "if all goes as expected, we need to start talking about a national tour." She cupped her hand on the side of her mouth, like she was letting me in on a big secret. "We've already gotten some interest from Chicago and Boston."

Wow. I guess I really wasn't fired.

"Great!" I said, deciding to get the hell out quickly and not press my luck. "I'll see you tonight."

"Oh," Bettina said as I turned to leave, "don't worry about playing piano at the cast party. I decided to hire someone after all."

"Great," I said, completely miffed.

"It's gonna be so-o-o-ome party!" She shimmied her shoulders and/or had a mini-stroke. "I just want you to concentrate on having a good time."

She sat smiling and waving as I walked out.

Wow. Maybe her doctor mixed up her recent brow lift with a lobotomy.

Mmm. It smells delicious in here. My dressing room is *filled* with bouquets from my dad/Mitzi, my mom, Traci Lyn, Dianne, and the Geisenshlaags (!).

I have a ton of opening night cards to read that I think I'll save for after the show.

Ooh, someone's knocking.

* * *

$\mathcal{T}$hat was Jackson. He gave me a great opening-night present: an enormous coffee-table book that had a Broadway story on each page from all the greats. He inscribed it—

"A fabulous story about *your* career is sure to be in the next edition (I'd better be mentioned in it!) . . . Love, Jackson."

It was so sweet. I though about how far we've come since the summer days we rehearsed *Seesaw* during the day and did *Applause* at night. I thanked him sincerely and then noticed he looked excited but stressed.

"Jackson, are you still upset about Ronald being potentially evicted?" I asked.

"Yeah." He shook his head, mournfully. "No one's ever gonna hire him. It's such a downer to be worrying about it on opening night."

"Listen," I said, putting my arms on his shoulders. "I think I may have solved it."

He immediately brightened. "You did? How?"

I disengaged my arms. "I want to wait to see if it works out, but you'll find out soon enough." (This goes for you, too, dear readers.)

He looked at me quizzically. "You're very mysterious . . . but I like having it off my shoulders." He hugged me. "Thanks, Stephen." He turned to leave and then turned back.

"By the way, are all brass players straight?" he asked.

I laughed. "Why?"

"Because I think the French horn player asked me out," he said with a big grin.

I was so excited. "He's totally cute! Go for it!"

He rubbed his hands together, greedily. "I intend to!" He exited with a little wave.

I'm sorry I haven't explained the possible Ronald job, but I don't want to jinx what could be *amazing*.

Karen just called half hour! I have to get into my "blacks," hand out these gifts, and give my orchestra a thank-you speech. This night has arrived at last!

INTERMISSION OF FLOWERCHILD

So exciting! I got to the pit early so I was able to scan the audience for a while. There were a ton of Broadway stars intermingled with pop stars from the '60s (because we were doing a lot of their songs). It felt like such an event!

Right before the overture I saw my father and Mitzi. She waved girlishly and my father gave me a thumbs-up. Then I looked two rows down and saw Mason. He looked so cute in his tuxedo. Unfortunately, so did Jason. That was sobering. The only good news was that Jason was animatedly talking to the woman sitting next to him so I didn't have to wave to him. Mason gave me a big smile and blew me a kiss. I tried to accept the kiss platonically, which took quite a bit of subtext.

Dianne looked great in the dress I secretly had made for her by Juanita, our costume designer. After Christmas, I gave Juanita three pix of Dianne and asked her to design something fabulous for the opening. After Dianne and I had breakfast I asked her if she'd come with me on a quick errand and we went to Juanita's shop. Juanita had put the dress on a mannequin with a sheet over it. When I introduced them to each other, she grabbed Dianne's hand, flipped off the sheet, and said with a flourish, "*Thees* is for choo!"

It was a deep black with a low-cut bust, a slit up the side, and beads on the bodice. Dianne didn't know what was going on. She just stared at it and then at me for help. I told her it was really hers and when she finally accepted that fact, she became so happy she literally jumped around the shop (which must have hurt because she was wearing new shoes she just got at Nine West that had crazy-ass high heels).

Dianne tried on the dress. Juanita had to take it in a little (thanks to Dianne's new Pilates regimen), and now, sitting in the audience, Dianne looks like one of the *Sex and the City* girls (if they ate more than just water).

Finally, I saw my mother (arriving late, as usual). She got there just as Karen called the houselights cue over my headset. As they started to dim, the audience started applauding and my mom, who had just sat down, quickly jumped out of her seat, turned around, and started to bow. It seemed like a message from above that even though the times may be, *she* ain't a-changing. I made the final decision to do this show for myself.

My red cue light went out and I started the overture to wild applause. All through Act One, every time I'd think of Mason or my mom or even Craig, I'd focus my mind on the joy I got from doing what I loved best, and I'd suddenly feel completely connected to the music.

Oh! It's places for Act Two!

*G*et ready.

The show went great. We got a standing ovation (typical for opening night, but it seemed like it wasn't just out of obligation).

The backstage area was crazy. The cast was running around getting glammed out, plus there were a ton of well-wishing visitors crowding every vestibule.

I retreated to my dressing room to take a shower and put on my new Marc Jacobs suit.

As I was tying my tie, someone was knocking.

I opened the door and Mason rushed in and lifted me in the air.

"Stephen, the show's gonna be a smash. I can feel it!"

I laughed, caught up in his enthusiasm. "I hope so, Mason! I want to conduct it for years!"

"Well, now that the Geisenshlaags are scared shitless, you could!"

He suddenly looked like he'd said too much.

"What are they scared of?" I asked.

He shifted his eyes. "The bill for Bettina's next procedure?" he offered.

I sat down. "Nice try, Mason. Spill."

He sat next to me on the couch. "Oh, I might as well. I mean, it's all because of you . . ."

"Huh?"

He took a deep breath. "Yesterday Karen called me and told me what the Geisenshlaags were up to." He started to sound angry. "Trying to screw you over because of that dumb-ass clause in your contract."

A lightbulb went off in my head. "So that's it!" I said. "No-nonsense Karen gave Bettina such a scary talking to that she reneged on my firing." It all made sense. "I knew her bitchery would pay off somehow."

He looked embarrassed. "No, not really. Karen didn't have much swing with Bettina, even though she tried."

The lightbulb flickered and went out. "So, what went down?" I asked. It seemed weird that stuff happened without me knowing it. I had no idea that Karen, let alone Mason, knew what was up.

He got his second wind. "After Françoise came to you she told Karen, who phoned Bettina right away and was told to butt out. Karen then called me."

So it really wasn't Karen. "Then who got me my job back?" The only other person with a big mouth was Kris, but I can't see him having much sway over the Geisenshlaags.

"Uh . . . I did," said Mason finally.

Mason who won't even send a hamburger back when it's raw and filled with salmonella? Mason who's always had the back-bone of pasta? And not even al dente, but blatantly overcooked pasta?

"How did *you* scare the scariest people in the world?" I asked, completely baffled.

He got an intense look in his eyes. "Well, when I heard what happened, I called them—" He searched for the words. "—in a rage . . ." I don't think he's ever used that expression about himself before. "And I told them that if they fired you I would *never* work with them again." He was getting riled up. "Of course, Bettina ignored me and started talking about the cast party and I promptly cut her off by saying that she had a half hour to rectify the situation or I would tell my agent to cancel *all* negotiations with them on my new play and that they could kiss the play, the movie rights, *and* my ass good-bye."

I was speechless.

He went on. "They agreed that you'd stay. And just to make sure, I had my agent add a clause to the new deal with them that if you were ever fired off of this project, the contract would be null and void."

"But, Mason . . ." I said, finding my voice. "You've never . . ."

"Had a spine? I know." He shrugged. "But I told you I've been working on it, and I guess I finally got the thing that could change me."

"What?" I asked. "A show on Broadway?"

He smiled and looked away, embarrassed. "No, Stephen, I fell in love."

I looked at him.

"With me?" I asked, just to make sure.

He laughed. "Yes, Mr. Literal."

He sat there smiling. He was so cute . . .

No! I couldn't! Oy, what a nightmare.

"Oh, Mason, I think I love you, too . . ." I said, getting up and walking to my dressing mirror. "But I made a vow not to get involved with anyone involved with someone else."

"But . . ." he said slowly, getting off the couch. "I thought your vow was never to get involved with anyone you work with?" He walked over to me. "You know, the whole number-one rule. That's why I quickly agreed not to pursue anything. I didn't want you to betray your beliefs."

That lie?

"Forget that," I said, waving it away. "That was just something I said because I was trying to cover up . . ." This was it. No more lies. I took a deep breath. "I was secretly dating Craig up until a month ago. And I was too embarrassed to tell you."

He was quiet. "Why couldn't you tell me?" he finally asked.

I started talking a mile a minute. "Because I knew it was sleazy. And I knew it was hurting Jeffrey, as uptight as he is." It was humiliating, but such a relief to finally tell him. I decided to say it all. "And . . . I didn't want you to think less of me."

He looked me in the eye and grabbed my hand. "I don't think less of you. Everyone's made mistakes in their love life."

He was so sweet.

"So . . ." He let go of my hand. "If you were lying about not getting involved with people you work with, why did you say we couldn't be together after the hot chocolate incident?"

Didn't he just hear me say I thought cheating was sleazy? "Because, I don't want to do that anymore!"

He sounded frustrated. "Do *what* anymore?"

Now *I* sounded frustrated. "Be with someone who already has a boyfriend!"

He still looked confused. "So?"

"Like you!" I yelled. I said each word with emphasis. "I can't date you while you have a boyfriend!"

He shook his head, as if to clear it. "But Stephen," he said. "I don't have a boyfriend."

Oh, please. Semantics. I flitted my hand in the air. "Lover, partner, whatever."

He grabbed both of my shoulders. "Exactly, Stephen. None of the above."

What? "Hello! Don't forget how long I've known you, Mason. You've been living with Jason for ten years," I said, to refresh his memory.

He nodded, laughing. "Yes, you idiot! Because he's my *brother!* Didn't you know that?"

I think the earth temporarily stopped rotating because I lost all sense of equilibrium. I started to think back. When I knew Mason at Rose's Turn I knew they were living together because of that annoying outgoing message. *For Jason press one, for Mason press two* . . . And when I met Jason at Gypsy of the Year I did notice they looked alike, but chalked it up to codependence. When you assume, you make an ass . . .

"Why didn't you tell me he was your brother when I met him?" I asked.

He snorted. "You only let me get out around three words. Then you went scurrying after that usher." That was true. I was so anxious that day I was cutting him off right and left.

"But how come you hardly talked about him to me?" I wondered.

"Please! You acted so weird when you met him, I thought you hated him! I assumed you had some anti-lawyer thing." Hmm . . . that does sound like me. I once boycotted *The Nanny* for two years just because I had a terrible blind date seeing *The Beautician and the Beast*. I actually loved the movie, but felt I had to take some action, and Fran Drescher was an easy target. Don't ask—it made sense at the time.

"And," Mason said sheepishly, "I guess I was embarrassed about the whole apartment rent thing and I didn't want another lecture from you."

I guess I am sort of a nag.

But wait a minute!

"Why didn't you ever talk to me about being single?" I asked suddenly.

"Why didn't you?" he threw back at me.

Oh, yeah. "Well," I said, embarrassed, "I didn't want you to figure anything out about me and Craig."

He nodded. Then softly said, "And I didn't want you to figure anything about . . ."

What? "About what?"

"About me and you." He averted his eyes. "I thought you'd know how I felt about you right away if I talked about romantic stuff with you."

I smiled and made him look at me. "Mason . . . how long have you liked me?"

"Um . . . why do you think I used to come to your piano bar so often?"

I was shocked. "Are you serious? Why didn't you ever say anything?"

"Well, I was shy, and it was just a crush then. Also, I knew I was about to go off to graduate school for a while. But as soon as I saw you at that audition with Traci Lyn the crush started taking off at hyper speed."

Wow. Why didn't I notice? Oh, right. Craig was like a bad case of cataracts.

"So, you've been living with your brother since college?" I asked.

"Yeah, my parents sort of instilled in my head that it's my job to take care of him. But," he said, with a huge grin, "it's finally ending!"

"Because of your new backbone?" I asked, excited.

"Actually, no." He said. "More because he's moving in with his girlfriend. She was sitting next to him tonight." So that's who Jason was talking to.

"Well, whatever it takes . . ." I said, with a laugh.

"So . . ." he said, standing awkwardly.

"So . . . you're available," I said quietly.

"Yes . . ." he said, trailing off.

Hmm . . . He was available. *And* interested in me. Or "in love" with me, as he just said. And I felt . . . what?

I had assumed my feelings for him were so strong because of his unavailability. And now that we can be together . . . I decided to take my "feeling temperature," as Monikah calls it. Let's see, I feel . . . palms sweating, thoughts spinning, heart bursting . . . happy!

More than that: *Overjoyed!*

I looked at him sternly. "Mason, you are *not* available . . ." He looked confused. I hugged him around his waist. ". . . to anyone but *me!*" Eyu! My annoying pause was a Ryan Seacrest/*American Idol* specialty: "Nicki, you are NOT staying . . . in the bottom. You're safe!"

He bear hugged me and planted one right on the kisser. And this time, it didn't end with proclamations of how "wrong" it was. It ended with more smooching!

"Dating my own brother! "Number-one rule . . ." He laughed. "Your mind is crazy!"

"I know," I said, defensively. "But I'm changing!"

"Don't change too much," he said, taking my arm and walking me out of the dressing room, into the throngs of people going to the party.

The party was a blur. Anike looked gorgeous and finally introduced me to Hugh, who was clearly smitten with her. Vince was getting tons of attention from the photogs there, and Jackson was sitting and talking animatedly to Hudson, the French horn player.

Kris walked up to where Mason and I were sitting. "Congrats to all!" he said, giving us each a kiss on the cheek.

"Sorry about Jay—" I began.

"Save the 'sorrys' for the deserved. I already have my eye on someone new . . ." He pointed to a CUTE waiter maneuvering through the crowd, holding an enormous platter of sushi. "He offered me yellowtail and I intend to take him up on the offer!" The pun didn't quite make sense, but the sassy line reading made up for it.

I saw my dad and Mitzi on the food line.

"Wonderful, Stephen!" Mitzi said, giving me a peck on the cheek.

"Yes, son," said my dad. "I'm proud of you." I gave him a hug and scurried away as he started arguing with Mitzi about whether the pasta was rigatoni or penne.

I walked by the bar and noticed a red-faced Craig arguing with Jay. Boy, Craig was loud. What happened to quiet time?

"There you are," said my mother, appearing out of nowhere and sweeping me in an embrace, but leaving her face turned out in case anyone was taking a photo.

"You did a wonderful job!" she said, cupping my chin with her be-ringed hand.

"Thank you," I said, trying to appreciate her praise while not expecting more. She will not change, I reminded myself.

"This is Aaron. Aaron Schwartz," she said, a little stiffly, introducing me to a handsome man in his early sixties with a nicely groomed salt-and-pepper beard. He was exactly her height but much broader.

"Uh . . . nice to meet you," I said. They were holding hands. Wait? Wasn't my mother still in love with my dad?

"Your mother talks about you quite a lot," he said, and even though it sounded clichéd, I believed him.

"Oh, stop it, you," she said, letting out a laugh that highlighted her still-extensive soprano range.

He gave her a quick kiss on the lips.

"Aaron's retired," she said.

"Civil engineer," he said modestly. Two words that meant nothing to me, but I knew were some kind of a job.

"So," she said, as if it weren't the biggest deal in the world, "Aaron's coming on tour with me."

What? That motley crew hasn't had a cast change in twenty-five years! So now the tour would be my mom, my dad, Mitzi, and Aaron. Wow. I guess things do change, even if they probably still result in me getting complaining phone calls from both parents.

I guess she really was going to continue touring even though I was on Broadway.

I walked away feeling the hole I always felt after being with my mom.

I walked by a mirror and saw myself. I had a five o'clock shadow. I wasn't an 11-year-old boy anymore wanting my mom to love me.

Yet, I still felt depressed.

OK, I heard Dianne's voice in my head ("*Stephen, will you always be a sub?*") and decided to make a conscious effort.

Instead of leaving that hole empty waiting for my mom to fill it one day, I forced myself to let in everything else in my life. My career, my friends, Mason, everything. (I conveniently left the Geisenshlaags and Craig outside the hole.)

Hmm . . . depressed feeling dissipating . . . fulfilled feeling taking its place.

Holy shit! I hadn't realized how much I had been ignoring! My life not only filled the hole, it overflowed it! From now on, every phone call from my mom will have to be followed by a conscious hole-filling (please leave the unfunny sex jokes to *Married . . . with Children* ex-writers).

The Geisenshlaags entered. He was in a Ralph Lauren tuxedo with a custom-made ascot that said "Flowerchild" down the front of it, and she was decked out in a Juanita Specialty. Well, the shape of it was all Juanita, but Flo had decided to make it '60s style by tie-dying it red, white, and blue! Have you ever seen a formal evening gown that's been tie-dyed and then put over a rectangle with heels? I couldn't tell if she looked like a dressy hippie or a flag-draped coffin. As soon as they entered the center of the room people got quiet.

"Well," Bettina said, standing by the ice sculpture (1969 surrounded by sushi). "The reviews are in and it looks like we're gonna run for a *long time!*"

Everyone cheered.

Wow. Instead of the unreliable subbing I've been doing, I'm finally going to be spending all my "nights (except Sundays and Mondays) on Broadway." I knew the title would pay off eventually!

She quieted them. Fritz whispered. "They're not 100% raves," she interpreted, "but there are *many* wonderful quotes . . . especially for the lovely Anike"—everyone applauded—"and Broadway's newest star . . . Vance!" She gestured towards Vince and everyone pretended that she had said his name correctly. "Although some papers think the show is simply fluff, they *all* say you can't help but enjoy yourself! Let's thank our creative staff, Kris, Stephen, and Mason!" It was so wonderful to see everyone's smiling face clapping in our direction. She held up her champagne glass. "As you know, it only takes one gosling to become a goose." Silence as everyone pondered what was lost in translation. "Next stop, the Tonys!" Relieved applause. Everyone toasted and began to chat.

Suddenly, I heard her voice cut through the noise.

"I want all the positive reviews cut out and pasted on 8 x 11 sheets for tomorrow's eight a.m. marketing meeting. *And* I'll need my Hermès scarf picked up *before* then from the dry cleaners. Don't worry, they open at seven."

She walked by me. "Thanks for the recommendation, Stephen." She motioned in back of her. "With a little more training, he'll be a great assistant." Ronald accepted the compliment and gave me a smile tinged with sadness and karma. Bettina turned back to him and barked, "Fetch my fox stole from the office so I can wear it as I walk to the limo."

Ronald turned on his heels and raced out the door. I thought about how we all benefited: he'd have the money to pay his mortgage, Bettina had a new punching bag, and I had a delicious sense of justice.

All right, that's it for now. I have to stop writing. Mason just got out of the shower and he's coming to bed.

I have a feeling he's not going to want "quiet time."

EXIT
MUSIC
- - - - - - - - - - - -

Thirty-Five

*M*ason and I got up at 11:00 and went to breakfast right near the theatre. There was the delicious sight of a line of people buying tickets. Not the longest line in the world, but a line nonetheless! The box office said they've already shot up 75% from last week!

"By the way, Stephen," Mason said as we strolled down Broadway, holding hands. "I got an offer to direct a workshop of a new musical slated for Broadway next fall. Do you think you'd have the energy to conduct *Flowerchild* at night and rehearse a new show during the day?"

I smiled. "Only if you promise not to keep me up all night."

He nuzzled my neck. "Sorry, no promises . . ."

I finally saw Monikah late afternoon and read her all that happened.

"So," I said, closing the book cover. "I guess the diary paid off."

I waited for the non-response response.

"Yes," she said.

Wait. Was it a trick? I had to have her qualify.

"Monikah, do you mean 'Yes, Stephen, I think the diary paid

off, too?' or 'Yes, Stephen, I'm agreeing that you indeed think that.'"

She laughed.

She laughed! I don't think I've ever seen her laugh before. Things are definitely different.

"I mean, yes, I think it's paid off." She gave me a "good for you" smile. "Congratulations. I see a lot of progress."

"You do?" She actually made me feel proud of myself!

We talked about how far I've come from when I was first seeing her and complaining nonstop about being a sub or else professing my undying love for Craig.

Before long, it was almost the end of the session. I started to get up and suddenly realized there was one thing that hadn't changed . . .

"Monikah." I decided to finally be direct. I spoke slowly and clearly. "Are you now or have you ever been on the Atkins Diet?"

She smiled and paused.

Finally. "No, Stephen, I have not."

Ah! The relief!

I had the answer I had been waiting for!

I put my coat on and said good-bye with a bounce in my step. As I was walking out I noticed an empty container of a Myoplex shake in the garbage. Was it from her or another patient, and what was it for? The door to her office shut. Wait a minute! That's what people drink who are on "Body for Life." I think that's the diet that combines protein *and* carbs each meal, so I guess she could have had her Atkin's-style hamburger without the bun that I noticed in her fridge forever ago *combined* with a healthy carbohydrate that I somehow overlooked. *Why* wasn't I more observant! I started to sweat a little. Maybe she's been on "Body for Life" this whole time.

Oh, why wasn't I clearer with my question! I should have asked, *Are you now or have you ever been on ANY diet, and if so, which one?* I've *got* to find out!

Wait. Monikah says I focus compulsively on minute details to help me escape from my feelings.

She's right. I'm going to stop thinking about Atkins or Body for Life and be in the present.

The present.

Although, they *also* make a low-carb version of Myoplex that's perfect for the South Beach Diet.

I'll try to get her to 'fess up at my next appointment.

The End?

About the Author

*S*ETH RUDETSKY wrote the opening number for the 1998 Tony Awards, was a comedy writer on *The Rosie O'Donnell Show* (three Emmy nominations) and was voted "The Funniest Gay Male in New York." As a musician, he was the artistic producer/conductor for the Actor's Fund CD of *Hair* with Jennifer Hudson, and the 20th Anniversary CD of *Dreamgirls* with Audra MacDonald. He has been a sub pianist on fifteen Broadway shows including *Les Miz*, *Ragtime*, and *Phantom*, and, in the Fall of 2007, he made his Broadway acting debut in *The Ritz*. He is currently the daily host of *Seth's Big Fat Broadway* on Sirius Satellite Radio.

www.sethsbroadwaychatterbox.com